But it seemed she had read Heather's expression incorrectly. Toni found herself flipped onto her back. "You're gonna pay for that, Ms. Ljanjovich."

"How so?" Toni looked up at the woman who straddled her stomach, somewhat impressed that Heather rolled her surname off her tongue so easily—most people she met had to ask for it to be repeated at least twice. At that moment, however, Heather's pronunciation skills took a backseat to her more physical attributes. Toni watched the bulge of biceps and the pleasing line of taut triceps when Heather lifted her arms to again adjust her twist tie. A healthy dose of lust reared its head. Along with it came her second wind.

She was ready.

"Maybe like this." The muscular arm descended and disappeared behind Heather's back, her hand probing the space between Toni's thighs.

A groan emerged as Heather's fingers found their target. Another burst forth as she began a slow grind over Toni's stomach, pace quickening in time with Toni's undulating hips.

The bed shuddered and shook. Toni shuddered and shook. She lost her second wind then gained a third. And a fourth. They spent the entire Saturday afternoon in bed. And they stayed there well into the evening.

D1059127

Visit

Bella Books

at

BellaBooks.com

or call our toll-free number

1-800-729-4992

REALITY BYTES

JANE FRANCES

Bella
BOOKS

2007

Copyright© 2007 by Jane Frances

Bella Books, Inc.
P.O. Box 10543
Tallahassee, FL 32302

All rights reserved. No part of this book may be reproduced or transmitted in any form or by any means, electronic or mechanical, including photocopying, without permission in writing from the publisher.

Printed in the United States of America on acid-free paper

First Edition

Editor: Christi Cassidy
Cover designer: Stephanie Solomon-Lopez

ISBN-10: 1-59493-079-1
ISBN-13: 978-1-59493-079-9

In loving memory of Virgil

Acknowledgments

Sincere thanks to all who provided me with advice, encouragement and support during the writing of *Reality Bytes*: Aline, Caroline, Don, Elise, Fleur, Joelle, Joey and Lee.

And special thanks to Christine at Bella Books.

About the Author

The daughter of a teacher, Jane was brought up with books from as early as she can remember, and to this day continues her love affair with the written word and its ability to transport the reader to places unknown.

Jane was educated in the traditional fashion, taking the path directly from school to university and gaining a Bachelor of Business with major studies in Marketing. Her studies took her to the marketing department of a city-based educational institution where she spent over a decade working in a creative and supportive environment.

English-born and Australian raised, Jane currently lives in France where she is taking every opportunity to absorb the sights and sounds of a culture steeped in history and brimming with romance. Totally inept to master the native tongue, she also daydreams of the day the "neighbors from across the channel" invade, and declare English to be France's new official language!

Reality Bytes, the sequel to *Reunion*, is Jane's second novel.

CHAPTER ONE

Emma Walker poked her head around the half open door. "See you in three weeks, Pete."

The lone occupant of the storeroom held up his hand. As requested by the gesture, Emma stayed, leaning against the doorframe while Pete finished counting the cans in an open carton of diet food for cats.

Emma sighed audibly, irked at the activity she was witnessing. Pete was supposed to be on his lunch break but instead was doing the weekly stock-take. Why anyone would select Saturday, typically the busiest day in a suburban veterinary practice, as the day to take inventory was beyond Emma. But then Colleen Wells, veterinary surgeon, recent divorcée and, for the five weeks since taking over the practice, the bane of Emma's existence, probably wasn't in her right mind. The woman was hell in high heels—who in her right mind tottered around a vet practice in heels, for goodness' sake?—and she and Emma clashed almost from day one. Luckily,

Emma had booked her impending vacation leave well before the sale of the practice was announced. She was hoping, come the end of her vacation, she'd have another position lined up.

"All done." Pete slotted his pen behind an ear, shaking his head as he turned to Emma. "You're completely mad, you know."

"Probably." Emma knew he was referring to the very large favor she was doing for Tricia, a fellow vet and friend from her university days. Tricia was desperate to attend the upcoming Veterinary Association's annual conference. She was also very persuasive. Emma crumbled, so now nearly half of her vacation days would be spent working as a locum in Tricia's practice. Each time Emma kicked herself for being such a pushover, she consoled herself with thoughts of the extra money. Every cent provided that bit more of a safety net if things got to breaking point and she told Colleen to shove her high heels and Saturday stock-takes where the sun didn't shine. "Here's a tip for you," Emma said. "Never, *never* tell anyone you plan to spend your vacation doing nothing more than pottering 'round the house."

"You're just a big softie, Em."

Their hug was swift, friendly. Emma would miss Pete over the next few weeks. Only nineteen, he was mature for his age, and his love of animals evident. He took his position as veterinary assistant very seriously, arriving early for shifts and, as she was witnessing now, even working through his break. Emma knew he felt the same discontent with the new management as she did. She also knew, unlike her, he was already actively job-seeking. Emma decided she'd put in a good word for him with Tricia, probably right about the time she laid out feelers for herself.

By two p.m. Emma was turning her station wagon into the driveway of her home. She'd made good time. Usually Saturdays saw her working well past her scheduled one o'clock knockoff, but today it seemed the Goddess was smiling down upon her. No emergency presented itself between her good-bye to Pete and the short walk to the back door of the practice so she was able to make a guilt-free getaway. Emma jangled her keys happily as she walked up the path to her front door. Despite having to report for duty at Tricia's practice on Tuesday, she was in vacation mode. A brilliant sun shone in a cloudless Western Australian sky, and she would be seeing Justine in less than two hours. Life was good.

The front door was hardly open when a cold nose pressed into her leg.

"Hello, my beautiful girl." Emma laughed delightedly at the welcome, despite coming home to the same greeting for over three years. She stood at the entrance, unable to get past the threshold until the ritual was completed. Emma hunkered down to doggie level and ran her hands down the length of Kayisha's long, floppy, golden retriever ears. "How was your day, Kai?"

The large golden mass of fur happily woofed in response, excitement at the return of the center of her universe evident in the whole of her body wag.

"That good, huh?" Emma scratched Kayisha's ruff and returned to human height.

Kayisha was at her heels as Emma walked the length of the hallway, jealously pushed her snout into Emma's hand when Emma called a hello to Malibu and wagged her tail frantically as Emma stripped out of her work gear to don a pair of running shorts and a T-shirt.

"Come on, girl." Emma adjusted the harness around Kayisha's middle, snapped on a lead and slipped a plastic poo bag into the space between fur and the thick leather collar. "It'll just be a quickie today. Mum's got to go out again soon."

Just under an hour later, Emma hummed softly as she patted herself dry. A hot shower had washed away the perspiration from her run around the local lake. It also washed away all the veterinary smells of the morning. Once dressed in fresh jeans and T-shirt, she left her bedroom in search of Malibu, at last in a state deemed suitable to say hello.

"Hi there, Mal." Emma plopped onto the couch next to the six-year-old Burmese and held her hand out to be sniffed. On the subsequent passing of inspection—Emma had long ago figured there was no point trying to go near Malibu while she still smelled liked a menagerie—she picked up the black bundle for a cuddle. Most days Emma would be rewarded with a purr, but today Malibu was having none of it, wriggling from Emma's arms and shooting a dismissive stare as she padded away, tail held high.

Emma watched Malibu disappear into the kitchen, getting the distinct impression she had just been treated to a brown eye. Obviously she had not yet been forgiven for the worm paste administered that morning.

Emma gave Kayisha a quick stroke as she headed toward the front door. "See you soon, Kai." With Kayisha's doleful look, Emma stooped to give a lengthier pat. "Don't worry, girl. I'll be home to give you dinner."

Although, Emma thought happily, *if all goes well, it'll just be a quick stop home on the way back to heaven.*

Heaven was located just a few doors away. Eighteen months ago an angel had arrived in Emma's street, and Emma had been knocking on heaven's door ever since.

The angel came in the form of Justine. Dear, sweet Justine, arriving in a cloud of black smoke, her old Celica barely making the journey from her previous home on the south side of the river, the other side of Perth. A loud backfire had diverted Emma's attention from her watering of the pot plants on her front veranda, and curiosity at her potential new neighbor held her attention as the Celica drew up outside the empty house a few doors down. Only minutes after the Celica shuddered to a stop, the new-neighbor theory was confirmed. A removal van pulled into the red concrete driveway and two men swung open the van's doors to begin spewing forth its contents.

Emma had steered clear of the house's previous occupant, a little weasel of a man with a very bad case of halitosis and a gaze that couldn't lift above chest height. From her current vantage point, however, Emma could quite plainly see New Neighbor was neither weasel-like nor male. She was too far away to tell if New Neighbor also suffered halitosis, but a quick appraisal told Emma

4

it was unlikely. New Neighbor looked a good few years younger than Emma's thirty-six years and she had the waif-like appearance of the infamous actress, Winona. New Neighbor displayed a pert little denim-clad bottom as she leaned into the passenger side of the car to tug at an overflowing cardboard box. She cursed a loud "Shit, shit, shit!" as a lamp base dislodged from the top of the box and dangled by its cord, dangerously close to smashing distance of the curb. Emma, watering can still in hand, rushed over to see if she needed some help.

Five minutes later Emma was in love with her new neighbor.

That same night, as Emma replayed the afternoon in her head—an afternoon of lugging boxes and shifting furniture—she told herself she was not in love at all, she was just rebounding from the three-and-a-half-year relationship that had ended only a couple of months prior. "Bloody Chris." Emma punched her pillow into shape for the third time. "How dare you leave me for a metal-mouthed trollop." Emma punched her pillow again, recalling how she naïvely echoed that sentiment to the totally tactless girlfriend of a friend helping her through the first days of the breakup. Her eyes had opened wide on discovering why a tongue stud could be so appealing, and then she burst into tears as images of the trollop doing *that* to *her* Chris flashed through her mind.

By the next morning her pillow had been well and truly pummeled and a bleary-eyed Emma hauled herself out of the house for Kayisha's morning walk. New Neighbor, Justine, called to her from the front step. A coffee and breakfast later Emma was convinced this was no rebound. It was love. Pure and simple.

It had to be love. Why else would she, to this day, force herself to swallow the burnt offerings Justine served up in the guise of food? The first breakfast—of congealed eggs, charcoal bacon and fossilized toast—was surreptitiously fed to Kayisha, who lay under Justine's kitchen table, while Justine busied herself cleaning the disaster she managed to create in the preparation of such a simple meal. Subsequent offerings were suffered with smiles at the time, and Quick-Eze once home. Justine just couldn't cook. But Emma didn't care. She'd chew through a five-course journey to indigestion if it meant spending one more minute in heaven, in the presence of her twenty-eight-year-old angel.

Even though heaven opened its gates to men.

Yes, Justine was straight. But it was an obstacle Emma chose to overlook. Initially it was a detail easily dismissed, the landscape dotted with men who appeared on the scene and left only a few days or weeks later—however long it took Justine to tire of them (or maybe for them to go in search of a decent meal). That was, until the arrival of Paul.

Emma learned of Paul during morning tea on a Sunday just over a year ago. Justine had poured tea and passed Emma a plate that contained, much to Emma's pleasure, shop-bought biscuits. Then, much to Emma's displeasure, no detail of Justine and Paul's "date" was spared.

"Please, Justine." Emma really had no desire to hear of the length or girth of Paul's appendage. And she certainly didn't want to hear of what he had done with it. "Can we leave something to the imagination?"

Justine appeared surprised, as if providing the neighbors with a lowdown on the boyfriend's anatomical "gifts" was an everyday occurrence. "Okay." She nibbled on her biscuit, a smile forming as she obviously remembered some other detail of the night. Justine launched into a description that left nothing at all to the imagination.

"For God's sake, Justine." Emma rose from her chair. "I told you, I don't want to hear about it."

Again Justine looked surprised, told Emma to sit back down, that she promised not to say anything more. Then she asked if Emma had a boyfriend.

It was Emma's turn to be surprised. She just assumed Justine knew. Emma took a deep breath, preparing herself. God, it had been so long since she'd done the coming-out thing, she had forgotten how nerve-wracking it was. "No, Justine. No boyfriend."

"Oh." Justine gave Emma a *poor you* look. "Never mind."

Obviously Justine had not caught on. Emma was going to have to spell it out. "I'm not in the market for a man."

"Oh," Justine said again. The *poor you* look was also repeated. "Burned, huh?"

Emma squinted in disbelief. Dear, sweet Justine. Absolutely clueless. Emma took a really deep breath, having no idea how Justine would react to her news. "Burned, yes, but not by the male of the species."

"Oh," Justine said for the third time. Silence drew between them, Justine giving Emma an overt once-over—maybe to see if there were any visible markings to give away the fact she was a lesbian. Seemingly satisfied, she picked up the plate sitting in the middle of the table and held it out. "Would you like another biscuit?"

Emma couldn't make up her mind if she was glad or disappointed. Glad, yes, that Justine finally figured it out and seemed not to care a whit over it. Disappointed she seemed not to care a whit over it, Justine's affections well and truly aimed at Paul.

Paul.

Emma didn't like him at all. He was a fraction taller than Justine, but that still left him a good couple of inches shorter than Emma. And, Emma couldn't help noticing one hot day as they all sat in her backyard sipping on cold beers, for his size he had big feet. Big, hairy feet. Emma renamed him The Hobbit. But of course she never told Justine that.

During one of Paul's absences—he had a fly-in, fly-out job at one of the underground mines in the state's interior—Justine and Emma rented the final installment of *The Lord of the Rings* on DVD, and Justine, more than once, exclaimed how cute Frodo was. The Hobbit name was quickly dropped and Emma now privately referred to Paul as The Troglodyte.

To Emma's mind, Paul's troglodyte occupation was the only redeeming factor in his sorry troglodyte existence. For, while he would hang around for two drawn-out weeks at a time, when he flew back to the mines, he was gone for three glorious weeks. Three weeks that Emma had Justine all to herself.

Sort of all to herself.

Well, not all to herself at all really. Unfortunately Justine saw Emma as nothing more than a neighbor and friend.

At least that's what Emma had thought. Until the night of the fight.

The fight was only three nights ago, halfway into Paul's latest stay in Perth.

Emma heard the fight from her house. She was sure the whole street heard it, neither Paul nor Justine holding back in the decibel department. But she was the only one who ventured outside to check on Justine's welfare. Emma stood in the shadows of her veranda, thinking what a sad state of affairs it was—how, these days, the world hid inside, too fearful for its own safety to intervene, or too disenfranchised from its immediate society to care.

In between the "fuck yous" and "fuck offs" being tossed around by both parties with amazing frequency, Emma gleaned the disagreement was over . . . she listened more intently . . . over sex, money, domestic skills or lack thereof, politics, religion, golf . . . Essentially they had polarized views on every single topic.

Emma jumped at the crash of metal hitting concrete, her body coiling into fight mode, ready to charge at Paul if he dared lay a finger on Justine. But Justine was more than holding her own, the crash coming from his set of golf clubs as they were tossed out of the front door and onto the driveway. The clubs were followed by his mountain bike, then by a noiseless flurry of clothes—jeans, shirts, socks and jocks went flying.

Finally Paul too was tossed out, although not literally. He received a few good pushes from Justine but crossed the threshold of his own accord, hurling a string of expletives as he went; a string of the same was hurled back at him. "Fuck off, you fucking bastard!" The door to Justine's home was slammed, leaving Paul on the step.

Emma watched Paul gather his belongings and shove them into the back of his four-wheel drive, cursing as a pedal of his mountain bike caught on the rear bumper. Then she watched his vehicle pull out of the driveway and disappear into the night. She let a minute pass before making the short walk to Justine's front door.

An angry voice came in response to her knock. "Fuck off, bastard!"

"Justine, it's me, Emma."

The front door opened and Justine threw herself into Emma's arms. For the first time Emma felt just how slight Justine was, and she marveled at the strength displayed in her golf club and bag toss, the whole kit and caboodle being hurled a good few meters in one impressive throw.

"Are you okay?" asked Emma.

"Fucking bastard," Justine repeated, seemingly at a loss to say anything more. "Fucking fuck of a fucking bastard."

Given the current limitations to Justine's vocabulary, it was pointless trying to eke an explanation, so Emma busied herself preparing what her mum called the salve to every problem—a good hot pot of tea. She didn't know if her mum still thought of it that way, as they hadn't spoken in years. Not since Emma took Chris home to meet her parents. That was a day she wouldn't forget in a hurry. It was the day she placed the key to her childhood home on the dining table and left it there, along with any hope of acceptance by the two people she most wanted acceptance from.

But her parents' reaction to Chris and Emma's relationship was not of current concern.

"Here you go." She placed a cup at Justine's elbow.

Emma sat at the kitchen table, opposite Justine, also at a loss for words. She was not well versed in post-fight etiquette. She and Chris had rarely raised their voices to each other. Even their breakup had been very civilized, Chris calmly announcing she had been seeing The Trollop for a month and that she was moving out to be with her. Shocked, numb, Emma just nodded and left the house while Chris packed. On her return, it was as if Chris had never been there, except of course for Kayisha. Kayisha had been the runt of an unwanted litter, deposited in a cardboard box at the back door of the vet practice. Lots of love and lots of attention

9

from both Chris and Emma saw her thrive. But obviously The Trollop didn't have the time, space or inclination to take her on. Which was just as well. Emma would have walked over hot coals to get custody of their baby and she was overjoyed to find no battle necessary.

Feeling old anger at Chris once again rise to the surface, Emma concentrated instead on the etchings in Justine's kitchen table. Not really graffiti—the kitchen table had become a guestbook of sorts, and the etchings the entries. Justine liked each new visitor to her home to scratch their name, the date of their first visit and a byline into the tabletop. Justine called it an historical record. Emma saw it more as personalized notches on a horizontal bedpost. A little of her heart bled with each male name she read.

Justine swiped at her eyes. "How the hell am I supposed to go to work tomorrow? I'm going to look like shit in the morning."

Emma took her attention from the "Paul" etching in her immediate line of vision. Justine's cheeks were streaked with tears. Her anger subsided; she now looked tired and drawn. "You look fine."

"Can you write me a sick note, doc?" Justine managed a smile through her tears.

Emma smiled back. "If you don't mind the excuse of having either worms or fleas."

Justine hiccuped a giggle and Emma's heart bloomed in her love. She took a quick sip of her tea and spooned more sugar into it.

"Do you like a little tea with your sugar?"

"Huh?"

"Your tea." Justine pointed to Emma's cup. "You've put about six spoonfuls in there now."

"I like it sweet." Hoping to disguise her embarrassment, Emma took a sip, nearly gagging on the sugar hit that assaulted her taste buds.

Justine saw through Emma's pretence and pried the cup from her hands. "I'll get you another."

Emma watched Justine rise from the table, pull a fresh cup from the cupboard above the bench and pour from the pot.

The cup placed in front of her was left untouched as Justine said, "I'm sorry you had to see that."

Emma knew Justine was referring to the fight, not the tea pour. "It's okay." She shrugged. "Everyone has . . . disagreements . . . once in a while."

"Fucking bastard." Justine reverted to her earlier chant. "He can go to hell."

Emma just nodded, wondering if that was indeed the last they'd see of Paul.

It turned out she didn't need to ask, Justine volunteering the information. "The bastard had better watch out if he comes round here again." She folded her arms. "I'll take his fucking golf clubs and shove them down his throat."

"That might be a bit difficult," Emma offered. "I think they're all bent now."

"It was a pretty good throw, huh?" Justine's scowl disappeared and she grinned.

"If it was an Olympic sport, you'd have won the gold."

Justine laughed and again Emma's heart soared.

On a roll, and encouraged by Justine's improved humor, Emma continued, "Your jockstrap toss was quite impressive too."

That comment prompted a raucous shriek from Justine. Her cup left the table as it was knocked by her hand, her reliving the moment she hurled Paul's clothes outside.

"I'll get it." Emma was immediately off her chair and to the site of the damage.

At the same time Justine scraped her chair away to squat beside the broken china. "It's okay, I'll get it."

"Shit!" A dual curse emerged as their heads knocked together.

Emma rubbed the point of collision, it taking a moment for the pain to register. "Ouch."

"You okay?" Justine reached to touch Emma's head.

"Yeah, fine." Emma briefly met Justine's eyes but lowered her gaze, focusing on the china that lay in a spreading puddle of tea.

"Emma—" Justine's hand flattened against Emma's forehead, slid across her temple to her cheek.

Wordlessly, Emma lifted her gaze once again. What she found were eyes filled with . . . want? Or maybe it was confusion? Or maybe it was just sympathy for the poor lesbian who was in love with her straight neighbor. Whatever it was, Emma couldn't hold the look. She groped for the broken china, not looking at Justine, not looking at the floor.

"Shit." Pain sliced through her middle finger and reflex brought it to her mouth. She tasted blood. Jesus, she was pathetic. Tears sprang to her eyes and she stumbled to her feet, wanting to escape an atmosphere that was suddenly suffocating.

Justine rose with her, capturing her hand and examining her finger. Five minutes later Emma's finger stung from the antiseptic that had been applied and throbbed from the "Simpsons" plaster wrapped a little too tightly around the wound. Once home Emma would rip the plaster off and put a fresh one on, but for now she just sat, uncomfortable, at the kitchen table, feeling quite the fool.

"I'll get going home then." Emma stood, her middle finger held up in what would normally be construed as an insult. "Thanks for the first aid."

Justine smiled at Emma's single finger salute, a casual arm circling her waist as they walked to the front door. "Thanks for coming to my rescue." Emma's waist was given a squeeze. "You're a good friend."

"Anytime."

"Emma?" Justine caught Emma's elbow just before she stepped onto the veranda.

"Yes?"

Justine's hand dropped away and she shook her head. "Nothing. It's okay."

"What, Justine?" If Emma was pushing, she didn't care. Her finger throbbed, but more from the force of blood coursing through her body than the tightness of the plaster.

"Nothing," Justine repeated. Emma was in the middle of nodding a dejected "Okay" when Justine piped up again. "Oh, what the hell . . ." Justine pulled her closer and Emma found she had been kissed.

On the mouth.

Quickly.

But *on the mouth.*

Now, as Emma walked the short distance from her house to Justine's, she clutched onto the thought of the kiss and the possible intentions behind it. The physics of the kiss were fading, it too fleeting to register a permanent place in Emma's memory. It had been three days since they had spoken. That was how long it had been since the fight . . . and the kiss.

The kiss *on the mouth.*

Physical memory was fading, but the promise of new memories beckoned. Emma vividly recalled the phone call she received at the surgery just that morning. Justine had been breathless on the line as she invited Emma to her home that afternoon. Breathless as she announced she had something important she wanted to tell her.

Emma rolled her shoulders, releasing some of her tension before she knocked.

"Just a minute." The voice of the angel sounded through the wood. Emma gave another shake of her shoulders, relaxing but immediately tensing again when the door opened. The lips that had kissed Emma *on the mouth* moved to say, "Hi, Emma, come on in." Emma was no sooner in the door than slender arms drew her into a hug. "Emma."

Joyful, Emma hugged Justine back. "Justine."

"You'll never guess."

"What?" Emma inhaled deeply. Justine smelled so good. Good enough to eat. Emma wondered if the rest of her tasted like her mouth. Not that she'd really tasted her mouth, but she knew when she did, it would be sweet.

"Paul came back this morning and we had a long talk."

Emma imagined Justine living out her promise and threatening to shove his golf clubs down his throat. And then telling him it was over. She couldn't see Paul taking the news too well. Emma almost felt sorry for the man. Losing Justine would leave a hole like . . . well, like nothing she could imagine. "How did it go?" she asked.

"Better than I expected," Justine said as she held Emma at arm's length, her eyes sparkling. "Emma, he asked me to marry him. And Emma"—Justine's laughter rang like bells as she pulled her close again and squeezed her tightly—"Emma . . . I said yes!"

If there was a moment when the world turned black and everything was sucked into some airless void, then this was it. Emma stood motionless, aware she should be hugging Justine, giving her congratulations and admiring the stupid ring (no doubt cubic zirconium, Paul too much of a troglodyte to even think of buying a diamond that large) thrust in front of her face. Numbly she went through the motions, her brain telling of the need for a cigarette, although it was a habit she'd given up nearly three years prior. She'd puffed like a steam train for weeks after The Trollop completed her home-wrecking, but that didn't count. Anything to do with The Trollop counted for nothing.

The lie slipped from Emma's throat and over her tongue with surprising ease, "That's great, Justine. I'm happy you two sorted things out."

CHAPTER TWO

Sensation focused sharply, then eased and spread, dissipating to all points, fingertips to toes. "Oh . . ." Toni fell into the mattress, her head hitting a goose-down pillow that would benefit from a good plumping. It had been plumped on entry to the bed that afternoon, but the hours since then had seen the pillow clutched at, pushed into the headboard and generally squashed by heads or feet or arms or whatever other part of the anatomy was at that end of the bed at the time.

Pillow plumping was, however, not currently high on Toni's agenda. She concentrated on regaining her breath and running a limp hand across her brow. The film of perspiration coating her body was more prominent on her forehead, and her hand came away quite damp. Toni wondered if her blood sugar was low. It crossed her mind that a burger would go down well. A burger with the lot, including bacon and double cheese.

"Here you go." A sports bottle with the insignia of the gym Toni was a member of was held out to her.

Toni gratefully accepted the bottle and chugged the remains of the contents, the water now lukewarm, but at least wet.

"You want another?"

Toni accepted what she assumed was an offer of a new bottle of water. At least she hoped it was a water offer only, as she was unable to find the energy to go another round.

"You poor thing." Heather's laughter washed over Toni as a quick kiss was aimed in the general direction of Toni's lips. "Is my little accountant all worn out?"

Whether Toni's reply registered or not would remain a mystery. Heather swung her legs over the edge of the bed, not bothering to don any covering as she headed out of the bedroom, presumably to the kitchen. Toni watched her depart, at once admiring the toned and tanned body that moved with the litheness of a cat, at the same time admitting the fascination she had with that body was no longer quite enough.

The empty drink bottle was rolled dispiritedly in Toni's palms.

Three weeks.

Toni wondered if that was an appropriate amount of time to make an accurate judgment. Maybe she was being too hasty, wanting too much too soon.

No, Toni admitted to herself as the bottle came to rest insignia-side-up between her palms, she and Heather just didn't mesh. At least not outside the bedroom. Or the gym. Or anywhere else that provided a workout opportunity.

Heather was a fitness fanatic. As a gym instructor it was her job to promote the healthy lifestyle, but she didn't hang up her healthy hat with her microphone headset at the end of class. She lived it twenty-four-seven.

Three weeks ago that fact had been Toni's prime attraction. Actually the attraction happened a lot earlier than that, Toni fast becoming addicted to the "BodyPump" class offered at the gym. Four times a week Toni's endorphins surged, not only from the choreographed weight workout, but also from the woman who led her and the other "Pump" disciples in their quest for tone and buff.

Months passed with Toni huffing and puffing in the second row, awed and fascinated with Heather and her biceps, before she worked up the courage to approach her after class and suggest they have a coffee.

Heather readjusted the twist tie that held her brown hair in a high ponytail and flashed a whiter than white smile. "I'd love to, but I have another class in half an hour. Maybe after that?"

Toni considered doing the next class but decided she'd be a limp, useless ball of aching muscles by the time she finished, so she had a spa and sauna instead. An hour or so later she discovered Heather didn't drink coffee—would Toni like to go back to her house? Apparently Heather grew her own wheatgrass and could whip up a few shots in no time. Toni agreed, swallowed the shot of bright green chlorophyll and then, without much further ado, they wound up in bed.

What a workout that turned out to be. Heather approached sex with the same enthusiasm and energy she gave her gym instruction. More than once Toni congratulated herself on her decision to soak and steam instead of taking Heather's second class. She was just at the point of saying, "Enough, no more," when Heather, in a rare moment of stillness, cast an appraising eye over Toni. "You know, you're starting to get some great definition."

To Toni, this was the highest compliment that could be bestowed by her gym guru. Puffed with pride—obviously her months of four-times weekly gym attendance was beginning to show results—she ran her hand the length of Heather's flawless thigh and over an almost washboard stomach. "Thanks. I just wish I could say the same about you." The arched eyebrows received in reply caught her by surprise and for some reason she felt she had to explain herself. "I was only joking."

But it seemed she had read Heather's expression incorrectly. Toni found herself flipped onto her back. "You're gonna pay for that, Ms. Ljanjovich."

"How so?" Toni looked up at the woman who straddled her stomach, somewhat impressed that Heather rolled her surname off her tongue so easily—most people she met had to ask for it to be repeated at least twice. At that moment, however, Heather's pronunciation skills took a backseat to her more physical attributes. Toni watched the bulge of biceps and the pleasing line of taut triceps when Heather lifted her arms to again adjust her twist tie. A healthy dose of lust reared its head. Along with it came her second wind.

She was ready.

"Maybe like this." The muscular arm descended and disappeared behind Heather's back, her hand probing the space between Toni's thighs.

A groan emerged as Heather's fingers found their target. Another burst forth as she began a slow grind over Toni's stomach, pace quickening in time with Toni's undulating hips.

The bed shuddered and shook. Toni shuddered and shook. She lost her second wind then gained a third. And a fourth. They spent the entire Saturday afternoon in bed. And they stayed there well into the evening.

The only problem was, they hadn't moved far from there since. The reality was that Toni and Heather shared great sex, but little else. And while great sex was . . . well . . . great, it wasn't enough.

Toni knew what she wanted. She wanted a relationship based on mutual trust and understanding, a relationship where sex was integral, but not the be-all and end-all. She wanted a lover but also a friend. She wanted to discuss and debate every topic under the sun, and she wanted to be comfortable just being silent.

She wanted the fairytale.

She wanted the lot.

With bacon and double cheese.

That last thought made Toni salivate. She really could go for a burger.

Toni sighed, remembering the look of absolute horror on that first night, when she suggested they make a trip to her favorite fast-food joint to fuel up.

It was at this point that Toni discovered, in addition to her no caffeine regimen, it had been five years since Heather had consumed any sort of dairy. Red meat was also off the menu. Prepackaged foods—forget them. And alcohol was a definite no-no. It seemed Toni had been poisoning herself with almost every bite of food since birth. And she was putting the largest organ in her body—her liver—under enormous strain.

"Your liver keeps the rest of your body clean," Heather explained as she pulled the ingredients for a vegetable stir-fry from the fridge. "The more junk you feed your body, the harder your liver has to work to clear it away. Every piece of rubbish you consume is shortening your life."

Toni listened to Heather's "love your liver and live longer" epiphany, watching as the vegetables were tossed in an oil-free wok. She agreed that Heather's dietary beliefs made sense, even if they did seem a bit drastic in the long-term. Although, Toni conceded as her eyes followed the movements of a body glowing with good health, Heather's long-term practice of her beliefs certainly didn't appear to be doing her any harm.

While Toni silently thought loving your liver might not make you live any longer—it would just feel like it—she had to admit the plate of steaming, still-crisp and brightly colored vegetables presented to her certainly looked appealing. She tucked in and it was delicious. Despite being hungry again an hour later, she decided to give liver-cleansing a go.

So, for the past three weeks she had followed the principles to the letter, even forgoing her absolute favorite meal, the chicken Caesar salad, at the restaurant she and her boss—Cathy Braithwaite—visited at least once a week for lunch. Toni considered ordering the salad so it was "liver-friendly," but by the time the non-hormone-free chicken was removed, as well as the parmesan cheese, the bacon and the anchovy dressing, there was little left but cos leaves and croutons. And probably the croutons had been cooked in non-liver-friendly oil and would also have to be discarded. So she'd ordered the grilled fish and a dressing-free garden salad instead. It was nice enough. As was her long glass of mineral water with a wedge of lemon.

Cathy questioned the menu choice; Toni had been ordering the

Caesar salad for practically the duration of the five years they had worked and lunched together. She initially laughed at Toni's explanation, but overall she was supportive, telling Toni how well she was looking and even forgoing her usual glass of red wine in favor of a pineapple juice.

The compliment cemented Toni's determination to stick to her new healthy eating plan. And she was very successful, having only one slip-up in three weeks. The slip-up occurred only the day before. It was the day the lure of a Snickers bar overshadowed her long-term aim of being a trim, taut and terrific centenarian.

Toni had woken feeling tense and fidgety, and hungry for something sweet. Her resolve faltered not far from the corner store she drove by every day on her way to work, and before she knew it, she had pulled into a parking bay outside the store. Once back in the car, will power returned and she resisted the urge to rip the wrapper off the Snickers bar, instead tossing it into her briefcase. When she stepped out of the lift to the reception of the accountancy practice where she worked, Cathy was talking to Sue, the receptionist. Toni nodded a greeting and hurried to her office, sure both of them were staring at her briefcase, knowing contraband was being smuggled.

The Snickers bar played on Toni's mind the entire morning and throughout her lunch of tuna salad and organic wholemeal bread. Finally unable to stand the thought of it any longer, she checked that her office door was properly closed and dug into her briefcase. The wrapper was torn open and the bar consumed in guilty rapture. Throughout, Toni kept an eye on the door, sure this would be the time Heather, who had yet to pop in on Toni at work, would choose to make her inaugural visit. Either that, or Cathy would suddenly change her idea of office etiquette and barge into Toni's sanctum without knocking.

The bar was scoffed without interruption and Toni leaned back in her office chair, patting her tummy, which felt replete for the first time in weeks. But the smug sense of satisfaction accompanying the celebration in her stomach did not last long. She picked up the Snickers wrapper and stared at it, wondering why on earth she, a grown woman, was sneaking around like a thief for the sake of a chocolate bar.

Toni put it down to pride. She didn't want to admit to what she saw as failure. That ill-placed pride also made her bury the wrapper right at the bottom of her wastepaper basket—just in case Cathy or one of her other coworkers paid a visit, rounded her desk and looked into the bin. She knew the odds of that occurring were less than slim, but she did it anyway. She also knew the notion that the cleaner would notice the buried wrapper and tell Cathy her employee had blown her diet was even more ridiculous. But that didn't stop her from retrieving the wrapper and putting it in a zip-up pocket deep inside her briefcase.

The wrapper was still there.

Toni placed her empty water bottle onto the bedside table. Even now, a whole day later, and with the briefcase miles away in her home office, the hidden wrapper taunted her. It became almost symbolic, a sign she was heading down a road she just didn't feel right traveling upon. Why was she molding herself to fit another person's idea of what was right? And, if she were to be honest with herself, she would admit that—apart from regular orgasms—Toni found her relationship with Heather, on the whole, unsatisfying.

Upon hearing Heather pad back down the hallway, Toni sat upright, tugging at the sheet that lay in a knot at the end of the bed. She shook her head at the fresh water bottle that was offered.

"Heather," she began, arranging the sheet so it covered her breasts, "I think it's time I went home."

Heather glanced to the clock sitting on her dresser and furrowed her brow. "But it's only three-thirty. Virgil won't be howling for her dinner just yet."

"I know." Toni took a deep breath, in a split second her mind constructing and deconstructing numerous explanations. "I wasn't thinking of Virgil. Heather, I just don't think this is working out."

Heather's brow furrowed further. "What do you mean?"

"I mean—" Toni raked fingers through her hair. God, she hated doing this, almost as much as she hated having it done to her. "I mean, I don't think we should see each other . . . like this . . . anymore."

"But, why?"

Toni blinked. Heather looked genuinely confused. Surely she didn't see what they had as a fulfilling relationship? Or maybe she did. Maybe she read more into their great sex than Toni did. Toni took another deep breath, this time acutely aware of the potential to cause hurt. "Because . . ." *Because I want someone I can talk to as well as have sex with. Because I want to go out to dinner and not worry my menu choice will turn into a lecture. Because sometimes I'd rather go to the theater than lift weights. Because . . .* Oh hell, everything sounded terrible. But it was all the truth. Toni raked her fingers through her hair again. "Because . . ."

Not too much later, Toni turned her car into her leafy, tree-lined street.

"Hi, Virg." Toni was only halfway from her driveway to the front door when Virgil trotted up to rub against her legs. She scooped the part-Burmese, part-moggie female cat with a male name into her arms for a cuddle. "Mum's home early for a change, isn't she?"

Her answer a satisfied purr, Toni carried her feline friend to the entrance, cradling her so her back legs stuck up in the air.

It was only when Toni opened the fridge to peer inside that Virgil leapt from her arms. Virgil stood on her hind legs, front paws on the second-to-bottom shelf, also peering in, her nose twitching at a rate.

"Pretty poor pickings, huh?" Toni scanned the liver-friendly contents, no longer hankering for a burger, but hungry enough to hope some delectable treat would materialize.

Nothing did. Toni closed the fridge door and Virgil, having moved away fast enough to avoid being snap-frozen, looked up to her servant and gave a short "what's up?" meow.

"Oh, Virg." Toni leaned down to give Virgil a nose-to-tail stroke. "You won't be seeing Heather over here anymore."

Having left Heather's house directly from the bed, Toni left Virgil in the kitchen and headed for the shower. Her shower was long enough that the water began to run cool. Most of the time was spent deep in thought, water streaming over her short, dark hair.

Her thoughts took her back to those last few minutes in Heather's bed. She had stumbled through her explanation for wanting to leave, head bent low, feeling worse with each reason she gave.

"You want the fairytale."

More than a little surprised to hear her own, unspoken, sentiment articulated, Toni lifted her gaze to find Heather regarding her with an almost sympathetic look. "Yes," she said softly.

Heather shifted to sit cross-legged in front of Toni. "Sweetheart." Toni found the hand that cupped her cheek was warm, but the expression she received was almost cold, and it was totally humorless. "The fairytale doesn't exist. It's just that. A fairytale." Heather seemed to sense Toni was about to argue the point, continuing before she could get a word in, "And anyone who tells you otherwise is either a liar or delusional."

Toni was immediately intrigued, more than a little curious at the circumstances that had led Heather to this conclusion. She wanted to break open the shell, find what was lurking inside. The ego in her said she could be the one to save Heather from herself; she could be the one to show her true love did indeed exist. But that thought was fleeting. Heather was not a project to be worked upon. "Then I guess I'm just delusional."

Heather gave what appeared to be a genuine smile. Her palm brushed Toni's cheek again. "My little accountant turns out to be a romantic." She tsk-tsked. "And I thought we were having such fun."

"We were having fun . . ." Toni quickly corrected herself, not wanting Heather to think her performance was in question. "I mean, we still are . . ." Shit, that wasn't right either. "I mean . . ." Toni slid off the bed and bent down to pick up her clothes while she tried to figure out just what she meant. "I mean . . . it was great, Heather. Really, it was."

Still sitting cross-legged on the bed, Heather watched Toni get dressed. "You know, we could still have fun together—while you go looking for your romance."

The thought made Toni hesitate. Heather was the first physical contact she'd had with a woman since . . . since a long time, almost a year. She took her attention away from the buttons of her shirt and asked, "No strings?"

Heather crossed her heart. "No strings."

Unexpected tears welled in Toni's eyes. She quickly blinked them away. A no-strings relationship had been the carrot she dangled in front of Cathy. And that had ended in disaster, primarily because Toni had been unable to keep her side of the bargain. Instead of keeping her emotional distance, she'd fallen in love. "Sorry, Heather. I'm just not built for no-strings. Been there, tried that."

"The fairytale got in the way?"

"No." Toni stooped to give Heather a last soft kiss on the lips. "Reality got in the way of my fairytale."

Heather twisted so her legs dangled over the end of the bed. "Reality bites."

"Sure does." Toni plucked her car keys from the dresser, turned and left the bedroom.

Now, shower-fresh and dressed, but still hungry, Toni did another sweep of the fridge contents. Nope, still nothing. Maybe the pantry held some delicious secrets. Toni did a cursory scan then delved deeper, rifling through packets of dry goods—brown rice, wheatgerm, corn and spinach pasta spirals, wholemeal flour— and shunting aside cans of crushed tomatoes, beans, beans and more beans. Toni picked up a can and screwed up her nose. What had she been thinking? The can was put back on the shelf; maybe one day she'd make her own falafel, or hummus, or whatever else one did with a can of chickpeas.

Toni hit pay dirt on the very top shelf. A packet of digestive biscuits was retrieved. The biscuits had been there long before the start of her liver-cleansing regime, and let's face it, they were not the most exciting members of the biscuit family, but to Toni they could have been manna from heaven. Like the Snickers bar of the day before, the packet was torn open.

Toni loped down the hallway to her home office, packet in one hand and biscuit with a big bite out of it in the other.

"Let's go see if there's anyone interesting online."

Virgil followed her servant to the study, more likely due to the promise of some crispy crumbs than any interest in Toni's keyboard globetrotting.

Late afternoon in Perth did not make for an exciting chat-room session. As usual there was no one else from Western Australia anywhere to be found, and it was still only early evening in the Eastern States so things wouldn't heat up on that end for a few hours yet. The other side of the world was also relatively quiet, probably getting late for even the most dedicated night owls. Toni had a quick exchange with Minxy, a New York art student who, no matter what time of the day or night Toni logged on, was also online. She then found FallenAngel and Rabbit—from Adelaide and New Zealand respectively—in the "Hot Tub" but after a few unanswered hellos figured they were, as was usual, in a private room and not available for communal chat. Five digestive biscuits and six empty chat rooms later, Toni put her computer to sleep. "Well, that was about as boring as bat shit."

Virgil's wide-mouthed yawn showed exactly what she thought of the whole affair.

"Come on, Virg." All of a sudden lonely for some human company, Toni eased Virgil from her lap. "Let's get you some dinner. Then I think your mum might go out for a while."

CHAPTER THREE

The moment Cathy opened the door to her home, the aroma of cooked onions and garlic filled her nostrils. Her afternoon running around a tennis court had made her hungry, and now the enticing smell made her stomach growl. She ran up the stairs to the main living area, wondering what fabulous creation—Italian, no doubt—Lisa had whipped up this time.

"Mmm, something smells divine." Cathy rounded the island bench to give Lisa, who was busily stirring what appeared to be a roux, a hug from behind. She settled her chin on Lisa's shoulder to peer into the pan. "What's cooking?"

"*Ciao*, honey." Lisa moved the pan off the heat and reached for the carton of milk and whisk sitting on the bench beside the stove. The milk carton was offered. "You pour. I'll stir."

Cathy slowly added milk to the roux while Lisa whisked it to a smooth white sauce.

"What're we having?" Cathy didn't really need to ask. She

could quite plainly see the rich Bolognese sauce in another pan, and the oblong baking dish and sheets of pasta sitting farther down the bench. Lasagna was obviously on the menu. But she wanted to hear Lisa say it. In her very bad Italian. It was a practice Lisa had adopted a couple of weeks ago, ever since Cathy announced they would be celebrating their first anniversary in Italy. Lisa had promptly bought herself an Italian phrase book and now many of her conversations comprised a splintered combination of English and Italian. No thought was given to syntax or grammar; if the phrase wasn't in the book, individual words were just replaced. The result was shockingly inaccurate, but Cathy loved it.

Lisa continued to whisk, silent for a moment as she considered. *"Lasagne e insalata mista e rosso vino. E tiramisu* for *dolce."*

Cathy laughed delightedly, and not just at the mouthwatering promise of pasta, salad and a decadent tiramisu for dessert. Lisa topped off her bad Italian with what she called her "George voice," a very broad Italian-Australian accent, picked up years ago from her boss at the time, George Giavanni. Before they left for Italy the coming Friday, Cathy would suggest Lisa tone it down a bit, but for now she kept silent, finding the total effect hilarious. "Have you made the salad yet?"

Lisa took the few steps to the island bench to grab her Italian phrase book, flipped a couple of pages and scanned. The book was tossed back onto the bench. *"Non ancora."*

Apparently not yet. "I'll do it if you like."

"No, no, no," Lisa said as Cathy was ushered from the kitchen with a pat on the bottom. "This is my dinner. You go freshen up. I'll have a *bichierre* of *vino* waiting for when you get back."

Cathy didn't argue, the lure of a hot shower followed by a glass of wine silencing any further attempts to contribute to the chores. "Okay, honey." Her sports bag and racquet were retrieved from the floor and she headed up the stairs to the bedroom level of their home.

Their home.

The phrase had a lovely ring to it. And it was finally a phrase

Cathy could utter with accuracy, their shared living arrangement becoming official that very morning. At eleven a.m. the last box had been carted from Lisa's home to Cathy's. As soon as it had been deposited in the garage they rushed to the street for a little name-changing ceremony at the mailbox.

"Bravo!" Cathy applauded as the label with her name was removed and a new one—*C. Braithwaite and L. Smith*—was inserted into the clear plastic casing.

The label change marked the end of nearly a year of shuttling between their two homes, a coin toss finally deciding the debate over which house they were to live in. Lisa won the toss and announced her desire to shift permanently into Cathy's house overlooking the ocean.

Despite the fact that Lisa's house was to be rented fully furnished, the move was still a protracted one, most evenings seeing them sorting and packing, carting and unpacking. Her yard also benefited from a spruce-up—garden beds were weeded and turned, shrubs pruned and lawns mowed—and of course every room given a thorough spring cleaning. Their efforts, while leaving them both worn out as they combined it with their normal workloads, were worth it, the agent confident of a quick rental at a good return.

"But it's our first afternoon together," Cathy had argued when Lisa shook her head at the suggestion she give her recently joined Saturday afternoon social tennis club a miss.

"You can't, honey. It's your first turn as afternoon tea provider, remember? There'll be a riot if there's no tea and tiny cakes to nibble on." Lisa screwed up the old mailbox label and put it in her pocket as she said, "You go whack some balls around. I'll stay here and get a few more of my things organized."

"And then I'll take you out to dinner to celebrate?"

Lisa shook her head gravely. "I was thinking we could grab a movie, have an early dinner and an early night."

Cathy nodded, her response just as grave. "An early night is probably a good idea. You'll be tired from all that organizing."

"And you'll be exhausted from passing all those tiny cakes around."

"Absolutely." Cathy shook the hand held out to her. "Okay, it's a deal."

Cathy had been looking forward to their evening all afternoon. Actually, she'd been looking forward to some unstructured time alone for what seemed like weeks now. Their combined work schedules were demanding of their time; Cathy's accountancy practice, although she had eased off on her historically long hours, was as busy as ever, and Lisa's tiling business was thriving. Add to this their social commitments, their sports and their hobbies and in the last three weeks, the distraction of combining two households, and it seemed there was rarely time for them to just be together and do nothing in particular. Even tomorrow, Lisa's thirty-third birthday, was not their own. They had wanted to keep the occasion quiet and low-key, but Joel—Lisa's friend, business partner and party-planner for most of the decade they had known each other—was having no such thing. Since there were only five days between her birthday and them flying out, he thought it a prime opportunity to have a knees-up.

"Girlfriend." He sniffed, looking to Cathy for support. "If you think you're going to run away to an Italian love shack for a month and not let us give you a decent send-off, then you've got another think coming."

So late morning would see Lisa and Cathy, and over a dozen of their friends, descend upon Joel's house for a Champagne brunch. Then it was off to Lisa's parents' place for a birthday dinner. Most of tomorrow was therefore written off as far as quality couple time was concerned.

All the more reason to make the most of tonight.

Fresh from her shower, Cathy pulled track pants over her hips and a lightweight pullover over her bare shoulders. "Did you end up getting a movie?" she called as she headed back down the stairs, not really caring if Lisa had or not.

"Yep." The answer came from the kitchen that opened to the

living area that looked out to the ocean. "It's on top of the television."

With no further clues coming from the kitchen, Cathy detoured to the living area to check on Lisa's choice. It was Audrey Hepburn's *Roman Holiday*. Cathy smiled. Lisa was well and truly in Italian mode.

Well over a month ago, while sitting at traffic lights on her way to work, Cathy decided Italy would provide the perfect backdrop for their first anniversary. By that same afternoon she had booked the flights and spent most of her time in between appointments surfing the Internet, checking out hotels and working on an itinerary. Throughout the day, Cathy was confident she had made the right decision in overriding her and Lisa's joint plan to celebrate their first year together at a beachside resort in Broome. Her confidence remained as plans fell into place over the ensuing days; travel arrangements, accommodation and activities were confirmed. It wasn't until the arrival of a reminder that passports needed to be sighted before tickets could be issued that Cathy's confidence wavered.

"Damn," Cathy had muttered under her breath. A seasoned traveler, she knew the legalities involved with international travel but had until this point ignored them, entertaining instead the fantasy of making the holiday a real surprise. Cathy imagined deviating at the last moment from the domestic to the international air terminal and whisking Lisa onto the plane, their journey timed with such accuracy Lisa would be unaware of their destination until the captain did his *welcome aboard* spiel just prior to takeoff.

A nice fantasy. But not really practical. Especially since Lisa's travel wardrobe would now need to consist of more than the shorts and bathers she planned on taking to Broome. Cathy slipped the reminder notice into her briefcase and worked on how to break the news of the change in plan.

That night saw them toss the coin for their living arrangements, so they were both too preoccupied with the details of that project to worry about what corner of the globe they would be jetting off to.

Cathy stretched out her temporary reprieve until after dinner on Sunday. Still seated at the dining table, Lisa was scanning the moving house to-do list they had constructed, eyes darting from item to item on the page they had managed to fill. "Do you reckon we can get all of this done before we go? It's only four weeks until we leave."

Cathy squirmed in her chair. No brilliant ideas for breaking her news had occurred, so this opening was as good as any. "Actually we haven't quite got that long. We fly out on a Friday."

Lisa shook her head sorrowfully, "Cathy, you're getting vague in your old age. We leave on a Sunday."

Lisa's eyes had opened wide when Cathy told of her plans. "Italy? But I thought we were going to Broome? We've already made the bookings and everything."

"I thought maybe your folks might like to go to Broome." Now that she was started, Cathy's words spilled out in a rush. "We could give the holiday to your mum as an early birthday present. I mean, they wouldn't have to stay the whole four weeks—we could alter the hotel and flights for just a week or two, or whatever." The travel papers that had been burning a hole in her briefcase all weekend were placed on the table. "I can cancel these if you like, but I thought Italy might be nice."

"Nice," Lisa repeated dumbly, staring at the Italy itinerary before shifting her gaze back to the to-do list, sitting next to her left elbow. "We'd better get cracking then." Lisa looked again to the itinerary. "If we're going to get me shifted in properly before we leave . . ." She grinned when she finally shifted her gaze to Cathy. "For Italy."

It was at that moment Lisa's obsession with all things Italian began. Along with the phrase book came an Italian cookery book, and Italian fare had since featured on the menu for many a home-cooked meal. Lisa's atlas was the first item to be brought to Cathy's, and she pored over the maps, cross-referencing them with their itinerary. Cathy had visited the country twice before and so was questioned incessantly, despite protestations the visits had been with her parents, prior to her teenage years.

31

"I can't remember honey," Cathy would remind Lisa of this fact when yet another question was fired. "The details are fuzzy."

"So it will be like we're both discovering the country together." Lisa appeared pleased at the thought.

"That's right." Cathy's heart tugged almost painfully. Her feelings for the woman sitting next to her were so strong, sometimes it felt she couldn't breathe.

But breathlessness wasn't currently a problem. Cathy again inhaled the lingering smell of cooked onions and garlic. Lisa was busy sprinkling grated parmesan on top of the assembled lasagna. "That looks good enough to eat."

"Not quite. It'll take about forty minutes to cook. If I start heating up the oven now we'll be eating by six-thirty. Will you be hungry by then or is that too early?"

"I'm already starving to death."

Lisa smiled at the exaggeration, switching on the oven and indicating with a nod to the open bottle of red and two glasses arranged on the island bench. "Can you pour? I think it's had enough time to breathe."

Two generous glasses poured, Cathy settled onto one of the chrome stools that flanked the island bench and clinked her glass against Lisa's. "*Salute!*"

"*Salute.*" Lisa stood on the other side of the bench, the makings of a garden salad laid out in front of her. "You do realize"—Lisa glanced at Cathy as she swapped her glass for a cook's knife—"I haven't yet had a proper welcome-home kiss."

"I would have given you one"—Cathy scraped her stool away and padded barefoot to Lisa—"but it looked like you'd already made yourself so at home, there was no need."

The knife was laid onto the chopping board and Lisa turned to Cathy, eyes alight as she reached out to her. "Come here, woman, and give me the welcome I deserve."

Surrounded by Lisa's arms, Cathy smiled into her eyes. "*Benvenuto casa*, Lisa."

"*Grazie.*" This time there was no exaggerated accent. Lisa's voice was at once gentle and full of longing. "*Ti amo*, Cathy."

Cathy experienced the heart-skip that came whenever a moment of complete understanding passed between them. How she loved this woman. "*Ti amo*, Lisa."

More oft-experienced reactions followed. The quiver of anticipation in the moment before their lips met, the involuntary groan as Lisa's hands swept under Cathy's pullover, fingers skimming beneath the waistband of her track pants to settle lightly on her hips. The reaction of Cathy's hands was no surprise either. They mimicked Lisa's, sliding under Lisa's T-shirt but heading in the opposite direction. Her fingers soon found Lisa's breasts. Softness filled her hands. Lisa gasped as Cathy tweaked an already taut nipple between thumb and index finger.

Then the phone rang.

"Ignore it."

"Ignore what?" Cathy asked. She had no intention of speaking to anyone, her mouth eagerly seeking Lisa's, her fingers continuing their play over Lisa's breasts.

The phone fell silent midway through a ring, its sudden halt magnifying the sounds of breath and kisses and lovers' desires.

"Let's turn the oven off," Lisa suggested.

Cathy nodded and began them on an entwined crab-step toward the oven. Food was no longer a priority. Both she and Lisa were already panting softly, bodies drawn tight, need expanding with each touch. The bedroom beckoned, and if history was anything to go by, dinner would be a burnt offering by the time they reemerged.

"Ignore it," Lisa repeated her earlier instruction when a mobile took over from where the landline had left off. The ring tone told Cathy it was Lisa's, and its volume said it was some distance away, probably charging via the power-board tucked behind the entertainment unit in the living area.

They continued their crab walk, coming to a halt less than a foot from the oven. As if choreographed, they reached together to turn the oven off, and in unison stood upright again. Every part of their bodies that could touch, did touch.

The house again descended into silence as whoever was trying to get through gave up.

"Cathy." Lisa drew a hand to Cathy's face, cupping her cheek. Cathy met eyes heavy-lidded with desire, and she heard the want in Lisa's voice. "You are so very beautiful. It's no wonder I can never get enough of you."

"Please, Lisa." Cathy ached in her need, Lisa's expression so profound she felt her heart would burst. "Make love to—" Her words were cut short, her mouth encased.

"Jesus Christ!" Lisa was suddenly gone from Cathy's lips and she scowled. Cathy's mobile, dropped on the island bench along with her keys when she arrived home, had begun to ring. "Whoever that is sure is determined to get through."

"Ignore it."

Lisa nodded, but this time her kiss was distracted. "I can't." She pulled away and stalked to the bench. "What if it's some emergency?"

Cathy couldn't think of anything more urgent than her current need to have Lisa inside her, but she caught the tossed phone, quickly reading the name on the display. She also coughed, hoping to clear the "I was just about to have sex, so piss off" tone from her voice. "Hi, Emma. What's up?"

"Justine's . . ."

Cathy frowned and moved a few steps. The reception was bad, of late a problem occurring with increasing frequency. She made a mental note to add a new mobile to the shopping list. "Sorry. What?"

"Justine's getting . . ." Again Emma's voice trailed away. Cathy was almost sure she heard her sniffle. But maybe not. The phone crackled.

"Wait a moment, Emma. I'm just going to move outside." Cathy quickly crossed the floor. The sliding doors leading to the balcony were not locked, so it was only a matter of seconds before the phone was at her ear again. "Justine's getting what, Emma?"

This time the sniffle theory was confirmed. The reception was much clearer now, but the sniffle was all that came.

"Emma?"

Lisa, who had followed Cathy outside, raised her eyebrows. Cathy could only shrug, not able to convey what was happening, as she didn't know.

Maybe Emma would tell Lisa. While Cathy had known Emma for years, both of them longstanding members of a women's wine club, it wasn't until the arrival of Lisa that they extended their friendship beyond club activities. Lisa and Emma were fast friends, having "clicked" from the first time they met. "Emma, I'll put Lisa on, okay?"

The phone was passed over and Cathy leaned against the toughened-glass and stainless steel railing, designed to provide a wind barrier while maintaining an almost unrestricted ocean view. The sound of waves was distinct, only the road that followed the curve of the sand dunes separating them from the shoreline. Cathy tuned out the ocean noises, concentrating instead on Lisa's half of the conversation. She wilted when Lisa said, "Sure, Emma, come over." Immediately Lisa silently mouthed, "Sorry." It was voiced out loud when the call ended a few moments later. "Sorry, Cathy. Emma's in a right state. What else could I do?"

"It's okay." Cathy gleaned from Lisa's side of the conversation that something had happened with Justine, the woman Emma had been lusting after for goodness knows how long. Cathy looked through the balcony doors in the general direction of the kitchen. "I guess we may as well get dinner on the go." She sighed. "And set the table for three."

"There's no great rush." Lisa took the step necessary so their bodies were back in contact. "Emma's already downed a few drinks. She said she'd catch a taxi . . ." Cathy's hands were guided back under Lisa's T-shirt, to her breasts. "After she's had a shower. So we've got at least an hour. What's say we take this upstairs?"

Cathy laughed, nodding toward the street. "Or at least, take it back inside."

"Mmm." Lisa's lashes fluttered, her nipples hardening under Cathy's palms. "Sounds like a plan."

Although in agreement they should go indoors, neither

appeared in any hurry to do so. Cathy was pinned against the railing, Lisa's mouth at her neck, her hands roaming everywhere.

"Please—" Cathy's body twitched, reacting sharply to the thigh Lisa pressed between her legs. "I can't stand this anymore. Let's go inside."

This time they stuck to their mutual agreement for retreat, turned toward the door and fell in step. But something instinctively told Cathy they had spent just that bit too much time on the balcony. Sure enough, by step three an electronic chime echoed from inside the house, signaling someone was at the gate that barricaded the driveway from the road.

"Shit, what now?" Cathy said as she rolled her eyes skyward. Unless Emma had caught a jet-propelled taxi, it surely couldn't be her.

They turned back to the street.

"It's Toni's car." Cathy didn't know why she was whispering, especially since they were both in quite plain view.

"Maybe she hasn't seen us," Lisa suggested hopefully.

"Yeah, right." Cathy harrumphed. The sun was setting upon them and their only protection was waist-high clear glass. They would have been seen. Sure enough, a hand emerged from the driver's window and waved. Cathy waved back, stretching her mouth into a smile. Her forced smile turned genuine, wickedly so, once focused on Lisa. "I bet you any money she's on her way to Heather's. She won't stay long." Cathy laughed out loud when Lisa turned on her heel and announced she was going to switch the oven back on and set the table for four. "And she definitely won't hang around for dinner, she's *liver-cleansing*, remember."

Toni followed Emma onto the balcony, pulling up a chair to sit opposite her at the outdoor table. The balcony lights were off, but enough light filtered from the lounge room that they could easily see each other. Well, at least Toni could clearly see Emma. She was not quite certain what Emma could see at the moment, the bottle of bourbon that had been her constant companion all evening now almost two-thirds empty. To be fair, not all had been consumed by Emma. Toni had taken a shot before dinner and another before the play button was pressed on the DVD. Now, with the movie on pause while Lisa took a trip to the bathroom, Toni followed Emma outside to beg another swig.

The bottle was pushed to Toni's side of the table even before she had the chance to ask. Toni took a chug, a liquor burn quickly spreading down her throat, to her stomach. She handed the bottle back. "Thanks."

"You want one?" A cigarette packet, also half empty, was offered.

Toni hesitated before plucking a cigarette from the packet. She rolled it between thumb and forefinger, again considering. The decision was made and she nimbly adjusted it to sit between index and middle finger. The actions of a smoker came back to her as automatically as if she'd only had her last cigarette the day before, Toni leaning forward and cupping her hand around the blue gas flame Emma also provided. In reality her last cigarette had been a good nine years ago, a particularly bad bout of the flu completely removing the desire to smoke.

Not all the smoker's actions came automatically. Toni drew back too fast and the smoke choked in her throat, making her cough violently. It tasted awful too. Toni's eyes watered and she coughed again, stubbing the cigarette into the ashtray Lisa had grudgingly supplied.

Now that that particular activity was aborted, Toni didn't quite know what to do. Never normally at a loss for words, she found she was currently rather tongue-tied. Something was up with Emma. She didn't know what, and she felt she didn't know Emma well enough to ask—which was rather a shame since tomorrow, Lisa's birthday, marked a full year since they had met. But, if one were to draw a line in the sand, it would clearly show Emma and Lisa on one side, and Cathy and Toni on the other. While Cathy and Lisa's partnership saw a merging of their social circles on the bigger occasions, for the most part their get-togethers were either with one set of friends or the other. So the odd party or large-scale dinner had been the extent of Toni and Emma's involvement, and even then they never had a real one-on-one conversation; their chitchat was trivial, the type that occurs when socializing as part of a group.

Toni studied her companion. Emma was hunched forward over the table, eyes cast downward, ash in danger of falling onto the table as her cigarette dangled in one hand, forgotten.

It has to be a woman, Toni decided. Toni also decided Emma must have been on the receiving end of whatever had happened. One didn't react this way when they were the bearer of bad tidings. Such melancholy came only as the recipient. Toni knew this from firsthand experience. She had been through the devastation of loss, the heartache that comes from loving but not being loved in return.

Sighing inwardly, Toni turned her attention to a point just past Emma's shoulder, to the interior of the house, made visible by the floor-to-ceiling expanses of glass. Returned from the bathroom, Lisa had resumed her position on the couch—arm slung over an armrest, legs sprawled over Cathy's. They were in the midst of some conversation, Lisa punctuating a point by poking Cathy in the ribs and both of them bursting into laughter. Toni watched the pair. Tomorrow marked more than the anniversary of meeting Emma; it was also a year to the day Toni lost Cathy to Lisa.

But that was a whole other story and not one Toni wanted to dredge up at this particular moment. Still, a twinge of regret couldn't help rearing its head as she continued to watch the pair. Lisa was playing the clown, her cheeks puffed out, arms spread in a wide circle as she bobbed up and down in her seat. Whoever or whatever she was imitating, Cathy obviously found it hilarious, her whole body shaking with laughter.

Toni was not immune to the contagious nature of laughter, even when witnessed from a distance. Feelings of regret gave way to the beginnings of mirth. But the smile hadn't quite reached her lips when Emma's voice broke into her thoughts. Toni returned her attention outside. "Sorry, what was that?"

Ash from Emma's cigarette dropped onto the table but Emma didn't seem to notice. The movement of her head as she indicated inside the house was more a sway than a nod. "You never had a chance with her, you know."

Toni blinked, not quite sure she'd heard correctly. "I beg your pardon?"

This time Emma used her cigarette as a pointer. The action made whatever ash was still attached fall to the tiled balcony floor. She sucked on the cigarette but it had gone out, burned right to the filter. Emma squinted at the dead cigarette in surprise, and ground it unmercifully into the ashtray. "I said"—she reached for her cigarette packet—"you never had a chance with her. She was Lisa's all along."

"I know that," Toni said without emotion, so unprepared for the directness of Emma's words she didn't know how to react to them. But Toni's reply was lost on Emma. She just kept right on talking, pausing only to light the fresh cigarette she pushed between her lips.

"Oh, you may have thought you had her. A word here, a hug there . . . a kiss." Emma stopped talking and drew in deeply, smoke billowing around her. "But not just a kiss between friends, a *proper* kiss . . . on the mouth." The bourbon bottle was pulled closer and Emma fumbled with the screw-top lid. "Fucking thing." The bottle was pushed in Toni's direction, obviously meant for Toni to open. Toni did so, silent as Emma continued, "It's the little things, you know, make you think you're in. But you're not, and you're a friggin' idiot for thinking you are."

Emma clutched the now open bottle, lifting it in the cheers gesture before tilting her head to down a good few mouthfuls. Toni watched her drink, a whole spectrum of emotions rising to the surface, fighting for supremacy. She didn't know if she wanted to laugh or cry or just plain lash out at . . . at this horrid woman who, with just a few choice words, managed to cut right to the bone.

Yes, Toni knew she was never Cathy's. Over the years Toni had called her boss, they'd also become the best of friends, and that's exactly where it should have stayed. But Cathy turned to Toni in her time of need and Toni, long besotted with her employer, offered her comfort in the form of a lover. Their brief time together saw Toni's crush quickly turn to love. And then, just as quickly, it all fell apart. Cathy's heart lay well and truly with Lisa and, as the saying goes, you can't stand in the way of true love. Yes, yes, yes! Toni knew all this, and she'd dealt with it all a year ago. She didn't want or need to deal with it again now, and she really didn't want or need to hear about it from some drunk.

Toni stood and, without another word or glance at Emma, left the balcony.

"Lisa, stop it!" Doubled over with laughter, Cathy took a hand from her stomach to swipe at her eyes. "You're terrible!"

"I can't." Lisa bounced around in her seat even more violently. Her demonstration of Teletubbies mating was reaching its climax. "I'm almost there."

Lisa had caught the children's show *Teletubbies* while packing up the contents of her lounge room and was immediately appalled by its four stars—tubby, jumpsuit-clad creatures with bloated faces, button noses and television screens where their tummies should have been. She said if she'd seen the show as a child she'd have been totally freaked out and scarred for life by the disturbing little creatures. Since then, Cathy had been treated to intermittent impersonations of them in various situations, none of which would be suitable for viewing by children, and always with the same result—the grim end for the Teletubbies.

Today was no exception. Lisa bounced right off the couch. "My cathode can't take any more. My tube's gonna blow!" Lisa issued a loud *ka-boom!*, combined it with flailing arms and concluded by lying prostrate on the floor, legs twitching.

Once finished with her death throes Lisa sat up and shook her hair into place.

"And that, my friend, is why Teletubbies must never, *ever* be allowed to reproduce."

"Amen to that."

"Jeez." Lisa checked her watch as she hauled herself back onto the couch. "What are those two doing out there? Growing tobacco and setting up a still?" Cathy received yet another poke in the ribs and Lisa winked at her mischievously. "Or maybe they're getting it together. Toni *has* been following Emma around all night."

"Ooh, you lie! She has not. This is the first time all evening Toni has gone outside."

"They sat next to each other at dinner."

"You told them where to sit," Cathy reminded her, smiling. "Anyway"—she stole a glance in the direction of the doors leading to the balcony—"I don't think either of them is in the mood for a new romance at the moment. Plus, I reckon if it was going to happen it would have happened by now."

"Not necessarily," Lisa countered, slinging her legs onto Cathy's lap. "Em's been blinded by bloody Justine for so long she couldn't see straight, and Toni's been . . . well, you know . . . up until Heather, not looking. Maybe now their blinkers are off—"

"Why don't you just throw them into the guest room together and see what happens?" Cathy suggested dryly. "Honestly, Lisa, I reckon I'll have to have a stern word to Steph." Steph was one of Lisa's closest friends. Happily partnered in a relationship spanning over a decade, she liked nothing more than setting others on the road to coupledom. "She's turned you into a real little matchmaker."

Lisa puffed out her chest. "It's my duty as half of a committed couple to ensure all singles are appropriately paired up."

Cathy knew she was being baited. Lisa was well aware how Cathy felt about the numerous attempts made by well-meaning couples to alter her previous long-term single status. She hated it.

"And it's my duty as the other half of the committed couple to ensure you keep your nose out of it."

Lisa folded her arms. "Can't blame a girl for trying. It would be convenient though—de-single two friends in one fell swoop."

"Very convenient." Cathy decided the quickest way to get Lisa to let go of the notion was to agree. Another surefire method was also employed. Cathy crooked her finger in the come-hither fashion. "Give us a kiss, cupid."

Their embrace was fleeting, cut short by the smooth-sounding roll of the balcony door sliding open.

"Sorry to interrupt, guys." Toni looked somewhat embarrassed as she approached the couch.

Lisa stretched for the remote sitting on the coffee table. She and Cathy had long resigned themselves to the fact that the evening, for now anyway, was no longer their own. "You ready to watch the rest?"

"Umm." Toni shuffled her feet, thrusting her hands deep into her jeans pockets. "Actually I think I might get going."

"Don't you want to see Audrey and Gregory ride into the sunset on their groovy little scooter?"

"I've seen it before." One of Toni's hands escaped a pocket and raked through her hair. She yawned. "Anyway I'm tired. I think I need an early night."

Cathy gave her friend careful consideration. Hair-raking was a habit Toni displayed whenever nervous, and the yawn, well, that was quite obviously forced. Something was wrong, and it was more than just feeling out-of-sorts over her breakup with Heather. "Why don't you stay and have a coffee?" Cathy was sure Toni would agree. After all, she had broken every other rule of her liver-cleansing this evening.

"No." Toni was insistent. "I really do want to go."

"You probably shouldn't be driving, you know," said Lisa.

"That's right," Cathy agreed. Toni wasn't drunk, not even showing any signs of being tipsy, but over the course of the evening she'd helped empty the better part of two bottles of wine,

42

plus she'd had at least three shots of bourbon. "It's not worth the risk." Cathy glanced quickly to Lisa, who understood and nodded almost imperceptibly. "You can always stay here. The guest room's made up."

Toni's eyes flicked upwards as if the guest room, located immediately above them, was visible through the ceiling. "Is Emma staying?"

Emma's lodging for the night had not been discussed but Lisa piped up, making the decision for both of them. Cathy was sure she could hear a trace of laughter in her voice. Cupid was back. "I think she probably will be."

"Well, I'll catch a taxi then."

Cathy raised her eyebrows at Toni's decisive tone. So, too, did Lisa. Cathy could almost see her cupid's arrow doing a U-turn, striking her right in the backside. Another split-second decision was made, and Cathy said, "Look, why don't I drive your car home? I can taxi back."

"You've been drinking too."

"Two glasses. And I'm already on the coffee." To prove her point Cathy pointed to the half-empty cup on the coffee table.

"Don't you want to watch the rest of the movie?"

"It's a weekly rental. We can watch it later." Lisa made a shooing motion with her hands. "Just agree, Toni. You two can have a private conversation on the way." She winked at Cathy. "And Cathy can tell me all about it when she gets back."

By the time Cathy returned from dropping Toni at home, the house was in semi-darkness. She trotted up the two flights of stairs to the bedroom level. As she ascended, she noticed the kitchen was clear of dinner's debris. Lisa had been busy.

Cathy poked her head around the half-open door of the guest bedroom. Emma was on her back, covers drawn up to her chin, seemingly fast asleep. One foot poked from the bedclothes to rest on the floor, a sure sign she had been suffering from the spins.

Emma was motionless and quiet, so, feeling all the responsibility of a babysitter with a newborn, Cathy approached the bed to check she was actually breathing. While still a few steps away, Emma drew the sharp intake of air indicative of oxygen starvation. Recognizing it as the sleep apnea of a drinker who has overdone it, Cathy decided to turn Emma onto her side. It turned out there was no need for her intervention, Emma shifting of her own accord. Cathy crept out of the bedroom.

The next door, the one leading to the master bedroom suite, was also ajar. Cathy could quite plainly hear the rush of water. The spa was being filled.

Cathy smiled. The night was not yet over.

She found Lisa sitting on the step leading to the large oval spa bath. Legs splayed, her elbows rested on her knees and she was seemingly lost in thought. So much so she seemed startled when Cathy stood in front of her.

"Hi, honey." Cathy nodded to the room down the hall. "I see you've been playing den mother with our charge. Was she a handful?"

"No more than anyone who's downed almost an entire bottle of bourbon in the course of an evening. She's going to have one hell of sore head in the morning." Lisa grimaced. "Poor woman. I remember what that feels like."

Cathy nodded, having experienced Lisa's hard-drinking, hard-partying days many years prior. This was their second time around the dance floor, the first almost twelve years ago, back in their university days. Cathy had graduated; Lisa had not. She left university at the same time she left Cathy, the lure of pubs and clubs and those who frequented them greater than her desire to continue their two-year relationship.

Over a decade passed before Cathy would see Lisa again. A late-night chase after Toni's wayward feline revealed Lisa lived not only in the same suburb as Toni, but in the house immediately behind, their properties separated only by a lane. Then, as chance would have it, Toni picked Lisa's tiling business at random from the phone book when they were in the process of acquiring quotes for Cathy's planned office renovations. So circumstance saw them meet up again, and destiny drew them back together.

If anything, the separation was probably the best thing that could have happened to them. In the intervening years both forged their careers, Cathy as an accountant and Lisa—once she dragged herself out of her unemployment lethargy—as a professional tiler. The years also saw them develop their own interests and opinions, try on new relationships, change and grow. When the time did come for them to meet again, they were both ready for what the other had to offer.

The only blemish on the perfection of their reunion was the hurt Cathy caused Toni along the way. Cathy knew no good could come from having an affair with an employee, knew the situation would only be worsened by the fact that that same employee was also her best friend. But she pursued the relationship anyway, desperately attempting to block out her feelings for Lisa by running roughshod over Toni's. Toni had been rightly upset when Cathy, realizing she could not rest until her attraction to Lisa was resolved, ended their short-lived relationship. Toni left not only work, but Perth, for three months, taking extended leave and returning to her hometown of Melbourne.

Cathy missed Toni terribly over those months. She missed the companionship Toni offered, missed the way she talked as much with her hands as with her voice, missed the woman who was not only highly competent in her profession but also a kind and thoughtful individual. Cathy fretted often during this period, hope of Toni's return fading with each week that passed. When the day came that Toni did step back into the offices, Cathy was overjoyed. But her joy was short-lived. Toni was largely aloof and remote, keeping to her office during work hours, displaying little of her effervescence of old when she accepted Cathy's invitations to lunch or Friday afternoon drinks. Cathy was sure she had lost the friendship forged over their years of working together. But again, just as Cathy's hopes were fading, Toni slowly let down her guard and allowed Cathy back into her life. To Cathy's delight, she also allowed Lisa into her life. Lisa and Toni began their friendship reluctantly, both practicing civility purely for Cathy's sake. It took time, but eventually both seemed to realize, if not to admit, the other had likeable traits and they could enjoy, as opposed to endure, each other's company. It helped they were both fond of hefting weights; they met at Toni's gym on at least a weekly basis for Pump class. Although, Cathy surmised, that activity would be coming to a temporary halt. Lisa would be in Italy, and Cathy doubted Toni would be attending any of Heather's exercise classes for a while.

"How was the drive?" Lisa asked.

"Good. The roads were pretty quiet. Too early for the pubs yet, I suppose."

"And Toni?"

"She was . . . upset." Cathy had managed to coax the truth about halfway through the twenty-minute journey. "Emma said some things . . . about me and her."

Lisa raised her eyebrows, her interest clearly piqued. "Like what?"

Cathy related all that had been revealed in the car and Lisa immediately came to Emma's defense. "She was drunk. And it sounds to me more like she was transferring her own issues onto Toni. I don't think it was a personal attack."

"I know." Cathy's thoughts had run along much the same lines. "I tried to tell Toni that, but I think she's a little raw at the moment." The water was almost at the right level and fragrant bath foam frothed on the surface. Masses of luxuriant ylang-ylang and sandalwood bubbles would appear within moments of activating the jets. "Needless to say, Emma's not her favorite person right now."

"Toni's not dumb. She'll realize Emma just wasn't herself tonight. She'll get over it." The taps were turned off and Lisa tested the temperature by swishing a hand through the water. "Bloody Justine. I tell you, if I get the chance I'll—"

Cathy folded her arms, smiling at the outburst. Lisa was unerringly loyal to Emma, but she was also well aware of the potential problems in bawling out one of Emma's neighbors. "You'll what, honey?"

46

"I'll—" Lisa paused to pull her fleecy rugby-style shirt over her head. "Oh, I don't know." The shirt was tossed to the far corner of the bathroom. "It just makes me so mad, her leading Emma on like that."

Cathy watched Lisa disrobe. Track pants and underwear were also tossed aside, fully revealing the work of art that was Lisa's body. Cathy was not shy in her outward appreciation of it as she removed her own attire. Almost matched in height—Lisa had the advantage by an inch or so—they were both blessed to be taller than average, but not tall enough to tower. There the similarities ended. Broader at the shoulder than the hip, Lisa had the physique of an athlete. Cathy was softer, more curvaceous, her trim build kept in check by the occasional run and weekly tennis. But while Cathy's sedentary occupation made planned exercise a necessity, Lisa thrived on all things physical, flinging herself around by choice. The demands of her job as a tiler not enough, Lisa also ran, swam and, via Pump class, tossed weights. The results were spectacular. Long limbed, Lisa had muscles that were lean and well defined. And she had legs to die for. Dressed in her work boots and shorts, she turned many a head of both sexes.

Cathy was dark—dark brown hair, dark brown eyes, skin quick to color when touched by the sun. Lisa was fair. A natural blonde, she inherited skin requiring extra care in the harsh Australian climate. A set of impossibly blue eyes shone from an open, friendly face. Even when her brow was furrowed, as it was right now, Cathy thought her a knockout.

Lisa was obviously still absorbed by thoughts of Emma and Justine. Cathy decided to play devil's advocate. "Maybe Justine wasn't even aware she was leading Emma on."

"Oh, come on." Lisa snorted. "She knew *exactly* what she was doing." The furrow turned into an outright scowl. "God, I hate those kind of women."

"And what kind of women is that?"

"You know." Lisa flashed Cathy a look that said she shouldn't need to explain this. "The kind who flirt around the edges. Bored heteros titillated by the attentions of another woman. And then, when the heat gets too hot, they flee the kitchen and have the gall to say, 'Me? I never did anything wrong. It wasn't *my* fault she got the wrong idea.'"

"Maybe Justine really did have some sort of feelings for Emma. Maybe she was just as confused by the whole thing." Cathy had never met Justine so was willing to give her the benefit of the doubt. "A lot of women try on the lesbian thing for size. And for some it fits. Just like some women who identify as lesbian try being with men." Cathy screwed up her nose. "God knows why."

"Because they're probably bi."

They were heading way off topic. Time to take the plunge. Cathy grasped Lisa's shoulders, pointing her in the direction of the water. "Unlike card-carrying, flag-waving, dyed-in-the-wool, dykes like us."

"That's right." Lisa turned to Cathy and grinned. "Bags I get the side with the good view."

"And which side is that?" A well-worn line of Lisa's, Cathy already knew the answer.

"Why, the side where I get to look at you, of course!"

Lisa stepped in after Cathy, her behind not even touching bottom before the button to the jets was pushed and bubbles appeared as if from nowhere.

The appearance of an increasing mountain of bubbles invariably evoked a childlike response in the both of them. After a brief period luxuriating in the massaging effects of the jets, they began to splash around like two kids at bath time. Lisa hooked her thumbs together, slapping her palms hard and flat on the water surface. The result was an instant tidal wave that soaked any part of Cathy that was still remotely dry. Cathy responded by paddle-kicking her feet madly in Lisa's direction. It had the same effect as the tidal wave.

Bubble construction was next. Cathy piled handfuls of foam onto Lisa's head and began what she thought was a pretty good interpretation of the Arch of Constantine. She even managed to excavate two of the three arches without her construct totally collapsing. Lisa's effort was less successful. Originally planned to be the tall, chimney-like Trajan's Column, the physics of bubbles failed her and it began to slide to one side. Not to be outdone, Lisa announced it was always intended to be the Leaning Tower of Pisa.

"*Magnifico!*" Given the Italian theme of their bubble buildings, Lisa slipped back into her Italian interjections. She sat back to admire her handiwork as it slowly slid off Cathy's head.

The jets had been going full-pelt throughout their play and the expanding mass of bubbles was creeping over the rim of the spa. Some had already fallen onto the top step. If they didn't want to be wading through a wet mess on the floor, it was time to turn off the jets.

With no motor whirring, the only sounds were the gentle lapping of water against porcelain and the crackle of thousands of tiny bubbles popping. Cathy became transfixed with the bubbles, each displaying a rainbow in miniature. She caught a handful in her palm, lifting it to the light. The foamy mass shimmered and shone, the bursting of one bubble revealing another, perfectly formed rainbow sphere underneath.

Lisa's toes wriggled against the soles of Cathy's feet. "Come over here, honey."

Cathy blew the foam from her hand. A splotch landed right on Lisa's nose. Cathy smiled. She couldn't have done any better if she'd taken careful aim. She eased her way across the spa. "Why?"

"So you can tell me about the rest of your day." Lisa gathered Cathy into her arms, arranging her so she sat with her back resting against Lisa's chest. She wrapped her arms around Cathy's waist and lay her chin on Cathy's shoulder. "How was tennis? Did you win?"

"It was good. A lot of people went. Because it was such good weather, I suppose." Cathy relaxed her muscles completely, letting buoyancy lift her limbs while her torso was kept anchored by Lisa's arms. It felt wonderful. "I got partnered with Belinda for a couple of rounds."

Lisa tilted her head so her mouth was right at Cathy's ear. "She's the one who plays competition?"

The warm breath tickled to the point it made Cathy shudder. "Uh-huh. Club pennants and State grade."

The tip of Lisa's tongue lazily traced the outer edge of Cathy's ear. "So you two wiped your opponents off the court?"

"Sort of. She wiped while I watched." Warm breath, a warm tongue and, now, the soft nibble of teeth on Cathy's earlobe were sending her into sensory overload. Talk was fast becoming difficult. Lisa was well aware of the effect she was having. Her hands joined in on the tease, moving slowly across Cathy's stomach and down, ever so slowly down. Lisa laughed softly when Cathy's legs opened in response. "She plays a hard game though. Too hard for me."

"I thought you liked a good game." Lisa worked her lips up and down Cathy's neck, slid her hands up and down the length of Cathy's thighs.

"I do." *Keep going.* Cathy tried to send mental messages to Lisa's hands. They were on the inside of her thighs now, inching upwards before retreating in the direction of her knees. "But her only aim is to win."

"Isn't that what the game's about?"

"In competition, yes. But in round-robin social tennis, no."

Warm breath was back in Cathy's ear. "Tell me how you like to play."

Cathy's mind tried weakly to construct sentences. It wasn't easy; all she could concentrate on was Lisa's hands and mouth. "Sometimes fast . . . sometimes slow. Make the most of each point. Rally a bit."

"And throw in an occasional ace for good measure?"

"Yes." Cathy moaned as fingertips found her slick and swollen. She longed for them inside her. "The occasional ace is good."

Cathy's mind was thick with desire and Lisa's voice swam through it, low and sultry. "So beautiful . . . my *bello* . . ."

"Please, Lisa." Cathy could take the tease no longer. She

strained against Lisa's fingers, but they never made more than a whisper of contact.

Light laughter washed over Cathy again. Lisa loved every moment of this. But she complied, releasing her hold so they could both stand.

Numerous attempts at spa sex had taught them that, while the premise was awfully romantic the reality was a different matter. Water could wash away even the most amorous of flows, and lying half-in, half-out of the spa was uncomfortable, especially with a tap sticking in your back and cold tiles making your bottom go numb.

Bed was much better.

With fluffy bath sheets draped around their shoulders, they practically ran toward the bed. Lisa veered to the door and snapped the privacy lock on, saying, "Just in case Emma decides to sleepwalk."

The bath sheet slipped from her shoulders as she climbed onto the mattress. Cathy had but a moment to again admire Lisa's physique before long, lean limbs were entangled in hers. Lisa lay right on top of Cathy, holding her upper body erect by virtue of the hands she anchored on either side of Cathy's ribcage. Those blue, blue eyes pierced with their intensity.

"My love." Lisa bent to Cathy's lips. "My beautiful beloved."

Welcome home, Lisa. Cathy was sure, even though she did not voice her thoughts out loud, Lisa understood.

Confusion crossed Lisa's eyes just moments later. She cocked her head to one side. "Did you hear that?"

"What?"

"Listen."

Cathy strained her ears. Nothing. She was just about to say so, when Lisa placed a finger over Cathy's lips.

"Shh."

Yes. Cathy heard it. A muffled retching came from beyond their bedroom door. Oh, great. "I think Em's bourbon has come back."

"Poor Em."

Yes. Poor Emma. But there was little they could do about it.

She would just have to suffer the consequences of her overindulgence. "I bet she'll be off the grog for a while," Cathy said.

"Hmm." Lisa traced a line around Cathy's lips with her index finger. "Now, where were we?" She smiled and winked. "Oh yes, that's right. I was just about to do something a little like this . . ." Cathy's mouth was captured, but only momentarily. Lisa's whole body went limp in a gesture of defeat. The effect was heightened by the repeated banging of her forehead against Cathy's shoulder. "No, no, no!"

Cathy knew exactly what was wrong. She couldn't block out the sound of retching either. Just as water washed away an amorous flow, so too did the echo of vomiting erase an atmosphere of romance. "Shall we make sure she's all right?"

Just moments later, donned in track pants and T-shirts, they headed from the bedroom.

"I guess this just wasn't our night," Cathy said morosely.

"Seems not." Lisa's voice was dark. "I tell you, if I get my hands on that bloody Justine—"

Cathy was frustrated beyond reckoning. "You hold her. I'll hit her."

Both knew neither would do anything of the sort, but it served to lighten the mood. Lisa turned in mock shock to Cathy. "Why, Cathy! I never knew you had such a violent streak."

"You better believe it, baby." As they entered the guest room Cathy noticed the clock radio on the bedside table tick over to midnight. "Happy birthday, Lisa."

"Hmph." The birthday girl pushed open the door to the *en suite* bathroom and squatted next to Emma, who knelt in front of the toilet bowl. She rubbed Emma's back and pushed hair back from her forehead. "You'll be okay, Em. Just let it all out."

Cathy busied herself finding and filling a glass with water. She sat on the bathroom floor, back against the vanity unit, glass at the ready whenever Emma needed to take a sip. Sympathy for Emma collided with more selfish sentiments. Cathy wished they'd stayed in the spa, preferably with the jets whirring at full pelt. A cold, numb bottom and a tap in the back didn't seem such a hardship now.

Lisa must have heard Cathy sigh because she turned and winked. "*Uno settimana.*"

"*Sì.*" One more week and they'd be together, alone. Cathy couldn't wait.

CHAPTER FOUR

Toni watched her business card holder fall to the floor. Not all the cards went with the holder; at least a couple remained at desk height, clutched by a chubby hand. But those cards too met their end, the fat little hand taking them to a small mouth so their corners could be chewed.

"I'm sorry."

"Don't worry about it." Toni waved away attempts by the woman sitting on the other side of the desk to bend down and pick up the fallen cards. The woman's hands were already full with the toddler she held in her arms—or rather, tried to hold in her arms. In the fifteen minutes of their appointment to date, Chloe, a two-year-old redhead, had twice escaped her mother's lap, both times being retrieved to sit squirming, red-cheeked and fractious. "I'll get them later."

At least business-card chewing momentarily stilled Chloe. Toni, making the most of the temporary reprieve, glanced quickly to the page of notes she had prepared and launched straight back into her interrupted explanation of dividend imputation. "So you see, when a company has already paid Australian company tax, shareholders are able to claim a tax rebate on the dividends." Toni turned the sheet around so it faced mother and daughter, using her pen to point as she explained, "It means tax isn't paid twice on the same profits . . ."

Toni trailed away as the pen was sharply knocked, leaving a slash of black ink across her neatly written figures. Card-chewing had obviously lost its appeal, the pen targeted as the next interesting plaything.

"I'm so sorry," the mother repeated, hoisting the toddler farther onto her lap and running a gentle hand through the red hair. She quietly appealed to her daughter to sit still for just a little while longer. Chloe responded by sneezing violently. A wide-eyed hiccup quickly followed.

The mother apologized yet again, removed a tissue from her sleeve and wiped the strand of mucus that dangled from Chloe's nose. A fresh tissue was then used to wipe the front of Toni's desk. During this intermission Toni stole a glance to her watch. Twenty past nine. What a start to a Monday.

At nine forty-five the sound of Cathy's voice came from Toni's half-open office door. "Are you okay?"

Toni glanced up from her self-administered temple rub. Her appointment with Chloe and her mum had ended fifteen minutes early, Chloe becoming more and more unmanageable. Finally, when Chloe had again wriggled from her mum's arms, found a stack of blank CDs on a low bookshelf and thrown them across the room, her mother declared the appointment over.

"What happened in here?" Cathy crossed the room, avoiding the disks that lay scattered across the floor and settling into the chair previously occupied by mother and daughter. Her head momentarily disappeared as she bent to retrieve the business card holder. It was placed back on the front edge of Toni's desk, along with a couple of bent business cards.

"A two-year-old happened." Toni released the last of her tension with a roll of her shoulders. She tossed the bent business cards into her wastebasket, screwing up her nose as a couple of soggy chewed ones followed them into the trash. "Honestly, Cathy, I don't know how mums do it. I certainly don't have the patience."

"Oh, I don't know about that. I seem to recall a certain person dominating all the cuddle time at Christmas."

"That's different." Cathy's brother and his family had been visiting from the Eastern States over Christmas and New Year. Apart from a festive season get-together, the visit had been to show off the latest addition to their little family, their second boy. "Holding a sleeping two-month-old is a lot easier than wrestling with a two-year-old wriggle worm. Besides"—Toni smiled—"I seem to recall a certain aunt continually interrupting my cuddle time so she could have a go."

Cathy gave the expected reaction, huffing and folding her arms. "Well, I had to, since Aaron decided Aunty Lisa was much more fun to play with than Aunty Cathy."

Toni continued to watch her employer from across the desk. A wistful expression crossed Cathy's features, as it now did whenever the subject of children was brought up. Toni was slowly getting used to this relatively new aspect of Cathy. She had always known of Cathy's love for her first nephew, soon to be six. She'd played the long-distance but devoted aunt since Aaron's birth. Christmas proved a turning point. The causal observer would still see a doting aunt, but if one looked a bit more closely, they would see Cathy's affections were laced with a quiet yearning, a need for something more. There was no other way for Toni to describe it. Cathy was clucky.

Toni wondered if Lisa had also noticed Cathy's shift in thinking and if the two of them had talked about it. It seemed whatever had or hadn't been discussed, Cathy obviously didn't want to enter into it now. The topic was quickly changed from motherhood to more mundane matters. "So, did you get your gardening done?"

"Some." Toni smiled sheepishly.

Come midafternoon on Sunday, Toni had left Lisa's birthday

brunch, full of food but also full of plans to make the most of a sunny autumn afternoon by tackling some chores in the garden. By the time she had driven home, her tummy had expanded, so instead she collapsed with a groan onto the couch, loudly cursing gay men and their catering abilities. Joel and his partner, Scott, had laid on a veritable feast. Toni indulged accordingly, avoiding the liver-friendly fruit and vegetable platters, instead piling her plate with mini blue-cheese and asparagus tarts, Danish pastries and a myriad of other delectable brunch-type treats. She undid the top button of her jeans, swung her legs onto the couch and lay flat. The couch was located under a window so she had a good upside-down view of the outside world. Thin wisps of cloud hung in a blue sky. It really was a beautiful day. Toni fell asleep with grand plans of weeding the garden beds and deadheading the roses still drifting through her mind.

By the time she awoke, her upside-down view of the world revealed light to be fading. Toni hauled herself upright and headed to her garden shed in search of some secateurs. She'd deadheaded two rosebushes before it got too dim to see clearly. She could have turned on the front security light and continued under artificial rays, but she didn't, choosing instead to retreat indoors and check out what was happening on the World Wide Web. The chat rooms were jumping and Toni clocked up a late night in front of her computer screen. But she didn't want to admit that to Cathy.

"I got some of my roses done but that's about it." Toni switched the focus away from herself. "How about you? Did Lisa drag you straight to the nearest duty-free store to get her digital camera?"

Birthday presents within Lisa's group of friends had traditionally been a group affair, everyone banding together to purchase one larger item rather than small individual gifts. This year had been no different, except this year, given the impending trip, it was decided the collective monies should be given as a contribution toward the digital camera Lisa was hankering over.

"She didn't get the chance. Most everyone stayed long after you'd gone." Cathy re-crossed her legs and smoothed the material of her slacks. "And given the day was held in Lisa's honor, we couldn't just walk out. As it was, we didn't even go home before we headed to Lisa's folks' place for dinner."

The hint of irritation in Cathy's tone didn't altogether surprise Toni. On Saturday night, only minutes after Cathy deposited Toni on her doorstep, Toni realized she had interrupted their first official evening at their now shared home. So caught up in her own worries, she completely forgot it was a hallmark night for the pair and had trundled over, expecting to be entertained. That Emma also barged in on their privacy less than an hour later was of no consequence. Toni still felt bad for not remembering. "Oh, well, only four more sleeps and you can forget about all of us for the next month."

"Sounds divine. By the way, how are you fixed for appointments on Friday morning?"

The Palm Pilot that housed Toni's schedule was retrieved. "Nothing until two. Why?"

"I thought you might like to take us to the airport. If you want, you can keep your car in our garage and use the company car while we're away."

Toni's smiled brightly. She relished any opportunity to drive the BMW Cathy leased on behalf of her business. "Just tell me the time and I'll be there."

"Great." Cathy stood, looking like her request had been accepted a lot easier than imagined. "The plane leaves at nine-fifteen. So that means I'll see you Friday morning at—"

Toni groaned, realizing what she had just agreed to. Travel to Italy was not as tightly controlled as travel to the United States or England, but still it required checking in at least two hours before takeoff. Add forty-five minutes to drive to the airport and that meant, "Six-thirty."

Left alone in the office, Toni continued with her mental arithmetic. To be at Cathy's by six-thirty meant she'd have to be up by . . . Gods, five forty-five. If she'd been awake that time of the morning in the recent past, she'd blocked it from her memory. Toni made a mental note to check her clock batteries and turn the alarm volume up as far as it would go.

CHAPTER FIVE

Lisa bounded up the stairs leading from the garage three at a time, calling as she went, "Honey, look what the cat dragged in."

Toni took the stairs at a much more sedate pace. Putting one foot in front of the other was all she could manage at such an ungodly hour of the morning.

Lisa had greeted her at the door fresh-faced and grinning, traits of the morning person that left those with closer attachments to their cozy beds, such as Toni, diving under the covers for protection. Toni was not the morning type—she had enough trouble getting to the office at nine a.m. And she rarely made it to her fortnightly eight-thirty meetings with Cathy on time. This morning's five forty-five alarm was utter torture, not at all aided by the headache she woke with, probably caused by the previous night's stress of checking and rechecking that her alarm was correctly set and operating.

Toni rubbed her temples as she mumbled a hello to Cathy, who, as much the early bird as Lisa, trotted down the stairs, toting two pieces of cabin luggage. They were dropped next to the pair of suitcases already zipped, locked and tagged.

"Hi, Toni," Cathy said, giving a lopsided grin. Obviously Toni looked as much like she had been dragged out of bed backwards as she felt. "You made it."

"Of course." Toni rubbed her temples again, hoping the headache pills she'd swallowed before leaving the house would kick in soon. She glanced pointedly at her watch, just to drive home the fact she was not only on time, but a whole two minutes early. "Are you about ready?"

"I think so." There was a final check of tickets and passports. "Let's go."

Once Cathy and Lisa had checked in and been issued their boarding passes, Toni accompanied them as they walked past the airport's souvenir shops, news agency and cafés.

"Are you sure you don't want to have breakfast with us?" Cathy asked, indicating a café from which the enticing smell of freshly brewed coffee emanated.

"Positive," Toni said, shaking her head. "I still have to feed Virgil." She glanced down to her track pants and fleecy jacket. "And I'm not exactly dressed for eating out."

They stopped at the entrance to departures. Once through the security check, Lisa and Cathy would head for the lounge reserved for business and first-class ticket holders. Despite her headache, Toni could not help but smile when she turned to Lisa. The woman looked like she could almost jump out of her skin. Initially floored when Cathy's last-minute surprise upgrade from business to first class was announced, now, if possible, Lisa was even more excited about the trip than before. For Cathy's sake Toni hoped, but doubted, there was something in the departure lounge that could help Lisa burn off her excess energy before she boarded. Toni definitely didn't envy Cathy sitting next to a Mexican jumping bean for the twenty or so hours they would spend in the air.

"Well, here we are guys, point of no return," Toni said.

"Thanks so much for doing this for us." Cathy drew Toni into a hug. "And for holding the fort while I'm away."

"No worries." Toni pulled away, her skin inexplicably tender. She assumed it was another side effect of throwing her body clock all akimbo. Toni jangled Cathy's car keys, BMW tag dangling. "Anyhow, I think I got a pretty good deal out of this."

Toni also drew away from Lisa's hug. Hopefully the shower she hadn't yet had time for would help her touchy skin.

"Have a *fantastic* time, you two, and I'll see you both in a month."

Once home and parked in her driveway Toni leaned into the leather headrest and closed her eyes. God, her head hurt. She decided to stop at the chemist on the way to work and pick up some industrial-strength painkillers. For now she had a cat and a troop of birds to feed, plus a shower to have and clothes to iron. Why, oh why had she not laid out her clothes the night before? Oh, well, for the moment she was boss, so no one could tell her off for being tardy. Toni sat with eyes closed for one more minute. She really was not feeling very well. Maybe Heather had been right. Maybe she had overindulged once too often and her liver was packing it in, unable to cope.

With more than a little reluctance, Toni hauled herself from the luxuriously comfortable interior of Cathy's car and headed inside. She left Virgil alone in the kitchen to crunch on a breakfast of professional formula cat biscuits and set about performing her least favorite task of the day, emptying and washing the litter tray. Virgil was curfewed from sunset to sunrise but spent the day with access to the outside world via the cat flap that swung from the back door. Toni left the tray to drain in the laundry trough and retrieved a bag of birdseed from the cupboard above the washing machine.

Lisa had encouraged the continued residence of a family of rock doves in her garden by feeding them daily for the last seven or so years. Toni had agreed to take over the task now that Lisa had moved from the house that sat immediately behind her own. Keys to the gate that gave access to the rear lane were plucked from their hook and Toni adjusted the deadlock so she could shut the back door without latching it. Once outside, the bag of used kitty litter was tossed into the wheelie bin and Toni headed to the rear of her yard.

She stopped short of the gate, pocketing the keys. The doves, although having a reputation for being minors in the intelligence stakes, had already realized the seed now appeared in the lane instead of in Lisa's backyard. Toni did not need to announce birdie-breakfast by entering the lane; she could just toss it over the fence. Sure enough, moments after rustling the bag and throwing the first handful, rock doves fluttered from the branches of Lisa's lilly pilly tree. A couple even landed on the fence itself, cocking their heads to one side, seemingly sizing up their new benefactor. Or maybe they were just waiting for Toni to leave so they could retrieve the seed that had fallen short of the fence and lay scattered on the grass.

Toni slowly took a few backward steps to see what the fence-sitting doves would do. By step ten the pair fluttered down to the grass. Pleased at the display of trust already being shown by a typically wary species, she continued her slow retreat, turning around only when more than halfway to the back door. The sight of Virgil outside and on the grass surprised her. Toni's eyes darted to the door, which, sure enough, was open at least a foot. The little sneak must have nosed it open. Either that or the wind that gusted occasionally around Toni's ears had been enough to push at the timber. Regardless, Virgil was now on the wrong side of the door for dove-feeding time, and she looked like she was making the most of the opportunity. Her stance was that of the feline hunter, body flat to the ground, one paw inching its way ahead of the other, tail slowly sweeping from side to side. Luckily, Virgil was not renowned for her hunting abilities. She'd get so excited at the prospect of a bird that she emitted what could only be described as a loud staccato meow. Toni could hear her doing it right now. It was such a comical sound she was unable to keep her voice stern as she scolded, "Virgil! Get back inside, you naughty girl."

Virgil's ears flicked, indication she heard Toni, but chose to ignore her.

Toni repeated her order, this time with increased command. "Virgil! Get inside. Now!"

Again she was ignored.

Virgil's slow stalk suddenly accelerated, limbs barely apparent as her belly skirted the ground. Toni watched in morbid fascination as Virgil launched off her back legs. For a moment she seemed suspended in midair and in that moment, Toni thought Virgil a picture of feline grace and beauty. The moment was shattered by the fluttering of a dozen set of wings, every dove in the vicinity, regardless of which side of the fence they were on, taking urgently to flight.

All doves except one.

"Virgil!" Toni rushed forward. The dove caught under Virgil's paw struggled frantically, wings beating against the earth as it made a desperate attempt to free itself. "Virgil! Stop!"

Toni appealed in vain. Virgil took the dove between her teeth and, ears back, trotted past Toni, a low growl warning Toni away.

Appalled by the base animal instincts her companion was displaying, Toni set after Virgil, hoping she would retreat indoors and hence give a chance to coax the release of her prey. Virgil did head for the back door and she slunk up the three concrete steps.

Toni felt the sudden gust of wind and saw the back door swing on its hinges. What she wasn't prepared for was the slam of the door. It was loud enough one could be mistaken it had been shut forcefully in anger. Nor was she prepared for the howl of pain that accompanied the slam.

"Virgil!" Toni screamed in horror as she saw a length of fur poking between the closed door and the jamb. Her bag of seed spilled to the lawn. "Virgil!"

Toni ran to the back door, choking back tears as she ascended the steps. Virgil howled again, and Toni was almost physically sick. The length of fur was still attached to her companion—Virgil's tail was caught. Toni pushed as gently as she could on the door but the action evoked a blood-curdling yowl from the other side. Toni immediately realized that her attempt at gentleness was only causing more pain. A tooth-pulling approach was needed. She swallowed the bile that rose in her throat, closed her eyes, prayed silently to the Goddess and gave the door a good, swift push.

"I'll get that, Maggie," Emma called to the veterinary assistant who was in the rear of the premises, cleaning out the cages that housed their post-operative patients. She turned the sign on the door to *Open*, snapped the latch to unlock the door and hurried to the reception desk to answer the phone.

"My Best Friend's Veterinary Service, Emma speaking." Emma placed a hand over her ear so she could hear above the high-pitched yapping coming from the back room. The cocker spaniel recovering from yesterday's surgery was in high spirits, probably as much to do with the attention Maggie lavished on her charges as finally gaining relief from the grass seed that had worked its way into his ear canal. Emma grinned when the caller announced himself. "Hey, Pete. How are you?"

"I'm good, Em." Pete's voice was low, evidence of an illicit call. Colleen frowned upon personal calls being made or received during work hours. Hell, Colleen frowned upon everything that didn't maximize her profits. She was the most non-vet-like vet Emma had ever come across. "I have to keep this short. The boss has just ducked out to the loo."

Emma's smile dissolved as Pete quickly related his reason for phoning. Apparently Colleen was on the rampage and Emma was the target. While doing the monthly accounts, Colleen noticed a discrepancy in the bill for Blue, a five-year-old Border collie owned by Frank, a retired postman. Frank's wife had recently passed after a long struggle with cancer. Her ongoing treatment had all but decimated their savings so Frank was now not only grieving, but trying to survive on what remained of their retirement nest egg while the authorities shuffled the piles of paper associated with his pension application. So when Blue was brought in, bent and bloodied from an altercation with a car reversing too fast out of its driveway, Emma was unable to further add to Frank's burden. She waived all of Blue's costs except the initial consultation charge. "What's Colleen's problem?" Emma frowned into the phone, wishing she had also waived the consultation fee and hence left no paper trail, "Hasn't she got a single compassionate bone in her body?"

"Seems not. She's *really* ticked off. I just wanted to let you know because you're likely to get a call from her sometime today."

Emma rubbed her left temple. Colleen wouldn't get much joy ringing her at home since she wasn't there. "Thanks for the warning, Pete. I'll work on my defense today and be ready for her tonight."

"I don't think you've got that long. Em, she also knows you're working. And where."

Oh, great. Emma grimaced, although she didn't have anything to worry about on that count. There was nothing in her employment contract stating she couldn't work at more than one practice. And it wasn't as if she was encouraging her regular clients to come to her while she was working as locum for Tricia. "How did she find that out?"

"I have no idea. Probably one of her cronies saw you slipping in the back door or something." Pete's voice lowered even further and it sounded muted, like he was cupping his hand over the mouthpiece. "I have to go, Em. I can hear her click-clacking up the hall."

"Okay, Pete. Thanks for the warning." The words were hardly out of Emma's mouth when the connection was terminated. Emma returned the receiver to its cradle, leaned back in the office chair and assumed her thinking position—elbows on the armrests, fingertips resting against each other.

In retrospect, Emma really should have told Colleen she had waived Frank's bill and why. After all, Colleen was the owner of the practice and it was therefore Colleen's equipment and supplies used in Blue's treatment. Emma had undertaken the work in unpaid overtime—let's face it, all her overtime was unpaid—but Colleen would no doubt be untouched by that argument. In Colleen's eyes she was probably already branded a thief. And, even if Colleen did not ordinarily take such a dim view of pro bono work, in this case it probably provided exactly the excuse she was looking for to oust Emma from the practice.

Emma sighed. She may as well start drafting her letter of resignation right now.

What a wonderful start to the day.

Actually, Emma's day had already begun badly, Justine waylaying her on the return from Kayisha's morning walk.

"Hi, Justine." Still unable to look Justine in the eye, Emma had crouched down and pretended to adjust Kai's harness. She hadn't seen Justine since Saturday's marriage announcement, deliberately avoiding all contact, even changing the route of her walks with Kayisha so she didn't have to pass Justine's house. However, this morning Justine came charging up the road before Emma could escape to the safety of her veranda.

"I'm so glad I caught you." Justine seemed breathless, as if she'd been running a lot farther than the few dozen steps from her front door.

"What do you want?" Emma didn't intend the sharpness of her tone; it just came out. She stole a glance from her protracted pretend harness adjustment to find Justine sporting a bewildered expression. Guilt surfaced. It wasn't Justine's fault Emma had fallen for her, and it wasn't as if Justine had ever hidden the fact she was straight. Emma had simply misinterpreted an innocent kiss. *On the mouth.* "Sorry, Justine," she lied. "I'm just a bit tired. I didn't sleep too well last night."

Justine's recovery was swift. She broke into a broad grin, literally bubbling with excitement as she danced happily on the spot. "Me either. And Paul flew back to the mine this morning . . ."

What a shame, Emma thought. Her hopes rose. Why would Justine be so pleased at this? She remembered when her partner

Chris, a public relations consultant, went away on business trips—the time of departure was certainly no cause for celebration. Not for Emma, anyway. Probably a different matter for Chris though, who no doubt used the time away to publicly relate with The Trollop.

For goodness' sake, woman. Focus. Emma snapped her mind back to the present.

" . . . and be a bridesmaid."

"Sorry? What?" Emma must have tuned out for longer than she thought. She had no idea what Justine was talking about.

"At our wedding." Justine either missed the fact Emma sported a confused frown, or she chose to ignore it. "We want you to be a bridesmaid." A petite hand had been placed on Emma's forearm, exerting a light pressure on her skin. "Oh, please say yes, Emma. I have no sisters and you're the best friend I have . . ."

Now, as Emma replayed the morning's conversation in her mind, she dreamed up at least five alternative responses to the one she had given: "Yes."

What had prompted such a response? Was it sudden sympathy for a woman who probably had few female friends because none dared let "her man" within striking distance for fear he may be seduced by her charms? Or was it because Emma herself was still so seduced by her charms she was unable to say no to anything Justine requested of her? Or was it because the pressure of Justine's hand on her arm got her brain so muddled it had mistakenly activated the nerve endings in her groin?

Emma didn't have time to figure it out. The buzzer attached to the front door announced the arrival of a customer. Problems with Justine and Colleen would have to wait. For now she had a veterinary practice to run.

When the door opened, recognition came immediately, as did the blush that burned Emma's cheeks.

Toni.

Emma had not been so drunk she had forgotten the utter fool she made of herself on Saturday night. According to Lisa when she dropped Emma at home the next day, she had also upset Toni quite considerably. Emma had not seen Toni since. She hadn't attended Lisa's birthday brunch, far too hung over to do anything but sit in a shaft of sunlight on her lounge room floor and feel abjectly sorry for herself. So the chance to apologize in person had been lost, and each time Emma picked up the phone to call Toni via Cathy's work number, nerves at the possible reaction got the better of her. Now, however, was not the appropriate time to ask forgiveness. Toni was obviously not here to pick up pet food or a flea collar. The woman was distraught to the point she was shaking. And in complete contrast to Emma's heightened embarrassment, it appeared all the blood had drained from Toni's cheeks.

"Virgil." The cat carry cage Toni clasped was lifted almost to the height of the reception console. "Her tail . . . she's hurt. Please." Toni looked past Emma to the corridor leading to the consultation rooms. "She needs help."

Emma rounded the reception desk. She knew from experience most people would not release hold of their pets until it was time to put them on the examination table, so she made no attempt to take the carry cage from Toni. Instead she placed a guiding hand on her shoulder, "Come this way."

Once in the consultation room Toni placed the carry cage directly onto the stainless steel bench but faltered when Emma reached to open it. "Aren't you going to wait for Tricia?"

"Tricia's away at the moment, Toni. I've taken over while she's gone."

There was no disguising the surprise that crossed Toni's features, or the slight narrowing of her eyes. Emma realized Toni had not known of her profession, and it was quite obvious she was dubious of her abilities. Not really surprising, given Saturday night's performance.

It seemed distress won over distrust. "Please help her."

"I will," Emma reassured her, opening the carry cage and reaching carefully for the mottled bundle that lay huddled at the far end. "Now you say she's hurt her tail . . ."

For the second time in as many hours, Toni leaned against the headrest in Cathy's car and closed her eyes. The adrenaline that had kept her going for the last hour finally seeped away, and tears the adrenaline refused to allow while action was required welled behind her closed lids. Now that there was nothing more she could do for Virgil except wait, she succumbed to her tears. They flowed freely, hot and salty as they ran down her cheeks and into her mouth.

The last hour had been one of the worst in Toni's life. She remembered every detail—the howls of pain when Toni pushed open her back door, Virgil fleeing under the couch the moment her tail was freed. Toni was unsuccessful in trying to coax Virgil from her hiding place, instead having to drag her out, Virgil's claws scratching against the wooden floorboards. Then there was the shock of seeing Virgil's tail—her beautiful tail—all mangled and bloody as Toni fed her into the carry cage retrieved from the top of the laundry cupboard. "It's okay," Toni repeated throughout the drive to the vet, as much to convince herself as to try and calm the distressed mewing coming from the cage securely belted onto the passenger seat. "You're going to be okay."

The fact that Toni was greeted at reception by Emma hardly registered, her only concern to get Virgil the help she needed. However, once she discovered that Tricia, Virgil's vet since she was a kitten, was not available and Emma was her replacement, Toni hovered over the decision to stay or go. Even if, as Emma claimed, she really was a qualified vet, that didn't necessarily mean she was a *good* vet. For all Toni knew, the woman carried a hip flask and chugged on it throughout the day. She probably even had a cigarette dangling between her lips as she performed surgery.

Reason overrode Toni's doubt. Tricia wouldn't put her practice at stake by letting an incompetent loose on her clients. Whatever Toni thought of Emma personally, professionally she was probably as able as Tricia.

Nevertheless, Toni watched carefully for any signs of professional inadequacies while Emma performed her examination. She didn't find any. Emma appeared in calm control, hands moving with surety over Virgil's spine and abdomen, voice steady as she announced there was no sign of any other injury, internal or otherwise.

Emma did quirk an eyebrow when Toni's response to her "How did this happen?" was that Virgil's tail got caught in a door when Toni chased her inside trying to get a bird out of her mouth. But if Emma thought Toni an irresponsible pet owner she didn't show it, nodding quietly and continuing with her examination.

"How bad is it?" Toni asked nervously, for the first time looking closely at the damage. It was awful. The skin at the end of Virgil's tail had gloved over itself, exposing raw skin and bone.

"It looks a lot worse than it is." Emma indicated the vertebra third from Virgil's tail tip. "But this bone is crushed beyond repair. Unfortunately, the only solution is to remove this section of tail."

"Oh, my God," Toni's hand flew to her mouth and immediately doubts of Emma's abilities resurfaced. What if she botched it up and Virgil lost the ability to walk? "Is that really necessary?"

"It's okay, Toni. It's quite a simple procedure." Emma seemed to sense the reason for Toni's distress, and she smoothed her hand down Virgil's back to the point where the tail began. "Cats tails consist only of bone, muscles, ligaments and tendon. The spinal cord finishes here." Emma pointed to what she announced was the fifth lumbar vertebra. "So it's not affected by tail injuries. Toni, Virgil will be okay—she'll have to get used to life with a slightly shortened tail, but she will be fine. Trust me."

So Toni had laid her trust in Emma. She left her best friend behind and walked out of the premises with the promise she would be called if necessary. Otherwise Toni could pick Virgil up after ten a.m. the next day.

Toni checked her watch through tear-blurred eyes. It was only just going nine a.m. How was she going to make it through the next twenty-five hours? She rubbed her temples. Her headache, forgotten as she attended to Virgil's needs, had returned with a vengeance. She checked herself in the rearview mirror. God, she looked as bad as she felt. Her teary session certainly hadn't helped; her skin was red and blotchy. Toni frowned at her reflection. What was that blister-like lesion between her eyebrows? She'd have to ask the chemist when she picked up her painkillers.

Toni turned the key in the ignition and reversed from the parking bay. Chemist, home, shower, dress, work, wait, worry. She rang the office from her mobile, announcing she would be later than expected. Sue, the receptionist, sounded like she wasn't at all surprised, but her sarcasm dissolved when Toni tearfully related the reason.

"Do you want to take the day, Toni? I can cancel your two o'clock."

"No, it's fine." Toni swiped at her eyes. Sitting at home all day would only cause her to worry more. Work was as good a time-filler as any. "I'll be in as soon as I can."

CHAPTER SIX

The plane touched down on schedule, but by the time Lisa and Cathy made it through the scrutiny of customs, survived a hair-raising taxi ride from the airport to the hotel and checked in, another two hours had elapsed. Cathy would not adjust her watch to Italy time, the six-hour time difference an easy enough calculation to do in her head. It was three-thirty p.m. Saturday in Perth. Nine-thirty a.m. the same day in Rome.

Luckily the electronic swipe card that gave access to their room worked the first time and they tumbled into what would be their quarters for the week spent in Italy's capital. Cathy's immediate reaction to their accommodation was positive. The hotel, a recent addition to the Roman landscape, seemed to deliver everything promised by its Web site. From her position near the door, Cathy could not see the bedroom or bathroom, but if the lounge/dining area was any indication, those two rooms would also be modern and elegant, with stylish furniture and fittings. Apart from its pleasing aesthetics, the hotel also won Cathy over by its location. It was within easy walking distance of a number of Rome's most famous attractions—the Pantheon, Trevi Fountain and Piazza Navoni. It seemed Cathy's choice won favor on both counts. A visit to the Trevi Fountain topped Lisa's Rome "must do" list and having it so close guaranteed more than the required three coins would be tossed over her shoulder and into its waters. And if the excited exclamations coming from the other rooms were anything to go by, the suite would be a welcome sanctuary after their days of sightseeing.

Cathy walked into the bedroom, humming happily as she deposited her cabin bag next to the bed. On the few occasions they had stayed in hotels over the last year, Lisa revealed an enthusiasm for her surrounds that Cathy found both refreshing and contagious. On entering a hotel room Lisa would immediately rush around, opening drawers and poking in corners, exclaiming over each new item she found. Whatever the room offered, Lisa would make sure it was utilized. If fluffy bathrobes and slippers were supplied, they would be worn; if there was a balcony, they would sit out on it. The only thing she refused to touch was the minibar, declaring it a total ripoff. Apart from the fact they had to forestall having a glass of wine until they had found the local liquor merchant, Cathy loved this aspect of Lisa, loved that she was not afraid to display her enthusiasm.

True to form, Lisa called excitedly from the bathroom, "Honey, we've got a bath. And they've provided cleanser and toner and a mudpack. We'll have to give each other facials. And you should see the showerhead. It's almost as big as a dinner plate." A short silence ensued, followed by a snicker. "Cathy Braithwaite's work, I presume."

"What's that?" Cathy entered the bathroom and smiled. The hotel management had not forgotten her special request. Lisa stared at a large bowl of tomatoes. They were ripe, very red, and from what Cathy could see, perfectly formed and unblemished.

Lisa selected a tomato from the bowl, tossing it in her hand as she turned to Cathy. "You're not going to ever let me forget, are you?"

"Not in this lifetime." Cathy laughed out loud, as she did every time she remembered. This Monday it would be a year to the day—their anniversary—that it happened. Sitting in a café overlooking the ocean, Cathy could not keep her sentiments in any longer and blurted her love for Lisa. That Lisa was unprepared for the announcement was an understatement. Her sudden shocked movement caught the edge of her fork and sent the remains of her meal—a single cherry tomato—flying into the air and straight into the wineglass of a fellow diner. Their exit from the café was hasty, their subsequent entry to Cathy's bed just as fast, and the rest, as they say, was history.

Cathy thought this trip, given it was a celebration of their first year together, as good a time as any for a reminder. So she'd arranged with the hotel management for a bowl of tomatoes to be left in the room in place of the customary flowers.

Lisa took a bite of the tomato and held it out to Cathy, an offer to try it. "Mmm, this is delicious." She nodded to the shower recess. "I vote we have a nice hot shower and a lie-down."

Cathy took a bite of the proffered tomato. Lisa was right. It was juicy and bursting with flavor. "You know, the best way to beat jet lag is to keep to local hours. If we sleep all day we'll be awake all night."

Lisa placed the partially eaten tomato on the vanity, freeing her hands so they could work on the top button of Cathy's shirt. "Who said anything about sleeping?"

Cathy glanced at fingers nimble with practice. She made no attempt to halt them. "What about your fountain? I thought you were desperate to toss some coins and ensure your return to Rome?"

Button number two on Cathy's shirt was popped open. "Tell me again when it was built."

Cathy tilted her head to give Lisa's lips access to her neck, "Around the early seventeen hundreds, I think."

"Well, if it's survived this long, I'm sure it will still be there in another few hours."

Cathy's giggle came out as a gasp, Lisa's attentions sending shivers all the way down her spine. "What about our luggage?"

"Honey." The last of Cathy's shirt buttons was freed and Lisa slid her hands under the material, drawing it open. "You don't need any clothes for what I plan to do to you."

A flash of reason sliced through Cathy's already sensation-muddied mind. "We didn't put the chain on the door. And the porter will just let himself in if we don't put the *Do Not Disturb* sign up."

The nibbling at the soft skin of Cathy's earlobe stopped, but Lisa's lips did not break contact. "You're a spoilsport, Cathy."

"Just practical." Cathy reluctantly extricated herself from Lisa's arms, wondering when the physical attraction between them would eventually wane. Or, more accurately, if it ever would. It had been a whole year and still they reacted as quickly and as strongly to each other as ever. If anything, they had stepped up a notch. Maybe not in frequency—it seemed something or someone forever needed their attention—but the moment they were alone, sparks flew. The both of them were relishing this time away together; now if the damned porter would just hurry himself up, they could relax and officially begin their holiday. "I'm guessing our luggage will arrive any minute. Tell you what, why don't you ring your folks and let them know you've arrived okay. I'll take care of the door."

Lisa screwed up her nose, but she headed for her cabin bag. Sure enough, just as Lisa was connected to her mum, a knock sounded. Cathy oversaw the depositing of luggage onto the racks, tipped the porter, hung the *Do Not Disturb* sign on the outer handle and slid the safety chain across.

"How are your mum and dad?" Cathy sat next to Lisa on the edge of the bed.

"They're good, said to say hi." Lisa frowned at the phone's display. "I've got a bunch of messages here. Shall I deal with them now or later?"

"Let's do it now." Cathy imagined there'd be at least a couple of messages waiting for her too. "Get it over and done with."

Cathy retrieved her own mobile while Lisa accessed her message bank. Both phones had been turned off since the departure lounge at Perth. They hadn't turned them on since, even during their short transit stop in Singapore, both of them too busy packing in as much leg-stretching activity as possible before boarding for the long haul to Rome.

"I wonder what's happened now?" Two of the messages, one from Emma and one from Toni, requested they call as soon as possible. Both messages had been left on both phones.

Lisa grinned wickedly. "Maybe they've rung to announce they've run away together."

Cathy rolled her eyes, not even prepared to comment on Lisa's continued cupid quest. She'd heard enough last night, when, despite their seats being turned into comfortable in-flight beds, Lisa was unable to sleep. Tiredness and boredom sent Lisa's imagination into overload and Cathy was treated to a succession of whispered matchmaking schemes, not to mention grotesque plans for the elimination of the Teletubbies. "Let's find out what's up. You take Emma. I'll take Toni."

Five minutes later Lisa hung up from her call, her expression disbelieving. "Emma's chucked in her job. She's cut off Virgil's tail and she's going to be a bridesmaid."

Cathy nodded at the first piece of news. It was not too much of a surprise, Emma frequently voicing her unhappiness with the new management. She'd heard about Virgil from Toni, and the bridesmaid business, well, she'd get details on that later. Not that she didn't care, she just had bigger things to worry over. "Lisa, have you had chicken pox?"

"What?"

"Chicken pox. Toni's got it."

"What?"

"Chicken pox," Cathy said for the third time. "Toni's got chicken pox."

"Yes, I've had it . . . but you have too, haven't you?"

"Yes."

Cathy could pinpoint the moment the penny dropped with Lisa. Having paced around the perimeter of the bed while on the phone, she now sat down heavily. The possibility of them contracting chicken pox wasn't the issue. The operation of Cathy's accountancy practice in Toni's absence was. "How long will Toni be off work?" Lisa asked.

"I don't know. Apparently it's quite severe. It's worse with adults, you know. They're talking at least two, maybe three weeks."

"Shit."

"I know."

"What are you going to do?"

"I don't know." Cathy had hung up from Toni with a promise to call her back after she'd spoken to Lisa.

From the corner of her eye, Cathy could see Lisa doing a visual sweep of their suite as she asked, "Are we going to have to go home?"

"I don't know yet," Cathy said honestly. During Toni's extended leave last year Cathy had hired an accountant from a temping agency and Cathy shouldered Toni's workload while the temp came up to speed. With both of them away, however, Julie was the only accountant left at the practice. Julie, although she had only graduated less than eighteen months prior, was proving herself more than able, but she couldn't be expected to run the entire ship until Cathy or Toni returned. Cathy guessed she could always just tell Sue, the receptionist, to cancel everything in Toni's schedule and hope her clients would rebook for a later date. But by the time Cathy returned, they would be spearheading into the busiest time of the year—tax time. Servicing all Toni's cancelled clients as well as the flurry of business the end of tax year creates would be . . . a challenge.

A prod in her upper arm made Cathy glance up. Lisa stood in front of her, the bowl of tomatoes in hand.

"Here, honey, have one of these." The bowl was held out. "It will help you think."

"Thank you." Cathy selected one of the larger tomatoes, munching on it thoughtfully as she watched Lisa disappear into the lounge room with the bowl. Lesser women would have kicked up a fuss, insisted some solution be found in their favor. Not Lisa. Instead she offered fruit.

Cathy made up her mind and, as was her way, she acted on it immediately. Her mobile was retrieved and for the second time she dialed Toni's number.

CHAPTER SEVEN

After much experimentation with different postures and positions, Toni finally managed to get herself relatively comfortable on the couch. When a knock sounded on her front door, Toni carefully turned her head in Virgil's direction and asked, "I don't suppose you want to get that for me, do you?"

The response that came from the armchair farthest away from Toni was an ear flick and an icy glare.

Toni didn't really blame Virgil for giving her the cold shoulder. She obviously interpreted the events of the last forty-eight hours as a series of inexplicable punishments inflicted by her servant. When Virgil had arrived home from the vet, Toni did try explaining that the plastic cone collar and total curfew were only temporary measures, designed both for her own good and to protect her heavily bandaged tail. Without the cone collar Virgil would soon chew through her bandage, and with the cone collar her vision was restricted—not good for a fence-hopping feline. Virgil, if she did understand, still did not justify Toni's actions and responded by flicking her ears disgustedly, marching into the laundry and defiantly pissing next to the litter tray instead of in it.

"I guess that's a no then." Toni grimaced at the pain that shot through the back of her legs as she carefully lifted herself from her half-sitting, half-lying position in the couch.

Successful in not rubbing too many of the fiery red lesions that now coated most of her body, she walked slowly to the front door.

She was expecting the young woman who stood on the other side of the threshold. "Hi, Julie. Come on in."

She was also expecting the reaction. It was one of wide-eyed shock. Toni was expecting it because every one of the visitors she had received since word of her chicken pox got 'round reacted in the same way. Julie also followed the same pattern as the other visitors, immediately trying to mask her *you look terrible* expression with a bright smile. She, as with most of the others, failed. Her smile faded at the edges, "Oh, Toni." Julie made as if to hug her but took a step back, reconsidering the contact. This was just as well. It hurt to be touched; even the light pajamas Toni wore felt like they tore at her skin. "You poor thing."

"Well, you know." Toni shrugged, purposely keeping her expression neutral. She was lucky the lesions on her face weren't as numerous as those covering her body, but still it felt like her head was massive with blisters. "I'll do anything to get out of work."

This time the smile that crossed Julie's features was approaching genuine. "A bit drastic, even for you." Julie followed Toni into the lounge room, shaking her head at Toni's offer of a drink. "You sit down and relax. I'll get you a drink. What would you like?"

"Just water, thanks." Toni pointed Julie in the direction of the kitchen and gratefully sank back onto the couch, the short walk to and from the front door more exertion than she could currently cope with. She could honestly say she had never felt this unwell in her life. Unfortunately, according to her doctor, it was only going to get worse before it got better. She related this to Julie, who on her return settled in the armchair not occupied by Virgil. Toni also related Virgil's tale of woe. "So between the two of us we make a very sad and sorry pair," Toni concluded.

"Not at all." Julie's words contradicted her pitying tone. "So have you any idea yet how you caught it?"

"None at all." Toni's first thought was the obviously unwell two-year-old from last week's Monday morning appointment, but that hadn't been the case. The mother confirmed Chloe was ill, but with nothing more than a cold. Luckily Chloe had already had a bout of chicken pox about six months earlier, so Toni didn't have to live with the thought she had passed it on to the child. Her subsequent rash of phone calls to everyone she could remember being in contact with over the past three weeks also came up empty. Luckily, or unluckily, depending on how Toni looked at it, it seemed she was about the only adult in the whole of Perth to have escaped childhood without having had the disease, so she wasn't going to be the cause of an epidemic. She told Julie, "Apparently you're contagious for a couple of days before any symptoms appear, so I guess it could have been anyone, anywhere."

"So right now there are probably people walking around unwittingly passing it on?"

"I guess so. And in a few days they'll be looking as bad as me."

"You really don't look that bad, Toni." Julie just wasn't a good liar. She avoided Toni's eyes by digging into her carryall, pulling out a bulging envelope and passing it over. "This is actually for Virgil, but I thought you may like to open it for her."

"Thanks." Toni was not disappointed the get-well card she extracted was for Virgil. She had already taken delivery of a card and a massive bunch of flowers from the office. Flowers had also arrived from her mum, and just this morning a bouquet from Cathy and Lisa landed on her doorstep. "Look, Virg." Toni held out the small, soft cloth-covered ball that had caused the bulge in the envelope. "You've got a new toy."

Virgil did her ubiquitous ear flick, yawned widely and ignored Toni completely.

"She's not talking to me at the moment," Toni explained, placing the ball and the card on the coffee table. "But I'm sure she'll come have a sniff at it as soon as I'm not looking. Thanks, Julie."

"No worries, but as the card says, it's actually from the whole office." Julie shrugged and smiled wryly. "Which at the moment means me and Sue. Speaking of which"—her hand dipped into her carryall again and retrieved a spiral notebook—"are you feeling up to doing this?"

"Sure."

Toni's response must not have sounded very convincing. Julie placed the notebook on her lap and covered it with her hand. "Actually, this can wait until you're a bit better. And I can always ring Cathy tomorrow."

"No, it's okay, really." Toni sat up a straighter, the motion making her temples pound with the headache even her extra-strength painkillers didn't completely ease. "It won't take us long, and anyway tomorrow's their big day. I doubt answering the phone will be high on the agenda."

"I guess so." Julie still didn't look sold but picked up the notebook and flipped it open. After another dig in her bag a pair of reading glasses was slipped over her ears. "I was in the office today so I checked your schedule and printed your appointments for next week . . ."

Half an hour later Toni was literally exhausted, but her mood was surprisingly buoyant, especially given her initial concern over Cathy's decision to put the short-term operation of the practice in Julie's hands. As Julie's mentor, Toni met with her weekly and they touched base daily, so Toni felt she knew her capabilities, as well as her limitations, better than Cathy. While Julie was proving herself a valuable asset, she still occasionally revealed the nervousness that plagued her early days at Cathy's practice. Toni couldn't count the number of times she had needed to calm a distraught Julie when Toni found an error in the accounts presented to her. Julie would invariably pale and then question her career choice, as she was obviously going to send every client into bankruptcy, or get them in strife with the tax department, or both. Over time, Julie's confidence grew and her bursts of self-doubt became rare. Toni attributed a lot of Julie's professional growth to her expert tutelage, but while her self-congratulatory pat on the back was not unwarranted, Toni also knew she wasn't a miracle worker. Less than eighteen months in the profession was an awfully short amount of time for someone to successfully take the reins of a busy accounting practice, albeit only for two to three weeks. Cathy had disagreed, arguing during a phone conversation that it was a real opportunity for Julie to prove herself. After all, Cathy had cleared almost everything on her own client list, leaving Toni with only a few outstanding items. Also, the temp she planned to hire could pick up most of Toni's workload, especially if she managed to again obtain the services of Marian, who had filled Toni's position for three months last year. Not too long after this conversation ended, Cathy called Toni again. She had contacted the temp agency and Marian was coming back on board. She couldn't start until the following week but was available for the rest of the month if need be.

"Okay then." Toni still wasn't entirely convinced, but it *was* Cathy's practice, and she could make whatever decisions she saw fit. Cathy wasn't exactly short of money either, so as long as they kept the reputation of the practice intact she wasn't going to worry over a few weeks' worth of decreased revenue. "Do you want to tell Julie or shall I?"

"I'll try ringing her now. Are you up to doing a bit of a handover with her?"

"Sure. Tell her she can call whenever she's ready."

Julie had phoned within the hour, and much to Toni's surprise, she sounded more excited than nervous during the call. Cathy must have intimated that the offer was made at Toni's suggestion as Julie thanked Toni for the opportunity at least four times and promised she would do everything possible to keep things running smoothly. It looked like Julie was going to live up to her promise. She had spent most of the day—Sunday—in the office, doing her own work to free up time during the week. During the handover, Toni watched for signs of panic as pages were filled with notes.

However, if Julie's insides were all aflutter, outwardly it didn't show. Julie nodded as she wrote, occasionally interrupting to ask a question or to pause thoughtfully, pen tapping lightly against her cheek. When Toni eventually ran out of things to tell her, Julie had snapped her notebook closed, removed her glasses and smiled so easily one would think she'd been doing nothing more than writing the weekly grocery list. It took Toni a good moment to remember the woman was only twenty-two. She suddenly seemed a lot older.

"Thanks for all of this, Toni. I won't let you down, I promise."

"I know you won't." Toni allowed herself to smile, surprised to discover she was telling the truth.

"I'll probably have to call on you again. Maybe lots of times as things come up."

"That's okay. I'm not going anywhere anytime soon."

Fresh concern entered Julie's tone and expression, "Are you going to be okay here by yourself? Shouldn't you have someone to look after you?"

"I'm fine." This time Toni told only a half-truth. Her mum had wanted to hop on the next plane from Melbourne as soon as she heard the news, but Toni had declined the offer. That had been on Friday night, when she felt sick but not too sick. Now she kind of wished she had said yes. She could do with a bit of mothering. "Mum offered to come over but she'd drive me mad after a day with the way she fusses . . . and I've had lots of people pop in . . . and Monica brought me a pot of chicken soup when she picked Virgil up from the vet."

"But you haven't had any of it, have you?"

"No." Toni wondered how on earth Julie knew. Oh, dear, maybe she had empty-stomach bad breath. And here she'd been breathing all over the poor girl for the last half-hour. Toni covered her mouth with her hand.

Julie's hands went to her hips. "Why not?"

Toni spoke through her hand. "I'm not hungry."

"Toni," Julie scolded. "You have to eat or you'll end up even sicker."

"I know. I will." Toni half smiled through her hand. "Eat that is."

"I'll get you a bowl now."

Without the energy to argue, and not wanting to blow more potentially bad breath in Julie's direction, Toni just nodded. As soon as Julie turned for the kitchen, Toni cupped her hand and blew into it. *Ee-eww!* Normally a stickler for oral hygiene, Toni was mortified. She announced a need to go to bathroom, and as fast as her sore body would carry her, fled to the nearest bottle of mouthwash.

Five minutes later Toni had minty fresh breath. She also had a bowl of Monica's chicken soup sitting in front of her, along with firm instructions to eat it. Despite the mouthwash somewhat tainting her chicken soup experience, in another twenty minutes there were only a few spoonfuls left in her bowl. Virgil had also been presented with an early dinner and a clean litter tray, and seed had been tossed over the fence for the rock doves. Julie returned to the lounge room. From the noises coming from the kitchen in the last few minutes, Toni assumed Julie had also taken out the trash and done the dishes left by the sink since the previous day. Again Toni was mortified. Julie had never visited her house before so wasn't aware Toni didn't normally live like a pig.

"Sorry the place is in such a mess," Toni said by way of an apology. "It's not usually like this."

"Yeah, right." Julie leaned over the back of the armchair she had previously sat on and retrieved her bag. "I've seen your desk at work, remember."

Toni opened her mouth to retort. Her desk wasn't *that* bad. She knew where everything was, even if it wasn't as anally retentively organized as Julie's and Cathy's work spaces. Julie, however, didn't give her the chance to argue. Her bag was slung over her shoulder and keys jangled in her hand.

"Okay, Toni, I'm heading off now. I'll call you sometime tomorrow, to see if there's anything you need me to bring over after work."

It was on the tip of Toni's tongue to say another visit wasn't necessary, but the social side of her personality thrust itself forward. "Okay."

Once alone, Toni arranged herself on the couch, finding that relatively pain-free position again. Her headache still lingered but her tummy was comfortably full.

She dozed.

Then she woke to a scuffing sound. It was Virgil's cone collar knocking against a leg of the coffee table. Toni squinted and pretended she didn't see the paw come up and pat on the tabletop until the new cloth ball fell to the floor. She also pretended not to see Virgil softly tap at the ball with her paws and begin chasing it around the room. She definitely didn't acknowledge the warm, furry body that eventually settled itself at the far end of the couch, next to Toni's feet. Inwardly, Toni smiled. She was on her way to being forgiven.

CHAPTER EIGHT

Julie kept her promise, ringing Toni often. Toni didn't mind the calls. Not feeling well enough to do anything much for herself, even to read a book or flick through a magazine, the calls made a welcome distraction from days filled with nothing more than the drudgery of daytime television.

The first call had arrived Monday morning. Julie was gushingly apologetic. Apparently she'd been saving up her questions so she wouldn't have to annoy Toni too often, but this particular query couldn't wait. Toni quirked her eyebrows as she checked her watch. It had only just gone nine a.m. Julie must have been at the office at sparrow-fart to have already racked up a set of questions.

Julie rang six more times that day. On Tuesday she interrupted Toni's television marathon five times; on Wednesday four times, but only twice on Thursday. Now it was Friday. Toni wondered how many calls she'd get today. If the pattern of the week was followed, she guessed only one.

Even if Julie's calls were declining in frequency, her visits weren't. She'd made an appearance every evening after work, each time toting something new to tempt Toni's taste buds. Each time Toni would shake her head and say she wasn't particularly hungry, but each time a plate would be placed in front of her anyway. And each time Toni surprised herself, her stomach growling at the sight of the food. It helped that every one of Julie's choices were toward the top of Toni's list of favorites. On Monday a Bento box of assorted sushi, miso soup, tempura vegetables and chicken teriyaki appeared. Tuesday a creamy Malaysian curry with roti was on the menu. On Wednesday they shared a foot-long steak and cheese Subway sandwich, and the fridge was currently hiding the remains last night's Chinese takeaway feast.

Julie's visits did not comprise only a food courier service. The operation of the office and the string of clients who had come in that day dominated a good part of their dinner conversation. At these times Toni slipped into her mentor role, and if it weren't for the fact Toni was in her pajamas and nibbling on delicious treats, their interactions would have been no different than mentoring sessions held over the past eighteen months. But unlike sessions held at the practice, once talk of work was done, instead of Toni or Julie retreating to their own space, they moved onto topics that lay beyond account balances and taxation law.

During the course of these conversations Toni found herself wondering what had caused the change. Had Cathy been right? Had handing the reins to Julie been the catalyst to drawing her out of her shell? Or maybe it was the change in scenery. Maybe, out of the office environment, Julie felt more comfortable with Toni. After all it would be hard to feel threatened by anyone donned in flannelette pajamas sporting a Tigger print.

Whatever it was, Toni was glad of the change, discovering a Julie she had not known existed. More than once Toni wondered at how she had spent eighteen months with no real notion of the personality that lived behind the quiet, soft-spoken and sometimes nervous employee that fronted for work each day. Toni admitted it was because she had never really bothered finding out. Even when Julie attended Friday afternoon drinks, she usually sat quietly listening to the banter between Cathy, Toni and Sue, her interjections rare and seemingly well considered.

But there had been nothing rare or well considered about Julie's conversations over the course of the last few days. Whatever topic they turned to, whether art or history, music, television, politics or religion, Julie had an opinion, and a theory to accompany it. She had no recollection of how they had gotten onto such topics, but Toni learned that Julie lay in the "man never really made it to the moon" camp. She was also adamant that while Elvis may or may not have died at the time, he surely must be dead by now, and even if he wasn't he surely wouldn't be wandering around in his white jumpsuit and cape. And—this was a theory Toni had pondered while lying awake just the night before—that hell was not fire and brimstone, it was right here, right now, and everyone would keep dying and coming back as "earthlings" until they got it right. Once they did get it right they'd tootle off to some planetary paradise reserved for the higher beings. Last night, lying as still as possible so as not to knock her lesions, Toni could not discount Julie's "hell on earth" theory. In fact, with stabs of pain shooting through her skull and her fever leaving her at one moment burning hot and the next shivering with cold, Toni believed every word of it. Last night had been her worst since falling ill. She rose often from her bed, pacing the house until sheer exhaustion drew her back to her mattress. Then, miserable, feverish and in pain, tears rolled down her cheeks and she'd prayed for dawn to sweep away the darkness.

Thankfully, morning brought a turning point and Toni woke from her broken sleep, tired but without the headache that had plagued her for days. She slipped from under the covers and opened the curtains, blinking at the not-yet-too-bright early morning sunlight. Outside birds trilled, a light breeze rustled the leaves of the peppermint trees that lined the street, and a neighborhood child was playing on his front lawn, making the most of a sunny morning before being bundled off to school. Toni found herself smiling as she turned from the window. She was already formulating her argument to debunk Julie's theory, hell on earth no longer seeming an apt description.

Debunking theories was soon put to the bottom of Toni's list of priorities. Relieving the itch was put to the top. Mary Lucas, Toni's doctor, warned of the itch during her last home visit. Mary pressed her fingers to a couple of lesions on Toni's face, noted they were not getting infected and announced they would soon begin to dry up, turn brown, then black, then fall off. It was at that stage they would really begin to annoy, and that was when Toni had to be careful not to scratch. It may provide temporary relief, but it would also leave scars. Toni had nodded in agreement. A little itch was not worth it.

But right now Toni was one big itch, just begging to be scratched.

Toni soon decided she had to keep her hands occupied. She tried sitting on them. That didn't work, fingers giving into the temptation to pick at a particularly annoying spot on her right bottom cheek. She tried petting Virgil, but Virgil went to petting heaven and began kneading Toni's thighs, claws exposed and biting into already tender skin. Toni yelped in pain and shooed Virgil from her lap. Since then Virgil had again refused to acknowledge Toni's existence, so Toni retreated from the lounge room, scouring the house for something to keep her hands busy. At the very back of her bottom bedside drawer she found a battery-operated de-pilling machine she had completely forgotten she owned. The next hour was spent in a de-pilling flurry. Every jumper Toni owned got the treatment, then she moved onto her stack of T-shirts. T-shirt number four was just about to have all the nasty little balls of fluff whisked away when the machine began to splutter and slow.

"Bugger," Toni cursed as the machine's teeny blades stopped altogether halfway down the left arm of the T-shirt. The batteries had gone flat. A search through her kitchen drawers revealed an unopened packet of D batteries, but no spare AAs. "Bugger," she repeated, her thoughts turning to Julie. Maybe she could ring and ask her to pick up some spares?

Toni checked her watch as she contemplated making the call. It was only ten-fifteen a.m.—hours before Julie could deliver some batteries, even if she made a special lunchtime visit. Toni put her big ideas of de-pilling her entire wardrobe aside and thought hard for something else to do. She tugged open the doors of her pantry and peered inside. Maybe cooking something would take her mind off her itchy skin. She plucked a can of chickpeas from the shelf, screwed up her nose and nearly put it back. Thoughts of her non-liver-friendly eating habits and total lack of exercise in the last week stopped her. She hefted the can in her hand, gauging its weight. Satisfied, she sifted through the shelf, found a second can of chickpeas and took them both into the lounge room.

"Watch out, Virg," Toni warned as she stood in front of the television, arms extended, a can in each hand. "It's been a while. I might drop them."

Later, her chickpea exercises long over and a long cool bath in pine tar solution leaving her less itchy and in clean pajamas—this time white with black cat paws all over them—Toni checked her watch again. It was now past midday and still Julie hadn't called. Usually by this time she had rung, Toni had answered the latest query, Julie would apologize for the interruption and then ask if Toni needed anything picked up before she came over. So usually by this time Toni had argued that Julie didn't need to come over again, Julie would say it was no trouble, and Toni would hang up the phone secure in the fact she'd have some company that evening.

As yet that hadn't happened. Toni shifted position on the couch. While feeling terribly unwell, her only marker of time was whatever program happened to be on the television. Even then, occasionally she would find the program had changed without her being consciously being aware of it. Mornings slipped into afternoons in some pain-fuzzied blur, and as a result, her solitude also went largely unnoticed. Now that she was on the mend the lack of social contact was beginning to wear at her. Toni may have lived alone ever since moving to Perth five years ago, but she was still a highly social being.

She mentally skipped through the pages of her address book, trying to think of someone who may be free for a visit. Unfortunately, what was usually a plus now worked against her, the majority of her friends working the nine-to-five. The exceptions either worked the night shift and wouldn't take kindly to a call at this time of day or, as in the case of Becky, had pre-school-aged children in tow, and just going to the store for bread and milk was a major operation.

Toni thought she might ring her mum, but even with the two-hour time difference between Perth and Melbourne, it was still a good hour before her shift finished at the lunch bar she had worked in since her "bastard of a husband" left her and Toni to fend for themselves when Toni was seven.

I'll just ring to see how everything's going at the office. As Toni dialed she remembered her dead de-pilling machine. She chuckled as she wondered how Julie would react to a request for some batteries to replace the ones she had run flat in a small, vibrating appliance.

The call was diverted to reception.

"Hi, Sue. It's Toni."

"Toni!" Sue was her usual exuberant self and immediately full of questions. Was Toni feeling better, when was she likely to be back, how was Virgil? It took a good five minutes before Toni could state the reason for her call.

"Is Julie available?"

"She's with someone at the moment. Do you want me to get her to ring you?"

Toni thought quickly. Sue was the biggest gossip she had ever met, her life revolving around who was with whom, who was no longer with whom, who had said this or done that. So, although Sue was very much aware Toni and Julie were required to communicate with each other for business purposes, if Toni announced a desire just to speak to Julie about nothing in particular, it would send Sue's gossip antennae twitching. Especially given Sue's knowledge of the infatuation Julie had developed for Toni in early autumn last year. Although the crush was old news and over—Julie's girlfriend of six months would likely attest to that fact—she could only imagine the reaction if she asked Sue to pass on the message about flat batteries and a vibrating appliance. The line from reception to the outside world would run so hot it would likely melt. Toni made up some work-related message that seemed to satisfy Sue and hung up the phone.

Sudden guilt swept through Toni. Here she was, thinking only of her own needs. Julie probably hadn't called because she wanted to spend some time with her girlfriend instead of attending to an invalid colleague. Toni had actually voiced that exact thought on Tuesday night, right after Mary Lucas left with the prognosis she would survive her illness. Julie had shrugged off Toni's protest, explaining she never saw much of Anna during the week, her job as a primary school teacher dominating her days and her position on the state water polo team keeping her busy by night. At the moment Anna was full swing into training for competition with one of the other state teams, so, if anything, visiting Toni was more a pleasure than a chore.

But Toni doubted Anna would train every night of the week. She probably got at least Friday and Saturday nights off. Toni decided that when Julie did return her call, she would make it quite clear she wasn't expecting her to visit, that she was actually capable of rustling up something to eat and no, she didn't need anything brought over.

That thought sorted, Toni discovered she had absently been scratching at the back of her neck. Her head was itchy too. She let herself scratch at her scalp as she walked to the bathroom, figuring a few pocks wouldn't show through her short, but thick, dark hair. Toni shed her pajamas, dotted a fresh layer of Calamine lotion over all the body parts she could reach and studied her reflection.

At five foot six she wasn't overly tall, and combined with a medium build, she was never going to grace the catwalks. Not that she had any desire to be a wafer-thin clothes hanger. She was just being realistic. Despite not meeting the ridiculous ideals of a body-obsessed society, she was usually pretty happy with the way she looked. Third-generation Australian, but born of parents of Macedonian extraction, she inherited the olive skin tones and dark hair synonymous with the people of her heritage. She was lucky enough to have inherited her maternal grandmother's Irish-Australian green eyes. She also inherited her grandmother's tendency to gain weight easily, but regular exercise and a reasonably healthy diet kept that in check.

What the bathroom mirror currently revealed was depressing. Her skin had assumed a grayish, yellowish pallor. That is, the skin that could be seen beneath the lumps and bumps, blisters and layer of Calamine lotion. Toni lifted her arms so they formed a right angle at the elbow. The tone she had acquired through her months of Pump was already on the decline. If she wasn't careful, her upper arms would soon resemble a bat's wingspan. Her eyes, while still green, looked tired, the whites, instead of clear and bright, shot with red. Toni bared her teeth. At least they hadn't changed. Her mum had scrimped and saved to get her the braces she needed as a teenager, so her teeth, naturally very white, were now also very straight. Toni considered them her best asset and was meticulous about keeping them that way. Toni poked out her tongue. Yep, still coated . . . and yep—she smacked her lips together and tasted her mouth—it was still gross. Bereft of the thought she would ever look or feel like a normal person again, she donned her pajamas, cleaned her teeth and headed to her home office.

Going online would satisfy two objectives. The typing would keep her hands busy and she'd enjoy the banter, no matter how inane the chat topic. There was also the added advantage of physical anonymity, so no one could see just how bad she currently looked.

Toni had switched to broadband Internet access at the beginning of the year so there was no need to dial in to the server. The monthly charge was a lot higher than a regular dial-up account, but she figured the extra cost worthwhile. The connection was exponentially faster than dial-up and her account allowed unlimited downloads, both of which made expanding her MP3 music collection a breeze. Plus, because broadband utilized a different part of her phone line than the phone itself, she could still make and take calls while connected to the Internet. A very useful feature, especially since she didn't have to explain to disgruntled friends why her phone line was always engaged. These days she spent a reasonable—although she didn't consider it an excessive—amount of her spare time in online chat. While she enjoyed it, she also knew of the stigma attached to the activity, and broadband allowed her to indulge her habit without appearing to be a loser to those who never entered the virtual world.

Toni woke her computer from sleep mode, opened her browser and went straight to her favorite chat site. It was a dedicated gay and lesbian site, with two "floors," one for the men and one for the women. Toni entered her user name and password, navigated to the women's floor and scrolled down the list of "rooms." She occasionally clicked on a room name in the drop-down list, the action bringing up a list of the people currently inside. Minxy, the ever-present New York Art student, was in the "New York" room with FairBriar, a dog breeder from Kentucky. A month or so ago, Toni and FairBriar had had a heated argument in relation to tail-docking. Toni thought that the practice of either shortening or completely amputating a dog's tail was both cruel and unnecessary, a thought doubly reaffirmed by Virgil's recent tail accident. FairBriar argued back it was necessary to remain true to the breed. They had not ended on friendly terms, so Toni clicked away from the New York room and continued her search. Two other rooms Toni frequented, the "Australian" room and the "Professional Women" room were completely empty. The "Spa" room was full to bursting, it being a favorite with many members, especially the younger set. It was notorious for those looking to flirt, or for a little bit more, and the conversations held in there varied from deadly dull to covertly suggestive to outlandishly bawdy. Toni considered "hopping into the spa" but decided against it. She wasn't feeling particularly flirtatious or bawdy. She continued scrolling.

TracieQ and Maddox were in the "Secret Garden." Toni liked the Secret Garden, it tended to be populated with the thirty-somethings, the age bracket Toni had entered the year prior. She also liked TracieQ and Maddox, both women hailing from different ends of Britain, and both with careers in fields relating to Toni's own. TracieQ worked as a bank teller; Maddox was a financial advisor. It had just gone six a.m. in England so they had apparently logged on for a prework breakfast chat. Toni double-clicked on the room and immediately a new window spawned, along with her username, Pookie.

> *TracieQ:* hi pookie
> *Maddox:* hi pookie. early for u?
> *Pookie:* not at work 2day
> *Maddox:* mental health day?
> *Pookie:* no. genuine. on the mend tho. how r u?
> *Maddox:* cant complain. weathers bad, as usual
> *TracieQ:* i'm fabulous
> *Pookie:* TQ—g/f back?
> *TracieQ:* 2nite. wont b speaking 2 any of u 4 a while lol

TracieQ was full of the news of her girlfriend's return from Newcastle. She was first to log off, begging the need to shower and dress for work. Maddox logged off soon after, but by then two others had joined the room. Toni settled in her chair, happy to interject as the newcomers dominated the conversation. Three more women entered and soon a number of different threads of conversation were flowing. Toni sipped from a glass of water as lines of text appeared in quick succession on the screen.

It wasn't exactly enthralling stuff, but it was a way to pass the time.

CHAPTER NINE

It was around midday when Emma turned the key in her front door. As expected, a cold nose pressed into her leg.

"Hi, Kai." Emma hunkered down to doggie level and ran her hands the length of Kayisha's ears. "How's your Friday been so far?"

Kayisha's response was gratefully received both for its enthusiasm and for the normalcy the ritual offered on this very non-normal day.

The long, floppy ears were tugged gently. "Let's go for a run, eh, girl."

That suggestion was greeted with more wild doggie enthusiasm so Emma quickly changed into her running gear and they headed out. Thoughts of opportunistic thieves got the better of her before they reached the end of the street and Emma turned back, spending a few minutes carting the contents of her station wagon into the house. Kayisha lay on the grass next to the driveway, snout between her paws, giving Emma doleful "we were supposed to be going out" glances each time she passed by, arms laden.

"This is the last of it, I promise." Emma said as she struggled under the weight of a box of veterinary reference books. It was placed on her bedroom floor next to the box containing her coffee mug, toiletries and other personal items used during her eight years at what was now Colleen's veterinary practice. Turning her back on the boxes, Emma trotted down the hallway and closed the front door behind her. "Come on, Kai." She ran past her best friend. "What are you waiting for?"

Emma started out hard but soon slowed to a more heart-friendly pace, her body settling into a pleasant rhythm. Once in her stride she was aware of her forward motion and of likely obstacles—other runners, cyclists, tree roots and fallen pine cones—but there was no effort to her movement, no pain in her limbs or gasping for breath. It was at these times, with the endorphins having kicked in and Kayisha trotting happily by her side, that Emma seemed to melt through the landscape, often finding herself finished with the lake circuit, or even back at her front gate, without consciously realizing where her feet had carried her.

Today her feet had carried her most of the way around the lake when a single word entered her thoughts and jerked her back to reality. *Colleen.*

Immediately Emma became aware of her feet pounding against the footpath and of her position in the universe. The water fountain that marked the point where Emma would veer from the lake and begin her return journey was a mere fifty meters ahead.

The thought reappeared. *Colleen.* Emma frowned and a drop of perspiration fell into her left eye, making her squint. She swiped the sweat from her forehead with her hand, then wiped the sweat from her hand to the side of her shorts. *Bloody Colleen.* Emma picked up speed as she mentally reviewed her week.

Colleen had called last Friday morning, the same morning Toni had brought Virgil in for treatment. Emma was actually performing Virgil's surgery when the call came through, Maggie passing

on the message to ring Colleen "immediately she was available."
Emma had purposely waited until late afternoon to return the call,
as much to prove she wasn't going to ask how high when Colleen
gave the order to jump as to give herself a bit of time to think. Her
protest, however, did little. If Colleen was annoyed at Emma's
delay tactics, she didn't let on, and the hours between the calls
brought no brilliant excuses for what Colleen described as "blatant
theft of company resources." Apparently—even though Emma
promised to have a check covering the full amount in the very next
mail—she was lucky Colleen didn't press charges.

At the conclusion of the call, Emma returned the handset to the
cradle, took a deep breath and closed her eyes. Despite the dress-
ing-down she had received, a smile formed. She'd just done what
so many dream of but few actually do. She'd just told her boss
exactly what she could do with her job. Emma's smile spread and
she laughed out loud. She was free.

Emma's post-resignation euphoria was short-lived. "What have
I done?" she had worriedly asked herself as she paced her kitchen
floor that same night, stopping more than once in front of the
drawer where she knew a half-empty cigarette packet lay.

What was she thinking, throwing in her job with nothing else
lined up? True, she had some small savings, and true, even after she
repaid Colleen the cost of Blue's treatment she would have a reasonable leave payout coming to her.

But that wasn't going to last forever.

And she had only more four days as the locum at Tricia's practice.

And vet vacancies in Perth were few and far between.

And Colleen would probably put out a general bulletin to every
vet in the vicinity advising not to hire Emma.

Panic rose. She'd probably never get work in this city again.

Emma finally opened the drawer and dug out the cigarette
packet. Smoking would help her calm down. Another dig in the
drawer and her lighter was also retrieved. Then both packet and
lighter were tossed disgustedly onto the kitchen bench. Smoking

wasn't the answer. She had to stop turning to it each time she became stressed. She reached for the wall phone instead.

"Damn." Lisa's mobile phone was turned off, even though, by Emma's calculations, she and Cathy should be in the midst of their Singapore transit stop. Emma had left a message on Lisa's voicemail. Then she tried Cathy's number. Again she was switched to voicemail. Another message was left and Emma tried three more friends' numbers. Again they either rang out or she was directed to their message banks. Glum, she stared out of her kitchen window. Since Friday was Justine's half-day at the city-based duty free store at which she worked, it was likely she was home by now. Emma could go talk to her. "No way," Emma told herself firmly. In the mood she was in she was likely to burst into tears, declare her undying love and generally make a complete idiot of herself. Still staring out the window, she groped along the bench until she found the cigarette packet and lighter. Smoke trailed behind her as she headed to the buffet in the dining area. On the bottom shelf she'd located the remains of her bottle of bourbon, placed there purely in case of thirsty visitors, because at the time she had vowed she was never going to touch alcohol again.

Needless to say, she had woken on Saturday morning with a very bad hangover, a severe case of smoker's mouth and an unquenchable thirst.

Now, just the thought of last weekend's dry horrors reminded Emma she was currently in need of some water. But the water fountain was well behind her and Kayisha. They were already nearly a third of the way around the lake again.

Another fountain should be somewhere around the next bend. Emma glanced to the golden mass of fur keeping pace with her. "What do you reckon, Kai? Shall we keep going or shall we turn back?"

Kayisha's happy woof indicated she could keep this up all afternoon. They committed to their second circuit of the lake, stopping briefly for a water break.

Despite the distance already covered, Emma continued onward

at a respectable speed, driven by continued thoughts of the past week. The weekdays had gone by without incident. Her last four days at Tricia's practice passed in a flash, the only noteworthy event an "I'm back, how did it all go?" call from Tricia on Thursday night. Emma truthfully related all had gone like clockwork. She didn't mention her resignation, deciding to keep that piece of information until she saw Tricia in person. Which would be this coming Sunday, Emma having accepted the invitation to Tricia's home for a "thank you" rib barbeque.

This morning—Friday—had been the big one for Emma. It was the morning she went to Colleen's practice to clear out her locker. Emma had approached the morning with dread, tossing and turning for much of the night, anticipating the worst. She even imagined Colleen having the police waiting for her, handcuffs at the ready because she had decided to press charges after all.

Luckily no such thing happened. Emma's departure from the practice was low-key and quiet. All the staff knew why Emma was leaving and they watched in embarrassed silence as Emma packed up her personal belongings. Colleen followed a few steps behind Emma throughout her journey through the practice's rooms. That was the most humiliating part, being watched by the boss as if she would souvenir some item not her own.

"I'll miss you, Em," said Pete, who, under Colleen's continued scrutinizing eye, had helped Emma pack everything into the back of her station wagon. He stepped forward and drew Emma into a hug. "I'll call you tonight."

"Sure thing." Emma blinked back tears. The reality of leaving the place she'd put her heart and soul into for so many years was finally hitting home. This was only the second practice Emma had worked at since finishing her training, and prior to Colleen's taking over the helm, it was the practice she'd envisaged staying at for a good few years to come.

"Bloody Colleen." The stress and humiliation of the morning enveloped Emma as she continued to run. *Bloody Colleen*. Emma mentally repeated her mantra with each step. *Bloody Colleen*. *Bloody*

Colleen. "Bloody high-heel-wearing, money-hungry bitch of a woman, Colleen."

That last curse took Emma all the way back to her front gate. Exhausted, she bent down, hands on her knees, chest heaving, lungs hungrily sucking in oxygen. For her part, Kayisha flopped onto the pavement, tongue dripping as she panted heavily.

"That's it." Emma managed to squeeze out a few words as she fought to regain her breath. "No more ciggies for me. My lungs can't take it."

By the time she stepped under the shower her breathing had returned to normal. She soaped down under a cool stream and rinsed off under bracing cold water. The shock of cold cleared her head and, newly enthused, she sat in front of the computer that resided in a corner of her lounge room.

Left for extended periods without use, the plastic dust covers were removed from both the keyboard and monitor. Like a car that has been sitting idle for too long, the computer seemed to struggle and groan when Emma booted it up. She half expected to see black smoke coming from the back of the monitor, or whatever part equated to its exhaust.

No smoke appeared and Emma rubbed her hands together in preparation for her selected tasks. She was going to get her résumé, eight years out of date, into order. Then, so long as the automatic deduction from her credit card was still reaching her Internet service provider, she was going to check the Web site advertised in the veterinary association's newsletter. The Web site apparently featured a nationwide employment section. This seemed as good a starting point as any for her job search.

Thankfully, although her résumé was over eight years old, it had been saved on a floppy disk conveniently labeled "Emma: Résumé," so it was not hard to locate. Kayisha settled on the floor next to Emma's chair and Emma absently scratched the top of Kai's head as she reviewed the document.

"Well, that's well and truly out of date, Kai." Emma selected the text that announced she was twenty-nine years old. She deleted the reference to her age altogether, recalling a conversation with someone at some party somewhere who announced it was actually against equal opportunity law to base an employment decision on a person's age. As the text disappeared, Emma couldn't decide which was more depressing—being of an age where she was thankful she wasn't required to reveal it, or attending a party where equal opportunity was the hot topic of discussion.

She took heart from other changes she made to her résumé. She surprised herself with just how much experience she had acquired in the years since the document was edited. What was now Colleen's practice was a state forerunner in the field of veterinary dentistry and as a consequence she had gained opportunities of which few vets in Western Australia could boast. A particular highlight was working as an occasional part of the veterinary team at Perth Zoo. Emma would never forget the mixture of awe, exhilaration and pure terror when looking directly into the gaping jaw of an anesthetized tiger suffering from a toothache.

As if knowing Emma was writing of a distant cousin, Malibu jumped lithely over Kayisha and onto the computer desk. Engrossed in her task, Emma mumbled a distracted "Hi, Mal."

Malibu, however, had decided she wanted Emma's undivided attention. She plopped neatly on top of the keyboard. Emma's résumé now announced she had successfully removed a tiger's "hyula67." That might impress someone ignorant of the finer points of large-cat dentistry, Emma thought, but it wasn't going to cut the mustard with her peers.

"Sit here, Mal." She lifted Malibu off her keyboard and plonked her onto her lap.

For a while Malibu stayed where placed, stretching as only cats can stretch, head and front paws dangling over the side of Emma's thigh, haughtily taunting Kayisha by her mere presence. It wasn't too long before passing contemptuous looks to the floor-bound canine lost its appeal. Malibu stood, two paws on each of Emma's thighs, arched luxuriously and stepped back onto Emma's keyboard.

"Malibu!" Emma shrieked as the contents of her word-processing window suddenly disappeared. Malibu was shooed from the desk and Emma hunched over the computer screen, hoping that by staring at it the lost words would magically rematerialize.

They didn't.

"Shit, shit, shit!" All that work wasted. Emma didn't even know if she had a hard copy of the original floating around somewhere.

She sat back in her seat and assumed her thinking position. Wait a minute . . . She sat forward again. The file name "Emma-Résumé" still blinked at the top of her word-processing window. The file was still there. Empty, but still there. She pointed her mouse at the edit menu and clicked "undo" from the selection.

"I'm a frigging computer genius." Emma congratulated herself as her résumé reappeared. "Just as well for you, my girl." She turned to Malibu, who had taken up position on the back of the couch. Malibu was unconcerned at the potential disaster she had created, concentrating instead on licking the point between her back legs.

Emma returned her attention to the monitor. The "save" button was quickly pushed, and she made a note to keep pressing it every couple of edits. After another half-hour, numerous edits and numerous saves, she was reasonably happy with the result. She read her résumé in its entirety, decided it was pretty damn good, printed out a copy, which she then read through once again, and closed the file.

Emma stood and stretched, grabbed a fresh glass of water and settled back down. The computer thought long and hard about connecting to the server, but the modem eventually made the correct sounds and she was in. Now all she had to do was access the veterinary association Web site, find their employment section and get the details of practices in need of a vet. Simple.

Not so simple. Emma's prediction of a lack of vet vacancies in Perth was quickly confirmed. "Shit." Emma cursed at the screen. She hadn't expected it to be this bad. There was absolutely nothing. She widened her search to the rest of Western Australia and stared at the single entry. An equine specialist was required in the south of the state. But when they said south, they meant almost as far south as you could get. Not exactly commuting distance. Emma sat with elbows on the armrests and fingertips resting against each other. Was there any point in even applying? She'd spent more time astride horses than treating them, her daily experience more geared to cats, dogs, goldfish, budgies and the usual mix of household pets. Not exactly what you'd call an equine specialist. And then there was the distance. If she did get the job, she'd have to uproot herself and relocate. And leave . . . what? She rented her house, so although she'd carried the lease over ten years and called it home, it wasn't really hers. She had no lover; she had no job. Her parents chose not to speak to her, but they lived a few hundred kilometers north of Perth so didn't really enter the equation. She had Malibu and Kayisha, but they would go with her. That left a few close friends and . . . Justine. Emma considered the pros and cons while she downed what remained of her glass of water. She decided that if she got the job, at least she'd have an excuse not to be a damn bridesmaid. She placed her glass on the table, clicked on the "apply here" button, wrote a brief cover letter and sent her résumé into the virtual ether.

Her primary objective achieved, Emma browsed some other sections of the site, found a few interesting articles, downloaded them for reading offline and clicked on the cross on the top right of the browser window.

"Are you sure you want to disconnect?" asked the dialogue box that appeared.

Emma decided she may as well make the most of her session, clicked the cancel button, navigated to a search engine and typed the first thing that entered her head.

Lesbian.

Of course, this wasn't the first time Emma had entered this search query. On taking delivery of the computer a couple of years ago, she and Chris had sat side by side as they accessed the Internet. They'd typed in the same query and were rewarded with pages and pages of results. Closer inspection revealed most to be pornographic sites. After the first four, Emma decided she'd had enough. Erotica was one thing, but these sites . . . She doubted any were owned and run by women. They were quite obviously meant for men to engage their distorted women-on-women fantasies.

The same type of results appeared in this search. She scrolled through the first screen, found nothing, advanced to the second. Again the results were spectacularly awful. Then she spied a title halfway down the page that announced "Lesbian Chat. In real time. Around the globe."

Emma had heard of chat rooms. She'd seen stories on television, read articles in the newspapers and magazines. One of her friends—Amanda—was currently into them. Emma had never seen the appeal, but now she wondered if this was the chat room Amanda frequented. Amanda had relocated to Sydney last year, so getting in touch via the Internet was appealing. It would certainly save on long-distance call charges.

Emma clicked on the link and waited.

She was confronted with a registration screen. She briefly wondered if she could be bothered, decided she could and began entering her details. Halfway through she got a case of the jitters, went back to the home page and read the privacy policy. Once certain her details wouldn't be put on public display by registering as a member she reentered her details, answering only the fields deemed compulsory. The profile field, the one that asked her to briefly describe herself, was thankfully not mandatory so she left it blank. The user name field was, however, required. Emma typed "Emma."

Then she deleted it. No way was she going to use her real name. She tried Sara. That was already taken. Then she tried Tara, then Belinda, then Cara, and even Lisa and Amanda. All taken. Obviously any name ending in an A was already used. So too it seemed was just about every other female name she could think of. As a last resort she entered Kayisha. The user name was accepted.

Great, Emma thought wryly. *Out to meet the girls under the guise of my dog.* At least Amanda would recognize her. She shrugged, clicked the "Enter Chat" button and waited.

"Jeez, does this ever end?" Emma asked herself. She'd selected the Women's Floor from the two options available, expecting this time to be in. Instead she was presented with a long list of "rooms." She scrolled down the list, balking at some of the room names. Even if Amanda frequented the "Leather" room or the "Dominatrix" room or the "Swingers" room, Emma would never know it, mainly because she had no intention of entering any of them. She was at the point of chickening out of the whole exercise when one caught her eye. The "Secret Garden." That sounded innocent enough. She followed the instruction at the top of the screen, double-clicking on the room name. She blinked as a new window opened. Maybe she had done something wrong? No, the title bar read "Secret Garden."

The window was divided into three panes. To the right was a list of names, hers included. To the left was a bigger pane where text was appearing as if by magic. It seemed the room occupants were acknowledging her presence. A string of names followed by "Hi, Kayisha" appeared.

Emma assumed the final pane, the one that said, "Type your text here," was where she should try typing. She moved her cursor to the text field and typed, "Hi, everyone." As soon as she hit the enter key her words appeared in the main pane. Emma smiled at her success. This was going to be fun.

After the initial flurry of hellos was over, however, the room occupants went back to typing at whomever they were typing at before. Emma watched the flow, trying to unravel the different threads and figure who was talking to whom. It wasn't easy. Apart from herself there were fifteen in the room and words scrolled by almost as fast as she could read them. Eventually she figured there were four different conversations happening. The one between Shygirl, Pookie, Vixen and Osmosis seemed the most entertaining, or rather, the least innocuous. In a rather disjointed fashion, and with a lot of acronyms Emma found quite meaningless, they were giving their opinion about the book *Angels and Demons*. She too had read Dan Brown's prequel to *The Da Vinci Code*, and along with all but Vixen had loved it. However, with no idea of the etiquette of a chat room, Emma was unsure if she should barge into the conversation and add her opinion. Just as she'd made up her mind she would, after all, what was the worst that could happen— maybe be ostracized by a bunch of people she couldn't see and had never met—Vixen began them on a discussion of a book she had actually enjoyed, *Life of Pi* by Yann Martel. Emma had never even heard of it, although according to Vixen it deservedly won the Mann Booker prize.

An instruction below the list of room occupants caught Emma's eye as she continued to sit silent, fingers poised over the keyboard. "Click on a name to view the profile." Maybe if she could find common ground with someone in the room she could strike up a conversation of her own. She clicked on Vixen. Her profile read, "Chicago. 29, independent, fun-loving, no games. No pvt."

No pvt? What on earth did that mean? Emma clicked on Shygirl. It appeared she wasn't too shy after all. "Petite 36D Sub. Cum let's have some fun." Hmm . . .

Next she tried Pookie. No profile appeared. Maybe she hadn't clicked properly, or maybe, like her, Pookie had not entered a profile. She tried again anyway, this time giving two clicks in quick succession.

Oh, dear. Emma had no idea why yet another window materialized. It was devoid of the list of room occupants and for a moment was completely empty. Text suddenly blinked.

Pookie: hi kayisha

Emma discarded her worries over the technical foibles of a chat room, glad someone was finally speaking to her.

Kayisha: Hi Pookie.

Pookie: u wanted 2 speak 2 me in pvt?

Pvt. There was that "word" again.

Kayisha: What's pvt?

Pookie: lol where we r now. u brought me in

Kayisha: How? What's lol?
Pookie: new 2 this?
Kayisha: First time.
Pookie: u 2x clicked on my name n brought me in. this is a private room. no 1 can see wot we say
Kayisha: Oh. Sorry. I didn't know.
Pookie: i did it 2 when new. frightened the life out of me LOL
Kayisha: lol?
Pookie: lol = laugh out loud. where u from kay?

Since it was obvious everything in this virtual world was written in some funny shorthand, Emma wasn't too surprised Pookie abbreviated her user name. She decided not to return the gesture. Being referred to as "Poo" might not go down too well. Emma hesitated over her answer. The chat site was apparently worldwide. Should she say Australia, Western Australia or Perth?

Kayisha: Perth
Pookie: perth scotland or perth wa?
Kayisha: WA
Pookie: which side of the river?

Emma quickly deduced Pookie must also be a "Perthite." Anyone who asked that question was obviously a local and knew of the ongoing debate over which side of the Swan River was best. North residents thought North best; South voted South. In this debate anyone who resided East or West didn't count.

Although it was nice to think she had happened across a woman from her own town, Emma found herself in a conundrum. Had Pookie been from deepest, darkest Africa Emma would have no trouble revealing her approximate location, but knowing she was in the same city, maybe even in the same suburb, raised alarm bells. Pookie may be a charming psychopath. Dear Lord, she may even be a he.

Emma typed in what she thought was a suitably obscure answer and waited for the response.

❧

Toni smiled when she read Kayisha's reply to her "which side of the river" question. Her answer, "The good side," proved she was a local. Finally, after all these months of chatting, Toni had bumped into someone else from Perth. She had begun to feel she was the only one.

> *Pookie:* so we have something in common
> *Kayisha:* You live on the good side too?
> *Pookie:* now i do. when i arrived i lived on the other side but i crossed over. still work on the other side tho
> *Kayisha:* A double agent.
> *Pookie:* lol i guess so
> *Kayisha:* Arrived from where?
> *Pookie:* melbourne
> *Kayisha:* I love Melbourne. But I think I put on five pounds during my last visit. It's definitely not a place to go when on a diet.
> *Pookie:* the refrain of a lygon street victim
> *Kayisha:* Spaghetti heaven stretched out on a street.

Toni smiled again, never having heard Lygon Street, famous for its plethora of Italian restaurants, described in such a way. Her fingers flew across the keyboard, running off a string of her favorite Lygon Street haunts. To her delight Kayisha declared two of them as "must visits" when in town. She even went into raptures over the same "to die for" spaghetti marinara. Toni found she was smiling yet again. She decided she liked Kayisha.

Much later, the phone rang. Toni was so engrossed in the words on her screen she jumped at the noise. A glance to the time display revealed it was nearly five-thirty. Goodness, last time she checked it had only been three forty-five. She typed an apology before reaching to answer the phone, and she used it as a chance to introduce Kayisha to another piece of chatter jargon.

> *Pookie:* brb = be right back
> *Kayisha:* ok

Toni was still watching the screen when she stopped the phone from its shrill ringing. "Hello?"

"Hi, Toni."

"Oh, hi, Julie."

"Sorry I didn't get back to you earlier. It's been all go over here."

"Back to me?"

"You called and left a message with Sue."

"Oh, yes." Toni closed her eyes so she could concentrate on something other than her computer. "But you didn't need to call back."

"That's okay. I wanted to see if there was anything you particularly felt like for dinner tonight."

"Honestly, Julie, it's fine. You don't need to come over again. I'm feeling much better today."

"It's really no trouble, Toni."

"I was going to rustle up something for myself. Forget about me and go enjoy your weekend."

"How about a Caesar salad?"

That was it. Julie hung out the bait and Toni took it. Of all foods known to womankind, Caesar salad was Toni's absolute favorite; even more so than Lygon Street spaghetti marinara. "Okay."

"Great. I'll see you in an hour or so."

"Okay. Oh, and Julie, do you think you could pick me up a couple of AA batteries?"

Julie didn't ask what they were for. Toni was a bit disappointed. She wanted to use her flat battery and vibrating appliance comment.

All Julie said was, "Sure thing."

Toni found the telephone handset by touch, eyes already refocused on the screen as she returned the receiver to its cradle. She had at least another half an hour to chat before needing to log off and make herself presentable.

Pookie: back

The screen sat silent. Toni waited a good minute before trying again. Kayisha may have used Toni's retreat to have a bathroom stop, or take a call or, anything really.

Pookie: u there kay?

111

Still no reply. Toni tried again but only her own words blinked back at her. Toni moved the private window to the far side of her monitor and refreshed the original window underneath. The membership of the room had turned over since she had moved into private, only Shygirl remaining. Kayisha's name was gone from the list. More than a little disappointed, Toni closed the private room window and returned to the main room.

Pookie: still here shy?

Shygirl: <g> waiting 4 u pook

Toni didn't currently feel like chatting to Shygirl. She had a habit of always alluding to sex, once even offering Toni a "pvt session she wouldn't forget." Toni had no idea how Shygirl could get turned on by what was simply a load of words flitting across the screen, but apparently she did, and apparently she'd soon get Toni typing with one hand too. Shygirl, having witnessed Toni's prolonged private session with Kayisha, would find it hard to believe that the last hour or so had been spent just chatting. But that's what Toni and Kayisha had done. Their conversation flowed easily from topic to topic, but, as if by some unspoken agreement, neither touched on anything remotely personal. Food, its preparation and consumption dominated a good amount of their time, and then it was onto movies and music. So Toni knew Kayisha loved to eat and listened to everything from jazz to rock to classical but couldn't fathom the explosion of rap. She also discovered they shared similar tastes in movies and they both despised Tom Cruise. On the other hand, she had no idea how old Kayisha was, if she was single or attached, what she did for a living, if she was a student, unemployed or maybe even retired. She also had no idea if she'd meet up with her again.

Toni knew people appeared and disappeared in this virtual world. Normally she didn't hassle over it; it was just the nature of the beast. But this time . . . Maybe it was because Kayisha was a "neighbor" that made the difference. Which was a silly notion, really. The world outside her front door was full of beautiful, vibrant and interesting women. Why she should worry over one hunched over a computer terminal, who didn't have the courtesy to give so much as a "by your leave" before dropping out of sight, was beyond her reckoning.

Pookie: speak 2 u later shy

Shygirl: look forward to it pook <wink>

Toni exited the room and signed out of the chat site. Now, with time to kill before Julie was due to arrive, she decided to pay some bills online.

Ten minutes later Toni had guaranteed the continued supply of electricity to her home, insured her car for another year and paid the balance of her VISA card. The one bill she was unable to pay online was the vet bill. The standard terms were settlement in seven days, but Toni figured a day here or there wasn't going to cause much angst at the practice. Virgil was, after all, a long-term client and Toni her usually prompt-paying guardian. She wrote a check, addressed an envelope and leaned it against her printer as a reminder to take it to the post box when she eventually ventured outdoors again.

Toni thrummed her fingers against the edge of her desk, staring at the Google search screen she had set as her home page. In less than a minute she had navigated back to the chat site, logged in again and was scrolling through the list of rooms. The Secret Garden was now devoid of any life. She found Shygirl in the Spa but there was no sign of Kayisha, there or in any of the other rooms she clicked on. Feeling rather obsessive and stupid, Toni closed down her browser, put her computer back to sleep and turned her mind from the virtual world to the real. She smacked her lips together, found her mouth again tasted disgusting and aimed for the bathroom to freshen up.

"Let me in, God damn it!" Despite the curse, Emma held her hands together in the prayer position. Her modem made the correct dialing sounds, rang three times, went silent for a moment and then, infuriatingly, gave an engaged signal. "Stupid, damned ISP."

Her Internet service provider received yet another verbal sledging. Out of the blue, just moments after Pookie had halted their conversation with a promise to be right back, a "You have been disconnected" dialogue box appeared on Emma's screen. She had been trying ever since to reconnect, but on each attempt she got the busy signal. By now Pookie probably thought she was the rudest person to walk the earth, just disappearing like that. "I've a good mind to ring up and complain."

Emma didn't get a chance to carry out her threat, her attention diverted by the chime of the doorbell. Halfway to the door, her phone also began to ring.

"Just a minute," Emma called to whoever was on her veranda. "Hello," she said into the telephone receiver. "Oh, hi, Pete." Emma remembered he said he'd give her a call. "You finished work already?"

A low rumble of laughter echoed through the phone line. "It's nearly six, Em. I'm home and ready with a six-pack if you're interested."

Emma glanced at her watch. My goodness, was it that late already? She must have lost track of all time. "Sounds great, Pete, but just hang on a minute, will you? There's someone at the door."

She left Pete hanging on the line and dashed up the hallway. Justine was on the other side of the door, a large white folder in one hand, bottle of sparkling wine in the other. Emma assumed the folder was Justine's wedding scrapbook, mainly because of the bright pink *Wedding Ideas* splashed across the cover.

Justine flashed an enticing smile and edged past Emma and Kayisha, obviously making the assumption the open door was an invitation to enter. "I've found some fabulous papers for the wedding invites and I got some sample menus faxed to me today at work."

Oh, yay. Emma rolled her eyes as she followed Justine down the hallway. "I'll be right with you, Justine. I've just got someone on the phone." She picked up the receiver as she watched Justine toss her scrapbook on the coffee table and head for the buffet. The subsequent clink of glass indicated Justine had found and helped herself to Champagne flutes. The woman certainly had a nerve, making herself at home like that. At the same time Emma knew, if there was the slightest possibility Justine wanted to make herself at home on a more permanent basis, Emma's door would be flung open so fast it would fall off its hinges. She pressed her ear back to the receiver. "Sorry about that." In the background a cork popped loudly from the bottle.

"What was that?" asked Pete.

"I've just had a friend arrive with a bottle of bubbly."

"If you're busy we can always make it another time—"

"Don't be silly," Emma interrupted quickly. Maybe with a bloke in the mix Justine would be distracted from wedding talk. "Come on over. The more the merrier."

"You sure?" Pete's tone gave him away. He obviously thought the bubbly-toting woman was a love interest.

Emma accepted the glass Justine held out to her. She smiled wryly. *If only he knew.* "Positive."

"Gee thanks, Em." Pete divided the contents of the last can between two glasses. "If I'd known we'd be sifting through piles of colored paper I might have thought twice about coming over."

Emma laughed as she sat back down. It was after nine-thirty and Justine had just left, bustling out the door, scrapbook in hand and chatting excitedly. Pete's presence had done little to quell the wedding talk. In contrast, it completely dominated the conversation. Emma slipped off her shoes and tucked her feet under her thighs. She took a sip of the freshly poured beer. It was cold and it was malty. Surprisingly good for a mid-strength brew. "I think you did rather well, actually. Justine certainly was impressed with your knowledge of colors."

Pete harrumphed. "Any fool could tell you black ink will not read well on red paper. He grinned. "I did like her idea of red invites in black envelopes though."

Emma laughed again. She knew Pete was speaking more from a standard bloke's distaste of pastels than an appreciation of the Japanese theme Justine had decided she wanted to pursue. "At least now I don't have to write all the invitations in whiteout."

"Yes." Pete snickered. "Very generous of you to offer, Em."

"Yeah, well." Emma adjusted her feet under her legs. It was a shame she couldn't kick herself from that angle. Now, in addition to being a bridesmaid, she also had to print all the invitations. Justine hadn't asked; Emma had offered. After all, it was much more economical than getting it done professionally, and, Emma reminded herself, she was a frigging computer genius so it shouldn't take too long. "It's not like I've got anything better to do with my days at the moment."

Emma immediately felt the mood dampen. Pete stared sullenly into his glass. "It's so wrong what Colleen did to you, Em. I'm tempted to tell her that too."

"Don't you even think about doing that, Peter Jamieson," Emma said sharply. "You'd be joining me in the unemployment line before you knew it."

Pete shrugged like he didn't care.

Emma wasn't about to let him lose his job because of some misguided protest. She untucked her feet and sat up straighter. "If anything, I caused this. I shouldn't have tried to sneak Blue's treatment through the books. Colleen had every right to be angry."

"Regardless, she should just have let you pay the money back and then forgotten about it. You're a good vet, Em. She's going to regret letting you go." Pete looked up from his glass, briefly meeting Emma's eyes before quickly averting his gaze again. "I don't like working for her any more than you did. But at least having you there made it bearable."

"Give it a week and you'll wonder why you ever thought that." Emma was touched by Pete's shy admission of affection. "And anyway, Judith's still there. She's just as good at getting you into line as I ever was."

"Judith isn't happy either. She told me she was thinking of moving on."

Judith, although a good decade older than Emma, was the practice "junior." Loathing her job as a high-level public servant, she gave up the associated salary and downshifted to become a vet assistant. Having dealt with the bureaucracy and melting pot of characters in government, she cruised through the mix of human personalities that walked through the practice each day. Emma had just assumed that, while Judith may or may not like Colleen personally, she would sidestep her feelings and get on with the business of caring for the non-human personalities that walked or crawled or swam or flew into the practice. That Judith was also thinking of leaving . . . well, at least it proved Emma wasn't alone in her inability to warm to Colleen.

"Sounds like Colleen will wake up one day and find she has no staff left."

"And then she'll have to sell up." Pete's expression showed a certain amount of glee at the thought.

"Yeah," Emma agreed, trying to picture Colleen in her high heels, scraping out the night's litter trays. "Because she sure won't do any of the dirty work herself."

"I can see the advert now." Pete grinned. "Vet practice going cheap. Owner desperate. All offers considered."

"And wouldn't it piss her off if one of us bought it." Emma laughed.

"Or both of us."

Emma nodded, caught up in the dream. "Or both of us."

"We could, you know."

Emma looked sideways at him. "You're not serious?"

"Why not? I don't necessarily mean Colleen's practice. Or any other established practice for that matter. But we could start one of our own."

"Do you have any idea how expensive that is?"

"No. But I'm guessing from your expression it's not cheap."

"More than I've got in the bank, buster."

"But maybe not more than you and me have put together."

Emma had no idea how much Pete had squirreled away, but she knew the state of her own bank account. If she didn't land another job in the next six weeks it wouldn't look too pretty. "I think maybe it would be."

"That's what bank loans are for."

"It's a nice thought, Pete, but it's not going to happen."

"Only because you don't want it to."

"It's not that at all." That comment raised Emma's hackles. "I would *love* to have my own practice, but unfortunately I don't have a money tree growing in my backyard."

"Okay, okay." Pete raised his hand in surrender. "Don't get shitty. It was only an idea."

"A damn good idea too," Emma admitted, her flash of temper disappearing as quickly as it came. "Tell you what, when I win Lotto you're the first person I'll call."

"I wonder how much money Judith has?" Pete mused. "Maybe the three of us could go in together."

"You don't give up do you, Peter Jamieson?"

He downed the last of his beer in one big swallow. "Not usually."

"Would you like another? I think I've got a bottle or two floating round in the fridge."

"No, thanks. I'm driving. A coffee would go down well, though."

"Coffee it is." Emma stood and headed for the kitchen. She stole a glance at the slender young man seated on her couch. Unaware he was being watched, he rolled his shoulders, reached for the *National Geographic* sitting on the far edge of the coffee table and idly flipped through it. Emma sighed. It was a shame the vet practice idea could never become a reality. She'd enjoyed working with Pete. They had made a good team.

"Thanks, Em." A few minutes later, Pete tossed the *National Geographic* back onto the coffee table and took the mug Emma offered. "Two sugars?"

"Yep." Emma sat down, tucking her feet under her thighs again. She took a sip from her mug. "So tell me how come a good-looking, smart young man like yourself hasn't got plans on a Friday night?"

Pete shrugged, grinning. "What do you mean? I'm here, aren't I?"

"You know what I mean."

"No, I don't know what you mean."

"I mean, why aren't you out on a date with a beautiful young woman? Surely you have them knocking down your door."

Pete shrugged again. "Maybe I prefer the company of an old lovelorn lesbian."

"Not so much of the old, thank you very much," Emma warned, hiding her smile behind her mug. She supposed that to a nineteen-year-old, anyone beyond thirty was ancient. She shifted in her seat. "And who said I was lovelorn?"

Pete guffawed. "Jesus, Em, if you had your mouth hanging open any more I'd have mistaken you for Kayisha. Complete with drool. Not that I blame you, though." He winked. "Justine's quite a looker."

Emma's face and neck became incredibly hot. She thought she had handled herself with considerable poise. But apparently not. And since Pete belonged to the gender not supposed to pick up on that kind of thing, it seemed she had silently screamed her feelings all evening. "Do you think she noticed?"

Pete guffawed again. "Of course she bloody well noticed. She feeds off it, Em. You can see it a mile away." Emma found Pete's hand on her forearm and she felt a slight pressure as he squeezed. Then he batted his lashes and raised his voice a couple of octaves. "Oh, Emma, are you *sure* you don't mind printing the invitations? It would be *such* a big help."

"Piss off." Emma snatched her arm away, angry and embarrassed. At herself. "Weren't we supposed to be talking about your love life, not mine?"

"She's getting married, Em. She's not interested in you. Deal with it."

Emma stared at Pete, stung and caught off-guard by his directness. Tears threatened, but she swallowed hard, refusing to let them reach her eyes. "I am dealing with it. In my own way."

❧

Toni pushed her plate away and sighed happily. "That"—she patted her tummy—"was the best Caesar salad I've ever had in my life. You do realize you've completely spoiled my lunchtime restaurant routine. Now I'll have to find something new to pick on the menu."

Toni wasn't exaggerating. Julie's Caesar was fantastic. Unlike the ready-made salad Toni was expecting, Julie arrived on the doorstep with an overflowing grocery bag. Once in the kitchen it was emptied of contents—cos lettuce, anchovies, streaky bacon, a block of fresh Parmesan and even an Italian Ciabatta for a variation on the usual white-bread croutons. The dressing had been a shop-bought cheat, but it was a delicious, decadent cheat, made all the better by the coddled egg stirred through it just prior to serving. Coupled with a glass of the crisp, dry white wine Julie also extracted from her bag, Toni felt she had entered culinary heaven.

"Glad you liked it." Julie stacked both plates in front of her. "It's one of my own favorites. I make it at least once a week at home."

"Let me clear that away," Toni said as she absorbed this new piece of information, once more experiencing a pang of guilt for not taking the time to find out Julie's likes and dislikes before now. "You know the rules. The cook never does the washing up."

"Which, as you should know, is superceded by the other rule."

"What other rule?"

"She who is sick must rest up and get better."

"But—"

"Stop it." Before Toni could continue the washing-up debate Julie swiped at Toni's hand. It was the fourth time she had done so this evening, this time as Toni unconsciously scratched at her upper arm. "You'll get scars."

Protesting, Toni was shooed from the table and she headed for her en suite bathroom, loudly complaining about now having two mothers instead of one. Julie had issued firm instructions Toni was not to worry about the dishes; that they'd be done by the time she emerged from the pine tar bath she also insisted Toni should have.

Despite the unpleasant odor of the pine tar and the fact she had already had a soak earlier in the day, Toni could have stayed in the bath for hours, the solution soothing her sore and itchy skin, but she made quick work of it, feeling odd bathing while a colleague puttered 'round in her kitchen. She splashed water onto her face, admitting that while it felt odd, it wasn't an awful odd, more of a pleasant odd. She was still mulling over that fact as she retreated to the bedroom to dot calamine lotion over her body. Feet, legs and bottom were first. Even her groin hadn't escaped unscathed, so that got a quick dabbing too. Her paw-print pajama bottoms were pulled on and Toni began on her upper body.

A soft rapping on her bedroom door stopped her mid-dab on her left breast. "Yes?"

Julie's voice was muffled through the wood. "Are you okay, Toni?"

"Fine." Toni's quick soak mustn't have been so quick after all. "I'm just putting calamine on. I'll be out in a minute."

"Do you want me to put some on your back?"

A little assistance would have gone down well. There was a spot right in the middle of Toni's spine she could never quite reach. *Yes, please.* "No. It's okay."

"You sure?"

No. "Yes."

"Okay."

As if on cue, the hard-to-reach spot on Toni's back started to itch. Damn, traitorous back. It knew Toni was funny about baring her body in public. She wouldn't even strip off in the change rooms at the gym, choosing instead the privacy of a toilet cubicle. It was rather an odd quirk, especially since she had no qualms about getting naked with a lover, even the first time. The itch got worse and Toni tried in vain to reach it with her fingertips. "Actually," she called through the door, "maybe I will get you to do my back. Just give me a second."

By the time Julie entered, Toni had tugged on her pajama top and done up the buttons.

Julie sat on the edge of the bed, Calamine bottle in one hand, cotton ball in the other. "Okay, Toni. Ready?"

Toni nodded but didn't move.

"Um, Toni . . . you're going to have to lift your top."

Toni lifted the back of her pajamas a little way, stopping as soon as she felt the material at the front begin to shift.

"It's okay, Toni. I can assure you, you have nothing I haven't seen before."

Toni was almost certain she heard a quaver in Julie's voice, despite the light delivery. She hoped her reply was just as light. "Maybe so, but you haven't seen mine."

Toni squeezed her eyes shut as Julie lifted her pajama top all the way up to her neck. The front stayed relatively intact, but just to make sure, Toni folded her arms protectively across her breasts. She shivered involuntarily each time Julie dabbed with her cotton ball. The lotion was cold.

All conversation ceased and Toni entertained the terrible thought her pajama bottoms weren't up far enough and Julie was speechless at the sight of her bottom crack. She wriggled a bit, trying to gauge exactly where the drawstring of her pajamas was sitting. To her relief it was well around her waist. But the move-ment prompted Julie to inquire, "Is that bothering you?"

Before Toni had a chance to reply, the waist of her pajama bot-toms was pulled and a dab of cold shot through the skin just above her left cheek. Now, Toni thought miserably, her bottom crack was well and truly exposed. She searched wildly for something to say that would distract Julie's attention from her behind. It occurred to her that she could ask if Julie had remembered to pick up her AA batteries. That idea was quickly dismissed. Now was not the best time to initiate a conversation about small, vibrating appliances.

"How's Anna's training going?" Toni asked, just for something to say.

"Good. They're only doing a light session tonight. Tomorrow's the big match."

"Are you going to watch?"

Another cold shot pierced the skin just above Toni's left kidney. "Of course." The dabs came to a halt and Toni felt the flannelette of her top fall over her back. Then she felt hands smoothing the material. They emitted hand-sized pools of warmth as they rested, just for a moment, on each side of Toni's waist. "If you're feeling up to it, you're welcome to come along."

"Thanks." Toni was disconcerted by the familiarity of Julie's touch. She was even more disconcerted at the flash of disappointment when the contact ended. Then she quickly decided she was just being a baby, that being "untouchable" for a week had left her in need of a cuddle. Especially since her usual source of comfort, Virgil, was still barely speaking to her, never mind being physically affectionate. Toni caught a glimpse of herself in the full-length mirror on the far wardrobe door. She looked a sight, the dark spots on her face still visible beneath the pink of the calamine lotion. "But I think I'll give it a miss. I don't want to frighten everyone out of the pool."

Only a matter of minutes later, Toni stood with Julie at the front door. Anna's training should be finished and Julie was going to stay the night at her apartment.

"Thanks again, Julie. That really was a great meal."

"My pleasure." Julie rummaged in her bag for her car keys. "Oh. I forgot about these." She pulled out a packet of batteries instead. "Here you go."

The batteries were handed over and once again Julie delved into her bag. This time keys were retrieved. "Remember, if you need anything over the weekend, just call."

Toni swung the small battery packet in front of Julie. "Now I've got these, I won't need anything."

Julie cocked her head to one side, curiosity flickering in her eyes. "Why? What are they for?"

Toni told her, pleased she was finally getting to use her small, vibrating appliance comment. She was doubly pleased at the reaction. Julie's eyes noticeably widened and color stained her cheeks.

"I'll ring you Monday," Julie stammered, suddenly intent on the keys in her hand.

"Okay." The laughter bubbling inside Toni burst forth as soon as Julie's old Ford Laser pulled out of the driveway. She was still laughing as she closed the front door behind her. Poor Julie. Toni knew she really shouldn't tease the girl, especially after all she'd done for her lately. On the other hand, it was good to know the shy, sometimes nervous young woman still existed underneath the confident exterior she now projected. It was somehow comforting.

Toni's laughter came to an abrupt halt halfway down the hallway, her mind snapping back to the light, brief pressure of hands on each side of her waist.

"Virgil," she called to her companion, refusing to allow the thought to linger. It was a silly thought anyway. It was quite obvious she was just in a state of touch deprivation. "Where are you? Mum needs a cuddle."

CHAPTER TEN

Cathy stretched her legs underneath the table located outside a café located at the edge of Piazza della Rotonda. Her feet were tired after another day of being on the go since breakfast. Today, Saturday, they had done the Capitol and Piazza Venezia. They'd climbed Michelangelo's long sloping steps to the geometrically paved Piazza del Campidologlio and spent hours in the Capitolene Museum. Once back in the piazza, they'd skirted the Palazzo Senatorio and discovered a terrace overlooking what was probably the city's best panorama of the Roman Forum. Needless to say, Lisa's digital camera memory card was filling fast.

"*Grazie.*" The latte placed in front of her was almost as welcome as getting the weight off her feet. Served in a tall glass, it had a creamy layer floating on top of robust coffee. She absently swirled the layers together with a long spoon as she watched Lisa conduct her own coffee ritual. Sugar was sprinkled over the froth of her cappuccino, the sugar stirred into the froth and finally the combination eaten with her spoon. All this was done on autopilot, Lisa's attention focused on the stream of humanity that passed by their table.

Cathy noticed the slight change in Lisa's expression, the twinkle that entered her eyes and the smile that crossed her lips. Wondering what had tickled her fancy, Cathy too turned her attention to the hustle and bustle of the piazza.

Not ten feet away, a couple were in the midst of an argument. Both were raven-haired Italians, both dressed fashionably and expensively, both young, maybe in their early twenties. The man was gesticulating wildly, beseechingly, the woman responding with her own exaggerated hand movements, a toss of her head. She turned sharply on her heel, folded her arms and held her chin high. In the woman's eyes, the conversation was obviously over. Not so in the man's opinion. He took her by the arm, spun her around, made some more wild gestures, then fell down on one knee and clasped both of the woman's hands. Whatever he said worked. Cathy saw the woman's features visibly soften and she raised her lover's hands, indicating that he should stand. He did so and within moments they threw their arms around the other, kissed passionately and continued across the piazza, arm in arm.

Cathy smiled behind her coffee, the incident reminiscent of the romantic Rome both she and Lisa had imagined but had rarely found. Yes, the city was steeped in history and brimming with "must-see" monuments and museums, but unfortunately every one of the tens of thousands of other tourists to the city each day also converged on the "must-see" places. Lisa and Cathy found themselves jostled from morning to night on narrow, badly maintained footpaths, not designed for the amount of pedestrian traffic they carried; they were constantly harassed by street vendors trying to ply them with cheap and nasty souvenirs; and apart from the restaurants contained within the walls of the expensive hotels, they found the cuisine on offer overpriced, unoriginal and disappointing. She could honestly say she had had the worst pizza ever in Rome, and Lisa's lasagna beat the one she'd tried over here hands-down.

Cathy was hoping the rest of their Italian odyssey would

unearth some of the true Italian culture that had seemingly disappeared from a tourist-wrecked Rome.

Come tomorrow they would depart for Capri and the Amalfi Coast. From there it was on to Venice, down to Tuscany and finally back to Rome where they would spend one more night before beginning the long journey back to Australia.

Despite the disappointment, Cathy admitted their week in the capital had flown by. The hiccup of Toni's illness behind them, they decided to live by the ethos "when in Rome . . ." and flung themselves into the tourist role by day. There was the Forum, with its churches and temples, arches and columns, and of course the Colosseum. Then there was Vatican City and its astounding collection of art. The Pope had not made an appearance during their tour, but in the big scheme of things, it was no great disappointment. Over the past few days they'd also shuffled their way through countless museums and galleries, awed at witnessing firsthand treasured artworks, sculpture and architecture.

Come late afternoon they usually found themselves ensconced at a café, reviewing their day, sipping on their drinks and, as they were right now, people-watching. This piazza, as with every other corner of the city, was touristy, but locals still gathered, probably due to the dramatic backdrop of the Pantheon, especially when lit up at night.

The only day sightseeing was well and truly off the agenda had been last Monday, their anniversary. Initially Cathy wondered if her hopes for a quiet day together would be shattered, Lisa leaping out of bed almost as soon as the first rays of light peeped through the break in the curtains. Cathy was mistaken. Within minutes Lisa was back in the bedroom, cups of instant coffee in hand to "tide them over" until the real coffee she'd ordered arrived.

Once their room service breakfast had been delivered, the *Do Not Disturb* sign was hung and the safety chain fed across the door. Cathy checked the contents of the breakfast trolley while Lisa found and turned both mobiles off, smiling engagingly as she headed back toward the bed. The white terry cloth bathrobe she donned to receive room service slipped from her shoulders.

"Here, honey." Lisa reached for the toast Cathy had buttered. "Let me take care of this for you."

Cathy handed the toast over. She had no problem being fed breakfast by a marvelously naked woman. No problem at all.

They didn't leave their room all day, again taking advantage of room service for lunch. Cathy could quite happily have stayed in their self-inflicted solitude for the duration of the evening as well, but Lisa insisted they at least poke their heads out of the door for dinner. They decided on the hotel restaurant.

Over dessert, Cathy presented Lisa with her gift. It wasn't greeted with quite the resounding enthusiasm she expected.

Lisa drew in her breath as she flipped the lid on the tightly sprung box. Inside was the Tag Heur watch she had drooled over in the duty free store but hadn't tried on, instructing the sales clerk to put it back in the display cabinet once he announced the two-thousand-dollar price tag. "This is the one . . . Cathy, when did you buy this?"

"Just one lunchtime last week." Cathy took the watch from its box, slipped it around Lisa's wrist and did up the catch. "It really suits you."

"You have to stop doing this, Cathy." Lisa turned her wrist and examined the watch. She stared at it, fingering the sports face. "You promised no more expensive gifts."

"Don't you like it?" Cathy knew she had sidestepped Lisa's request to stop buying costly gifts on a whim, primarily because Lisa could not afford to return the gesture, but she had been hoping for at least a little bit of enthusiasm. After all, it *was* their first anniversary.

"I love it." Lisa shook her head as she continued to examine the watch. "But it's just too much."

"Nothing's too much for you, sweetheart."

Lisa acknowledged Cathy's comment with a quick glance before looking again to her wrist. "Is this set to the right time?"

"Of course. Perth time."

Lisa reached inside her jacket and pulled out an envelope. "Present part one."

Inside the envelope were a dozen vouchers, each redeemable for a night's worth of whatever the holder desired at "Lisa's *casa di celeste piacere*"—Lisa's house of heavenly delights.

The vouchers had obviously been designed and printed on their home computer, each individually numbered and with an expiration date that just happened to coincide with their last night in Italy.

Cathy waved the small stack in front of her. "*Anything* I desire?"

"Uh-huh." Lisa nodded. "*Any*thing."

"You may live to regret that, my girl." Cathy laughed and put the vouchers in her purse. Part one of the present promised great fun. Loving to receive gifts as much as to give them, however, she was intrigued to discover what part two was. "What else did you get me?"

"You'll just have to wait." Lisa gave an enigmatic smile and turned attention to her chocolate mousse. She offered her spoon. "Try some of this—it's bloody fantastic."

It would be another couple of hours before Lisa relieved Cathy of her curiosity. They lingered over the rest of their meal. In between dessert and coffee Lisa begged a need to go to the bathroom. She was gone long enough that Cathy wondered if she had fallen in, or if she had dashed to the hotel gift shop to buy the second part of the gift she had alluded to, but she held back from commenting when Lisa finally returned. The waiter, clearing their plates, assured them it was a beautiful evening so they took a long stroll along streets still bustling with life.

"Let's go back to our room." Lisa eventually steered Cathy in the direction of their hotel.

"My God, Lisa." Cathy entered their suite to find it festooned with flowers. Vases of roses adorned nearly every surface.

Lisa took Cathy's hand and led her around the suite. They stopped at the dining table where a vase spilled over with white roses. "White is for the purity of my feelings for you. It's also for innocence"—she winked—"but we won't go into that one right now." One of the roses was plucked from the vase before they moved to the coffee table. "Pink symbolizes your gentleness and sweetness and the happiness I feel to be with you." Again one of the roses was taken and Cathy was guided toward the entertainment unit. A vase of yellow roses stood next to the television. "Yellow is for the bonds of our friendship and to show how much I care. And finally . . ." A stem was plucked and Lisa led Cathy into the bedroom. A vase of brilliant red blooms sat on the nightstand next to Cathy's side of the bed. "Red is a sign of my love. My deep and true love for you." Lisa took one of the red roses and added it to the small bouquet she now carried. She held the bunch to Cathy, giving the slight smile Cathy recognized as a rare flush of shyness. "I know it's not much compared to—" Lisa indicated to her wrist.

"Oh, Lisa." Cathy hushed her with a finger over her lips, scolding herself for even entertaining the thought that Lisa had dashed from the restaurant to purchase a last-minute gift. This was anything but last-minute. It was planned and it showed a real romantic side that Lisa liked to pretend didn't exist. "This is better than anything else you could possibly given me."

Lisa quirked her eyebrows slyly. "Anything?"

"Well, almost."

"And what would you find preferable?"

Cathy had sat on the bed and patted the mattress. She reached for her purse, which she had tossed onto the bed. "I think I want to redeem one of my vouchers now."

Cathy smiled into her latte, remembering the night. Lisa must have diverted her attention from the piazza as her voice broke into Cathy's thoughts. "You look like the cat that ate the canary. Just what are you smiling at, Ms. Braithwaite?"

"Just this place," Cathy said as she sipped on her coffee, the warmth that spread from her stomach to her limbs not entirely attributable to the hot liquid. "Although it stinks on so many levels, I'm actually going to miss it."

Lisa laughed at the combined reference to the bad food, sweaty crowds and pervading smell of urine evident on almost every exterior vertical surface. "Me too." Lisa reached across the table.

The little furnace Cathy's thoughts had ignited was fanned by the gentle stroking of Lisa's thumb across her palm.

"*Ti amo.*"

Cathy returned her own quiet "I love you" and sighed contentedly. At that moment she thought it impossible to be any happier. Rome would soon be a distant memory, and she was holding the hand of her favorite person on the entire planet. Life just couldn't get any better.

Except for maybe one thing. An excited squeal stopped Cathy from plumbing the blue, blue depths of Lisa's eyes and she turned her attention to a table two down from theirs, recently vacated by a stout couple with broad English accents and now occupied by a little family of three. Their tourist status was suspected from the Michelangelo T-shirts both adults sported and confirmed by a language Cathy quickly divined as being German. The family was obviously footsore from their own day of sightseeing. The mother gratefully accepted a tiny cup of espresso, watching with even greater gratitude as the father assumed responsibility for overseeing the consumption of a bright pink gelato by their daughter. It was the presentation of the gelato that caused the squeal of delight, and the blonde girl, hardly big enough to see over the tabletop, was in typical ice-cream-induced raptures. Judging by the already spreading pink ring around the girl's mouth, Cathy could tell the father had a long, sticky clean-up task ahead of him, but he appeared unperturbed, chatting happily with the mother as he intermittently wiped gelato away with a moist towelette. The mother reached over to smooth a stray strand of her daughter's hair, and the child accepted her parents' ministrations without fuss, little legs swinging under the chair as she continued to get more gelato on her than inside her.

The happy family scene was one played out any number of times all over the world, but as was usual these days, Cathy found herself emotionally torn as she looked on. Part of her was delighted. The other part, the little empty bit she discovered over Christmas, found it almost too painful to watch.

There was a pressure against her hand. "Hey." Lisa squeezed her hand again. "Now you look like you're a million miles away. What's on your mind?"

131

Cathy blinked once to refocus on Lisa. "I want to have a baby," she blurted.

There was a snort of derision from the other side of the table and Cathy saw eyes that only moments before had reflected concern crease with humor. Lisa lifted her coffee cup to her lips and took a sip. "Yeah, good one, Cathy."

A good minute passed, and in the silence of that minute Cathy watched Lisa's humor slowly fade, then return, then fade again. The cup was placed quietly onto its saucer.

"Are you serious?"

Cathy nodded.

Lisa tilted her head to one side, as if studying Cathy from a different angle would help her understand. It didn't seem to. Her brow creased with incomprehension. "In case you hadn't noticed, we're missing a vital piece of equipment for that."

"We don't need it, Lisa."

Lisa guffawed and her face relaxed. "Cathy . . . honey . . . I'm good, but I'm not that good!" Once again she lifted her coffee cup to her lips, this time sniggering into it. She wiggled her eyebrows suggestively over the rim. "But if you want to go to our room and give it a try, I'm up for it. I won't even call in a voucher."

"Lisa." Cathy spoke softly, then appealed to her without words, hoping to convey through her expression that she was not joking.

It worked. Lisa actually spluttered into her cup. Cathy's heart sank as she reached across the table to whack Lisa's back. The fact she was choking over the idea did not bode well.

"Thanks." Lisa coughed and wiped her watering eyes with a napkin. She sat back in her chair, again tilting her head and studying Cathy.

Cathy could not bear the silence. "Tell me what you're thinking."

Lisa shook her head. "I don't know yet." She pointed to Cathy's latte glass. "Are you done?"

Usually Cathy and Lisa took their time over coffee, sometimes ordering a second, but always lingering long after they finished their drinks. Over half of Cathy's latte remained but she nodded. "I'm done."

"Shall we go? I feel like a bit of a walk."

Cathy knew Lisa processed things best when in motion. "Sure."

At the exact moment they passed the happy-family table, the daughter emitted a high-pitched scream. Cathy's glance revealed why. The child now held an empty waffle cone and pink gelato dribbled over the mother's very new-looking Nikes and onto the pavement. Lisa smiled sympathetically to the parents, but when she next caught Cathy's eye, she conveyed an expression that clearly asked, "Do you really want one of those?"

Cathy's heart sank even further, and when they made it back to their room—in record time as Lisa had set a cracking pace—Cathy could not but help notice her roses were looking a bit sad in their vases. She busied herself with her daily task of changing their water. Even though this was their last night in Rome, she wanted to extend their life as long as possible. She caught Lisa watching her, leaning against the bathroom doorjamb as Cathy emptied water from the vases and replaced it with fresh.

"Cathy . . ."

"Yes, honey."

Lisa shifted her weight to her other foot. She scratched her head, looked around the room and opened her mouth as if to say something, then closed it as if reconsidering. She scratched at her head again. "Cathy . . . when you said you wanted a baby . . . did you really mean a *baby*?"

Cathy smiled. As opposed to what? A piglet? "Yes, Lisa. A baby."

"Oh." Lisa shifted her weight again. She didn't meet Cathy's eye, instead focusing on the clear glass vase Cathy held in her hand. "I might take a drink onto the balcony. Do you want one?"

"Sure." Cathy watched Lisa's retreating figure with concern. She quickly finished refilling the vases and gave their bases a wipe before placing them back around their suite.

A glass of Chianti was waiting when she stepped onto the balcony. Cathy moved to sit in the chair opposite Lisa, but Lisa beckoned her to her knee.

"I do love you," Lisa said as she placed her glass onto the small balcony table and wrapped her arms around Cathy's waist. "But I do wish you'd give me some warning before making your big announcements."

"It wasn't an announcement, Lisa. It was just an expression of a desire for a child. I haven't exactly picked out the nursery furniture yet."

"But you have thought about it, haven't you?"

"Well," Cathy admitted, "I have been turning the idea 'round for a while, yes."

"And when was I going to be let in on it?"

"I thought I just did."

"Yes, you said *you* wanted a baby. But in the whole time we've been together you've never asked if I wanted one or even brought up the subject of having children."

"I guess I just assumed," Cathy faltered. Making assumptions about Lisa and her behavior had caused Cathy problems just over a year ago. In fact, jumping to incorrect conclusions nearly prevented them from even getting together. And here she was, doing it all over again.

Over that Christmas, Cathy had been delighted by the rapport Lisa quickly developed with her older nephew, six-year-old Aaron. Aaron adored Lisa, who was not only willing to partake in the rough-and-tumble games of a young boy but seemed to enjoy them as much, if not more, than he did. The two of them, when left to their own devices while Cathy, her brother and the rest of his family went on a shopping excursion for baby clothes, transformed the lounge room into an elaborate fort. Cathy returned home to find Lisa emerging from a maze of sheets and cardboard boxes, a metal colander on her head and wielding a shield fashioned from a plastic bin lid. Lisa looked somewhat embarrassed being caught by the grownups, but it wasn't enough to stop her from mounting the broom that served as her horse and charging after Aaron, who was leading the crusade against the mutant penguins that had escaped their home in the freezer.

"I guess I just thought, since you're so taken with Aaron and you're so good with him, that you had thought about maybe . . ."

Cathy trailed away when Lisa shook her head.

In the ensuing silence, Lisa said, "Just because I like kids and they seem to like me doesn't mean I've thought about taking the next step. Jesus, Cathy, it's not like we can just decide to stop using contraceptives like other couples. It's a bit more complicated for us."

"So you don't want children then?" Cathy didn't plan for her voice to sound so petulant, but it did. So she wasn't too surprised at the touch of annoyance in Lisa's reply.

"I didn't say that." Lisa touched the tip of Cathy's chin with her index finger. "I'm saying I need some time to think this through . . . just like you already have."

Cathy nodded. She couldn't argue with that request. So, although she was bursting to discuss the issue at length, she knew it wasn't the right time. She moved the topic away from children and instead they discussed plans for their next stop on their Italian adventure, the Amalfi Coast. Tomorrow would be an early start, their coach to Sorrento leaving at six a.m.

Cathy glanced at her watch and said, "So we really should get packed before we go to dinner."

"I guess so." Lisa released her hold on Cathy's waist.

"Are you coming in, honey?" Cathy stopped at the balcony entrance when Lisa made no move to stand.

"Soon." Lisa picked up her glass of wine. Cathy decided to just let her be, even though she didn't come in to start packing anytime before they left for a local restaurant an hour later.

CHAPTER ELEVEN

"I'm sorry, Virg," Toni apologized as she held Virgil flat to the floor in order to stop her from running out the back door. She edged around the wood, only releasing her companion once the gap between the door and the jamb was becoming too narrow for her hand. "You know you're not allowed out here just yet."

It was a gorgeous Saturday morning. Toni had planned on having a read and a coffee in the sun, but Virgil's determination to escape as soon as the door opened made carrying anything outside impossible. So, while Toni had dragged one of her outdoor chairs from under the eaves and into a sunny spot in the middle of her lawn, she sat in it empty-handed.

"Oh, Virgil, don't look at me like that." To avoid looking at the mottled lump that appealed to her from the windowsill, Toni turned her chair so it faced the back fence.

It wasn't the most inspired view. The jarrah pickets that comprised the fence were broken only by the jarrah picket gate that gave access to the lane. A smattering of shrubs skirted the fence line, but apart from that grass grew right to the boundary. She did a visual sweep of the rest of her garden. That wasn't exactly inspired either. She never gave much thought to her backyard. Essentially it was all lawn, with a clothesline and garden shed flanking a side fence. A single plane tree had been planted off-center by whoever owned the place around twenty years prior. A deciduous tree, it provided welcome shade in summer and let the sunshine through in winter.

Toni gave an envious thought to the back garden immediately across the lane. The yard—Lisa's—had been fully landscaped. Before Lisa moved into Cathy's, her backyard was used as an extension to the house. She entertained there, relaxed there, even cooked there.

Toni did another sweep of her barren landscape, imagining what it could potentially look like if she put some time and effort into it. Her gaze came to rest on a small mound of dirt in the far corner. A now-dead rose lay across the mound. She had placed the flower there after burying Virgil's dove. The dove had no mark, no blood or signs of broken skin. The poor creature had no-doubt died of fright. Toni turned her mind to the two information sheets she'd found packaged with Virgil's bill. One detailed Virgil's respite care; the other was a fact sheet outlining the damage domestic and feral cats were doing to the environment, along with tips to pet owners for the responsible management of their feline charges.

Toni followed the respite care instructions to the letter, kept Virgil indoors, administered her antibiotics at the right times. The other sheet, well, Toni had always thought herself a responsible pet owner. She curfewed Virgil from sunset to sunrise and kept a bell on her collar. According to the fact sheet, these steps weren't enough. Apparently, many cats learn to hunt without their bells making so much as a tinkle, and even well-fed felines would hunt prey purely for the sport of it, not because they were hungry. The sheet recommended keeping cats indoors all the time. Toni

137

swiveled to look at Virgil, who was still sitting on the windowsill, looking longingly past the glass. Virgil had been given access to the outside world during daylight hours ever since she was a kitten, so suddenly stopping that privilege seemed cruel. Toni could only imagine the damage Virgil would cause to the house if her curfew became permanent. As it was, she protested the current state of affairs via her litter tray, kicking up the litter until it spread across the laundry, or refusing to use the tray at all.

The fact sheet also suggested building a cat run—essentially a cage running from the house to the outside world. Toni tried to imagine such a construct, and putting Virgil in it. It conjured images of a pussycat prison. But—she glanced once more to the dove's mound—she really had to do something. And considering the current emptiness of her backyard, there surely were some possibilities for a reasonably sized, non-prison-like run for Virgil. Toni stood and headed for her back door. Maybe there was some-one local who could supply such an item.

The fact sheet provided little guidance on the acquisition of a cat run, and Toni doubted she had the handywoman skills required to undertake the project herself. While she owned a fair set of tools—all housed in a gleaming red toolbox—none had really seen the light of day, except to tighten the odd screw or change a tap washer. She'd never even tried to knock up a spice rack, never mind cut a hole through an exterior wall of her house and con-struct an escape-proof wire module.

There was little point ringing Virgil's vet. If they had a list of contacts they would no doubt have been referenced on the fact sheet. So Toni tried a couple of pet stores. Her first call was answered by a shop assistant who sounded no more than fifteen years old. She'd never heard of a cat run and no, there was nobody else who could assist. Her second call connected her to a well-spoken woman who tried very hard to be helpful but wasn't. Apparently the store stocked a lovely range of quite large bird aviaries that might do the trick. Toni said thanks, but no, that wasn't quite what she was looking for. Call number three was answered by a gruff male who obviously had better things to do than try to solve a pet-related problem. "We have nothing like that here. I suggest you organize to have one built." Then the line went dead.

"Bastard." Toni looked incredulously at the receiver and banged it back onto its cradle.

Next she tried an Internet search. While it proved a lot more fruitful, it revealed no Perth-based companies that supplied ready-made cat runs. It seemed she would have to go the custom-built route. Probably costly. But—Toni patted Virgil, who had jumped onto her desk to see what she was up to—definitely worth it. And—Toni thought of her VISA card, which she had primed with funds just the day prior—it had been a while since she had splashed out on anything for the house or garden. She navigated back to a page that displayed an Adelaide yard nearing the dimensions of Toni's. The cat run was integral to the landscape design.

"That's what we're going to get done, Virg." Toni pointed Virgil in the direction of the screen. Virgil tapped at the monitor with a paw and banged her still cone-encased head against Toni's forearm. Given Virgil's seal of approval, and excited at the prospect of a new project, Toni typed another query into Google.

By midafternoon, some of her initial enthusiasm had waned. She had found and downloaded some free garden-design software but the program wasn't exactly user-friendly. The promotional blurb on its Web site made it sound like one just entered the garden dimensions, dropped some virtual shrubs here, some paving there, maybe a water feature in the corner and—*voilà!*—instant landscaping brilliance. But after struggling with the program for what seemed like hours, Toni decided you get what you pay for. In this case, nothing. It didn't matter where she tried to place her shrubs, they jumped somewhere else, and her attempt at drawing the outline for her cat run was nothing short of a disaster. Maybe she should have read the user manual. Oh, well, there was always good old pencil and paper. She stretched and yawned, closed her debacle of a design and glanced at her watch. She also refreshed the browser screen running in the background. Once the window recomposed she checked the contents. Nope, still no one in the Secret Garden. She had been checking intermittently over the past hour, just to see if anyone interesting came online.

Toni stared glumly at the empty room window, knowing she was really hoping Kayisha's name would appear.

For the second time in as many days, Toni felt obsessive and stupid as she browsed through the rooms, hoping to find Kayisha in one of them. This just wasn't like Toni. She had flitted in and out of chat for months, and never once had she worried if someone was online or they weren't. And never, ever had she gone on a room-by-room search for someone. "Shit, Toni," she muttered under her breath, "you're acting like an online stalker." She closed her browser, put her computer to sleep and glared at the black screen. Then she left the study altogether and made a BLT with the strips of bacon left over from the previous night's Caesar salad. She fed most of it to Virgil because she wasn't particularly hungry.

Twenty minutes later, having decided she may as well read the user guide before reverting to pen and paper for her garden design, Toni was back in front of her computer. The manual was as manuals are, dry and dull. Not the most stimulating reading.

"I'll just have one more little look." Toni reopened her browser, navigated to the Women's Floor and for the umpteenth time that day, checked to see who was in the Secret Garden.

Many topics had kept Emma awake overnight. Justine walked through her thoughts, as did Chris, her parents, Colleen and every other person who had crossed her path and tripped her up. All loomed larger than life, surrounding her and casting a shadow so encompassing it seemed impossible to emerge into the light.

"It's just so unfair." She lay on her stomach and screwed her face into her pillow. She flopped an arm over the side of the bed and Kayisha nuzzled her hand, woofing softly, offering comfort.

Emma lay that way until she could no longer breathe. She

flipped onto her back and stared at the ceiling. It was then that it happened. She sat bolt upright in bed, hands on either side of her, anchoring her into position. Her thought was astonishingly simple, so simple she wondered why it had never occurred to her before: *I am in control of my own destiny.*

Justine, Colleen, Chris, her parents. None of these people had any control over Emma except that which she allowed them. Her thought repeated, *I am in control of my own destiny.*

Here she had been passing control with gay abandon, blaming everyone else for everything that went wrong in her life. When in actual fact they were just convenient reasons to continue doing nothing, to mark time instead of moving forward.

Emma voiced her thought out loud. "I am in control of my own destiny." Then she called Kayisha onto the bed and hugged the mass of fur that leapt at the opportunity to tread on usually off-limits territory. "Tomorrow is the first day of the rest of my life, Kai."

That old chestnut sounded outrageously dated when she said it, but she didn't care. It was true. Tomorrow was a new day, and it would also be a new start.

She lay back down, her mind turning over all the fresh possibilities. She draped one arm over Kayisha while Malibu nuzzled into the crook of her other. Surrounded by the nonjudgmental warmth and love of her companions, Emma closed her eyes and tried to sleep, but her mind had become just too active. Although it was only two a.m. she rose from her bed, settled at her kitchen table with a pot of tea, some paper and a pen and began planning.

Now, midafternoon on Saturday, Emma had already made inroads into her new day/new life. At first light she'd stepped into her backyard, built a little fire and sat cross-legged in front of it. Next to her sat a pile of papers. One by one she picked up each sheet, read it, screwed it up and threw it onto the fire. One by one she watched the sheets burn, and with the flames, she willed herself to let go of the fear that held her bound to the contents. She even managed to wish Chris and her partner well in life without

141

referring to Bree as The Trollop. Paul still lived in the troglodyte category, but Emma refused to be too hard on herself. After all, it was still early days.

The fire doused, and her little ritual complete, Emma returned indoors. She fed Kayisha and Malibu, showered, dressed and retrieved the Saturday paper from her front lawn. She scoured the employment pages, found nothing, so read the magazine section while munching on toast and sipping on Russian Caravan tea. Midmorning she moved from the kitchen to the lounge room, from paper to screen. No new postings appeared in the Veterinary Association's online employment section. Despite her best intentions, panic rose.

"Not to worry." She swallowed it, moved quickly back to the search screen and entered a query requesting veterinary vacancies. Maybe not everyone listed with the association. She followed the links to a nationwide employment site that listed jobs in every conceivable profession. The position she applied for the day before was also listed on this site, as was her old position at Colleen's practice. Nothing else suitable was listed for Western Australia, so Emma widened her search to the rest of the nation. Vets were required in general practices in suburbs of both Sydney and Melbourne. Figuring a five-hour flight to the other side of the country was only a little more inconvenient than a five-hour drive to the south of the state, Emma duly wrote some cover letters and whisked her résumé down the phone line. No sooner had she done this than she received another "you have been disconnected" message.

The previous day's experience told her there was little point trying to get back online immediately, yet her stubborn streak made her try anyway. Not surprisingly, her attempt was fruitless, but she still swore at the screen, vowing to cancel the contract with her Internet provider first thing Monday morning. She turned the computer off in disgust, stretched her arms high in the air and considered going for a run.

She did head out with Kayisha, but her run soon became a walk, her leaden limbs complaining at the lack of rest the night before. Half an hour later she gratefully sank back into the chair in front of her computer. She hoped her ISP would now let her dial back in. It had just gone a quarter to three. If her memory served her correctly, that was about the time she'd entered the Secret Garden yesterday. So Pookie might be there. It was a long shot, thinking Pookie might log in at the same time and go to the same room, but there was no harm in trying. After all, Emma really did want to let Pookie know it wasn't her fault for just disappearing yesterday.

Plus it would be nice to talk to her again.

Emma held her breath as her modem beeped and blipped. Within a minute she was in, had logged onto the chat site and navigated to the Secret Garden. To her dismay it was empty. Maybe Pookie, unlike Emma, had a life and more to do on a Saturday afternoon than sit in front of a screen. "Stop it!" Emma rebuked herself for her creeping self-pity, aimed her mouse at the "close window" icon and . . . Pookie's name appeared.

Emma had no idea why her heart began to pound. She attributed it to her impending apology and fear at a rebuff. On second thought, that seemed silly. She was only dealing with words on a computer screen.

Pookie: hi kayisha

To Emma, Pookie's use of Emma's full user name indicated she was annoyed at yesterday's sudden departure. Emma bit on her lip as she typed.

Kayisha: Hi Pookie. I'm sorry for just disappearing yesterday. My ISP booted me off and wouldn't let me back in.

There was a pause before words appeared on Emma's screen.

Pookie: thats ok, i figured something like that happened. so u have dialup?

Emma had no idea what Pookie was talking about.

Kayisha: I don't know.

Pookie: do u connect 2 the server each time u want 2 go online?

Kayisha: Yes.

Pookie: then u have dialup. i switched 2 broadband last year

Kayisha: This broadband, it's good?

Pookie: i reckon it beats dialup hands down. now i stay connected 24/7. costs more but saves getting booted each time traffic gets busy

Kayisha: Do you think that's what happened?

Pookie: probably. the time u left all the kids would b home from school and online. ur ISP will have kicked u out when their lines got busy. first in, first out

Shygirl: hi kayisha. hi pook <wink>

Emma had almost forgotten she was in a public space until the appearance of Shygirl. Strangely enough, her appearance was irksome, but Pookie had already given her greeting so Emma added her own, following Pookie's lead in abbreviations.

Kayisha: Hi Shy.

Shygirl: every1 having a good nite?

Pookie: its day over here shy

Shygirl: how bout u k? wot time in ur parts?

Kayisha: Around 3 p.m.

Shygirl: 11 here. fri nite

Emma did a quick mental tour of the globe and figured Shygirl must be somewhere in the United States.

Kayisha: US?

Shygirl: texas honey

Emma raised her eyebrows at the endearment. She decided to throw it back.

Kayisha: Is Honey a town in Texas?

Pookie: <grin>

Emma's heart did a little flop at Pookie's virtual smile.

Shygirl: no honey. i meant u

Was the not-so-shy Shygirl flirting with her? It seemed a ridiculously pointless thing to do, given that they were on opposite sides of the planet. Emma sat with fingers poised over the keyboard, unsure how to reply. No further witticisms were forthcoming. Maybe she should just tell Shygirl thanks, but no thanks? A private room window appeared and with it a string of text from Pookie.

> *Pookie:* she tries it on with every1 kay. dont worry about it
> *Kayisha:* I'm not worried. Just a bit surprised. She doesn't know me from Adam.
> *Pookie:* doesnt matter. 15 mins in here can b a meaningful relationship
> *Kayisha:* I don't get it.
> *Pookie:* different reality. am going to go. will be in the fijian room if u want 2 keep talking

Emma kept looking at the private room window Pookie had taken her into, but no more text appeared. She shut it down, returning to the Secret Garden.

> *Pookie:* off now guys. speak later
> *Shygirl:* later pook
> *Kayisha:* Bye, Pookie.

Pookie disappeared from the room occupant list. Emma didn't know what to do next. Pookie had obviously extended the invitation to continue chatting in the Fijian room, but she couldn't just leave Shygirl in the Secret Garden all by herself. Could she?

Why the hell not? After all, as Pookie said, it was a different reality in here.

> *Kayisha:* I think I may get going too, Shy. Nice speaking to you.
> *Shygirl:* u 2 honey. bye

Luckily, the Fijian room was empty when Toni arrived. She sat in the room, but after more than a minute of nothing began feeling quite the idiot. Kayisha wasn't going to come. She'd no doubt been freaked out by the forwardness of Toni's invitation and had run away. Or maybe she had just been disconnected again. Toni scratched absently at her forearm as she continued to wait. She'd just realized what she was doing and clasped her hands in her lap when her screen sprang into life.

> *Kayisha:* Hi again.

Pookie: its quieter in here. that ok?

Kayisha: Fine with me.

Pookie: hows ur day been kay?

Kayisha: Long, but good.

Pookie: how come?

Kayisha: I had one of those nights where I couldn't sleep so I was up rather early and have got a lot of things done. How about you?

Toni wanted to ask why Kayisha couldn't sleep, but the question overstepped the unspoken boundaries set the previous day.

Pookie: been busy 2. working on sort of n extension 2 my house

Kayisha: The joy of renovations. I don't envy you.

Pookie: havent started yet. just in the planning stage

Kayisha: So the tears and tantrums are yet to come.

Pookie: lol yes

Kayisha: What sort of extension?

Pookie: a cat run

Kayisha: Good for you! How many cats?

Pookie: just 1

Kayisha: I've one and one. Cat and dog.

Pookie: do u curfew?

Kayisha: Cat is indoors all the time. Was brought up that way.

Pookie: so dog stays outside?

Kayisha: No. Got a doggie door.

Toni frowned. That didn't make sense. The cat must be pretty dumb not to have figured it could use the dog door. But then, maybe the cat and dog were restricted to different parts of the house.

Pookie: how does that work with the cat?

Kayisha: It's a special door that works electronically with the dog collar. It lets her in and out but nothing else. It self-locks.

That was a clever idea. For all her love of gadgetry, Toni had never heard of such a thing.

Pookie: great idea. doesnt solve my problem tho

146

Kayisha: You could just keep your cat indoors like I do.

Pookie: not if i want any peace. or a couch that isnt shredded

Kayisha: So it's used to its freedom?

Pookie: 5 yrs of nite only curfews

Kayisha: Cats are amazingly adaptable creatures.

Pookie: sounds like u speak from experience

Kayisha: I've met more than a few in my day.

Toni considered her next words. Should she use the opening to find out a bit about Kayisha?

Pookie: do u work with animals?

Kayisha: I did. I hope to again soon.

Pookie: so u do something different at the moment?

There was a definite pause. Either Kayisha was typing an extended response, or she didn't want to respond at all. Toni decided to fill the gap.

Pookie: sorry. didnt mean 2 pry.

Kayisha: That's ok. I'm sort of in between jobs at the moment.

They were only words on a screen but Toni could read the embarrassment that came with the admission. It seemed unemployment was not a state that sat easily with Kayisha. And unsatisfied curiosity was not a state that sat well with Toni. Should she ask what profession Kayisha sought work in?

Pookie: if u could do any job at all, wot would it b?

Kayisha: I'd be a vet.

Toni smiled. Just about every young girl dreamed of being a vet at some stage. Maybe, even though Kayisha was old enough to be "in between jobs," she was still young enough to hold onto the dream.

Pookie: i wanted 2 b a vet when i was around 9

Kayisha: What happened?

Pookie: i got hit on the head by an overaffectionate pony at the easter show. been scared witless of the species ever since. cant have a vet thats scared of its patients

Kayisha: I love horses. In fact I applied for a job to work with them just yesterday.

Two images ran through Toni's head. One of a female jockey, resplendent in her racing colors; the other of a jillaroo, in faded jeans and a khaki shirt, hair flowing as she spurred her mount across endless dusty plains. Toni liked her jillaroo imagery the best. She wondered if Kayisha fit her mental picture.

Pookie: so u ride?

Kayisha: Yes, but not much since I moved to the city. When I was at home I used to ride a lot.

Pookie: home?

Toni learned Kayisha grew up in Geraldton, a regional city a few hundred miles north of Perth. She also learned her childhood best friend lived on a combined sheep and wheat farm six miles out of the city. Along with wheat, sheep and the ubiquitous hens, they stabled a handful of horses. On weekends Kayisha would get up at first light, cycle to the farm and help with the chores just to speed up the time she and her friend could saddle up.

Kayisha: I lived and breathed horses. When I wasn't riding them, I was thinking about riding them. My room was plastered with pictures of them. I reckon, if I could, I would have slept in the stables.

Pookie: did u have a favorite?

Kayisha: A high-spirited stallion called Rafterey.

Something niggled at Toni's memory. Rafterey. Why did that name sound so familiar?

Pookie: is that the name of a racehorse? ive heard it b4

Kayisha: Think Radclyffe Hall.

Pookie: stephens horse in the well of loneliness?

Kayisha: Yes! It wasn't until years later, when I read the book, that I made the connection.

Pookie: coincidence?

Kayisha: I don't know. My friend's mum's sister apparently named him. She was married to another farmer in the area. But I guess that doesn't mean anything. I love the fact I was riding a horse named after the heroine's own in one of the most famous lesbian novels of all time.

Pookie: famous maybe, but rather a depressing read

Kayisha: True. I'm so glad I didn't have to read it in isolation. I mean, there's so much positive literature out there now, it must have been a real downer for the women back then who had nothing else to compare it to.

Pookie: and a real downer 4 those looking for a few boudoir tips <grin>

Kayisha: lol. No, not the most enlightening novel. Like I said, I'm glad I didn't have to read it in isolation. Or I wouldn't have had the slightest idea what to do when confronted with a naked woman.

Pookie: lol

Toni actually did laugh out loud. Kayisha's conversations were dotted with observations that appealed to her sense of humor. Toni imagined, in person, Kayisha would have a very dry delivery, that her expression would be largely unreadable, and for a second you'd wonder if she was joking or not. Toni liked that. She liked Kayisha. The little she knew of her, that was. Toni realized she was still no closer to finding out what Kayisha did, or used to do, for a living. Nor had she expanded on any snippets of information provided about other aspects of her life. Every time Toni seemed at the point of making a discovery, Kayisha veered off on a tangent. Not much, but enough to steer their conversation in a different direction.

Maybe a direct approach was needed. Toni was in the middle of typing "getting back to the horse thing, what job did you apply for?" when Kayisha changed the topic completely.

Kayisha: If I suddenly disappear, it's because I've been booted again.

Toni deleted her question.

Pookie: ok

Kayisha: I'm just warning you, because it happens out of the blue.

Pookie: ok

Kayisha: We can talk again later? If I get back in?

Toni smiled at the screen.

> *Pookie:* sure thing. how about 7pm in this room if u get the boot?
>
> *Kayisha:* It's a date.

Five minutes later Kayisha suddenly disappeared. Toni felt immediate disappointment. Then she remembered she had "a date." She checked her watch. In two and a bit hours she would be speaking to Kayisha again.

Suddenly hungry, Toni put her computer to sleep and went in search of food.

CHAPTER TWELVE

"Mum." Ashley's voice held a plaintive whine, despite the volume of delivery. He called from the media room, "Courtney's hogging the controls again."

"Courtney," Tricia called back. "Let your brother play."

"But, Mum." Another plaintive voice emanated from the media room. "He can't play properly. He mucks it all up."

Tricia assumed her end of discussion voice. "Courtney. I'm not going to tell you again . . . let your brother have one of the controls." She plucked a nearly empty bottle of wine from the ice bucket. It was tipped to Emma's glass. "I pray for the day they turn eighteen and move out. A top-up?"

"Not for me, thanks." Emma placed her hand over her glass, letting Tricia take the remnants of the wine. She leaned back in her sturdy jarrah chair, one of six that surrounded the outdoor table located under a pitched-roof gazebo. The remains of their Sunday lunch of barbequed ribs had been cleared away by John, Tricia's husband. He was currently busying himself with the dishes—an occurrence Tricia declared an absolute miracle and another reason she should go away more often. Her sons, nine-year-old Ashley and twelve-year-old Courtney, had found the lack of activity around the table outrageously dull and retired to the media room to squabble over the PlayStation. Emma took a sip of her wine. "You're a bit ambitious if you think they'll leave home at eighteen. Latest stats show boys are staying at home longer than ever. Some even until their thirties."

Tricia threw her head back and groaned. "God save me!"

Emma knew Tricia wouldn't be without her boys, all three of them if you included her husband. While she'd never voice it out loud in company, she had missed her family while away. It showed. The hugs for the boys that lasted just that bit longer than usual—which, when done in company produced mortified wails of "Mum!"—and the affectionate touches between husband and wife that said "I'm glad you're here with me again."

Emma laughed and said, "You'll be a wreck when they go."

"Not a chance. I'll be there with a cattle prod to help them out the door." Tricia downed the last of her wine, placed her glass next to the ice bucket and called in the direction of the house, "John, be a love and put the kettle on for a coffee."

Five minutes later Tricia accepted the mug and the kiss on the cheek that came with it.

"Thanks, sweetie." She offered Emma the plate of cookies John had also delivered. "You'd better take one now before the vultures get wind of them and descend."

Sure enough, within a minute Ashley and Courtney had pushed and jostled each other out the door, grabbed a cookie for each hand, shoved a third in their mouths and left nothing but their dust and a smattering of crumbs on the plate.

Emma watched the prepubescent tornado go through. No wonder Tricia stayed so slim, if she had to fight for every morsel. Emma took a bite of her cookie.

"So, Emma." Tricia left her own cookie dangerously unattended on her plate. "What are you going to do now?"

Emma took her time chewing. Within minutes of arriving at Tricia's she announced her resignation, but since then family, food and the veterinary conference dominated the conversation. She took a sip of her coffee. The proposal she had been rehearsing in her head was reasonable. Tricia's practice was busy to the point of being overly so. For one vet. But if there were two to share the load . . . Emma swallowed the cookie and coffee combination with some difficulty. She took another sip of her coffee before saying, "I've been applying for some jobs. One in Albany and a couple interstate. But I'd much rather stay in Perth if I could. I was thinking . . ."

Later that afternoon Emma hugged Tricia's husband. "Thanks again, John. Your ribs are just the best. And, Tricia"—in turn she hugged Tricia—"I'll see you Friday."

Tricia held Emma at arm's length, looking her straight in the eye as she asked, "And you'll think about the other?"

"I will." Emma nodded. She pulled keys from her jeans pocket, jangling them in her hand as she called down the hall. "See you later, boys."

A muffled duet came from the media room. " 'Bye, Auntie Em."

Emma slid behind the wheel of her station wagon, which she'd parked on Tricia's driveway. Her feelings were mixed as she reversed onto the street. She was elated at securing part-time work at Tricia's practice. Two days a week: Fridays and Saturdays. However, her hopes of walking into full-time employment were dashed.

"I just can't afford to take on someone full-time, Em." Tricia had gestured toward the house when Emma suggested the idea. "Not while the bank still owns most of this."

Emma nodded her understanding. Never mind feeding the hefty mortgage Emma knew Tricia and her husband carried on their house, she could imagine the boys also ate their way through a mountain of profits.

"But," Tricia continued, "my rooms are definitely underutilized. If you would consider buying into the practice . . ."

The thought of being part-owner of a practice, especially in partnership with someone she trusted on both a professional and personal level, was a dream come true. But still just a dream. Just as she'd told Pete, there was no money tree growing in her back garden.

Emma eased her foot off the throttle as she neared the end of Tricia's street, promising to do as Tricia said and give the idea some serious thought. For now she had another task to accomplish. She turned onto the freeway as if heading for home but got off one exit early. She was heading for Mt. Hawthorn, to Toni's. Her task was bridge repair.

Once parked, Emma double-checked the street number against the one written on the slip of paper she extracted from a shirt pocket. Confident she had the right house, she reached for her sturdy leather doctor's bag. Hopefully Toni would be softened to Emma's apology by a home visit to remove Virgil's stitches.

The rush of adrenaline Emma recognized as nervousness nearly sent her scurrying back to her car, but she walked through it and knocked on Toni's front door.

"Emma." Despite knowing the identity of her visitor due to the peephole she'd had installed just after Christmas, Toni could not disguise the surprise in her voice when she opened her front door. Her first thought was to wonder how Emma knew her address, but of course it would be on the practice's client database. Toni imagined the word *debtor* flashing across her details in big red letters, and her mind flitted to the envelope still propped against her printer. Then she wondered if Emma had taken on debt collection as one of her duties in Tricia's absence. Then she realized she should say something instead of standing at the entrance wondering all these things. "Hello."

"Hi, Toni." The leather bag Emma carried was hefted, just a little. "I hope you don't mind my dropping by. I thought I'd see how Virgil's doing. Remove her stitches."

"Oh." Toni stood aside to let Emma in. She adjusted the collar of her pajamas and raked fingers through her hair, flustered by the appearance of the last person she had expected to visit. Toni gave a quick thought to her friend Monica, who had stopped by that morning with a fresh pot of chicken soup and an offer to take Virgil to the vet after work on Monday. "I'd actually arranged with a friend to take Virg into the surgery tomorrow."

"Oh." Now Emma appeared flustered. She stood in the hallway, both hands grasping the handle of her doctor's bag. "Well, it's really no trouble. It will only take a couple of minutes."

"Sure. Come through." Toni figured she could ring Monica and cancel. She ushered Emma in the direction of the formal lounge, where she knew Virgil was sleeping. "Um, can I get you a drink of something?"

"Water would be good. Thanks." Virgil lay on one end of the three-seater couch. Toni watched Emma sit next to her and hold out her hand to be sniffed. "Hi, girl. How are you?"

When Toni returned to the lounge room, Emma gave a distracted acknowledgment to the glass placed in front of her on the coffee table. Her attention was focused on removing Virgil's bandage.

"It's still quite intact," she said as she snipped carefully with a pair of surgical scissors. "You've done well with her, Toni."

"Yes." Toni watched the removal of the bandage intently. What had Emma expected? That she'd just ignore all instructions and let Virgil loose on the world? Maybe Emma *had* expected that. After all, the "Cats and the Environment" fact sheet included with Virgil's bill was a sure indicator of what Emma thought of her pet-ownership skills. "I've kept her indoors since she got home. I did take the cone off her at mealtimes. Let her groom a bit. But it went back on as soon as she went for the bandage."

The last of the bandage was removed and placed onto the coffee table, next to the two cans of chickpeas Toni left there for her now daily exercise routine. Toni leaned forward for a closer look at Virgil's shortened tail. It no longer tapered at the end, coming instead to an abrupt, stumpy halt. But the skin appeared healthy and the wound was clean with no sign of inflammation or seepage.

"This has healed beautifully." Emma stroked Vigil from her nose to the base of her spine. To Toni's amazement, Virgil closed her eyes and purred. Emma reached into her bag and extracted another, smaller pair of surgical scissors. "Can you help me for a minute?"

"Sure." Toni knelt next to the couch and held Virgil firmly in place while Emma removed the stitches. "It's okay, Virg," she reassured her friend, who was, surprisingly, showing no signs of distress at the attention. The whole procedure was over in less than a minute.

"You're free to go, Virgil." This time Emma ran her hands from nose tip to tail tip. Virgil swiveled her head and nuzzled her nose into Emma's palm. Then she stood and stretched, jumped lithely off the couch and sauntered across the room, stumpy tail held high, as if showing it off.

Toni was so happy she almost cried. She would be eternally grateful to the woman who, in her eyes, had saved her best friend's life. "Thank you, Emma."

"My pleasure." The scissors were placed back in her bag and the bandage, stitches and cone collar bundled into one hand. "If you can point me in the direction of the trash can."

Toni pointed the way to the kitchen but followed behind her. "While you're here I've got the check for Virgil's bill."

In turn, Emma followed Toni to the study. Toni plucked the envelope from its home against the printer and handed it over. "I know it's late, but I was going to send it with Virgil tomorrow."

"Thanks, Toni." Emma seemed more concerned with the array of equipment in the room. She took a step toward the desk. "Wow, this is some setup you've got here."

"I updated last year." Toni stood next to Emma. "Certainly beats the old clunker I had before."

"I bet. I've still got an old clunker." Emma nodded toward the printer. "Is this one of those multifunction thingos?"

"Uh-huh. Fax, scan, photocopy, print."

The monitor was next for attention. "LCD screen?"

"Uh-huh. Twenty-inch."

"And of course it's Internet-ready?"

"Of course."

"Broadband?"

"Uh-huh."

"Is it really all it's cracked up to be? I was speaking to someone just the other day who reckons it beats dialup hands down."

"They're right. I'd never go back to dialup."

"What about the cost? It's expensive?"

"Depends what your needs are. Hang on a moment." Toni opened a drawer of her filing cabinet and pulled out a folder. From it she extracted the promotional brochure for her ISP. "Here, this is the company I use. You can have it if you like."

Somewhat surprised at the unlikely common ground they had found, Toni continued with the computer theme as they walked back to the lounge room. "So you reckon you may upgrade to broadband?"

"I'm thinking of it." Emma glanced to the brochure Toni had given. "Are you sure you don't mind my keeping this?"

"Go for your life."

"Thanks." Emma sat, perching on the edge of the couch to slip the brochure and envelope into her bag. She clipped the bag closed, her gaze settling on the two cans of chickpeas. If she wondered why anyone would keep tins of legumes on the coffee table, her expression did not give her thoughts away. Emma looked up, meeting Toni directly in the eye. "Toni, I wanted to say I'm sorry for the way I acted the other week. I was going through some . . . stuff . . . and I'm afraid I took it out on you."

"Don't give it a second thought." Toni waved the apology away with a lie. "It's long forgotten."

Emma extended a hand. "Friends?"

Toni matched the firmness of Emma's handshake. "Friends."

A few uncomfortable seconds passed where neither said anything. Emma's gaze wandered around the room, coming to settle again on the cans of chickpeas.

"So, have you heard from Lisa or Cathy lately?" Toni blurted, as much to fill the gap as to take Emma's attention from her pseudo hand-weights. She made a mental note to put them out of sight when they were not in use.

"Not since they first arrived."

"Me neither."

"They're probably having such a good time they've forgotten about all of us."

"Where will they be now?"

"Capri, I think."

Both sighed little envious sighs and echoed "Capri" in unison. Then they both laughed. Toni felt herself begin to relax. Emma the vet had more than proved herself. Maybe Emma the person wasn't such a bad sort either. "Do you have time for a cup of coffee?"

"I really should get going." Emma grasped the handle of her doctor's bag and stood, checking her watch. "I've got a . . . I have to get home and feed the troops."

Toni looked to her own watch. It was nearly six-thirty. She'd arranged to meet with Kayisha at seven so still had some time up her sleeve. But she had to feed Virgil and grab something for herself before then, so she didn't argue. "I imagine you've got a house full of animals?"

Emma shook her head. "Occasionally I do the Doctor Dolittle bit and baby-sit a litter of puppies or kittens, but for the most part it's just me, one dog and one cat."

The bit of Toni that was still slightly miffed at the inclusion of the cat fact sheet with Virgil's bill couldn't resist asking, "Does your cat live inside?"

"Yes, she does actually."

"Oh." Toni felt rather silly for having asked. Of course Emma would follow veterinary guidelines. "And she doesn't mind?"

"No. I brought her up that way from a kitten."

Maybe Toni really was the irresponsible one. It seemed everybody had done the right thing by their pets except her. She was tempted to invite Emma back to her study so she could show her the beginnings of her cat run design—just to prove she was making moves in the right direction. However, time was marching on. Toni reached for the latch on her front door, thanked Emma once again for everything she had done for Virgil and said her good-byes.

Just for a second, as she watched Emma descend the steps and walk down the path, Toni entertained an unbeckoned image of her mounting a horse and riding into the distance. Probably because of the jeans and khaki-colored shirt Emma wore. Plus, she did have a kind of country girl, jillaroo look. Healthy, tanned skin. An outdoorsy type. Toni wondered if Kayisha looked a bit like that. She decided she wouldn't mind if she did.

For God's sake, woman, Toni thought as she closed the front door behind her. *Get a grip.* If asked twenty minutes ago, she would have said Emma outside the veterinary surgery was rude and obnoxious. And now she was putting Emma's features onto the faceless person who spoke to her across cyberspace. She really must be losing it.

"I've got to get back into the real world," Toni told herself. She headed for the kitchen to fork some fresh cat food into Virgil's bowl. Then she made an omelet sandwich and carried it and a glass of pineapple juice to the study.

Tomorrow she'd venture outside in to the real world. But for now she had a date to keep.

CHAPTER THIRTEEN

"Em, that is such good news."

"Thanks, Pete."

"But I'll miss you if you get the job."

"It's just Albany. Five hours' drive. Or an hour by plane if you're really desperate to see me."

"What time do you leave?"

"I'll set off around one." Emma twisted the phone cord round her finger. It was Pete's rostered day off and she'd rung him at home to see if he would feed Kayisha and Malibu while she was away. She'd initially thought of ringing Justine and asking her to do pet-sitting duty but had a last-minute change of heart. Pete already knew to separate them at mealtimes to avoid Kayisha's nosing into Malibu's bowl. He also wouldn't forget he had the feeding duties to perform, unlike Justine, who could be distracted from her promise by something as simple as a bad movie on television. Or by a phone call from the troglo . . . from Paul. Emma twisted a bit more of the phone cord around her finger. It was a tight twist and her fingertip began to go purple. "I know it's short notice, but if you're not going to be home I can leave the key in a hiding spot around here."

"No, no. That's fine, Em. I was just hanging 'round the house anyway."

"Great. I'll see you a little after one."

Emma hung up the phone, released her finger from the cord's stranglehold and headed to the bedroom. She stood in front of her open wardrobe door, wondering what to pack for her trip. She'd wear what she currently had on for the drive but would need something warm for the night, something decent for her interview tomorrow and another change of clothes for the rest of the day. Finally, she'd need at least a change of underwear for the next morning. She didn't need to spend two nights away but decided she may as well check the lay of the land while she was down there, to see if she could live in the region were she offered the position.

Emma sat on her bed, feeling in a bit of a spin. Everything had happened so fast. Less than an hour ago she'd spoken to Frank, who announced himself as calling from Albany. Specifically, from the practice Emma had applied to last week. He was most interested in talking to her further—would she be available to come down for an interview, maybe Friday? Emma thought quickly. Friday she was scheduled to work at Tricia's. Tricia would understand, but Emma didn't want to lose a day's pay, and since she had no other commitments until then, she had suggested, "I could make it sometime tomorrow if that's convenient?"

Frank had agreed to the Tuesday meeting. So all of a sudden Emma found herself making preparations for a road trip to Albany.

Forty minutes later Emma was packed and she'd checked her car for oil and water. She would have been finished a lot sooner had her preparations not been peppered with regular trips to the lounge room to refresh her computer screen, each time hoping that Pookie might have entered the Fijian Room. Given the fact she had no idea what Pookie did for a living, she had no idea if

Pookie would log on at this time of day. Maybe she had restricted access to a computer when at work, or maybe no access at all during work hours. Or maybe she worked the night shift somewhere and so was currently asleep.

Now, with less than an hour before she was due to drop off her keys at Pete's, Emma sat in front of the monitor, closed her eyes and willed Pookie to come online.

Log on! Emma concentrated really hard, trying to send a telepathic message to wherever Pookie was. Which, Emma thought miserably, could be anywhere in the Perth metropolitan area. Why, oh why had she persevered with maintaining such anonymity? Since their original meeting, Emma had spent hours chatting with Pookie, and with each hour that passed, she felt more of a connection. But despite her heart telling her she could trust Pookie, her head told her to be careful. So, although they spoke at length about all sorts of topics, Emma stopped short of revealing personal details. She could tell Pookie found this frustrating. Pookie had hinted around the edges but, to her credit, she never pushed. And in turn, Pookie did not offer any details of her own.

"Sh-i-i-t!" Emma swore long and loudly when the disconnection message appeared. Briefly she thought of the broadband brochure still housed in her doctor's bag, but she doubted—even if the company Toni recommended had exceptional customer service—they could get her up and running in less than an hour. Emma leaned back in her chair and assumed her thinking position. Toni seemed a bit of a computer buff. Maybe she would know of some way to find out who Pookie was.

Emma immediately discarded the idea. Even if Toni did have hacking capabilities, Emma couldn't imagine asking her to tap into the back end of a chat site to retrieve someone's personal details. Toni would have her branded as a Froot Loop in two minutes flat. Which would completely undo her bridge repair from last night. That would be a shame, because Emma hadn't been giving lip service with her request to be friends. Over the course of last night's brief visit, she'd decided anyone who doted on their pet as much as Toni did had to be okay.

Also, she had looked awfully cute in those Tigger pajamas, even with her face covered in all those spots.

Emma swept her mind clear of that thought. It wasn't solving her current problem at all. She tried a different tactic, talking nicely to her computer instead of swearing at it. It worked, but Pookie still wasn't anywhere to be found. Emma kept trying until she was due to leave, considered delaying her trip, then thought better of it. She didn't want to be driving country roads at dusk. That was when the kangaroos came out to feed, and they had a habit of bounding across highways without looking. She'd just have to explain to Pookie in a few days' time why she didn't keep their usual seven p.m. meeting.

Emma said long good-byes to Kayisha and Malibu, checked her computer one final time, grasped the handle of her overnight bag and locked the front door behind her.

"Toni." Julie looked Toni up and down before she crossed the threshold on Monday evening. "You're dressed."

"Had to happen sooner or later. How was the game?"

"They won."

"Great." Toni sensed a lack of enthusiasm. "Isn't it?"

"Yeah, I guess."

Water polo was obviously not a popular topic. Toni stood aside to let Julie pass. As with all her other visits, she arrived with her arms laden. Tonight, in addition to her usual carryall, she held a plastic bag with the unmistakable insignia of a fried chicken chain.

Julie took another look at Toni's attire, loose-fitting track pants and a similarly loose T-shirt. "So I'm guessing you're feeling better?"

"Heaps." Toni followed Julie into the kitchen and pulled a couple of plates from an overhead cupboard. She placed them on her kitchen table, where Julie was extracting the contents of the plastic bag. The smell of fried chicken was delicious. Toni could feel her arteries harden just by thinking about eating it.

"I'm afraid it's not the most imaginative of meals." Julie was apologetic as she lifted the lid on mashed potato and gravy.

"Looks pretty damn good to me." Toni poured wine leftover from their Friday night meal. "I think this should still be okay." She clinked her glass to Julie's, hoping her glance to the kitchen clock wasn't too obvious. "Cheers."

As was usual, dinner conversation was dominated by talk of the practice. It was Marian's first day in her temping role, so much of Julie's time had been taken with the duties inherent with bringing a new staff member up to speed. That Marian had previously worked at the practice and was familiar with a number of her assigned clients was a real bonus, as was the fact she and Julie got on particularly well during her last stint.

"Marian must think I'm the slackest person around," Toni said glumly as she picked at a chicken bone. "Three months last year and now this."

"Don't be silly." Julie grimaced in the manner of someone who'd eaten more than her fill and pushed her plate away. "No one can exactly say you're faking it, and last year, well . . ." She folded her arms. "I don't blame you one bit for leaving."

Toni shot a look in Julie's direction. A little bit of her wanted her to elaborate—Toni's sudden departure last year was a seemingly taboo subject in the practice, so she had no real notion how anyone felt about it—but the other bit of her, the bit that was clock-watching, decided it could wait. Toni pressed a paper napkin to her mouth. It came away with transparent lip marks, an indication she'd consumed enough grease to keep her liver chugging for days.

"Julie, I know it's really rude, but I just remembered a bill that will be overdue if I don't pay it today. I can take care of it online. Do you mind? I won't be long."

"Go for it." Julie waved her away. "I'll do the dishes."

Toni smiled gratefully, looking to cardboard and plastic. Washing up was no major task this evening. "Thanks." She dashed to the study.

Her online bill payment was, of course, a ruse. It was an excuse to log on to chat, explain to Kayisha an unexpected visitor had dropped by and request they meet later in the evening. It was pretty much true. During Julie's midafternoon call she had established that Toni had not yet ventured to the shops and hence must be starving to death. She subsequently insisted on bringing dinner.

It was one minute past seven. Toni clicked into the Fijian room.

Kayisha: Hi Pookie. You'll never guess where I am.

Pookie: hi kay. where?

Kayisha: In an Internet café in Albany.

Toni blinked. Albany. What on earth was Kayisha doing there?

Pookie: wot r u doing there?

Kayisha: I don't have a laptop so I'm using one of their computers.

Pookie: i mean, wot r u doing in Albany?

Kayisha: Remember that job I told you I applied for?

Pookie: the horsey 1?

Kayisha: Yes. I got an interview.

Pookie: n its in albany?

Kayisha: Yes. They called today and I drove straight down. I didn't think I'd be able to get in contact with you, but then I found this cafe. It closes at eight though so we can't speak for long.

Albany. Toni's heart pulled unexpectedly. Albany was so far away. But then again, distance meant naught in this virtual world. Albany did lengthen the odds of ever getting to meet Kayisha in person though. Albany. It was Cathy's hometown. From Cathy's description it was a picture-postcard place, a port city surrounded by rolling hills. Kayisha would probably love it, accept the position and . . . Toni felt her heart pull again.

Pookie: actually i cant stay n chat 2night. had a visitor drop in n just logged in 2 let u no

There was a pause before Kayisha's reply blipped across the screen.

Kayisha: That's okay. Enjoy your night. I'll speak to you when I get back? Wednesday at 7 pm?

165

Pookie: sure thing. good luck with ur interview

Kayisha: Thanks. Oh and Pookie

Pookie: yes?

Kayisha: I'll miss speaking to you tomorrow.

Pookie: ditto. bye 4 now kay

Toni didn't log properly out of chat, she just closed down her browser completely. She stared at the black screen before hauling herself out of her chair and heading for the kitchen. Albany. She'd never been there, but already she hated the place.

"All done?" Julie asked upon Toni's return.

"Yeah." Toni sank into one of the chairs surrounding her kitchen table.

Julie sat opposite, watching her carefully. "Are you okay, Toni?"

"I'm fine." The kitchen walls seemed to shrink, closing in on her. "Do you want to go for a drive or something? I think I'll scream if I stay in this house one minute longer."

If Julie was curious about Toni's change in mood, she didn't let on. She just nodded and in no time at all they were on the entry ramp to the freeway heading toward the city.

"This car drives like a dream." Julie shifted into third, accelerating hard before slipping into fourth. She slid Cathy's BMW in and out of traffic with ease. Toni was surprised not only at Julie's driving skills, but also at her own confidence in them. Usually she'd be gripping onto the door handle for dear life and asking the driver to slow it down. "I've decided my next car's going to be a Beemer."

"Well, I did offer you the car while I wasn't using it," Toni reminded her. Passing the company car onto Julie had been cleared with Cathy, but the offer was declined. Julie lived in a block of units with allocated, but insecure, parking. She said she'd never forgive herself if Cathy's BMW was stolen or vandalized while in her care.

"And by now some asshole would be having as much fun driving it as I am." The car surged forward with such power that Toni was pushed back into her seat. Julie glanced in her direction. "Where do you want to go?"

166

With the window down and the car hurtling forward, the rush of wind on her face almost took Toni's breath away. While it was good to be outside, she was acutely conscious of her appearance. A number of her blisters had lived their life, turned black and fallen off, but just as many still remained. She shrugged, and said, "Anywhere relatively dark and quiet."

They ended up in Kings Park, parking along a stretch of road flanked by majestic Ghost Gum eucalyptus trees. The main lookout, buzzing with tourists clamoring for the panoramic city views it offered, was less than a hundred meters away. Their chosen position still offered stunning views, but it was free of tourists and their flashing cameras.

Toni lay on the grass, knees crooked and hands behind her head. A cloudless sky blinked thousands of stars. "It's a beautiful night."

"It is," Julie agreed. She mirrored Toni's position, lying beside her. "You'd never think winter's on its way."

"Sure beats a Melbourne autumn. If we were over there we'd be freezing our butts off. And it'd probably be raining."

Julie lay still, staring up at the sky. "Did you think of staying in Melbourne? Last year, I mean."

"I did for a while." The night sky blurred as Toni switched her vision to middle space, and the time she'd spent in Melbourne escaping the hurt of Cathy's breakup came into focus. In the space of a few seconds her three months back in the city of her childhood flashed by. She'd consumed a lot of alcohol and shed a lot of tears. She'd been on the receiving end of some high-end fussing and clucking by her mum and, once she was able to get through a day without crying at the drop of a hat, had caught up with some old friends. Daily life got better, brighter. One friend dragged her to her local gym and introduced her to the joys of Pump. Another thrust the employment pages of the daily paper under her nose and yet another would circle entries in the real estate section in red ink and leave the pages strategically placed so Toni was sure to find them. Secure in the fact she was very much loved and wanted, the temptation to stay was strong, but Perth had attractions of its own, not the least of which was its Mediterranean climate. On one dreary, drizzly Melbourne day she realized how much she missed Perth. She missed the sunshine, she missed her little house and she missed her office with its stunning city views. She missed Cathy too, but no longer in the aching, angst-ridden way of a jilted lover. Toni picked up Virgil, who had accompanied her on the plane in a cat carry cage, complaining the entire length of the continent, and asked if she was ready to go home. Virgil's nose nudge was interpreted as a yes. "But I eventually realized Perth had become my home."

"I hated her for a while, you know," Julie said bluntly.

"Who?" Toni asked as she rolled over to rest her head on her hand. She found Julie had already turned to lie on her side, facing her.

"Cathy."

"Cathy?" Toni couldn't understand why anybody would hate Cathy. Once Toni was over her own period of malicious thinking, Cathy resumed her ranking as one of the most likable people she had ever met. "Why?"

"For what she did to you." Julie picked viciously at the grass. Tufts were grasped between thumb and forefinger then flicked aside. "When she told Sue and me what happened and that you'd left, I was so angry with her I nearly quit on the spot."

"I did have a part to play in the whole thing, you know."

"She used you."

The venom in Julie's tone took Toni by surprise. "I never knew you felt that strongly about it."

"I know." Another tuft of grass was pulled. Julie studied it before letting it fall through her fingers. "You never even knew I existed. Every day I watched you fall all over yourself for Cathy when all the time . . ." Julie briefly met Toni's eyes, smiled ruefully then flung herself onto her back again. "I would have fallen over backwards for you."

"Julie . . ." This admission was totally unexpected and Toni didn't know how to respond.

"I don't hate her anymore."

"Well, that's a relief." Eager to lighten the tone, but still curious nevertheless, Toni asked, "What made you change your mind? About hating Cathy, I mean."

Julie lay silent, considering. "I think it was one of those cases where acting a certain way makes it so. You know, act happy and you'll be happy. Once I figured it probably wasn't a good career move to snarl at the boss every time she came near, and I decided I had to at least pretend I liked the woman, I found I actually did start to like her again." Throughout her explanation, she continued to look to the sky. But now she turned to Toni again and her tone was suddenly shy. "You weren't too surprised at what I just said."

Toni knew Julie was not referring to her act happy/be happy theory. "No. Not surprised. Not that I picked up on it myself though. I kind of got a tip-off from someone."

Julie visibly frowned, then groaned. "Let me guess . . . everyone's favorite receptionist, Sue."

Toni nodded.

"Bloody woman." Julie tore at the remaining tufts of grass. "She cornered me one day in the toilets and wouldn't let me alone till I admitted it. But she promised not to say anything."

"Seems like that's her M.O."

"She cornered you too?"

"Right in front of cubicle one. The first morning back at work after Cathy and I . . . got together. That was when she let slip about you too."

"Bloody gossip's got the eye of an eagle."

"I know. She never misses a trick."

Both Toni and Julie fell into silence, Julie concentrating on her grass-pulling and Toni's thoughts turning unexpectedly to a port city five hundred kilometers away.

Albany.

It must have been all the talk of Cathy that made her think of the place. She wondered what Kayisha was doing right now. Was she also outside somewhere, looking up to the night sky? Toni decided she probably wasn't. Apparently Albany got cold at night. Kayisha was probably in a motel room watching television. Or maybe scouring the real estate section of the local rag for a more permanent place to stay. Toni inwardly sighed. She didn't like that last thought at all.

The knowledge of eyes on her drew Toni's mind from the port city back to Perth. She found that Julie had sat up, arms wrapped around the knees she had drawn to her chest, and she was looking at Toni rather . . . oddly.

"What?"

Julie shook her head as if to stop any words before they could emerge. She looked out to the cityscape.

For her part, Toni suddenly realized the chill in the air and the beginning of dew on the grass. She sat, brushing at the arms of her windcheater. "It's getting cold and my bum's getting wet. Shall we go?"

"Sure." Julie jumped to her feet, seemingly thankful for the excuse to move. She held out her hands and Toni accepted them, letting Julie haul her up. "Is there anywhere else you want to go? Get a coffee maybe?"

Toni thought of the state of her face. "Home's good."

Back at Toni's, they stood together on the road next to Julie's car. The driver's door was wide open and Julie tossed her carryall onto the passenger seat. "Well, I guess I'll get going then. I'll give you a call tomorrow."

"Okay." Toni scratched fingers through her hair, uncomfortable because Julie seemed so uncomfortable. The drive home had been rather more sedate than the drive out, and their conversation was, at best, sporadic. Toni was getting the distinct feeling Julie was either desperate to tell her something, or desperately regretting her previous admission. "Thanks for dinner and the drive. The fresh air has done me good."

Julie nodded, looked around her and repeated, "Well, I guess I'll get going then."

Toni was in the middle of a nod when hand-sized pools of

warmth cupped her cheeks. A different kind of warmth spread across Toni's lips.

Then the warmth was gone.

"I'm sorry," Julie said as she smiled shyly. "But I've wanted to do that for ages."

More than a little surprised at the kiss, Toni tried very hard to put an authoritative tone to her voice, but instead it just sounded lame and croaky. "I think you should go home." She put her hand to her mouth so she could cough and clear her throat, but her hand was pushed away.

"Your breath is not bad, Toni."

Toni hadn't been thinking that at all, but Julie's words served as a reminder she hadn't freshened her mouth in a good couple of hours. She had no time to ponder the notion, however, her mouth once more enveloped. This time the pools of warmth settled on Toni's hips. And this time Julie's lips lingered—gentle, soft, insistent.

"Julie." Toni did an awkward little backwards waddle. "Stop it." Her fingers again fled through her hair. "You have a girlfriend."

"No, I don't."

"What?" Toni narrowed her eyes, disbelieving. "Anna . . . ?"

"Anna and I have split."

"What?" Toni repeated, finally piecing together the clues Julie had been dropping all evening. All the clues that pointed to her being one unhappy woman. "When?"

Julie had bent her head so Toni couldn't see her eyes, but tears must have welled because she swiped at her cheeks. "Yesterday afternoon."

"Come on, grab your bag." Toni waited for Julie to retrieve her carryall and lock up the car. She pointed her in the direction of the front door. "I'll make us a coffee."

"I'm sorry for acting like such a moron before."

"I don't recall any moronic behavior." For the second time that night they stood beside Julie's car. The time between Julie's first attempt at departure and now had been spent on the couch, Toni sipping on coffee while Julie tearfully related the incidents following Anna and her team's win. Apparently, despite Anna's promise of a private celebration once home, she had gotten totally wrecked on whiskey at the post-match party. Unable to talk due to her case of the hiccups, she poured herself out of Julie's car and into her apartment, staggered to the bedroom, fell asleep fully clothed, then slept most all of Sunday. When she did emerge from the bedroom, Julie was treated to verbal replays of the match and the three goals Anna had scored for her team.

"I'm sick of it." Julie sobbed to Toni. "I play second fiddle to a ball that floats."

Toni recalled how she had lasted only three weeks in the shadow of Heather's exercise obsession and assured Julie there was nothing wrong or unusual about the way she was currently feeling. She didn't offer any suggestions; Julie would have to figure for herself if she could live with Anna's sporting ambitions. But she did point out most balls do float. To her delight, that comment raised a smile. Within another half-hour Toni had extracted at least three more smiles, enough to declare the night a success.

"Thanks, Toni." Julie drew Toni into a hug but this time her kiss landed squarely on her cheek. "You're the best."

"You can tell that to anyone you like." Toni held the car door open as Julie stepped in.

"Even Sue?"

"Especially Sue. That way, soon the whole world will know it."

"Speak to you tomorrow." The car door closed and in seconds Julie's car had revved into life and disappeared down the street.

Toni let herself back into the house, turned on the television and stared at it, unseeing, instead wondering what would have happened if she hadn't told Julie to stop. She quickly surmised—even if Julie had pushed the issue—that nothing would have happened. Toni just didn't look at her in that way. A sigh of frustration escaped. She must be on the mend to be thinking about having sex with a coworker. Or, more accurately, thinking about *not* having sex with a coworker.

Toni turned off the television, took care of her nightly toilet routine and slipped between the sheets.

All thoughts of Julie fled when Toni's hand dipped between her thighs. Instead, the form that flickered behind her eyelids was of her own imagination. The woman of her making wore faded jeans and khaki. Toni could not define the planes of her face; they never came into sharp focus. The lack of clarity in the woman's features declined to be an issue as the jeans and khaki peeled away to reveal a limber, willing body. Toni groaned and pressed harder against herself, sensations causing her breath to first grow shallow, then stop. The rush of air that came from Toni's lungs as her body rippled in its pleasure contained a name. Toni curled on her side and sleepily decided to ask Kayisha what it meant when next they spoke.

CHAPTER FOURTEEN

As pre-agreed when Emma dropped Pete her spare house keys on Monday, she met him for lunch on Wednesday afternoon at a café close to his work. They were tied to Pete's scheduled one p.m. lunch break so Emma arrived directly from Albany, an unexpected delay caused by road works not leaving enough time to go home before the appointment.

After demanding an almost word-for-word description of the interview itself, Pete rested his arms on either side of the mug sitting in front of him on the café table and asked, "So what happens now?"

Emma stirred her hot chocolate with the spoon she would keep in the mug until the drink was gone. She hated how the chocolate settled at the bottom, so she redistributed it in between mouthfuls. "Apparently there are three others who've applied and they're being interviewed over the next week, so I'm not expecting to hear anything until at least next Friday."

"Are they locals?"

"I'm not sure. Frank didn't offer the information and I didn't think it the right time to ask. Although I'm guessing since the interviews are so spaced out, that at least one had to arrange time off to travel to Albany. And that probably means they'll get the job."

"Why?"

"You know how it is. They always pick the person who's working over the person who's not."

"But you *are* working, Em."

"Two days a week." Emma sighed. "And of course the question came up why I'd left the other practice."

"So you said it was because you couldn't stand working for the Wicked Witch of the West one moment longer?"

"Something like that." Emma watched Pete stir his own hot chocolate. "So I'm guessing things aren't all rosy in the Land of Oz?"

"Same old, same old." Pete waved his spoon dismissively in the air before licking it clean and dropping it back into his drink. "I don't suppose they're looking for any vet assistants down there, are they?"

"If I get the job I'll drop your name so often they'll wonder why you haven't been on the payroll long before now."

"So if you get offered the job you're going to take it?"

Emma shrugged noncommittally. The practice was a large one, dealing not only with domestic and herd animals but specializing in the equine arena and servicing a number of horse studs in the outlying region. Apparently a couple of racehorses worth millions were in their care. The practice facilities were extraordinary, reflecting its high-end clientele. Should she be offered the position, in addition to a company vehicle, she would have at her disposal equipment most vets would walk over hot coals to get their hands on. Salary had not yet been discussed, except to say the successful applicant would receive a package commensurate with their qualifications and experience. The principal vet, Frank, was affable and highly qualified. The other vet she met during her visit was also friendly, as was the assistant on duty at the time of her interview. Albany itself, while officially a city, still managed to retain the aura of a country town. Everyone she met, from the clerk at her motel, to the garage attendant who gave directions to the practice, to the Internet café owner and the waitress who served her evening meal, was unhurried and happy to chat. "If the temperature was anything to go by, it will be absolutely freezing once winter sets in, but apart from that I reckon I could live down there."

"So you're not even going to try and raise the funds to buy into Tricia's practice?"

Emma read the accusation in Pete's tone and immediately wished she hadn't mentioned Tricia's offer when she dropped him her spare house key on Monday. "I told you, Pete, the bank would probably laugh me off the premises."

"But you don't know that until you try."

Tricia had told Emma she'd have to speak to her accountant and get some accurate figures, but over their post-barbeque coffee on Sunday afternoon she'd given a guesstimate of the half-share value of the practice. It wasn't an outrageous figure but . . . Emma just could not see a bank approving her for such an amount, especially since she had no real assets to speak of. They certainly wouldn't be softened by a "but I promise I'm good for it" approach. "I'm taking an educated guess."

"I still think you should at least give it a go." Pete swallowed the last of his hot chocolate. "Really, Em, the worst they can say is no."

"You're a tyrant, Peter Jamieson."

"Maybe so." Pete pulled out his wallet and tossed enough for the two drinks and their lunch of chicken and avocado focaccias onto the table. "But I'd rather stay in Perth if I can, so I'm just looking after my own interests."

Emma really couldn't tell if Pete was serious or not with all his talk about following Emma to her next place of employment. She'd do her best to get him a new position whichever way the coin landed, but for now he wasn't going to allow her world to just keep turning. She sighed. "I'll ring the bank from work tomorrow."

An obvious glance was made to the wall clock behind the counter and Pete said firmly, "This afternoon."

There was still nearly three bank trading hours left. Emma nodded resignedly. "Okay. This afternoon."

"Promise?"

"I promise." Emma slid Pete's money back across the table and dug into her own wallet. She shook her head at his protest. After looking after her babies for two days, the least she could do was spring for lunch.

Ten minutes later she was home. Kayisha literally launched at Emma before she could get through the front door. Malibu came to see what the commotion was about but stalked away, demonstrating her disgust at the state of affairs over the past two days. In another ten minutes Emma had deposited her luggage on her bed, walked through every room in the house, found all was in order and admitted she had missed her little home, even for the brief period she was away. She stopped in front of her computer, also admitting the familiarity of home wasn't the only thing she had missed. She vowed, come seven p.m., she would drop her "woman of mystery" routine and, hopefully, Pookie would reciprocate. That decided, Emma thumbed through the phonebook, found the number of her bank's loan hotline and dialed.

Amazingly, she was not kept in a queue for an eon, being transferred to a loan officer almost immediately. Emma explained her requirements, outlined her assets, income and expenses, fidgeted while her situation was assessed, and slumped in her seat when the figure the bank *might* loan her was announced.

"This is only an approximation based on what you've given us," the sympathetic voice on the end of the line assured her. "I can set up an appointment with one of our lending managers if you wish."

Based on their approximation, Emma knew it was fruitless to arrange an appointment. She needed at least double what she'd just been quoted. She declined the offer, hung up the phone and dialed the number of her old practice.

Pete answered and Emma wasted no time letting him know what she already predicted. "I told you they'd say no."

Pete wasn't so easily discouraged, "Haven't you got any rich friends who might like to invest in you?"

Emma found the thought of approaching friends for money appalling, but Pete—just like Tricia when she'd asked Emma to act as locum in her absence—was persistent and persuasive. Despite her misgivings, Emma found herself on the end of a phone line to Italy. As expected, it was Cathy who answered.

"Em, Lisa's not here at the moment. She's on one of her marathon runs."

The mobile phone Cathy had purchased before leaving for Italy was obviously a good investment, her voice clear as a bell. If she didn't know better, Emma could have sworn Cathy was in the next suburb and not halfway across the world, but wondering at the marvels of modern technology was not her primary objective. "Utilizing her network" as Pete so eloquently described it, was. Emma called it "scabbing money off friends" but, whatever it was called, it left Emma with a dry mouth and a churning stomach.

"Actually, Cathy, it's you I wanted to speak to . . ."

Cathy snapped her mobile shut and placed it in the daypack that rested on the stonework next to the sun lounge. She adjusted the straps of her black bikini top before lying back down and closing her eyes against the glare of the Italian sun. It was still mid-morning, but already the sun had a bite intent on working its way through the layer of sunscreen Cathy had applied. She decided that, if Lisa hadn't returned from her run in ten minutes, she'd escape to the cool of their room and wait for her there.

By the time another body sat down next to her she'd turned over to lie on her stomach. Fingers pressed lightly on the skin between her shoulder blades. "I think you're done, honey."

Cathy turned over and smiled sleepily. Lisa's timing was perfect. Another minute or so and she would have dozed off, giving the sun ample opportunity to do its damage. "Hi there. How was your run?"

"Great." Lisa had the glow of someone still in the midst of an endorphin high, but she grimaced as she rubbed her thighs. "It's a killer climb back, though. Next time I think we should book a hotel closer to sea level."

"It does look like you had to work a bit hard." Cathy reached to brush a strand of wet-with-sweat hair from Lisa's forehead. "Tell you what, next visit I'll book us a tent on the beach."

"Sounds perfect." Lisa dangled an empty water bottle. "Have you got anything to drink? I finished this halfway up the hill."

"There should be one floating in there somewhere." Cathy pointed to her pack and within moments Lisa was breaking the plastic seal on a fresh bottle of water. She watched Lisa down half of it in large, thirsty gulps. "Emma called while you were gone."

Lisa swiped at her mouth with the back of her hand and offered the bottle. "Did you tell her I wasn't far away?"

Cathy shook her head at both the water and the question. "Actually, she called to speak to me."

Lisa's eyes widened in surprise. "Seems everyone's forgotten who's supposed to be friends with whom."

"Seems so." Yesterday morning Cathy had taken a call from Toni but was soon handing the phone to Lisa. Apparently Toni was planning some construction work and, since Lisa worked in a related industry, was hoping to get some names of reputable tradespeople.

"So, what did she want?"

Cathy frowned, recalling their conversation. "I'm not really sure. After she said she wanted to speak to me, she didn't really say anything at all. Actually, she went so quiet I had to check to see if she was still on the line. Then she just asked if we were having a good time, said she was insanely jealous and that she'd speak to us when we got back."

"And that was it?"

"Yes."

Lisa rolled the water bottle in her palms, eyes out to the horizon. "I wonder what's up?"

Cathy dug into her pack and held out her phone. "Give her a call and find out."

The mobile was considered but refused. Lisa turned her attention to the pool. "I'm hot. I think I'll have a swim first. Do you want to join me?"

It took Lisa less than five minutes to jog to their room, don her bathers and rejoin Cathy by the pool. She dove straight in but Cathy chose the more tortuous method of easing in slowly. By the time Lisa had swum a couple of laps Cathy's body temperature had equalized with the water. She waited by the edge of the pool, lazily kicking her legs until Lisa swam up to her.

"I think I've turned into a sloth." The water was particularly salty so there was little effort required to stay afloat, especially with her arms stretched along the edge. "I think I'll ring ahead to Tuscany and change our bike booking to a tandem so you can do all the work."

"You can do that if you like." Lisa pushed off the wall with her feet, gliding backward through the water before swimming a few forward strokes and stopping directly in front of Cathy. She tread water as her hands dipped below the surface, finding Cathy's waist. "I'll still think you're sexy, even with a big jelly-belly."

"Is that so?" Cathy pushed Lisa to arm's length, the comment seeming an opening for discussion on the topic that had not been mentioned since their last night in Rome. She wanted to ask what Lisa would think of her with a swollen belly, with fluid-filled ankles and probably a good layer of padding around her thighs. What she'd think if Cathy suffered morning sickness and had to make mad dashes to the toilet, and if Lisa would drive to the store in the middle of the night to satisfy some madder food craving. "You'd still find me attractive even if I was twice this size?"

"Even if you were four times this size." Lisa ducked her head under the water and Cathy felt lips slide along her stomach. Her head reappeared and golden hair was smoothed back. "But I don't think I have to worry about that for a while." Light lashes blinked away droplets of water and blue irises surrounded increasing pupils. "Because you're so damn sexy right now . . ." Wet lips slid across Cathy's neck to that most sensitive bit of skin just below her ear. They traversed Cathy's earlobe. "Damn, you look good in that bikini."

Their hotel was full to capacity. Sun-worshipers surrounded the pool and they shared the water with at least a dozen other guests. As Lisa's fingers slid between Cathy's thighs, a scantily clad woman eased into the water not more than a foot away from them. It was a very public place to be sharing such a private moment. Cathy stayed Lisa's fingers by grabbing her wrist. Desire clashed with disappointment at the missed opportunity for a baby debate.

Desire won. Cathy was already lifting herself out of the pool as she said, "Let's go to our room."

The room was cool, closed wooden shutters and thick stone walls providing efficient insulation against the heat of the day. Cathy stretched out fully, her thigh muscle twitching in response to the fingernails that traveled its length. She arched her back before settling, with a sigh, onto the mess of bedclothes. Once still, her stomach complained it was empty. It was no wonder she was hungry. Since she and Lisa had flung themselves onto the bed, their combined enthusiasm ensured an energetic workout.

"Shall we go get some lunch?" Cathy suggested.

"Mmm . . ." Lisa too stretched out on the bed, but her fingers continued their tour of Cathy's thigh. She completely ignored the new watch strapped around her wrist. "What's the time?"

The small clock on the bedside announced it was now past one. As if to prove a point, Cathy's stomach grumbled again. "Lunchtime."

Lisa ruffled Cathy's hair, pulled herself upright and leapt off the bed. "Okay, lazy bones. Let's go eat before you begin chewing on my arm."

Cathy headed for the bathroom.

Lisa announced, since it was now past seven p.m. in Perth, she'd give Emma a call.

Showered, Cathy emerged from the bathroom patting her still damp hair with a towel. "How is she?" she asked Lisa.

"I have no idea." Lisa's phone was tossed onto the closest

pillow. "She's gas-bagging to someone. I keep getting the engaged signal."

"You can try again later." Cathy stood in front of the closet, considering what to wear to lunch. She decided, since they were in Capri, that a set of Capri pants would be appropriate. She coupled them with a light sleeveless cotton shirt and headed back to the bathroom. She was pulling a brush through her hair when she caught Lisa's reflection in the mirror. Lisa was doing as she seemed to do every day now, leaning against the doorjamb, arms folded as she watched Cathy complete her preparations. And as was usual over the past few days, Cathy found Lisa's expression unreadable, and a bit disconcerting. "Are you going to have a shower before we go?"

"In a minute." Lisa leaned her head against the wooden frame and shifted her weight to her other foot. "I'm just enjoying watching you."

Cathy looked at Lisa's reflection in the mirror and smiled.

"You really are beautiful, you know."

Cathy smiled again. "Thank you."

"I reckon your children would be beautiful too. Good genes."

Cathy locked eyes with Lisa, her brush stopping midstroke. "Thank you," she repeated.

"But there's two sets of genes involved, aren't there." Lisa's gaze didn't waver from Cathy's reflection. "Who'd provide the other set, Cathy? Because it can't be me."

"I don't know, Lisa. I thought we could talk about that together." There was no response so Cathy pressed on. "Do you want to talk about it?" she asked softly.

Lisa's eyes held to Cathy's for one more second before she broke the contact. She unfolded her arms and looked down at her nakedness. "I think I'll have that shower now."

"Hi, Mal." Emma scratched Malibu under the chin before lifting her off the desk and onto her lap. "You sit here. That's my keyboard, not your cushion."

182

Malibu did a couple of three-sixty-degree turns before winding into a tight crescent of fur and emitting a gentle purr. Emma absently stroked her in between bursts of keyboard tapping. She glanced to the clock at the bottom of her screen. It was past ten p.m. With the exception of an enforced fifteen-minute "booted" break, she and Pookie had been talking for three hours.

Pookie had not been alone in the Fijian room when Emma entered. Shygirl was also present, as was Osmosis and FallenAngel. The conversation revolved around FallenAngel and her recent trip to New Zealand to meet Rabbit, the woman she had been talking with, both in chat and over the phone, for months. Apparently the trip had been a misery, the meeting in the flesh revealing that Rabbit was not the caring, sharing woman FallenAngel had been expecting. Rather she turned out to be quite the opposite, doing little to make FallenAngel welcome, and leaving her alone for extended periods while she retreated to globetrot on her computer. Finally having enough, FallenAngel booked into a motel for the last four days of her one-week stay and flew back to Adelaide, tail between her legs, ashamed at being so naïve as to fall for someone she had never met.

Emma contributed nothing to the conversation; she just sat watching, appalled at what she was reading. To think she'd been on the verge of lifting her veil of secrecy and offering Pookie insights into her life. A heavy weight of disappointment settled over Emma as the Fijian Room emptied of occupants. Shygirl hung around for a while, flirting with both Emma and Pookie, but eventually left, getting no reaction from either. Shygirl's continued pointless passes only served to reconfirm what Emma now knew to be true. This virtual world was purely that, a virtual reality that had the potential to suck you in and just as easily spit you out.

Finally alone, Pookie had been the first to speak.

Pookie: alone at last
Kayisha: Yes
Pookie: how r u kay? how did ur interview go?
Kayisha: Okay
Pookie: did u get the job?

183

Kayisha: Don't know yet. Three others applied.

Pookie: when will u find out?

Kayisha: Don't know. Next week maybe.

Pookie: do u want the job?

Kayisha: It seems like a good position and the people are nice.

Pookie: wot is the job exactly?

Emma thought carefully about how much she should reveal.

Kayisha: I'd rather not talk about it.

The delay on the screen indicated Pookie was also considering her response.

Pookie: ok then

Kayisha: I'm sorry, Pookie.

Pookie: wots wrong kay? have i said something 2 upset u?

Kayisha: No. Not at all.

Pookie: ok then

Emma stared at her blinking cursor, knowing Pookie was waiting for her to say something. Finally, she began typing again.

Kayisha: It's the FallenAngel and Rabbit thing.

There was another short delay on the screen. Pookie was either thinking carefully about her reply or typing an extended response.

Pookie: its sad. i spoke 2 fallen the day b4 she flew out. she was so excited 2 b finally meeting rabbit. i never guessed rabbit could turn out like that. even if there was no chemistry when they met she didnt have 2 b such a bitch about it

Kayisha: I'd never put myself in that position.

Pookie: i never thought i would either, until now

Kayisha: Now?

Pookie: ive been thinking about u a lot over the last few days kay

Emma held her breath as she typed. Her fingers spelled out, *I've been a thinking a lot about you too, Pookie,* but she quickly deleted the words and typed an alternative.

Kayisha: What were you thinking?

Pookie: that i missed u, n how strange that was since i really no nothing about u, n how i could pass u in the street n not no its u cos i have no idea what u look like, n how that may never happen cos u may get that job in albany n move away

Emma's heart thudded. Pookie had just verbalized her own thoughts during her time away. Both nights she lay on the bed in her motel room, wondering what Pookie was doing, where she was, who she was speaking to. She'd fall asleep trying to paste together an image of the woman who would later run through her dreams, and wake the next morning trying to capture fragments of the picture her subconscious had painted. For well over a year Justine had dominated her pre-sleep, post-sleep and dreamtime, and it wasn't until on her way home from her lunch with Pete and driving past Justine's house that Emma realized she hadn't given her a thought for the past forty-eight hours. While walking to her front door Emma thought of Lisa and how pleased she would be to discover the flame Emma had carried for so long was finally extinguished. Then she cringed at Lisa's likely reaction to the news that she was now plagued by thoughts of a faceless entity coming to her compliments of her computer's circuitry. Emma could think of at least one occasion when Lisa had threatened to call the men in the white wagon on her behalf. This bit of information would have her ready to sign commitment papers.

Emma typed slowly, the old saying "look before you leap" running through her mind. She read the words out loud, knew them to be true and, despite her better judgment, hit the enter key.

Kayisha: I want to know everything about you, Pookie.

Pookie: n i want 2 no everything about u

Kayisha: But at the same time I'm scared of finding out.

Pookie: i'm not like rabbit

Kayisha: I don't know that.

Pookie: give me a chance 2 prove it

Emma gave no response.

Pookie: lets start with some easy stuff. u can tell me 2 go 2 hell if it gets 2 personal

That sounded perfectly reasonable. And relatively safe.

Kayisha: ok

Pookie: my fav color is green. wots ur fav color n y?

They had covered a lot of ground in the hours since Emma revealed that her favorite color was blue. She told how the gas-lift chair she was currently sitting on was blue and that many of her interior design choices had been influenced by her preference. Pookie asked if her color preference extended to her bedroom and Emma told her to go to hell for getting too personal. But she went on to tell Pookie that her continental quilt was predominantly navy blue, and how she'd overhauled the whole room, including the color of the walls, in a post-breakup frenzy.

Given the opening, Pookie skirted around the subject of partners until Emma finally gave in and relieved her curiosity, announcing she'd been single since the woman who inspired the redecoration of her room. Emma then worked up the courage to ask of Pookie's status, hoping she was unattached, not quite sure just how she'd feel if she wasn't.

Pookie: i'm single

Yay! Emma silently cheered.

Pookie: have been 4 a year now. unless u count a 3 week fling

Kayisha: Why wouldn't you count that?

Pookie: cos we slept together, but not much else

Kayisha: So you reckon if you just sleep with someone it doesn't count?

Pookie: i didnt say that

Kayisha: What are you saying then?

Pookie: that she wasnt the right 1 4 me

Kayisha: Was she with someone?

Pookie: no

Kayisha: Have you ever been with someone who was with someone else?

Pookie: not as far as I no

Kayisha: My last partner was with someone else. She left me to be with her.

Pookie: that must have been hard

Kayisha: I hated her and her new girlfriend for quite a while.

Pookie: sounds reasonable. i went thru something similar last yr, but eventually got over it. lol i had 2 get over it. she was my boss

Kayisha: Really?

Pookie: still is

Emma jumped at the opportunity to discover what Pookie did for a living.

Kayisha: What do you do?

Pookie: at the moment i'm on leave

Kayisha: Holiday?

Pookie: sick leave

Kayisha: Not too serious I hope?

Pookie: i'll survive. should b back on deck next wk

It was the moment before Emma hit the enter key on her repeated "What do you do?" question that her ISP booted her out. In the minutes that followed, the question was forgotten, Emma too busy swearing and cursing at her screen. Finally the damned machine made the correct noises and Emma flew through the sequence that would take her back to the Fijian room.

Pookie: wb = welcome back

Kayisha: Thank you.

Pookie: u really need 2 get broadband

Kayisha: I'm going to ring first thing tomorrow.

Pookie: want the name of a good provider?

Pookie relayed the name of the same provider Toni had. Emma decided that, with two recommendations, the firm must be good. She reiterated her promise to organize the change the next morning and, remembering her as yet unanswered question, began composing it again. Pookie beat her to the screen.

Pookie: tell me kay, wot was it like growing up gay in geraldton?

Kayisha: I don't know. I didn't realize I was until I was in my twenties.

Pookie: tell me

And so Emma and Pookie swapped coming out stories. Their tales were very, very different.

Pookie spoke of a childhood as a rebel tomboy. Of preteen days spent with the local boys, playing ball and thumbing their collective noses at the "stupid girls," all the while Pookie thinking this or that girl really was quite nice and not stupid at all. She spoke of her twelfth birthday party and of her friend Melanie's dare, the dare that led her behind the shed and her hand up Melanie's skirt. She also told of her coming out to her mother sometime in the year she was fifteen. Pookie had arrived home from her first "full" experience with a girl. She was still giddy, hardly able to think straight and totally unable to keep the smile from her face. She was also dreading what her mum would have to say when she announced she was a lesbian. Her mum's reaction took her totally by surprise. "Thank heaven you've finally realized it. Maybe now we can both get some peace." Pookie soon discovered she had a mother who was not only accepting, but vicariously out and proud. Overly so. Whenever Pookie was with her mum and in new company, her mum would wind her arm around her shoulder. "This is my daughter. She's a lesbian, you know."

> *Pookie:* it was great having mum so behind me. but sometimes i wish strangers got 2 no me as something other than 'the lesbian'
> *Kayisha:* I wouldn't care if mum and dad shouted it to the rooftops. It has to be preferable to what I have now.
> *Pookie:* wots that?
> *Kayisha:* Nothing. They choose not to speak to "the pervert."
> *Pookie:* how long since u spoke?
> *Kayisha:* Nearly 5 years now.
> *Pookie:* how old r u kay?
> *Kayisha:* 37
> *Pookie:* u waited a long time b4 telling ur folks?

188

Kayisha: I guess. But like I said, I was also a bit of a late starter. I was actually engaged to be married. To a boy I went to uni with.

High school passed Emma by without any concerns other than riding her horses and doing everything in her power to ensure she got accepted into university. Determined it was her calling to be a vet, she concentrated on her books, paying little attention to either the boys or girls with whom she shared a class. She got into university, but it was a struggle. She was dedicated, even passionate over her love for animals, but the theory didn't come easily and she had to work hard to ensure that she passed.

Pookie: hang on a sec kay. u actually r a vet?

Kayisha: yes

Pookie: really?

Kayisha: yes

There was a slight pause before Pookie responded.

Pookie: ok

The first three years of Emma's degree came and went with her nose stuck firmly in her texts. It was in her fourth year that she looked up from her books and hooked up with Adam, a fellow student. Looking back, she wasn't altogether sure why she finally agreed to his constant pleas to go out with him. Maybe it was because all her friends were in relationships and being the odd cog was getting tiring. Whatever it was, she found herself suddenly attached. She let him do his thing. It hurt at first, but after a while she got used to it and eventually felt nothing at all. She knew something wasn't right; surely there had to be more to sex than this. All her friends certainly seemed to find their experiences pleasurable. At least that's the impression they gave. Emma decided not to dwell on this point, because although Adam left her cold in the bedroom, he was a kind, gentle man who shared her ideals when it came to animals.

Pookie: he was safe

Kayisha: Yes I guess he was. I think I subconsciously made the decision, if I had to be with a man, he was one who wouldn't make too many demands on me. So when he proposed, I said yes.

Pookie: y did u think u had 2 b with a man?

Kayisha: I really don't know. Just following what I'd been brought up to think was the natural order of things maybe.

Emma's notion of the natural order of things suddenly changed in her final year of study. She met Melanie.

Pookie: i wonder if its the same melanie i knew <grin>

Kayisha: lol maybe. If it was, I can see why you took her up on her dare. I couldn't think straight when I was around her.

Melanie was a graduate student doing her thesis on postoperative care for reptilians. Whether by coincidence or design, she was often in the university practice when Emma was rostered. They struck up a friendship unlike Emma had ever experienced. There was something about Melanie that made Emma come completely unglued. When Melanie came close, Emma felt ecstatic yet faint; when she moved away it was as if some electric current between them was jammed. On the occasions Melanie was not at the practice, Emma felt a deep-seated disappointment she knew she should feel when Adam wasn't around but didn't. When Adam wasn't around, all she felt was an empty relief.

It was a quiet Sunday afternoon that Emma's world turned upside down. Melanie's tone was more of an instruction than an invitation: "Come with me." And she strode ahead with Emma following. They ended up in the storeroom. And what happened there left Emma light-headed and unable to breathe. But unlike Pookie's first "full" experience, Emma *could* think straight. In fact it seemed her blinkers had been removed and she saw the world clearly for the first time.

Kayisha: It was like all the pieces clicked into place. Being with Melanie just felt so . . . right.

Pookie: n adam?

Kayisha: I'm ashamed to say I didn't handle it very well. I drove to his house that very night and told him I didn't love him and that the engagement was off. But when he asked me why I just couldn't bring myself to tell him. And instead of getting angry with me he cried. He really was a nice guy, Pookie. He deserved better than I could give him.

Pookie: so was melanie the woman u repainted ur house over?

Kayisha: No. Once I graduated we sort of drifted apart.

Pookie: and since then?

Kayisha: Since then I've had the usual experience. You know, a train smash followed by a pileup.

Pookie: any long-term relationships?

Kayisha: Just one. Three years. She was the one I repainted my house over. She was also the one who convinced me I should come out to my folks.

Pookie: do u blame her 4 wot happened with ur parents?

Kayisha: How can I? They would have reacted the same no matter who I was with when I told them. But I remember I did feel sort of pressured into coming out. I was happy to let sleeping dogs lie, but she was adamant I be politically correct.

Emma's parents—her father a welder and her mother a career housewife—had never had much money, but they had given her a happy home and she loved them both dearly. She could not grasp how the knowledge that she was a lesbian should change their love for her, but apparently it did. Her mother told her it would be the death of her standing in the community if the neighbors found out; her father wouldn't look at her as she held out the key he requested. She placed the key to her family home on the dining table and walked out the door with the word *pervert* echoing in her ears. She'd never been back since.

Pookie: i'm sorry kay. i cant imagine how it feels 2 b cut off from ur folks like that

Kayisha: Thanks, Pookie

Pookie: its their loss

Kayisha: That's what I keep telling myself too.

Emma stretched her mind back to that most awful day. Hurt beyond belief, she had left with head held high, determined not to let her parents see how deeply she was wounded by their reaction. Within a few days her hurt turned into anger—"How dare they . . ." As time wore on, that emotion too flagged and waned, morphing into a deep-seated sadness at her loss. Emma thought often of dialing her parents' number, but nerves always got the better of her and she never did. In turn, her parents had never attempted further contact.

All this was relayed to Pookie via a series of fragmented, typo-filled sentences.

Pookie: i dont know wot 2 say kay. i'm so sorry

Kayisha: No need to say anything. Thanks for listening though.

Pookie: i hate the fact all i can c is this damned screen

Kayisha: ditto

Pookie: i wish i could c u, see ur expression

Kayisha: ditto

Pookie: do u know what u'd c if u could c me right now?

Emma held her breath as she typed. Maybe she was finally going to get the physical description she was so desperate to discover.

Kayisha: no

Pookie: u'd c some1 who'd love 2 kiss u

Emma's heart stopped, started again, then bounced right out of her chest. She typed *ditto* then deleted it.

Kayisha: Go to hell Pookie

Twice Emma typed *I didn't mean that. Tell me again.* Then twice she highlighted the words and made them disappear.

Pookie: tell me wot Kayisha means

Midstream in her third attempt at retracting her statement, Emma overwrote her words. She was at once disappointed and grateful for the topic change.

Kayisha: It's actually a hybrid of two names, Kaila and

Ayisha. Kaila is Hawaiian and means "keeper of the crown" and Ayisha is African and means "woman" or "life."

Pookie: its a lovely name. i like the sound of it

Kayisha: And your user name?

Pookie: nothing as glamorous as urs. its the name of garfields teddy

Kayisha: You're a Garfield fan?

Pookie: he n my cat share a lot of traits

Kayisha: Is you cat called Garfield too?

Pookie: no. virgil

Emma blinked when the name appeared. That was also the name of Toni's beloved puss. But, she guessed, coming across two cats sharing the same relatively uncommon name was not that much of a coincidence. Just a couple of months prior, two children's pythons were brought into the surgery for treatment. Different owners brought them in at different times, but both were called Harriet.

Kayisha: He's the couch shredder?

Pookie: lol no, hasn't destroyed it yet. but he's a she

Emma stared at the screen. At least both Harriets were female. The practice of assigning male names to female animals was also not that uncommon, but to come across two female feline Virgils in the space of two weeks was pushing coincidence a bit far.

Kayisha: Does Virgil have part of her tail missing?

The screen was silent for what seemed an awfully long time. Then a single-word answer appeared.

Pookie: yes

Jesus. It's Toni. Emma swallowed hard and did the first thing that came to her head. She stabbed at the on/off button on the hard-drive casing and aborted the entire session.

"No!" Toni exclaimed loudly and thumped her fist on the desk in frustration. The sudden noise frightened Virgil from Toni's lap and she scampered out of the study. "Sorry, Virg," Toni called, staring miserably at her screen. What a time for Kayisha to get booted, right when Toni was on the verge of discovering her identity. Her very next question was going to be a direct "who are you?"—a question she felt she had every right to ask, especially since Kayisha obviously knew, or at least knew of, her cat, Virgil.

Now it would be a good fifteen minutes—the average timespan for Kayisha to get reconnected—before her curiosity would be satisfied. Toni took a large swig of water, swishing it around her mouth as she mulled over Kayisha's identity. Once again Emma came to mind. That had been her first thought when Kayisha announced she was a vet. At the time of the announcement Toni could have kicked herself. Kayisha actually revealed her occupation last Saturday, but Toni had been too stupid to pick up on it.

For the second time Emma was dismissed as a candidate. She wasn't the only vet in Perth; it was purely because Toni knew her that her name sprang to mind. Emma had seemed very interested in Toni's computer, however, and she *was* thinking of switching to broadband.

No. It couldn't be her. Emma had a job. Kayisha didn't.

But Kayisha knew of Virgil's tail injury. Emma was the one who had treated her, and the only other vet at the practice was Tricia. And Tricia was . . . just Tricia. So maybe Kayisha *was* Emma. Or maybe all the local vets got together to have powwows about their cases and Virgil had been the topic at their last meeting. In which case Kayisha could be a vet she had never met.

"Shit, I don't know." Toni swiveled 'round and 'round in her chair, knowing she was missing some vital clue. She brought her chair to a sudden stop, a fresh thought forming.

When Virgil was injured Emma was working as a locum at Tricia's practice. What if her stint was finished and she was now looking for another job? That would make Emma fit the profile.

"Oh, my God." Toni felt almost certain she had hit the nail on the head. "I think I've been talking to Emma."

A check of her screen revealed she was still the only occupant in the Fijian room. She swore under her breath. Now that she had a theory, she was eager to prove it. She couldn't stand the thought of waiting until Kayisha was reconnected. She wanted to know *now*. She reached for the phone. All she had to do was ring and ask to speak to Kayisha. If Emma was Kayisha then she'd say so, and if she wasn't then she'd probably say the caller had a wrong number.

But there was a fatal flaw in Toni's plan, and it wasn't the fact that Kayisha would be busy trying to dial back in so the line was likely to be busy. Toni couldn't ring because she didn't know Emma's phone number. She also doubted very much the after-hours answering service for Tricia's practice would give it out. She didn't even know her last name, or what suburb she lived in, so directory assistance would be no help. Toni thrummed her fingers on the desk. Her eyes darted to the computer's time display. Ten-thirty p.m.

Four-thirty p.m. in Italy.

Toni picked up the phone again and dialed.

Cathy held her phone out to Lisa. "It's Toni. She wants to speak to you again."

The book Lisa held open while she stared out to the sea was placed face down in her lap. She frowned as she took the mobile from Cathy's hand. "Hi, Toni."

The conversation was brief. Lisa relayed a number Cathy recognized as Emma's, told Toni she was welcome and said her good-byes.

Then she checked her watch and said, "How strange. Why would Toni want to ring Emma at this time of night? Come to think of it, why would she want to ring Emma at all?"

Cathy shrugged. "She sounded a bit flustered. Maybe Virgil's had a relapse and needs treatment."

Lisa nodded, but the nod turned into a shake. "If Virgil was sick Toni wouldn't muck around making international calls to get her vet of preference. She'd be straight out the door to the nearest twenty-four-hour practice. It has to be something else." She snapped Cathy's mobile back open and began pressing numbers.

"What are you doing?"

"I forgot all about ringing Emma. I'm going to do it now."

"Oh, no, you don't, Lisa Smith," Cathy snapped. Yet another afternoon of avoidance was driving her crazy. Lunch came and went without so much as a word about "the baby thing." Neither was it mentioned throughout their hike back up the steep slope to their hotel.

They had since settled on the balcony of their room, armed with books and a bottle of wine. The silence of their afternoon could have drifted by quite comfortably, except for the fact that Cathy was acutely aware that Lisa was not reading at all. Her book was held open, but she was in some other world. A world Cathy was not allowed to enter. Each time Cathy glanced in Lisa's direction, Lisa seemed to sense the gaze and turned pretend attention to the contents of the page.

Now, all the frustration of the last few days suddenly came to a head and anger flashed red in front of Cathy's eyes. "Don't you even *think* about making that call!"

"I beg your pardon?"

Cathy plucked her phone from Lisa's hand. "Take your nose out of other people's business and concentrate on the problems closer to home."

"Problems?" Lisa spun her head sharply to meet Cathy's gaze. "What problems?"

"For God's sake, Lisa." Cathy couldn't believe she had to explain it. Hurt mixed into her anger and the brew bubbled over in the form of hot tears. "You know *exactly* what I'm talking about. If you really feel that strongly against having children then just say so and I'll be okay with it. But please, don't keep shutting me out."

"I—" Lisa stopped short, slumped back in her seat and chewed on her knuckles.

Cathy sat gape-jawed at the reaction and a fresh surge of anger pushed itself up from her gut. It was at the point of spewing forth via a series of expletives aimed in Lisa's direction when Lisa sat forward again. Questioning eyes darted across Cathy's features.

"Would you really be okay if I said I didn't want children?" Lisa asked.

Cathy swallowed her unspoken tirade and swiped at her eyes with the back of her hand. What she would do if Lisa didn't want to be part of raising a family wasn't something she had seriously expected to need to consider. Now that she was forced to, she realized she already knew her answer. Lisa was more important to her than anything. "Yes," she said softly. "If that's how you feel then I have to respect that."

Lisa shook her head. "I'm not saying that's how I feel."

"What are you saying then?"

For a long moment of silence Cathy thought Lisa was going to do as she had for days now—shrug off the question and change the topic. She didn't, instead reaching for Cathy's hands, holding them between her palms. "I'm saying I'm frightened, Cathy. I know I haven't talked to you about it, but I've been thinking about it constantly. And I'm frightened."

This admission was totally unexpected. Lisa's ability to meet just about any situation head-on gave Cathy the impression almost nothing could scare her off. The silent appeal in Lisa's expression, however, conveyed the honesty of her statement. "Oh, honey . . . what are you frightened of?"

"Everything." Lisa broke eye contact, intent instead on her hands. They gently rubbed Cathy's as she appeared to be considering her words. Finally she took a deep breath. "I'm frightened that having a baby will change everything that's so good between us. I'm frightened of being responsible for a tiny life that's totally dependent on us, and I'm frightened when I think of all the things that could possibly go wrong. I'm frightened that it won't really be *our* baby; it will be yours and whatever you decide I'll have no say in it. I'm frightened of bringing a child into a world still full of prejudice against people like us and that the child will grow to hate us for it. And"—she stopped her now furious rubbing of Cathy's hands, instead tightening her grip on them—"I'm frightened you'll want to find someone who isn't so frightened by the whole thing."

"Oh, honey." That Lisa was so worried over the responsibilities that came with parenthood put her streets ahead of many who leapt without looking. "You're not going to get rid of me that easily."

Anxious eyes searched Cathy's. And the vicelike grip was loosened, just a little. "Really?"

"I love you so much, Lisa. I don't want to lose you, ever."

"And all the other stuff . . ."

"We have a lot to talk about." Lisa just nodded, so Cathy repeated her question from earlier in the day, "Do you want to talk about it?"

Lisa's book was closed and placed on the table. Her tone was uncertain, but she looked Cathy directly in the eye as she said, "Yes. Yes, I do."

Despondent, Toni returned the handset to its cradle. "Well, there's that theory down the drain." Despite repeated attempts, she had not been able to get through to Emma. The line was not engaged. It rang out, unanswered. Slumped in her seat, Toni turned her attention back to the monitor. She refreshed the screen, hoping Kayisha—whoever she was—might finally be back in. She wasn't, and Toni sighed, pushing at the floor with her feet to begin her office-chair swivel.

The chair swung in a slow arc. Having her theory disproved was only one aspect of her disappointment. That Emma wasn't Kayisha was the other. Toni really had begun to warm to the idea. Faded jeans. Khaki. Those strong, healing hands. Hands that saved her best friend's life . . .

Three loud raps came from the direction of her front door.

"Shit." Toni brought her chair to a halt and checked her computer clock. *Who'd be calling at this hour?* she wondered. Toni wandered down the hallway and put her eye to the peephole. And her heart came to a temporary halt.

She tried for a nonchalant door-opening but failed miserably. The door slammed against the hallway wall, the handle denting the plaster. Trying for a recovery, Toni leaned against the door and folded her arms. She realized her attempt at looking cool was somewhat hindered by her paw-print pajamas and ultra-fluffy slippers, so she removed her body from the door and stood up straight. Good posture was always a winner.

The woman on her doorstep suddenly bent to the ground, scooping Virgil into her arms. The little sneak had tried for a breakout but was foiled by quick reflexes. "Looks like you should ramp up work on your cat run."

Toni raked fingers through her hair and smiled nervously. Apart from Lisa, she had only told one other person about her planned renovations. "Hi, Kayisha."

Emma nodded. "Hi, Pookie."

CHAPTER FIFTEEN

Finally face-to-face with the woman who'd tormented her thoughts since their first virtual meeting, Toni completely forgot her manners and just stood, staring, etching Emma's features into her memory. Hazel eyes flecked with green; light brown hair tied in a loose ponytail. The beginnings of creases around her eyes spoke of frequent laughter, or maybe frequent squinting against the sun. Whichever, Toni thought it added character to the otherwise smooth planes of her face. Toni could well imagine Emma on her childhood friend's farm, those strong hands confidently running the flank of a horse before deftly sitting astride the creature.

"Um, Toni . . . Do you mind if I come in?"

"Sorry." Toni stood aside to let her pass. "Come on through. Would you like a drink?"

"Just water, thanks." Emma followed her to the kitchen, speaking quickly. "I know it's late. I wanted to ring but I couldn't find the piece of paper I had your details on and I wanted to speak to you tonight but not on the computer, so . . . thanks." Emma put Virgil down to accept the glass Toni offered. "So . . ." She looked around her before smiling wanly. "Here I am."

Toni followed Emma's cue and looked around the room, as if hoping to find something new in familiar surroundings. Emma was the only new item in her kitchen, so she settled her gaze on her. "I'm sorry, Emma, but you've caught me a bit off guard. I was actually waiting for you in the chat room."

"Oh." Emma's face fell. "I won't stay long."

"I didn't mean it like that." Toni backtracked quickly. Emma's expression, combined with the nervous sips on her water, indicated she felt herself to be an unwelcome visitor. "I'm glad you came over. I really am. It's just I wasn't expecting it." Toni ushered Emma in the direction of the lounge room. "Go make yourself comfortable. I'll be one minute, okay? I'm actually still sitting in chat so I'll just go log out."

Toni waited for Emma to nod unsurely, then turned and fled for the study.

Despite her promise, Toni was gone quite a bit longer than one minute, making a stop at her en suite bathroom to scrub her teeth. She also threw aside her pajamas in favor of track pants and a light pullover. Her fluffy slippers stayed. After all, she didn't want to look like she was making too much of an effort. Halfway down the hall she retreated to her bedroom again, scuffed off her slippers and pulled on runners. She also ran a brush through her hair, sprayed on some perfume and wondered if she should dress in something a bit better than track pants. But, while peering at the contents of her wardrobe, she realized Emma would probably be thinking she had been deserted in favor of whoever was in the chat room when Toni went to log off. She closed her wardrobe door. For better or worse, track pants would have to do.

Emma had taken a seat toward one end of the three-seater couch. Virgil had taken residence next to her and was getting a scratch on the chin. Toni tossed up where to sit. The choices were one of the two single chairs, the vacant space on the three-seater, atop the coffee table or on the floor. She opted for the vacant space on the couch.

"So," Toni said as she half-turned in her seat. "Here we are."

"Yes." Emma took another sip of her water. It was almost gone.

"Can I get you another?"

"No." The glass was placed on a coaster on the coffee table. "Thank you."

Toni scratched her arm, then stopped. She looked at Emma, who looked back, and they both smiled. Then they both looked away. Silence reigned supreme. Except for Vigil's purr. She was in raptures over Emma's extended chin-scratch.

"Toni, can I ask you something?"

"Sure." Toni sat forward, hands clasped in her lap. She would answer any question, anything to break this uncomfortable silence. Toni half-wished Emma had just logged back into chat. It was much less confrontational than having her here, in person.

"Why do you keep tins of chickpeas on the coffee table?"

Toni immediately wished she had kept her promise to put them out of sight in between uses. Her cheeks burned. "I use them as mini-weights while the gym is off-limits."

"Why? Have you been banned?"

"No." Toni pointed to her face but, seeing Emma's crooked smile, realized she was being teased. Nervous tension seeped away. "Not yet anyway."

"So you weren't discovered behind the lockers with your hands up some girl's skirt?"

"No." Toni grinned at the reference to their online conversation. "I prefer the back of a shed to the back of a locker."

Maybe it was the gloriously throaty quality to Emma's chuckle, or maybe it was the way the green flecks in her irises twinkled as the delicate skin around her eyes creased in humor. Whatever it was, when Emma laughed Toni felt an involuntary shiver travel all the way up her spine. She also had a sudden, sharp awareness of the woman sitting next to her and a firm desire to remove the physical barrier between them that Virgil currently provided.

Her opportunity came sooner than expected. Emma picked up her glass. "I think I will have a refill."

Toni's offer to freshen Emma's glass was waved away. As soon as

Emma left for the kitchen Toni picked up Virgil and plonked her onto her lap. "What do you reckon, Virg?" she whispered, now very much pleased Emma would be staying for at least the duration of another glass of water.

Virgil yawned widely but rested a paw on Toni's forearm. Toni took it as a sign of approval. From the corner of her eye she spied Emma on her return to the couch. As she watched her approach, the reality that Emma had been the person who'd captured her imagination across cyberspace finally hit home. All the things they'd talked about, all the common ground they shared. To think it was all with a woman she wouldn't have given the time of day to a few weeks prior.

Toni's whisper lowered even further. "Yeah, I agree, Virg. Sometimes truth is stranger than fiction."

On Emma's return from the kitchen, their conversation began to flow. Just as with their online sessions, topics rolled effortlessly into one another, but this was so much better than online chat. In contrast to her earlier thought, Toni discovered speaking that to Emma in person was not confrontational—rather, their communication was rich and complex, heightened by the ability to read expressions and tone.

They moved closer together as they talked, and quite by accident, Toni's knee brushed against Emma's. It caused a jolt like electricity, and Toni felt the freshly vacant air between their thighs positively hum when they both quickly shied their legs away.

Toni's reaction was more than just physical. It was in that brief moment of contact that she fully realized the burgeoning emotional attachment she felt in online chat had already increased exponentially. She liked Emma. A lot. The temptation to tell her so was almost overpowering, but she caught herself in time, instead asking if Emma would like to check out her plans for the cat run.

Emma said yes and followed Toni into her backyard. In the poor light offered by the single under-eaves globe, Emma peered at the design for Toni's proposed cat run. Then she paced the length of the run. Her paces took her well toward the back fence.

Toni paced alongside her. "What do you think?"

"It's an ambitious project." Emma squinted in the direction of the plane tree, where the main area of the run would be located. "And this section is huge."

"Well, I wasn't going to build it so she was on one side and me on the other, so I decided to make it big enough for us upright types too." Toni pointed to appropriate spots in the garden as she spoke. "Over there will be the decking. It will skirt the edge of the tree and down a few meters to just about that spot there. There'll be grass and a litter arrangement down that side. I'll be getting paving done from the back steps and the human-size entry will run off from it. And see the spot just to the left of the back door? That'll be where the hole is cut so Virgil will have access to and from the house. Once all that is done the rest of the yard will be planted out properly." She stood back, hands on her hips as her eyes swept the garden, visualizing her masterpiece.

"It's fabulous, Toni. You've covered everything—shade, light, a windbreak, a comfy sleeping spot and plenty of room so she can have a good run. Virgil sure is one lucky cat."

"Try telling her that at the moment." Toni grimaced. "I've got someone coming 'round tomorrow morning to give a quote on the work, but I'm guessing it will be a good few weeks before it's finished. Virgil will be climbing the walls by then."

"Cats are amazingly adaptable, Toni. She'll survive." Emma looked to her watch and asked, "What time have you arranged for the quote?"

"Around nine."

"It's late. I really should let you get some sleep."

"I'm okay." Toni knew it to be well past midnight, but she wasn't tired at all. And was that reluctance she heard in Emma's voice? She hoped so, because she really didn't want Emma to leave.

Not yet.

"Do you have anywhere you need to be tomorrow?" Toni asked.

"No."

"Then stay."

Emma tilted her head to one side as if considering. "I really should go."

"Why?"

"I . . ." Emma looked to the cat-run plans before rolling them into a scroll. "I don't know."

Toni took the scroll from Emma's hand and dropped it to the ground. "Then stay."

Emma stood silent for a moment. "I lied to you."

A little piece of Toni withered. Both online, and now offline, she'd been completely honest with Emma and had assumed the same from her. "When?"

"In chat. When I told you to go to hell. I didn't really mean it."

Emma had told her to go to hell more than once. "Which time?"

"When you said you wanted to kiss me."

"Oh." Caught in the moment, the words had just flown from Toni's fingers and landed on the screen. The reaction to her words made her instantly regret them and now, freshly embarrassed, Toni looked down to the ground.

"I wanted to kiss you too." Emma tilted Toni's chin with her index finger. "I still do."

At first their kiss was shy, hesitant. It deepened slowly, Emma's hands sliding to Toni's buttocks and pressing her closer to her hips. "Oh . . ." Toni took a breath before falling back into the embrace. Her tongue tipped against Emma's.

The touch was almost too much. The touch was not nearly enough.

Toni was gathered closer and Emma's hands skimmed under Toni's pullover. Fingers explored lightly, delicately, traveling up and around her waist, pausing briefly before continuing their journey. They couldn't seem to find a resting place, fingertips roaming over the smattering of dried blisters that still dotted Toni's skin. Toni stiffened, embarrassed at her condition.

Emma must have sensed the change in mood, her hands easing

from under the light wool. Her breath came in short gasps and she visibly swallowed. "Too much?"

It seemed Emma had misinterpreted her hesitation. Nevertheless, Toni nodded.

Emma held her at arm's length. "Are you okay?"

Toni nodded again.

"I think I should go."

"No." Toni reached for Emma's hands. She held them lightly, again struck by the memory of them running confidently down the length of Virgil's body. Toni enveloped them, feeling absolutely none of the calming effect they seemed to have on Virgil. "I don't want you to."

"I . . ." Emma's gaze wandered around Toni's backyard. Toni had seen the reaction enough times now to know it was Emma's equivalent of her own hair-raking habit. Her gaze finally came to rest on Toni's, and Emma asked, "Will you come out with me tomorrow? We could go to the movies, or maybe catch a show."

The knowledge she had effectively brought a halt to proceedings she desperately wanted to continue weighed heavily, but Toni wasn't going to force the issue. Emma had obviously made up her mind.

Toni's thoughts turned to her face. As with the rest of her body, most of the dried-up bits had fallen off. The new skin underneath was tight and pink and evidenced Toni's passing illness. On her mid-morning trip to the supermarket, she'd seen people stare then look quickly away. Some even walked a wide circle around her as if she carried some communicable disease. Well, chicken pox *was* a communicable disease, but not of *that* sort. "I'm not really up to a night on the town just yet . . . I really would like to see you though," she added quickly.

Emma tipped her head, as if wondering whether Toni's response was actually a yes or a no. Then she smiled. "How about you come to my place instead? I'll introduce you to the real Kayisha."

CHAPTER SIXTEEN

The number on the letterbox sitting atop a low fence paling matched the one Emma had relayed, but Toni did not cut the car engine straightaway. Instead she sat with eyes closed, taking a series of calming breaths. Her utter nervousness at the visit was yet another sure sign she was falling, and falling fast.

The day had been filled with signs. That Emma was the first thing on her mind when she opened her eyes that morning was one. The next thought, the one that wondered how on earth she was to survive the hours until their arranged six p.m. meeting time, was another. Then there was the fact she was showered, dressed and ready to leave a full ten minutes before needing to. Being ready early was strange enough, but being ready early despite having tried on every item of clothing she owned was nothing short of a miracle.

Deciding it was now or never, Toni cut the engine, did a check in the rearview mirror to make sure no renegade bits of food had escaped her protracted teeth-cleaning, picked up the two bottles of wine—one white and one red—brought to accompany their meal, and headed for the veranda of the California-style bungalow Emma called home.

The chiming of the doorbell prompted a large dog's *woof* and the sound of paws trotting on what must be bare wooden floorboards. Human footsteps soon followed and Emma's front door opened. Toni's already strangled attempt at a hello was completely cut short when a snout pushed its way right into her crotch.

"Kai! Stop it!" Emma scolded, pulling at Kayisha's collar and telling her to sit. The golden retriever did as she was told, her frantic tail-wag causing a thumping echo across the polished floorboards. The face that looked up to Toni was panting as dogs are wont to do, but this particular dog did it with an expression that gave Toni the distinct impression she was smiling. "I'm sorry Toni, please forgive my ill-mannered canine. She doesn't usually do that."

"Sure, Emma." Toni desperately hoped Kayisha's wet nose hadn't left a wet patch on the crotch of her carefully selected "I just threw these on" jeans. "I bet you spent months training her."

Toni's reward was a chance to listen to Emma's deliciously throaty chuckle.

She held out the bottles of wine. "I wasn't sure what we're having so I thought I'd cover the bases."

"Thanks, Toni." Emma accepted the bottles, smiling but apologetic in tone. "I've actually got someone here at the moment. We're in the kitchen." Emma ushered Toni down the hallway. "Having some tea." Emma's voice lowered to a whisper just before they reached the kitchen entrance. "Whatever you do, don't have a muffin."

Thoroughly disappointed they were not alone, Toni's smile was weak as she took a seat at the kitchen table opposite a woman Emma introduced as Justine.

Emma pulled a cup and saucer from an overhead cupboard,

placed it in front of Toni and sat at the head of the table. "Justine, this is Toni."

"Pleased to meet you." The young, finely featured woman picked up a Tupperware box and offered the contents. "Blueberry muffin?"

From the corner of her eye Toni saw Emma mouthing *no* and giving an almost imperceptible shake of her head. Despite the repeated warning, Toni dipped her hand into the box. Almost immediately she wished she hadn't. For its size, it was mighty heavy. Against her better judgment she took a bite and chewed. Were these hard pellets really blueberries? And was that a glob of uncooked flour filling her mouth? Toni continued to chew, well aware that Justine was sizing her up from across the table. Her peripheral vision caught Emma's expression. Her lips were pressed together as she desperately tried to keep a straight face.

Justine eventually packed up her Tupperware box of terror with an announcement that she had to get home as Paul, her *fiancé*, was down from the mines and would be home from his golf game any minute. Toni smiled at the tenth reminder that Justine was engaged to be married. The woman must be a homophobe. Either that or she was a closeted lesbian trying to convince the rest of the world how straight she was.

The two of them finally alone, Emma chortled as she pointed at the remains of Toni's muffin. "Are you sure you don't want this?" With Toni's vigorous head-shake she called Kayisha to the table and held out the cannonball.

Toni watched Kayisha wolf it down without chewing, wishing she'd thought of that method of consumption and wondering at the unlikely friendship between Emma and Justine. They were like chalk and cheese, not a pair she'd have guessed would hit it off. "How do you know Justine?"

"She's my neighbor. Lives just a few doors down."

"Oh." Toni watched Emma gather empty cups and saucers and rise to take them to the sink. She knew she should have offered to help, but the sight of Emma's behind wriggling in time with her cup-rinse was rather distracting.

"And you remember the night I drank myself stupid at Lisa and Cathy's?"

Toni harrumphed loudly. "Vaguely."

Emma turned from the sink and gave a half-smile, acknowledging Toni's dry humor. "She was the reason why."

The significance of Justine in Emma's life assumed a swift upward trajectory. And her closeted lesbian theory thrust itself forward. Or maybe not so closeted. Toni's mouth felt like it was still full of uncooked flour. "You went out with her?"

"No. I was just suffering a very bad case of misguided lust."

Toni stared at a muffin crumb in the middle of the table, thinking of the world of difference between Justine's looks and her own. "She's very pretty."

Emma sat back at the table, not quite sure how she felt when Toni announced Justine pretty. Emma looked nothing like Justine. Maybe Toni preferred the waif look to . . . to Emma's decidedly non-waif look. Then, when Toni's words were combined with their light delivery and the hesitant raising of the eyes to meet her own, Emma realized the comment for what it was. Toni was trying to gauge where she ranked.

Emma stopped herself from blurting a hackneyed, "She's not as pretty as you." *Pretty* was not an appropriate adjective for Toni. *Pretty* was reserved for woman such as Justine—petite and feminine. The word also held an implied simplicity. No, Toni wasn't pretty. Short hair with an unruly fringe accentuated the boyish quality to her features, but the long, dark lashes, full mouth and wonderful swell of breast screamed she was all woman. As for simple, that description was totally inappropriate. Toni had layers—layers, Emma knew, once peeled away, would reveal new, more complex ones underneath.

While still surprised she found features so different to Justine's

210

not only attractive, but downright sexy, Emma could not deny what she knew to be true. "Yes, she is very pretty."

"Shocking cook though."

There was no question about that one. "Terrible."

Toni stabbed at a muffin crumb with her finger. "I can cook," she said offhandedly.

Toni's efforts to elevate herself above Justine were incredibly sweet, but totally unwarranted. "Would you like me to arrange a bake-off so you can prove it?"

The repeated attempt to get the dry bit of crumb to stick to her finger came to a halt. Toni shot a glance across the table, color staining her cheeks in her obvious jealousy. "It's my green eyes," she smiled sheepishly. "It's an inherited trait."

"Come on." Emma scraped her chair from the table. "While we're on the subject of color, I'll introduce you to Malibu."

"Your black cat."

"Uh-huh."

"And you'll show me the blue room?"

Emma was sure every drop of blood shot straight down to her groin. The "blue room" was the name Toni gave Emma's bedroom when it was described in chat. "Maybe."

Toni concentrated on washing her hands with the pump-pack soap she found next to the basin.

Ordinarily, this being her first visit to a new bathroom, Toni would have studied her surroundings a bit more carefully. Ordinarily, she would have noticed that Emma used the same deodorant as her, that the pump soap, while being her preferred brand, was of a different fragrance, and that all the towels not only matched the bathmat but were hung neatly on their railings. All this and more Toni would have noticed. Had she been feeling particularly inquisitive, she might even have had a peek in the bathroom cabinet.

But right now, the aesthetics of Emma's bathroom were insignificant. Instead, Toni's attention was focused on analyzing how the evening had strayed so far from her expectations. Nothing had gone *wrong* exactly. The tour of the house, which did include a peek inside the "blue room," ended back in the kitchen. Toni's offer to assist with dinner was refused, so she sat at the table, watching Emma in her preparations. Emma was a calm cook. There was no hurry to her movements, no furious chopping or clanging of pots and pans, just a series of tasks efficiently performed. The result, chicken fillets accompanied by roasted Mediterranean vegetables tossed with rocket and olive oil, was delicious, and Toni gave it the praise it deserved. Their conversation throughout the meal flowed easily enough. There were a couple of periods of silence, but they weren't extended to the point of being uncomfortable. Their talk continued through the stacking of plates next to the sink and the journey into the lounge room.

They'd demolished the bottle of white over dinner, so the bottle of red was next targeted for consumption. Emma delved into her buffet unit for some fresh wineglasses while Toni pondered where to sit. She decided on the couch, a two-seater.

Nice and cozy.

"This is a good wine." Emma studied the label before cutting the metal around the cork. She smiled in Toni's direction as she twisted the corkscrew. "We did a tasting of it a couple of years ago at the wine club. It was good then, but they said at the time it would be fabulous if laid down for a few years. So this should be bloody fantastic."

Toni was surrounded by wine buffs; Cathy was a member of the same wine club as Emma. But Toni, while appreciating a good wine, considered herself more a quaffer than a connoisseur. She mentally thanked the wine merchant for his recommendation, nodded in agreement they should leave it to breathe a while and waited in anticipation of Emma joining her on the couch.

But she didn't.

Toni took a mental step back when Emma lifted herself from her kneeling position in front of the coffee table and hoisted herself onto the single easy chair immediately behind.

And what was worse, she stayed there. They talked of wine, and they how Emma had met Cathy through the wine club. Then they talked of Toni and the gym and Emma and her running. Toni explained how she always went to the gym after work because she was *so* not a morning person, and Emma explained how she often got up even earlier than she had to for her early starts at the practice so she could take Kayisha for a run. Not because she had to, but because she wanted to.

Toni was on the verge of saying, "So, apart from the morning thing we're perfect for each other," when Emma said, "Well, that's it then. Night owls are from Mars, morning people are from Venus. And never the twain shall meet."

Toni thought she had Emma's dry humor down pat, but this time, as she tried to read the intention behind the remark, she couldn't. Maybe it was because she was so damn far away from the woman, she couldn't see if that was a twinkle in her eye or just a reflection of the floor lamp that softly lit the room. Toni assumed the worst, and she assumed the worst because the woman was so damn far away and had made no moves to be otherwise throughout the whole evening. Throughout the whole evening Toni received nothing more than a brief hand-squeeze when she was pulled from her kitchen chair to go on a tour of the house.

So Toni escaped to the bathroom and now, her hand-washing complete, stood staring at herself in the mirror, analyzing the evening.

Green eyes stared back. Maybe it was the green-eyed monster that frightened Emma off. Jealousy was an ugly emotion and there she had been, sitting at the kitchen table going green over a neighbor. A neighbor who was not only outwardly straight, but engaged to be married.

Toni grimaced as another thought occurred. Why had she made the comment about wanting to see the blue room? In online chat, her naming of the bedroom hadn't been altogether due to the color of the walls. Dovetail that conversation into the admission she had spent three weeks having sex with a woman she had no

213

emotional attachment to, and it was no wonder Emma was wary. She probably thought Toni some sort of predator, just waiting to pounce.

Finally, Toni took attention from her eyes her skin. To her horror a dried blister, just near her left ear, was at the point of falling off. It hung like a leaf about to drop in autumn. Toni pulled at it, but it wasn't ready to budge. She stared morosely at the blackish, protruding lump. No one in her right mind would be attracted to someone who looked like she escaped from the infectious disease control unit.

Toni decided Emma had decided she was just not interested. Being too polite to tell Toni outright, Emma would see the evening out, but once Toni left she would shut the door, happy to see the back of her.

Toni took a deep breath as she opened the bathroom door, readying herself for the return to the lounge room.

"Thanks for a wonderful meal." Toni stood at the lounge room entrance. She noticed that in her absence Emma had managed to peel herself from her single seat and now knelt in front of the stereo, flipping through a stack of CDs. She waited for Emma to turn around before stretching her arms into the air, forcing a yawn. "But I'm pretty tired. I think I should get going home."

"Oh." Emma stood with little effort, brushing at the knees of her jeans. Her eyes darted to the nearly full bottle of wine on the coffee table and the almost untouched glasses. They also glanced quickly to the clock hanging to the right of the computer Emma used in the hours where she became Kayisha. Finally her nervous glance rested on Toni. "Okay."

Tell me you'd rather I stayed! Toni mentally screamed at Emma. *Tell me you really don't want me to go!*

Emma didn't say either of those things. So Toni left. She sat in the car, hand on the indicator lever, watching the house. Finally, Toni flipped the indicator lever down and pulled into the traffic-free street.

❧

214

Emma stared at the empty couch as the throb of the BMW engine faded into the distance. She wasn't quite sure what happened over the course of the evening, but she sure as hell knew it didn't pan out the way she had hoped.

FallenAngel and Rabbit and their disastrous meeting came to mind. "Lack of chemistry"—that's what Toni had said about their failed rendezvous. Maybe that was it. Maybe the energy Emma felt in Toni's company was all one-sided, maybe the meeting in the flesh was one big disappointment and Toni was just too polite to say so. After all, Toni was the one who suddenly went cold last night. At the time Emma assumed Toni was also so overwhelmed by the sheer pull of their attraction she needed to stand aside from it for a little while, to let the enormity of it sink in. It had not even crossed Emma's mind Toni felt nothing, or worse, repelled. Emma's insides shriveled in mortification. Toni had said no to a night out on the town. Maybe the invitation to dinner had been accepted purely out of manners.

But Emma was certain she had read Toni's reaction to Justine as one of jealousy. Why would she be jealous if she felt nothing? She'd as much as admitted it with her green-eye comment. Were Emma's instincts so off the mark she totally misread the tenor of the entire evening?

All evening she'd been in some almost indescribable half state. Half of her was at ease, finding the woman who sat at her kitchen table incredibly easy to talk to, articulate and entertaining. The other half was tightly wound, unnerved by her mere presence. Her hands were especially distracting. Toni used them as an extension of her voice, punctuating her words with expansive gestures. Emma couldn't keep her eyes off them. At one point, when chopping up an eggplant, she nearly sliced her fingers because she was so busy imagining those hands expressing themselves all over her body. She avoided damage, but to be safe, slowed her slicing and dicing considerably. Controlled movements in the rest of her preparations enabled her to avoid personal injury or breakage of crockery, but to her mind it was a wonder she managed to get a meal served up at all.

The consumption of dinner was unhurried and surprisingly relaxed. The downing of a bottle of wine between them no doubt helped lubricate the conversation. It also heightened Emma's desire to reach out, take hold of those expressive hands and press them to her lips. She resisted the urge. If Toni wanted to take things slowly, she was not going to foist herself upon her.

That's why, although she desperately wanted to, she didn't place herself next to Toni on the couch. Instead she sat in a chair opposite, every cell in her body calling Toni to make some sort of move. No move was made. Despite them both inching forward in their seats and pointing their bodies directly at each other, nothing happened. Instead, Toni begged a need for the bathroom, stayed there an awfully long time, then announced her desire to go home.

Emma slumped into the couch and stared at the bottle of red and two glasses left abandoned on the coffee table. Maybe Toni sat forward in her seat because she wanted to make her escape. Maybe it was only Emma who moved forward because she wanted to leap straight onto Toni's lap.

"Hi, girl." Emma scratched Kayisha's ruff and bent to nuzzle her head into her companion's. "You still love me, don't you?"

Kai's fur smelled fresh and clean, evidence of her morning bath. Kayisha had complained at the treatment, it coming a full two days early, Emma wanting her at her best for meeting Toni.

Kayisha grumbled quietly when the cuddle was halted. She followed Emma to the lounge room window, nosing her snout into Emma's hand as Emma stared out into the night. The floor lamp was on so all Emma really stared at was a reflection of herself. When she met her own eyes her mantra of less than a week ago replayed in her head. *I am in control of my own destiny.*

"Stop saying stupid things to yourself," Emma reprimanded herself as sat heavily onto the seat Toni had vacated. "You can't control how someone feels about you." From her vantage point, the computer Emma had spent so many hours in front of was in plain view. Were she and Toni really just more victims of its virtual reality? Were they just another FallenAngel and Rabbit?

Emma really didn't know. The signals she received over the last twenty-four hours were so mixed they were impossible to interpret.

Destiny and who controlled it—the thought again ran through Emma's mind as she headed for the kitchen. "Act in haste, repent at leisure" was her next thought and it almost stopped her from retrieving the car keys that sat on her kitchen bench.

"She who hesitates is lost." Emma actually spoke out loud as she grabbed for the keys and trotted to the front door, at the same time wondering if talking to oneself in a series of quotes was normal.

She decided it probably wasn't.

Fifteen minutes later Emma knocked on Toni's front door. When the door swung open, Emma didn't even give Toni the chance to say hello before she took a deep breath and started talking, "I know I'm making a habit of landing on your doorstep late at night but you forgot something when you left so I came over to give it to you."

Toni looked down to Emma's hands, empty except for her car keys. "What did I forget?"

Emma smiled weakly. "Me."

There was no immediate response and Emma had a sudden image of a cursor blinking on an empty screen. Maybe her intellectual dissection of the night had been correct and Toni was not interested. Her gut told her to press on. After all, she'd come this far. If she was making a fool of herself, she may as well make a good job of it.

"But if you left me there on purpose, I can always just take me back home again."

"I thought—" Toni lifted a hand to run through her hair but stopped, instead pulling Emma through the door and closing it quickly.

Emma thought maybe Virgil was trying for another escape, but a glance down the hallway revealed no feline in the vicinity. Warm hands cupped her cheeks, pulling her attention back to human height. Green eyes met hers and long lashes fluttered shut. Emma was still not sure what Toni had thought, but if this was any indication, it was all good.

Emma leaned into the kiss, one hand settling into the curve of Toni's waist as the other thrust car keys into her jeans pocket. Dear God. The sensation of Toni's tongue dancing across her own, combined with the press of Toni's hands against her cheeks, left her feeling at once faint, yet very much aware, very alive. All the fears of the evening were swept away, replaced by a fierce desire to be as close to this woman as possible. Emma wanted to step inside Toni's skin, feel what she felt, see what she saw, to know everything about her.

"I want . . ." Emma slid lips, moist and puffy from desire, across Toni's cheek, to her ear. "Please—show me your bedroom," she said breathlessly.

Emma heard the sharp intake of breath, felt the body that had molded so well into hers, tighten and tense. For an awful moment Emma thought herself trapped in some weird *Groundhog Day* world, where she was forced to live the same day over and over until she got it right.

"Toni?"

"I'm sorry." Toni looked down to the floor, shuffling her feet nervously.

Exasperated, frustrated, Emma tilted Toni's chin with her forefinger. "I don't understand. What's wrong?"

Toni just shook her head. "I'm sorry."

"Am I moving too fast? I . . . Toni, I'm getting some very mixed messages here."

"Please, Emma. It's not you. It's me."

Well, that was one of the oldest brush-offs in the book. Emma was disappointed Toni would use such a line. She had thought her bigger than that. "What a crock, Toni. If you're not interested then just say so, but don't patronize me."

Toni's eyes widened in surprise, then her face fell and her eyes filled. "Emma, believe me, please." She pointed to her face. "It's got nothing to do with you. It's me." She stabbed at the skin near her left ear. "It's this."

A good few seconds passed before Emma twigged onto what Toni was trying to say. It took that long because the thought had not previously crossed her mind. "You're worried that I'm worried over a few spots?" she said incredulously.

When Toni nodded, Emma was so relieved she burst out laughing. "You silly. A few spots are nothing. And besides, they're disappearing daily. Not that I'd mind if they didn't," she continued quickly, thinking Toni may have some other hidden, but permanent, blemish she'd then start fretting over.

"I know they're disappearing." As if proving a point, Toni scratched at her forearm. "They're falling off everywhere."

"That's good, isn't it?"

"I mean"—Toni shuffled her feet again before meeting Emma's eyes—"they're falling off *everywhere*."

"Oh." Emma grasped the full meaning of Toni's words. She nodded wisely. "I see."

"It's not funny."

"I didn't say it was." Despite trying not to, Emma grinned. She really couldn't help it; she was bursting with the knowledge Toni at least wanted to continue what they had started. Even if she wouldn't continue it right now. "Can I see your bedroom now?"

"But I just told you—"

"No funny business, I promise," Emma interrupted, holding her hands in the air in surrender. "I just want to be able to picture where you sleep. Okay?"

CHAPTER SEVENTEEN

"I'll fax those figures to you as soon as I can." Toni rose to shake the hand of Alexandria, a sixty-five-year-old ex-army nurse who, over the course of her working life, had amassed an impressive residential property portfolio. An imposing woman, she was not one to suffer fools lightly. Toni knew her to be soft as marshmallow on the inside, but her often gruff exterior could be quite intimidating. It was for that exact reason she had not handed her account over to Julie. "Thanks again for rescheduling."

"No trouble at all." Alexandria's eyes darted over Toni's face. "I'm glad you're feeling better. Although it looks like you didn't get it too bad. My nephew got chicken pox as an adult, and quite frankly, he looked like crappola for twelve months afterward. But I reckon he probably picked himself silly."

Toni smiled. Alexandria wasn't one to mince words. If she thought Toni looked like "crappola" she probably would have told her so within the first five minutes of their appointment. "It was tempting, I tell you. I had to bind my hands behind my back."

"It worked." Also not one to decline from physical contact, Alexandria ran her palm down Toni's cheek, "My little Macedonian is positively glowing. Is there some woman gave you special treatment on your sick bed?"

" 'Bye, Alex. See you next week." Toni ushered Alexandria out of her office with a laugh. She might tell her sometime soon, but not right now. Now was Toni's time to savor. She settled behind her desk, gladly noting she had a full hour before her next, and last, appointment of the day. As well as giving ample opportunity to pull the files she needed, it provided a bit of uninterrupted time to think, to dream, to remember. Toni swiveled her chair to the expanse of plate glass. Normally she would have a commanding view of the city, but today the rain that had fallen steadily since midmorning shrouded the cityscape. Still, Toni hauled her feet onto her low bookcase, put her hands behind her head and turned her attention outside the window. She smiled as drops cascaded down the glass. Nothing, especially a little rain, could put a damper on today.

Today was Thursday, a full week since her first dinner at Emma's place. She'd had dinner there three more times since then. They'd seen each other every day, replacing their online chats by spending alternate evenings at each other's homes. A couple of nights they ventured out—once to an art-house movie, and once to an offbeat performance at some independent theater in the middle of the Perth Cultural Centre. Still very self-conscious, Toni was grateful both events were staged in intimate venues with correspondingly small audiences.

On the nights they stayed in, one hour just slid into another. A tremendous amount of time was spent talking, their list of topics to be discussed seemingly infinite. Sometimes they watched television; sometimes they listened to music. They took Kayisha for long evening walks and they played with Virgil, tossing her cloth ball around the house and exclaiming delightedly when she trotted back to them with it in her mouth. Whatever they did, every evening ended in the same way: with lots and lots of kissing.

221

Toni could not recall ever spending so much time kissing a woman without it turning into sex. It was nice. It was more than nice. It was glorious. It was also frustrating beyond belief. Yes, Toni was quite aware she had inflicted the restriction upon herself, and on occasions, when the heat between them was building, the desire to take things to the next level was so strong she physically ached. But each morning, when she again had to get the Dust Buster and vacuum the bits of black left on the bedclothes, she thanked the Goddess for her restraint.

Just how long Emma's continued patience could hold was a source of constant concern and she found herself apologizing again and again.

"Shh, Toni." With face flushed and eyelids heavy, Emma's breath would wash over Toni in short, labored puffs and she'd return to Toni's mouth, temporarily ridding her fears, but fanning the flames of her desire.

Each and every night Toni turned to her own hand for release. "Emma," she'd call out in the darkness of her room, her bed all of a sudden very lonely.

But last night, when she called Emma's name, a voice responded, "I'm here."

The previous morning had been a joyous one, Toni standing with Dust Buster in hand, bedclothes pulled down, sucking up the one black bit sloughed off during the night. Once the sheets and her Tigger pajamas were thrown into the washing machine, her naked twirl in front of the mirror revealed that one black bit to be the last of many. She'd hardly been able to contain herself during the three phone calls she and Emma exchanged yesterday and she bit her tongue many times during their walk with Kayisha last evening. It wasn't until they were settled on the couch after dinner that Toni made it known things had changed.

They had been studying the brochure for the state symphony orchestra's winter season, but the brochure and list of concerts circled for attendance were long forgotten. Both had kicked off their shoes. Toni sat at one end of the couch, legs stretched across both seats, Emma sat astride her, one hand on the backrest, the other on the armrest. Toni was being kissed in Emma's inimitable way: slowly, methodically and thoroughly. As was usual, her kisses were driving Toni slowly, methodically and thoroughly mad.

In the limited space afforded by Emma's position, Toni scrabbled with her clothing, undoing the top two buttons of her button-down shirt. She took one of Emma's hands and placed it under the material, over her left breast. Emma drew back from Toni, eyes darting, questioning.

At first Toni thought Emma had misunderstood, her hand resting lightly without moving. Then . . . when Emma returned to Toni's mouth, her kiss held an increased intent and ever so slowly her palm brushed then pressed. Toni's nipple reacted immediately and Emma responded with a fevered kiss, her fingers stroking, teasing and tweaking until Toni could stand no more. She wrestled with her other buttons, pulling them loose and drawing back the material of her shirt to lay her breasts bare, open, for Emma.

Again Emma left Toni's mouth, gaze wandering over the gifts Toni was offering. "Oh." She breathed. "Magnificent." Her head descended and Toni moaned as the sudden, unexpected attention shot waves of pleasure to every pulse point. The pleasure escalated as hands and mouth expertly combined to make love to Toni's breasts. Fingers massaged and fingernails trailed, lips encased flesh and a warm, wet tongue flicked and swirled.

"Please." Toni pulled Emma back upward, her breasts so engorged with sensation it seemed all the nerve endings in her body had converged in the delicate tissue.

"Too much?"

"No." Toni greeted lips, puffy and red, with her own. "You make me . . . Oh . . ." A groan escaped the moment her tongue tipped Emma's. "Not nearly enough."

Vaguely she heard someone say something about taking someone to bed, but she didn't know if it was her own voice she heard, or if it was Emma's. Regardless, the suggestion went unheeded as the task of removing clothing became the new priority. Even that was largely unsuccessful. They got as far as tugging Emma's jumper over her head and popping the buttons open on each other's jeans. That was about it. The zipper on Emma's well-worn and faded Levis provided little resistance against Toni's hand and she slid inside, her already racing pulse quickening with the evidence of Emma's desire. In the moment of contact she saw Emma's eyes widen and her mouth open in a silent "Yes." Then she saw her eyes shut tight, her face a picture of ascetic beauty as she moved in time with Toni's thrusting fingers.

It all happened very quickly, and when a strong, sure hand slid inside Toni's jeans, Toni's release of pent-up energy was just as fast, her body exploding against Emma's in no time at all. She collapsed back into the couch, heart pounding, breath coming in ragged gasps.

"Are you okay?" Emma ran fingers through Toni's fringe, pushing it back from her forehead. The pleased smile that accompanied the gesture told Toni that Emma already knew she was more than okay.

Toni nodded, pulling Emma down. "Oh, yes." She closed her eyes instinctively for the kiss and she shuddered yet again at the touch of Emma's tongue against her own.

Now, a fresh shudder swept through Toni as memory again warmed her blood. She closed her eyes, allowing the indulgence of once more reliving the night. She'd already relived portions of it on the morning drive from Emma's place to her own, recounted it to Virgil while she sat on the floor and watched her crunch on breakfast, and relived portions over again as she tried somewhat unsuccessfully to concentrate in the limited time before her first appointment. Today, true concentration was impossible. Images of Emma would rush to the forefront of Toni's thoughts, and she'd find herself sighing, feeling for the world like she could just melt into a little puddle of happiness on the floor.

The night came back to her in a series of erotic vignettes: the two of them falling together into the bedroom, legs and arms tangled as they made slow, crab-stepping progress toward the bed. The fire in Emma's eyes as she pulled Toni with her onto the mattress, her knee rising to provide a fabulous, yet torturously teasing pressure between Toni's legs. The warm tones of Emma's skin as she turned to lie on her stomach, bathed in the soft light of the bedside lamp, dimmed to the point of almost-dark. Toni's own hand as it traveled Emma's spine, across the wonderful swell of buttocks and down the back of Emma's legs. The breath that caught in Toni's throat when the legs parted and hips rose to give Toni's fingers access to slick, willing heat. Much later, the sensation of erect nipples grazing over her skin as Emma slithered first down the length of Toni's body, then back again, with a long, leg-trembling stop in the middle. And later again, the taste of Emma—so deliciously intricate, complex and unique.

Toni felt her insides shift at the memory of it all. All the hours that passed between them before finally succumbing to exhausted sleep.

Toni awoke sometime in the middle of the night, momentarily disorientated by unfamiliar surrounds. Then realization dawned and she smiled, softly saying Emma's name just to hear the sound of it. She wasn't expecting a response, but one came.

"I'm here."

"You're so far away." Toni stretched her arm across the bed, finding Emma's waist.

Emma laughed at the gross exaggeration and shunted across the mattress. She rested her head on the same pillow as Toni, facing her. "Not anymore."

Neither got any more sleep for quite a while.

When Toni awoke the second time, the light that filtered through her still closed eyelids revealed it to be morning. She groaned and threw her hand over the side of the bed, wishing it were still dark. Her arm landed on something warm and furry. Something warm and furry that panted and, *urghh* . . . had doggie breath. Toni's eyes flew open to find Kayisha with front paws on the bed, black, glistening nose right in front of Toni's face. If Toni thought Kayisha had smiled at her before, this time she looked like she was positively grinning.

"She likes you." Emma's voice came from behind Kayisha. She

held a mug in each hand, and apart from a sleeveless T-shirt, she was naked. The T-shirt wasn't quite long enough to completely cover a thatch of light brown hair. Despite not even being properly awake, Toni felt the pull of lust in her groin. Emma's voice was gently commanding, "Kayisha, paws off the bed, please."

Kayisha did as told and Emma sat on the edge of the bed. One of the mugs was handed over and Toni yawned a thank-you. "Oh, dear." She glanced to the clock on the bedside table. It was eight o'clock. Luckily, her house was only fifteen minutes' drive from Emma's. Still, she had only one hour to get home, shower, dress, feed Virgil and the doves and drive to the office. Her first appointment wasn't until eleven, but nine was her official starting time. "I'm going to have to get my skates on."

Emma smiled over the rim of her mug. "I guess there's nothing I could do to persuade you to take the day off."

"Absolutely nothing." Toni shook her head vehemently, at the same time knowing it would take very little to persuade her. She purposely avoided looking at Emma's lips. They would be quite persuasive. She couldn't let her gaze drift down past the hem of Emma's T-shirt either. That would likely make her stay. Then there were those hazel eyes. Toni remembered looking deep into them last night, as they knelt naked in front of each other, touching in places . . . The coffee mug was relegated to the bedside table. "But I could be persuaded to be a little late."

Toni arrived at the office outlandishly late, even for her. It was all Emma's fault for being so downright sexy. As soon as Toni stepped into the reception, Sue tried to eke an explanation for the tardiness, but Toni refused to be drawn into conversation, begging the need to get ready for her eleven o'clock appointment. She doubted it would take Sue long to put two and two together anyway. The woman could sniff out a new romance at one hundred paces.

Toni smiled when she again opened her eyes to the world as seen from her office window. The rain had stopped, but rivulets of water still ran down the plate-glass window. A streak of blue sky was emerging between the clouds that lay over the city like a blanket. The blue reminded Toni of the color of Emma's bedroom walls.

"Ahh, Emma." Toni swung back to face the desk and leaned her chin on one hand, dreamily doodling little love hearts on the lined pad that lay in front of her. She imagined her fairytale coming to life. In the form of a woman who was not only willing to discuss and debate every topic under the sun, but who—as Toni had discovered after the cinema on Sunday night—liked her burgers with the lot. Bacon and double cheese.

A knock on her half-open door jerked her back to reality. Julie stood at the entrance, two coffee mugs in hand. She held one up as she said, "I thought you may like an afternoon pick-me-up."

"Thanks." Toni nodded to one of the chairs on the other side of the desk. She folded her arms over her doodles as a mug was placed next to her elbow.

"It's technically Marian's last day tomorrow," Julie said as she frowned quizzically at the now covered paper. "But I thought I'd check to see if you're ready to take on a full load yet. If not, I'll ask her to come in next week."

Toni had been eased back into work with a light schedule, Julie arranging only a smattering of appointments, well spaced throughout the day. It was a thoughtful move Toni took full advantage of, spending a good amount of her free time in long phone contact with Emma. Or thinking about Emma. Or, as with this morning, being with Emma. Toni looked rather guiltily at Julie. "I'll be ready to get stuck right into it next week."

"Are you sure? Sue told me you came in awfully late today. I thought maybe you weren't feeling too good." Julie looked pointedly at Toni's still covered pad. "Unless, of course, it was something else that kept you away."

Damn Sue. Toni cringed as her cheeks flamed. "Has the office gossip sent you in to do her dirty work?"

"Yeah, right." Julie folded her arms as if offended at the thought, but she broke into a grin. "You've got her going crazy out there wondering what's going on." She leaned forward. "Are you going to tell me her name?"

The question did not come as a surprise. Before Toni returned to work, Julie had persisted with her daily phone calls, still determined to keep her fed and entertained. Toni just wasn't a good liar and during last Wednesday's call had admitted someone "special" was occupying her evenings. The admission was difficult, primarily because at that stage Toni was still in the dark about Kayisha's identity. So, not only did she have to admit she met the special someone online, but that she had not yet met her offline. Nor did she know her real name, her age or what she looked like.

"How do you know she's a she?" Julie had asked.

"I . . ." Shit, that was something that never crossed Toni's mind. "I just know. She expresses herself like a woman."

"Uh-huh." Julie's tone told exactly what she thought of that argument. "Well, just be careful, Toni. I'll ring you again tomorrow."

"Okay," Toni had said guiltily, the knowledge that Julie was going home to an empty apartment—she and Anna still not having sorted their differences—weighing heavily on her mind. She almost told Julie to come over after all, but the part of her that could not stay away from Kayisha, and the words she relayed via a computer screen, stilled her voice.

Now, however, Toni was bursting to say that glorious name out loud again.

"Her name's Emma."

"Emma," Julie repeated softly. "Should I know her?"

"I don't think so. She's one of Lisa's friends. She fixed Virgil's tail."

"She's a vet?"

"Yes."

"So you were speaking to Virgil's vet and you didn't know it?"

"Yes and no. She's not Virgil's regular vet. She was a locum at the time."

Julie continued with her twenty questions and managed to extract the entire story. Eventually she seemed to run out of things to ask, and even though her coffee was long consumed, she made no move to leave.

Toni studied the young woman sitting across from her. She seemed to want to say something but didn't quite know how to get started. "How're things in your world, Julie?"

Julie picked up one of Toni's business cards, turning it over and over in one hand. "Anna came over last night. We talked."

So there *had* been a development in the Julie and Anna story. "And?"

"And she's up for selection in the national team."

"Oh." This did not sound like good news. Not for Julie anyhow.

"So she'll be going to Canberra next month."

"Oh," Toni repeated.

Julie blinked quickly. "If she gets selected she'll probably have to move over there."

"You'll miss her," Toni said matter-of-factly.

"I've been missing her since the day we met." A rueful smile crossed Julie's features. "Now there'll just be a greater distance to miss her over."

"You could follow her."

Julie shook her head. "It'd just be the same shit, different location. The reality is, I come second to that damn floating ball."

Toni nodded sympathetically. "I'm sorry."

The phone rang and Toni glanced quickly to the caller display. Her expression must have advertised the caller's effect on her heartbeat. Julie gave a knowing look as she rose from her seat. "I'll let you get that."

"Thanks." Toni's heart went out to Julie as she watched her leave. Then her heart pulled in a completely different manner as she picked up the receiver. "Hi, Emma."

"Toni . . . I've just had a phone call."

"From?" Toni prompted when the line went silent.

"From Frank."

"Frank?" Toni knew she should know who Frank was but her brain couldn't make the connection.

"From the practice in Albany."

"And?" Every muscle in her body tensed. *Please God,* she prayed, *let it be good news.*

It wasn't.

"And I've been offered the job."

229

Toni gripped tightly onto the handset. "Did you accept?"

"I said I wanted a bit of time to think it over."

Toni closed her eyes as hope rose, just a little. "And what are you thinking?"

There was a pause on the line. "I'm thinking it's a great opportunity. But I'm also thinking it's a big move. I'll have to completely relocate."

"It *is* a big move," Toni echoed softly. She opened her eyes to rid the unbidden image that flashed under her lids—the image of Emma astride a horse; donned in the ubiquitous faded jeans and khaki, riding into the distance. Leaving her.

"Yes, well . . . I just called to let you know. We can talk about it tonight?"

"Sure, Em." The flatness in Toni's tone sounded obvious, even to her own ear. "Congratulations, by the way."

"Thanks, Toni. Speak soon."

The phone rang again just ten minutes later. Toni grabbed for it, the display announcing it was Emma again. Had she thought it over already? "Hi."

"Toni, I've just had another call."

Maybe Frank had changed his mind. It was a selfish thought, but Toni's heart leapt at the notion. "Yes?"

"From a practice I applied to in Sydney."

Christ. Toni felt sick. Emma had not told her of any interstate applications. "And they want you too?"

"Not yet. But I've got a phone interview tomorrow morning, before I go to work. Because of the time difference between Perth and Sydney it'll start early. At six-thirty. Toni, I know we agreed I'd come to your place, but it'd just be a bit easier if I stayed home tonight. Do you mind coming over again?"

"No. No. I don't mind. I'll see you around seven."

The receiver was placed quietly onto its cradle and Toni stared at her page of love hearts. Albany. Sydney. Toni tore the page from the pad and folded it into four. The home she chose for it—a zip-up pocket deep in her briefcase—already contained an item. Toni pulled out the Snickers wrapper she'd placed there weeks prior.

Immediately Heather's words came rushing back: "Sweetheart, the fairytale doesn't exist. It's just that, a fairytale."

Toni swiveled her chair back to the window. The streak of bedroom-blue sky had expanded, the clouds parting and the sun breaking through. Toni decided it must be a sign. A sign that, were it written in some fairytale, would be seen as portent to something good.

Toni screwed up the Snickers wrapper and threw it into the trash.

At twenty-eight past six the next morning Toni asked Emma, "You nervous?"

"A bit." Emma sat fidgeting in her seat next to the phone.

Toni kissed the top of her head. "You'll be fine."

"Thanks." Emma smiled weakly.

When the phone rang, Toni left Emma alone, heading for the bedroom and her overnight bag. She'd shower and dress before going home to feed Virgil. Given the early hour, she'd have plenty of time for a cuddle and a play—if Virgil wasn't sulking too badly at Toni's absence two nights in a row.

The water quickly flowed hot and Toni stepped under the stream. She'd only just finished soaping down when the screen slid open.

"That was fast." Toni was fully expecting to be blowing Emma a kiss on her way out the front door. Then again, she had spent quite a bit of time with the bar of soap in hand, just staring at the tiles.

"Mmm." Already dressed for the day, Emma held the screen open, unperturbed at the water that splashed onto her clothes. "I told them straight up what Frank was offering and it seems they can't afford me."

Yay! Toni mentally cheered. But while Sydney was now off the agenda, Albany still loomed large on the horizon. From last night's discussion, she could see why the offer was being so seriously considered. Her eyes had opened wide when Emma whispered the cash component of the salary package in her ear.

"And you should see the equipment they've got, Toni. It's amazing." Toni could only nod. This type of opportunity didn't knock often.

But neither did the offer of being part owner of a practice.

Toni learned of Tricia's offer of a partnership when Emma spoke of the Albany job giving her the chance to save enough to be considered for a business loan. Twelve months of solid saving would put her in good stead, she estimated. Toni blinked at this new information and her mind began to race, looking for some faster solution to the funding problem.

Cathy came to mind.

"No." Emma shook her head, having apparently already considered that option. "It's too close to home. What if everything went pear-shaped and I couldn't pay it back?" Toni argued that was unlikely to happen, and even if things did go pear-shaped, then Cathy would be much less likely to foreclose than a heartless bank. She also pointed out that in twelve months' time, Tricia's offer may have expired. But Emma was adamant. "No, Toni. I won't do it . . . And don't you go getting any ideas about talking to Cathy on my behalf," she warned. Toni reluctantly promised, although that was exactly what she had thought of doing.

Emma's stance on borrowing money from friends was admirable, and probably very wise, but right now, Toni resented the fact a seemingly simple solution was being ignored. If only she had a large spare stash of cash, she'd have insisted Emma take it. Anything to keep the woman she loved in close proximity.

Toni blinked away the drops of water that fell from her fringe onto her lashes, surprised and caught off-guard by the admission she had just made to herself. Her head told her it was too soon, too fast, for such feelings. But when she met Emma's eyes and felt her heart swell to the point of bursting, she knew with surety, however fast love had come, it was here to stay.

The realization sent a sudden rush of vertigo, and Toni swayed slightly under the shower's stream.

"Are you okay, Toni?" Worry crossed Emma's features and a steadying hand reached to grab her shoulder.

"I'm fine." Toni was also suddenly desperate to share this new knowledge. "Emma, I—" The words were cut short, mentally stashed in her briefcase, along with her page of love hearts. The words were the truth, but saying them under these circumstances would only sound manipulative. Instead she said, "Emma, I'm glad you're not going to Sydney."

"So am I."

Toni stepped into the towel Emma held open for her. "I guess this means you're going to take the Albany job."

Emma wrapped the towel around Toni. "It's a great opportunity," she said softly.

"I wish they grew racehorses in Perth."

Emma's deliciously throaty chuckle surrounded Toni, and she found herself enveloped in Emma's arms. "Dear God, Toni. You are just gorgeous."

Not gorgeous enough to keep Emma in Perth though, it seemed. Once dressed, Toni left for home with a heavy heart. Emma did not say it outright, but Toni knew that sometime in the very near future she would be ringing Albany to say yes, she would be taking up the position.

Sure enough, when Emma arrived at Toni's house that evening she had not long been off the phone to Frank.

"How long before you leave?" Despite having just taken a sip of the bourbon Emma brought with her, Toni felt as if her mouth was again thick with uncooked blueberry muffin flour.

Emma raised her gaze from the tumbler she rolled between her palms. "Six weeks."

No! Toni stopped the words from crossing her lips by taking another sip of her bourbon, this time a large one. *Don't go. I love you. Stay here with me.* Knowing she could not keep locking away her words once alcohol loosened her tongue, Toni set the tumbler aside. "Oh, well," she said brightly. "At least that gives me plenty of time to arrange a ding-dong of a going-away party for you."

Emma just gave a weak little smile and poured another two fingers of bourbon into her tumbler.

Toni didn't give her the opportunity to sink it, rounding the kitchen table and prising Emma's fingers from her glass. She set the glass well into the middle of the table and straddled Emma's lap. "We'll have party pies and sausage rolls, and lots of balloons and streamers. And party games."

Toni got the reaction she was looking for, Emma smiling. "Sounds very adult."

"What do you mean? Isn't naked Twister adult enough for you?"

"*Naked* Twister?"

"Mmm." Toni nodded somberly. "Don't tell me you've never played?"

"Well, no."

Toni laughed at the dubious expression that crossed Emma's features. "I'm kidding you, silly. Although"—she leaned in to brush her lips along Emma's jaw line—"I'd play it with you anytime." They traveled to the edge of Emma's mouth. "Just you and me though. No one else is invited."

Toni interpreted Emma's soft whimper as agreement and covered Emma's mouth with her own. With each kiss came increased awareness that in six weeks Emma would be far away, and with this awareness came an urgent need to make each embrace count. Toni uttered her own incomprehensible whimper as their kiss deepened. The future and what it would be taking away was temporarily forgotten; for the moment nothing else mattered but the here and now.

The here and now saw Emma rise from her seat with Toni still attached to her lap and deposit her onto the table's polished wooden surface. Another whimper escaped from Toni as hands pushed on her behind, drawing her closer, encouraging her legs to wrap around Emma's hips. Standing, Emma had the advantage of height, and she eased Toni backwards onto the table.

We're going to do it on the kitchen table. Toni first giggled at the thought, then all of a sudden Emma's lips were at her throat and her humor evaporated, replaced by a surge of lust that made her gasp. Her legs tightened around Emma's hips and she thrust herself against her, squirming to find the position that would allow greatest contact. Finding it, she flung one arm out, looking for the edge of the table to grip onto.

Her forearm touched cold glass. Then there was a loud clatter as the bourbon bottle tipped over. Startled into inaction, Toni could only turn her head and watch as the bottle rolled to the edge of the table. She was mentally preparing for the crash when another arm—Emma's—shot out and caught the bottle by the neck just as it was about to disappear over the edge.

What a woman! Toni was impressed by this second display of Emma's lightening-quick reflexes. She looked up into the eyes of hazel and smiled. "I bet you couldn't do that again in a hurry."

The bottle was placed well away from Toni, next to her discarded glass. "I'm not going to give you the opportunity to let me try."

Toni found her hands clasped and she was pulled back into a sitting position.

"Toni." Emma slid her lips across Toni's cheek and whispered in her ear, "Take me to bed."

Maybe it was the words themselves, maybe it was the tone that delivered them, or maybe it was the warm breath that accompanied the request. Whatever it was, it left Toni weak with desire, and she could only nod wordlessly as she eased off the table and led Emma by the hand out of the kitchen.

The trip to the bedroom was long, punctuated by extended stops where slow, burning kisses accompanied the removal of yet another article of clothing. The hallway was littered with discarded items, both Emma and Toni in only their underwear and T-shirts by the time they reached the bed.

"Come here," Toni said, holding her hand out to Emma.

Emma joined her in the middle of bed, and there was a rustle of linens as they lifted themselves into a kneeling position. Toni felt that subtle tension that comes when a lover is still new, but she liked the sensation, fingers tingling and her body shivering when they laid their hands on each other.

Toni's eyes followed the course of her hands as they trailed over the thin material of Emma's T-shirt, and she drew in her breath when she felt the curve of breast and the hardness of nipples through the cotton. Toni watched Emma as her hands followed a similar course to her own. She saw her lips part slightly and her eyelashes flutter, but any uncertainty in Emma's eyes was replaced with desire as hands continued their journey.

Emma lifted her arms for Toni to remove her shirt and her chest heaved when Toni buried her head between her breasts. Toni shuddered when Emma bent to breathe in her ear and said, "Let me see you naked, Toni."

Again overcome by the words and their tone, Toni raised her arms. Emma's fingers lingered over her waist, never leaving contact with her skin as she slowly pulled Toni's top over her head. Her eyes wandered over Toni, hands sliding across her hips to slip under the seam of Toni's underwear. Her lips left a warm trail down Toni's stomach as she guided their removal, and she kissed Toni softly all the way back to her neck.

"God, Toni." Her voice was low, husky. "You are so sexy."

Toni locked eyes with Emma's. "Kiss me again."

Toni lost herself in the warmth of Emma's lips and shuddered as their tongues touched. They kissed tenderly and slowly, Emma's hands cupping Toni's face as she lifted herself to allow Toni to remove her underwear. For long minutes they kissed, desire growing as hands pressed bodies closer together. Toni felt her breasts against Emma's and their pubic hair brushed as they knelt together, hips grinding in a slow, sensuous rhythm. The heat that welled inside Toni threatened to boil over as her outstretched fingers explored yielding flesh. Then she pulled away and clasped Emma's hands, both of them panting softly.

"What do you want me to do?" Emma whispered.

"Touch me," Toni begged, guiding Emma's hand between her legs. "What do you want me to do?" she murmured, her mind awash with anticipation.

"Touch me." Emma's voice was thick as she placed Toni's hand between her parted thighs.

Toni cried out when Emma made contact and moved slowly over her. She buried her head into Emma's neck, her fingers gliding over Emma's exquisite wetness.

"You feel wonderful," Toni whispered when they eventually faced each other, increasing her pressure then coming to rest over swollen lips. "So wonderful."

"Don't stop," Emma begged. She groaned when Toni's fingers slid over her again and Toni kissed her in anticipation of the louder groan to come when she entered her. "Oh, Toni . . ." Emma moaned as Toni glided in and out.

Their mouths kept contact as excitement increased. Toni was breathing heavily from the expert attentions of Emma's fingers as they darted over her, and she pressed her lips harder to Emma's as she was taken to the edge.

"I can feel you getting close."

Toni nodded and Emma slowed, bending to encase one of Toni's breasts into her mouth. Toni increased the tempo of her fingers and felt Emma's breath hotter on her nipple as she drew to the same state. Emma's lips trailed back up Toni's skin. Then their bodies both stiffened and their backs arched. The room was suddenly filled with cries of pleasure.

"Emma," Toni mouthed when their eyes met again.

Emma just smiled in her pleased way and leaned in for another spine-tingling kiss. Her embrace could not silence the cries that emerged when she reentered Toni. Toni rested her forehead against Emma's as her pleasure was fulfilled, the movement of her hips becoming stilted as it all became too much.

"How was that?" Emma whispered.

"Oh, God." Toni clutched onto Emma's shoulders, nestling her head into Emma's neck as she fought to regain her breath. "As if you have to ask!"

Emma held her tighter. "Just making sure."

Toni tumbled backwards, pulling Emma down with her. "Just kiss me, you dag."

"Where?" Emma asked slyly, eyes twinkling.

"Anywhere you want."

"And what about me?" Emma questioned as she rained kisses over Toni's face.

Toni pecked her on the nose. "There you go."

Emma pouted. "Is that all?"

Toni shook her head. "If you turn around I'll give you a surprise."

"What sort of surprise?" Emma asked softly, rolling Toni over.

"I don't know . . . Why don't you just wait and find out."

They kissed again before wriggling around to lie end to end. Toni delighted in the firmness of Emma's thighs as she let her mouth and hands wander over them. Then they both sighed when their heads nestled between each other's legs.

Much later, Toni snuggled into Emma's neck. They still lay together on the bed but were finally at rest. "You know," said Toni, "I reckon you are *the* best kisser in the known universe."

Emma chuckled into Toni's hair. "Why, thank you, Toni."

"That's one of the things I'll miss the most. The kissing."

The fingers that had been stroking Toni's waist stilled and Toni heard Emma's sharp intake of breath.

"I mean—" Toni realized how that must have sounded. "I mean, it's not the only thing I'll miss. I'll miss everything about you."

That got no response at all. Toni lifted onto her elbow and met eyes that searched her own. What they were looking for Toni did not know, but eventually they slid away to stare at the ceiling.

"Emma?"

"So once I go to Albany, that's it?"

"Oh, Emma. No." Toni sat up straighter. Christ, she was a buffoon. A brainless buffoon. "I didn't mean it like that." She tugged Emma around to face her and took hold of her hands. Those hands. Toni studied them, turning them first palm up then palm down, her body shivering with the recent physical memory of them. The secondary rush that surged through her system was one of emotion and not of lust. It took every ounce of Toni's willpower to dam up the words she was so desperate to say, the words that might in the short term convince Emma to stay, but in the long term could turn into resentment at missed opportunities. "I meant I was just getting used to seeing you and touching you and kissing you and in six weeks that won't happen. Not every day I mean. We'll still get to see each other occasionally." Sudden uncertainty made Toni falter. "Won't we?"

Emma lowered her eyes again. "Do you want to?"

God damn it, woman. Can't you see how much I want you? "Of course I do."

Lashes were raised hesitantly. "So you'll come to visit me?"

"Every chance I get." Toni stroked Emma's cheek, smiling softly. "I reckon I'll get one of those Global Positioning thingos. I'll program it so all I need to do is type in 'Emma,' then sit back and have a snooze while my car drives itself down."

"I don't quite think that's how it works, Toni."

Toni already knew that wasn't how GPS worked. She shrugged. "Oh, well, I'll just have to sleep the whole time I'm there."

Emma wasn't buying into Toni's attempt at humor. "It's a long way for just a weekend."

"Would it sound really naff if I said it was worth it?"

"Totally." Finally, Emma smiled. "But say it anyway."

Toni leaned back toward those fabulously kissable lips. "It's worth it."

CHAPTER EIGHTEEN

The Web site Cathy discovered while arranging their Italy itinerary promised Tuscany by bike would provide an insight into the region that could not be matched from inside a vehicle. Despite the promise of a unique experience, plus an assurance the tour was suitable for those of only moderate fitness, misgivings surfaced the moment they were presented with their 18-speed hybrid bikes in Pienza, a picturesque Renaissance town near Siena. What had prompted the thought that someone in a sedentary occupation, such as herself, could cope with daily rides averaging fifty kilometers? In hilly, winding terrain. Lisa hadn't shared Cathy's doubt, anticipating this portion of their Italian adventure with relish.

On the first day Lisa covered much more ground than necessary, hurtling ahead before turning and pedaling back to Cathy, who rode at a more moderate, steady pace. Lisa's exuberance was her undoing. The next day Cathy's behind protested wildly at being put back onto the saddle, but her discomfort was minor compared to Lisa's. Obviously very stiff and saddlesore, Lisa grimaced as she cocked a leg to mount her bicycle for their second day of riding.

"Sore bum, honey?"

Lisa nodded as she secured the strap of her helmet under her chin. She was quiet that day, keeping pace with Cathy and not attempting any more of her hill sprints.

By day three Lisa's muscles had ceased their complaint and she and Cathy settled into a relaxed tempo, passing through one enchanting village after another. Little-used roads cut through countryside straight out of a Renaissance painting. Grassy plains gave way to stands of cypress trees, olive groves and, of course, vineyard after vineyard. Each morning they would strap a lightweight daypack over their shoulders and each night they would arrive at their accommodation to find their luggage waiting for them. The weather was more than kind, sunny days giving way to cool nights.

Today's ride took them from Sienna to Castellina in Chianti. Their accommodation for the night was exactly as Cathy had pictured a true Tuscan inn to be, with rooms laid out as a series of stone houses in a compound surrounded by acres and acres of woodlands. The next day they would saddle up for Florence, and their last night in Tuscany. From there it would a short flight back to Rome, then onto Australia.

After a dinner of homemade ravioli, they took the remains of their bottle of Brunello and headed down one of the paths leading through the woods. Not too far into their walk, they came across a clearing. It was largely devoid of vegetation, the brown earth hardened by the sun and pushing forth just a smattering of grass near a long-fallen tree.

Lisa led Cathy by the hand. "Let's sit for a while."

They settled onto the grass, the log providing a convenient if not altogether comfortable backrest. The bottle of wine was offered. With Cathy's shake of the head Lisa took a large swig, cradling it between her palms.

"This has been a wonderful holiday. Thank you, Cathy."

"It's not over yet." Cathy didn't look directly at Lisa, but in her peripheral vision she saw the wine bottle being turned round and round in Lisa's palms.

As if suddenly aware of her own compulsive actions, Lisa placed the bottle aside and sat on her hands. She looked upwards. "The first star should be out soon."

"Hmm." Cathy too looked up to the sky. Dusk was falling in its slow manner and it would be a good hour or more before the light of the day completely faded. Then, without the glow of a city to falsely light up the night sky, the stars would shine brightly against a black backdrop. The majesty of the universe was briefly considered before Cathy turned her thoughts much closer to home. Not for the first time that day she wondered at the cause of Lisa's latest shift in mood. All day Lisa had been quiet, and, if Cathy had to give a word to describe her demeanor, it would be . . . *agitated*. A couple of times during the day's ride Lisa reverted to previous behavior and set out on a sprint, her legs exploding into action. But instead of turning around at the end of her breakout, she would dismount and wait for Cathy on the side of the road. At each of these stops Lisa would look around her, seemingly sizing up the landscape, suggest a short break, then fidget until she announced a desire to get on the move again. On arrival at their accommodation her exploration of their room was notable for its lack of enthusiasm, and at dinner she declared the ravioli delicious but spent most of the time moving it around her plate instead of eating it.

Over dinner Cathy tried to eke an explanation for Lisa's erratic behavior but just received a long look followed by a shrug of the shoulders. "Nothing's wrong."

Cathy didn't push the issue, but in the silence began to formulate her own theories. She quickly decided it had to be baby-related. Ever since Capri, not a day went by where they didn't discuss the issue. They had talked at length about almost every aspect of starting and raising a family, from the pros and cons associated with each method of conception to their opinions on public versus private education. Their discussions revealed how each believed a child should be raised, but Lisa stayed silent about whether or not she actually wanted to raise one.

Cathy felt dinner churn in her stomach. Lisa's agitation indicated she had made up her mind and was working herself up to the announcement. It also pointed to a negative.

Wanting to get the news out in the open so she could begin dealing with it, Cathy tried once more to get Lisa to talk. "Honey, tell me what's on your mind."

Lisa pointed to the sky. "There. That's the first star."

Cathy's eyes followed Lisa's hand and could just make out a dot of light against still blue hues. She turned her attention to the woman sitting next to her.

Lisa had closed her eyes and was speaking very softly. Cathy strained her ears and heard, " . . . star bright, first star I see tonight . . ."

Lisa was wishing upon a star.

Despite knowing she wasn't supposed to ask, Cathy did anyway. "What are you wishing for?"

Lisa wriggled until she faced Cathy. What seemed a very long moment passed, during which Cathy was carefully assessed by a set of very worried-looking blue eyes. Cathy's dinner was just at the point of settling into a hard ball at the base of her stomach when Lisa reached into one of the deep pockets of her three-quarter-length cargo pants. She held out an open palm to Cathy. "That you'll say yes."

Lisa's palm cradled a ring. It glittered gold and sparkled with the gems encrusted on its surface. "Oh—" Cathy began, her breath catching in her throat.

Lisa's eyes shone as she said softly, "Some people search all their life to find that someone who lifts them up, makes them want to be a better person, be the best they can possibly be . . . I've found that person, Cathy. And it's you." She smiled shyly and plucked the ring from her palm, offering it. "I love you so much, Cathy. And it would do me no greater honor than to have you as my lifelong partner."

"Oh, Lisa . . ." Cathy wanted desperately to say something

243

meaningful to mark the occasion. But Lisa's proposal was so at odds with what she been expecting, all she could manage was a choked "Yes!"

Lisa's eyes widened as if she expected a different answer. "Really?"

"Yes," Cathy repeated softly. "I want to spend my life with you."

"Thank you, thank you, thank you!" Lisa slipped the band onto Cathy's ring finger before clasping her by the shoulders and kissing her fiercely. "Thank you." Lisa's hands moved from Cathy's shoulders to her cheeks. Her blue, blue eyes visibly softened. "And I want us to start a family."

Cathy's heartbeat echoed in her ears. Needing to know she had heard correctly, it was her turn to ask, "Really?"

Lisa nodded. "I'm still scared to death over the whole thing, but I think we'll make terrific parents."

"Oh, Lisa." Cathy wondered if it were possible to die of happiness. If so, she must be having a near-death experience. Her head swam, her heart still hammered, and if she didn't have the log supporting her back she was sure she'd fall backwards. "I love you."

"And I love you."

Lisa's next kiss began gently but quickly gained urgency. She tugged at the band of Cathy's Capri pants, fingers fumbling with button and zipper. What she found made her groan. "Sweet God,"

"Only for you." Sick with passion, Cathy didn't even bother with the button of Lisa's cargoes. She went straight for the zipper, sliding her hand inside and pushing aside underwear.

She moaned when Lisa moaned and they fell against each other, thrusting together, moving quickly to almost simultaneous climaxes that broke the silence of the still evening air.

Cathy fought to bring her breathing under control, her forehead resting against Lisa's. "Do you think anyone heard that?" she whispered, despite knowing that, if anyone had been in proximity, it was far too late for a hushed voice.

"If they did, I bet they're wishing they were me right now." Lisa rolled over, taking Cathy with her so she lay on top. She drew Cathy down to her lips. "Kiss me."

Light had all but faded by the time zippers had been rezipped, buttons rebuttoned and dirt brushed from each other's clothes.

"This is beautiful." Cathy sat between Lisa's legs, her back leaning against Lisa's chest. Despite the poor light she was studying the ring on her finger. A combination of diamonds and sapphires cut their way through the precious metal. The gold itself did not form the traditional circle; rather it tapered to two false ends on either side of the line of gems. "I've never seen one like it before."

"It's called a channel crossover. I had it made." Lisa's arms tightened around Cathy. "Especially for you."

"You designed it?"

"Mmm. It tells a story. Of us." Lisa took hold of Cathy's hand. "Those two smaller diamonds, they represent our first two years together, when we were at university. And count the sapphires."

Cathy eyed the line of gems. "Eleven."

"One for each of the years we were apart. And then . . ." Lisa ran the tip of her thumb over the stone set in the middle of the channel. Slightly raised from the others, it was also significantly larger. "One more diamond for the year we've just spent together. And see the engraved lines that run along the band? That's to signify a continuation." Lisa's voice cracked with emotion as she rested her chin on Cathy's shoulder. "For all the years that are yet to come."

No words could express the joy Cathy felt at that moment. She reached over to stroke Lisa's cheek.

Lisa leaned into the touch. "Do you know I've had that ring hidden for weeks now? I actually picked it up the day you announced we were going to Italy. I'd planned to give it to you on our anniversary as the sun set over Cable Beach."

"I'm sorry." Cathy felt renewed guilt for overriding their Broome plan without consulting Lisa. "From now on I'll let you in on my 'big announcements' before I actually announce them." Curiosity at Lisa's own change in plans—in terms of the timing of her proposal—prompted her to ask, "Why did you wait until now?"

"To ask you?"

"Yes." Cathy had a terrible feeling she may have stolen Lisa's moment with the presentation of the Tag Heur watch.

As if reading her mind, Lisa tapped on the sports face with her index finger. "It had nothing to do with this, if that's what you're thinking." Cathy was squeezed again. "I really do love it, by the way. I didn't ask you in Rome because . . . well . . . because neither of us were too enamored with the place, and anyway, I wanted something a bit out of the ordinary. Then I had this idea of asking you on our gondola ride, but that seemed such an obvious thing to do I decided to wait and see what Tuscany had to offer." Lisa ran her thumb over the ring. "I've been carrying this in my pocket all day, but each time we stopped for a rest in some picture-postcard place with a Tuscan sun shining down upon us, I got a case of the jitters." Lisa's laughter was self-derisory. "So I picked a patch of dirt in the middle of some trees. That's something to tell the grandkids, huh?"

Cathy smiled her agreement but soon sobered, still somewhat unable to grasp the evening's turn of events. She wasn't sure she really wanted to know the answer but she asked anyway, "Did you ever think of changing your mind?"

Lisa hesitated, and then took a long, slow breath before saying, "To be honest, when you said you wanted to have children, the whole image I'd painted of our lives together kind of fell apart. There was a selfish part of me that really didn't want to share you with anyone else. We have busy lives back home, Cathy, and I was worried a child would take away what little quality time we have together." She paused, pressing her lips to Cathy's hair. "But no matter how hard I tried to picture it, I couldn't imagine my life now without you in it. And I figured that damn beautiful heart of yours had enough love for both me and a little one. Or two little ones. Or three. Or—"

"Hang on a second." Cathy laughed delightedly. "Are you planning on having me barefoot and pregnant from now on?"

"Not just yet. I'm planning on having you all to myself for at least a little while longer." Lisa's voice assumed that delicious resonance as it lowered, husky with desire. "Can we go back to our room now? There's things I need to do to you that just can't happen on a hard patch of dirt."

Once standing, Cathy stayed Lisa from pulling her in the direction of the path. "Wait just one minute." She walked to the middle of the clearing and did a slow three-sixty-degree turn. "I want to be able to remember this hard patch of dirt forever."

The wine bottle was retrieved before they left the clearing. Cathy didn't care about the contents, but she didn't want to sully her sacred spot with their litter.

They held hands as they walked down the path, talking softly about life and love and happy-ever-afters.

Lisa grinned slyly. "Speaking of happy endings, I wonder how Toni and Emma are going?"

"Lisa," Cathy reminded her, "we don't even know if there *is* a Toni and Emma."

"I reckon there is," Lisa said assuredly. "I reckon it was Toni who was there for dinner."

Lisa had finally made her phone call to Emma a few days prior, during their lunch stop at a tiny restaurant that made a goat's cheese tart to die for. Her call proved unfruitful in terms of specifics, Emma admitting yes, she and Toni had become friends and yes, Toni had phoned Emma at home, but no, it hadn't been late at night after Toni contacted Lisa for her number. Then Emma said she had to cut their call short because the friend she was expecting for dinner had just arrived, and no, she wasn't going to tell Lisa who the friend was. But, Lisa should be happy to know, it wasn't Justine.

"It could have been anyone. Just leave it be, Lisa. You'll find out in a few days' time anyway."

"You could ask Toni when you call to remind her about picking us up from the airport."

"I could."

"But you're not going to, are you?"

Cathy laughed at Lisa's pout. "Nope."

"Are you going to tell Toni our news when you ring?"

"Nope." Cathy stopped at the door to their room, standing aside to let Lisa turn the key in the lock. "That can wait until we get back too. But for now, you've got duties to perform."

"Oh, yes." Lisa quirked her eyebrows. "I almost forgot." She closed the door behind them and held out her hand, palm up. "Well, hand it over."

"Hand what over?"

"A voucher."

Cathy just folded her arms, forming an expression to show exactly what she thought of that request.

"Okay, then." Lisa nodded generously. "I guess since it's a special occasion you're entitled to a freebie."

Cathy spluttered with mock outrage, pushing Lisa backwards onto the bed. "I'll freebie you, you right little . . ."

"So do you promise, Cathy?"

Cathy snuggled into the crook of Lisa's arm and breathed in the heady scent of sex. She still had Lisa on her fingers and could taste her on her lips. "Promise what?"

"That once junior comes along we'll still make time to be together, like this."

"Of course." Cathy ran her fingers through Lisa's hair. She grinned mischievously. "I'll buy the entire *Teletubbies* collection and leave junior in front of the televis—" She laughed as she was pinned to the mattress, Lisa straddling her hips and grasping both wrists. Her laughter gurgled in the back of her throat as Lisa launched into her anti-*Teletubbies* tirade and then verbally voided the remainder of Cathy's anniversary vouchers. "Okay, okay. No *Teletubbies*."

"Promise me." Cathy's wrists were pressed further into the mattress.

"I promise." Cathy laughed again. "But for your information I

248

used my last voucher days ago, so I've been living on credit ever since."

"Is that so?" Lisa raised her eyebrows in surprise. Her eyes wandered down Cathy's torso. They held a familiar glimmer when they returned to Cathy's. "So how much do you owe me then?"

"Let go of my wrists and I'll show you."

Much later, Lisa flung her head into the pillow. "Oh, my God. I think we're about even now." She checked her watch and groaned. "Look at the time. I'm never going to manage the ride to Florence tomorrow."

Cathy slid back up the bed and kissed Lisa hard on the lips. "Poor tired baby." She snuggled back into the crook of Lisa's arm. "Good night, honey."

"Good night, lover." Cathy was squeezed then released, Lisa sliding from the bed to make a bathroom stop. On her return Cathy found herself gathered into a hug. "Sweetheart."

"Yes?"

"Thank you for saying yes."

Cathy smiled and snuggled deeper into Lisa's arms. "Thank you for asking me."

Totally happy, Cathy fell quickly into a deep, dreamless sleep.

CHAPTER NINETEEN

Emma and Lisa stopped at one of the water fountains dotted around the lake. They were halfway through their second circuit, it taking that distance for Emma to tell Lisa what had been happening in the month she'd been away.

It was Tuesday morning, a full thirty-six hours since Emma had accompanied Toni to the airport to meet the flight from Rome. Emma had clearly read Lisa's "I told you so" look to Cathy as they entered the arrival lounge, and she laughed at the "You sly little fox" Lisa had whispered in her ear when they hugged hello. But once the ring on Cathy's finger was spied, attention was taken immediately from new bonds, focusing instead on the strengthening of existing ones. Despite the excitement, Emma and Toni both noticed the yawns of long-haul travel creeping in and, not long after reaching the house by the ocean, left Cathy and Lisa to unpack and settle back home in peace.

Cathy had returned to the office this morning and, technically,

Lisa should also have been at work, but a mix-up with a tile delivery meant a reprieve until at least lunchtime. So Emma had been both surprised and delighted at Lisa's phone call, asking if she was free for a visit. Both of them avid joggers, they had decided to go for a run around the lake near Emma's home.

"Jeez, and I thought we had some news for you." Lisa laughed as she dropped to the ground. "Now let me get this straight." She watched as Emma filled the shallow doggie trough that adjoined the fountain. "In the last four weeks you've resigned from one job, declined another in Sydney, accepted one in Albany and been offered a partnership in a Perth practice. You've fallen out of lust with your neighbor, agreed to be bridesmaid at her wedding, had an Internet affair and fallen in love with my partner's best friend."

"Well, I had to do something to keep myself occupied while you were away." Emma plopped next to Lisa on the grass and wrapped her arms around her knees, "Although I wouldn't exactly call it an Internet *affair*. All we did was talk. And," she said guardedly, "I never said I was in love."

Lisa snorted. "You'd make a rotten poker player, Em."

Emma pretended she was in sudden need of a stretch. She held her hands high in the air and twisted her torso from one side to the other. She purposely held her stretch as she looked toward the fountain, away from Lisa's penetrating gaze.

"You can't not look at me forever."

"I can try," Emma said stubbornly, still intent on the fountain. She *had* fallen in love with Toni, but if asked to pinpoint the moment it happened, Emma would stumble over her answer. The beginnings of love were there the night she paced Toni's cat run design. They grew roots the first night Toni came over for dinner, and they sprang into life over the course of their dating. Now, each time they kissed, each time they were together, each time Emma even thought of Toni, her love flowered.

The trouble was, her love came with such damnable timing. Ever since the feeling emerged, Emma had been a referee in the fight between her emotive side and her logical side. Emotion told her what she and Toni were sharing was too new, too fresh to survive so early a separation. The promise of regular visits from Toni, and vice versa, might be pure in its intent, but in reality the promise would prove difficult to keep. So her emotive side told her to stay in Perth, to keep her two days at Tricia's and continue her local job search. Her logical side said she would be foolish to pass up Albany and such a good job offer. Logic also told her that, if Justine could survive Paul leaving for three weeks at a stretch, then surely Emma could survive her own separation. Then emotion kicked in again and reminded her how Justine got Paul for a whole two weeks out of five, whereas Emma would be lucky to see Toni on alternate weekends.

So Emma's internal struggle continued.

At present, logic was winning. And it was logic, however warped, that told her so long as she didn't voice her feelings out loud, they didn't really exist and hence could be ignored.

"So I was wrong then?" asked Lisa.

Emma gave a tiny little nod.

"Strange." Lisa flopped backwards onto the grass. "I could have sworn I was right."

"Well, you weren't."

"Okay." There was an audible sigh, then a good long moment of silence. From her peripheral vision, Emma saw Lisa sit up again. "Hey, I'm a bit broke after my holiday. You want a game of poker?"

Emma's left obliques were begging an end to her torso twist. She complied with their wishes, giving a relieved expulsion of breath as she straightened up again. "I have no idea how Cathy puts up with you, Lisa Smith."

"Which translates to . . ."

"You were right," Emma said quietly.

"Sorry." Lisa leaned obviously closer. "I didn't quite catch that. What did you say?"

"You were right about Toni."

Innocence was feigned. "What about Toni?"

Emma took a deep breath. She was about to make it real. "I do love her."

"I knew it!" Lisa laughed gleefully as she launched across the grass, rolling Emma over with her. "I just knew it!"

Kayisha, who until that moment had been lazily snapping her jaw at passing bugs, leapt up and bounded around the pair, barking excitedly. Swans that had been peacefully paddling the calm waters of the lake turned long necks in alarm and took to quieter waters with a swoosh of water against outstretched wings. The male half of an elderly couple passing by muttered, "Disgraceful," and his wife nodded in acquiescence. But, once past the kafuffle Emma, Lisa and Kayisha were creating, the wife turned for a second look and smiled a secret, pleased smile.

"Get off me!" Emma half-heartedly tried to push Lisa away. As predicted, just by saying the words out loud, they crystallized, gained form, became real. The reality struck Emma right to the core. She had fallen in love. Fallen in love with a woman who wore paw-print pajamas and fluffy slippers, and who went through toothbrush heads twice as fast as the average person. A woman who loved her pet to the point of designing and building an extension to the house for its comfort. A woman who surrounded herself with every conceivable gadget, who grumbled every morning as she headed sleepily for the shower, and who was invariably at least a little late for work. A woman who was at once self-conscious about her appearance, yet uninhibited in the most intimate of settings. Yes, Emma was in love with a fabulously quirky and expressive woman, and it felt so damn good she had to join Lisa and laugh out loud. "You're squishing me!"

Once they'd finished rolling around on the grass, and Kayisha had calmed down enough to slurp the last of the water in the doggie trough, they resumed their lake circuit. Lisa was suddenly full of questions about Emma's planned relocation, forcing her to admit she had not yet done anything about canceling her lease or finding accommodation in Albany. When asked why, Emma explained she was only required to give four weeks' notice on her house and that Albany was sure to be bursting with empty rental properties, so there was no rush. That received a sideways look but no comment. Which was just as well. Emma knew her procrastination was purely to delay solidifying the fact she was actually leaving.

Finally Lisa spoke again. "I don't get it, Em."

Emma glanced warily to her companion. Obviously Lisa had discovered the gaping holes in her argument. "What?"

"Why you're going to Albany when it's quite obvious you want to stay here."

"Of course I'd rather stay here, but like I told you, Leese, Albany offers the chance for me to get a financial kick-start."

"In a year."

"Yes," Emma admitted.

"Why waste a year, and maybe have Tricia take on someone else as a partner, when you could potentially get in now?"

Emma sighed. Halfway through their first circuit of the lake her mouth had gone into autopilot and—despite promising herself not to say anything to Lisa—Tricia's offer became common knowledge. Lisa's initial reaction had been exactly the same as Toni's, and she suggested approaching Cathy. Emma paraphrased what she had told Toni, "I already told you, Leese, I can't risk losing a friend over money."

"Look, Em." Lisa spoke slowly as if explaining to a child. "I really can't see that happening. Cathy didn't get where she is today by being a financial slouch. She wouldn't just give you a pot of money without doing all the checks and balances. She'd expect you to present a business case and she'd want projections and cash flow and all that stuff. Then, if she's happy with what she sees there'll be proper contracts drawn up and if she's not, she'll let you know it's a no-go."

"But—"

"Tell me one thing, Em," Lisa interrupted. "If money wasn't an issue and you had a choice between the Albany gig and the partnership, which would you choose?"

Emma had already had this debate in her head. Guaranteed income aside, there really was no competition between being an owner over being a salaried employee. Whichever she chose, her skills would be used to the benefit of the animals she treated, but in hard, fiscal terms, ultimately they would either benefit someone else's pocket or her own. In a nonmercenary sense, being part owner also gave her the opportunity to contribute in a very real way to the overall direction of the practice. As an employee, she was constrained by the motivations of her employer, and her experience with Colleen illustrated the extent to which employer/employee motivations could be at odds. "The partnership."

"And tell me another thing. If Toni was out of the equation, which would you choose?"

This was another debate Emma had already had with herself. It usually wove into the argument over logic versus emotion. Well aware she tended to make emotional decisons, and how in the past those decisions usually blew up in her face, Emma was determined not to make the same mistake again. But despite trying desperately to separate Toni from the decision-making process, she couldn't. "I can't take her out of the equation, Leese. She's in my life now and I can't pretend she isn't."

For a moment at least, that comment seemed to satisfy Lisa, her nodding and giving a crooked "I hear you" smile. But the moment was short-lived. "So, if the mountain won't go with Mohammed, then Mohammed must stay with the mountain."

Emma picked up on the twist in Lisa's phrasing. Emma had never even considered what had just been implied. "I'm the one without my own home or a job. Why should Toni move?" she said defensively.

"I'm not saying that, Em." Lisa stopped running and stood with hands on her hips. "I'm saying everything you want is here in Perth, and if you'd get your head out of your arse for one minute, you'd do the figures and find out once and for all if this practice thing is a possibility."

Emma fought to keep a suitably insulting response from falling out of her mouth. Everything Lisa said was true—well, maybe not the head up the arse bit—so she had no argument. "I'll think about it, okay?"

"Better think fast. You're due in Albany in five weeks." Lisa did a couple of quick leg stretches and turned back to the path. She sniggered loudly as she picked up speed.

"What's so funny?" Emma asked.

Lisa sniggered again. "I was just thinking about you being a bridesmaid. What on earth prompted you to say yes?"

Emma cringed. The bridesmaid business was a prime example of how she acted on emotion instead of logic . . . and ended up the worse off for it.

"Shut up, Lisa." Emma adjusted her hold on Kayisha's lead and quickened her trot.

Lisa hooted with laughter. "Has Justine picked out your dress yet?" she called from behind.

Emma ignored both Lisa and her continued bridesmaid taunts for the remainder of their run. Once back in front of Emma's house she shooed Lisa into the cab of her tray-top utility. "And to think I actually missed you while you were gone. Go home and leave me alone. I've got things to do."

"Like go practice walking in high heels?"

"No. Like start checking out the rental market in Albany."

The disappointment in Lisa's expression was obvious.

Emma shrugged. "And *maybe* go work on a business plan."

Lisa visibly brightened. "Okay. I'd better leave you to it then."

It was Emma's turn to stand with hands on hips. She hoped she looked menacing. "Now, you promise you won't say anything to Toni about any of what I told you today?"

Lisa crossed her heart. "I promise."

"And you won't breathe a word to Cathy about the practice thing? *If* I do anything about it I want it to come from me."

Lisa turned the key in the ignition and the engine roared into life. "I won't. I promise."

Emma waited until Lisa's utility disappeared around the corner before letting herself into the house and booting up her computer. It was ten a.m. By ten-thirty she had scoured the sites of all the Albany-based real estate agents she could find. One had detailed rental listings, complete with photos, so she bookmarked the site for easy reference. The others advised that rentals were available but provided only a contact e-mail address or phone number for further information. By eleven a.m. Emma had e-mailed all the real estate agents, advising of her requirements. Now she sat, thrumming her fingers on her desk, address book open, considering the number that stared back up at her. It was the number of her landlord. One simple phone call and she'd be on the countdown to vacating her home of the last ten years. Instead, pages of her address book were flipped and a different number considered. This time Emma did dial.

Cathy answered on the third ring and, in contrast to her call to Italy, Emma launched straight into the reason. They agreed to a six p.m. meeting on Thursday. Toni would be well clear of the office, having already arranged with Lisa to meet at the gym that evening for her first Pump class since falling ill.

Shit. Thursday was only two days away. Emma knew she had to get her skates on if she were to come up with the goods. Another phone call was made and within five minutes Emma was in her car and on her way to pore over Tricia's accounts.

CHAPTER TWENTY

Toni was having one of those days. Her stars were obviously not only out of alignment, but it seemed her Venus had crashed into her Mars, or one of her ascending moons had run out of fuel and landed in her fourth house of harmony. Everything, but everything had gone wrong, from the moment she put her foot to the floor and stood on one of Kayisha's chew toys—a recently chewed chew toy, still glistening with doggie dribble—to the phone call received just minutes ago, advising her that the cat run plans needed to undergo some "modifications" before council would approve them.

The modifications were relatively minor—requiring only a small reconfiguration of the area closest to the house so the footings fell within the minimum distance of her outside faucet—but by that time she was ready to blow her stack. Either that or crawl into a little hole and hide until the planets decided to come to order.

Not that order seemed likely to come any time soon. Toni stared morosely at her computer screen; at the e-mail that had arrived from Emma just a few minutes ago. It was the third such e-mail to arrive in the past two days. This one, like the others, contained a description of a rental property that was available, or becoming available, in Albany. Along with the description was a short note from Emma, asking Toni her thoughts on the property.

While Toni knew that Emma had to make preparations to relocate, the evidence preparations had begun struck a chord deep inside. Add to this Emma's late arrival at Toni's on Tuesday night, and her distracted mood once she got there, and it was no wonder Toni had turned into a walking, talking disaster zone.

"Tricia's ultra busy at the moment so I'm just helping her out" was Emma's explanation. When Wednesday turned into a repeat of Tuesday, the same reason was cited.

Toni told herself not to worry, but despite her best efforts, she did. She had spent most of last night lying on her side, watching Emma sleep, wondering what was going on in that mind of hers. There seemed to be a lot. Emma slept restlessly, tossing and turning, occasionally mumbling something incomprehensible, occasionally frowning. So it was a groggy and very tired Toni who hauled her legs over the bed and started the day by stepping on a dribble-coated chew toy.

Toni shuddered again at the thought of it and was immediately glad to be distracted by the phone. It was Lisa.

"Bugger." Toni replaced the receiver a minute later. There went her buddy for her return to the gym. Lisa and Joel were running a good few hours behind schedule, no thanks, apparently, to the idiot who delivered the wrong tiles to their work site a few days ago. Oh, well, she could always go on her own. Although at the moment, the thought of a good stiff post-work drink was a lot more appealing than hefting weights in time to music.

Toni's phone rang again. It was Sue, coolly advising that her four-thirty—Alexandria—had arrived. Toni was not surprised at Sue's tone, given that Toni had snapped at her the moment she'd walked into the reception.

"Thank you so much for pointing that out to me." Toni had scowled when Sue advised her that she had only one minute before her *nine-thirty* was due to arrive. "Bloody woman," she muttered to herself as she stalked past the reception console without another glance.

Toni damn well knew she was late. Sue would be late too if she'd had to spend ten minutes vacuuming bird seed from her laundry floor after the plastic bag inexplicably burst at the seams, and another twenty minutes sponging down her kitchen cupboard doors and sweeping up shards of broken china because her morning cup of coffee just flew out of her hands.

"Thank you, Sue. I'll be out in two minutes." Toni tried to convey an apology for her earlier behavior by being extra nice and polite, but Sue was obviously still stinging and the line just clicked and went dead.

Thankfully, Sue was professional enough to disguise her current displeasure with Toni in front of a client. Although once her back was turned and Toni led Alex to her office, she was sure she felt a series of mental knives being flung in her direction.

Toni waited for Alex to ease her large frame into a chair before rounding her desk, settling herself and leaning forward. "So, nearly tax time again." She looked at the stack of manila folders Alex held in her lap. Experience told Toni that each folder would contain the in-comings and out-goings for an individual property, and that the contents of each folder would be categorized and in chronological order. It was still a good few weeks before the end of the tax year, but since Alex would soon depart for her annual trip to the Greek Isles, the paperwork was deposited with Toni early, along with details of any outstanding items. Toni wished all her clients were so organized. Hell, she wished she were so organized. "Comes 'round quicker every year."

"Wait till you get to my age." Alex put the folders onto the desk but placed a hand over them before Toni could pull the stack toward her. "*If* you get to my age. Which could be doubtful by the way you look today. What have you been doing to yourself, Toni? You look like crappola."

"Thanks, Alex." Toni slid her gaze away, tidying a sheaf of papers that didn't need tidying. Jeez, she didn't think she looked *that* bad. But then, maybe once one turned thirty, a single night without sleep made one look like "crappola." "Let's get started, shall we?"

"I don't give a horse's arse about this at the moment. And it looks like you don't either."

"I do, really." Never before intimidated by Alex, Toni was more than a little surprised at the quaver in her own voice. She tried for a smile. "Give a horse's arse, that is."

"Cut the bullshit, Toni."

Toni wondered if being sixty-five conferred permission to speak one's mind to relative strangers. Maybe it did. Toni considered confiding in Alex. It could be dangerous to her already fragile ego. On the flip side, Alex had probably seen it all and Toni could potentially benefit from her years of experience. "Alex, there's this woman . . ."

"You silly, silly girl." Once Toni finished her confession, Alex treated her to a look that said she was not only silly, but downright stupid. "You love the woman yet you haven't told her?"

"I told you why."

"Because you think you're being manipulative." Alex harrumphed. "What a cop-out. How does expressing what you feel make you manipulative?"

"Because if I say how I feel, it may make her stay when she really should go."

"From what you say, she's a big girl and able to make up her own mind. At least give her the choice."

"And have her end up hating me because she made the wrong one? Love doesn't pay the bills, Alex. She needs to get full-time work. And it's being offered in Albany."

"Does she love you?"

Did seeing your own love reflected in the other's eyes count? Or hearing it in their voice, feeling it in their touch? "If she does she never told me."

Alex folded her arms and harrumphed again. "Sounds like you're made for each other. Both stupid."

Toni felt her hackles rise. Alex had no right to call Emma stupid. "Don't make assumptions about someone you've never met," she snapped.

Oh, shit, Toni thought as she watched Alex set her mouth, unfold her arms and lean forward. *I've pissed her off and she's going to let me have it.*

Alex seemed to reconsider, settling back into her seat. If anything, her expression conveyed a pleased respect for Toni's defiance. "How long before she goes?"

Toni's computer time display blinked at her. Thirty-two days, thirteen hours and forty-two minutes. "A little under five weeks."

"Tell her how you feel, Toni. Believe me, once you get to my age you'll realize the words you regret most are the ones you didn't say rather than the ones you did. And the things you didn't do will leave a much deeper impression on your psyche than the things you did." Alex stood, checking her watch and patting the stack of folders. "I'll leave these with you. You can call me if you have any questions."

Toni nodded.

"I'm assuming I won't be billed for this appointment?"

Toni shook her head.

"And I'm also assuming they pay taxes down in Albany?"

Toni pushed out a smile. "You know what they say. There's only two things certain in this life."

"Just as I thought." Alex ran her hand down Toni's cheek, turned and headed for the door. She stood with hand on the lever. "Think about it."

Toni did think about it. And think about it. She turned to her window and pondered the view and she turned back to her desk and pondered the rest of her surrounds. She loved this office. She loved her job, and on most days, when her feet touched carpet instead of a chewed chew toy, she got on well with her colleagues. Including Sue.

Toni pushed her feet against the floor to begin her office chair swivel. As she spun slowly around and around, her thoughts tread tentatively around the idea Alex had planted in her head. She drew closer to the idea, backed away, drew closer again. Finally she reached out and touched it. Surprisingly, it didn't feel too bad. In fact, the longer she held onto the idea, the more appealing it became and she wondered why she hadn't thought of it herself.

Snippets of a conversation held in this very office only the week prior reverberated in Toni's head. "You could follow her," she had told Julie when discussing Anna's possible relocation to Canberra.

Toni ground her chair to a halt, deciding to take her own advice. Her computer showed it to be two minutes to six. Too late to go to Pump, but hopefully not too late to catch Cathy before she left for the day. Toni launched out of her chair and opened her door just in time to see Cathy at the end of the passage, heading for the reception.

Toni chased after her at a trot. At the entrance to reception she skidded to a stop, nonplussed to find Emma standing next to the console. Sudden dizziness convinced Toni she had been spinning around in her chair for so long she was hallucinating. That theory was quickly banished. Cathy wouldn't say hello to a hallucination, especially one not her own.

"Toni." Cathy turned surprised attention to her. "I thought you'd gone for the day."

"No, I . . ." Toni raked fingers through her hair, took a long look at Emma, then Cathy, and finally back at Emma. She hovered over her decision for a split-second before plunging in. "Emma, I love you. I can't stand the fact you're going away and I wish there was something I could do to enable you to stay here in Perth, with me. But there's not and to be honest, it doesn't make a whole lot of difference anyway, because I've decided to go and live in Albany too."

There was a splutter from the other side of the reception console. Sue had been sipping on a cola but now stood with the glass poised at her lips, her eyes wide as saucers.

They followed Toni as she turned to Cathy, and said, "Cathy, you know I love working here and you're the best boss in the world

263

but I've decided to hand in my notice. I know my timing sucks but I'll stay until we get through the worst of the tax rush, and I'd love to come and work back here when I get back to Perth. If you'll have me that is, and . . ." She began to run out of puff. "And . . . I'm sorry to be such a pain but"—she turned back to Emma—"I want to be where you are."

Emma opened her mouth, closed it again. On her second attempt some sound came out. "What about your house?"

"I can rent it out."

"And Virgil, your cat run?"

"Virgil goes where I go." Toni smiled. "As you like to say, cats are amazingly adaptable."

"And your office, your view?"

"I spend altogether too much time looking out that window." Fingers fled through Toni's hair and doubt crept into her voice. "Don't you want me to come with you?"

Emma's voice was so low it was barely audible. "I want to be where you are, Toni."

The ensuing silence was broken by the phone, but it was cut off on the half-ring, Sue never taking her eyes off Toni as she picked up the receiver and put it immediately back on its cradle again.

That distinctly unprofessional act may have been the catalyst to Cathy's cough. "Umm, Toni, you do realize you're holding up my client."

"Client?" Toni echoed, suddenly noticing Emma was not in her usual casual wear. She was dressed to kill in a business suit tailored to accentuate her curves. A crisp, white shirt complemented the navy pinstripe, and her hair, normally held in a loose ponytail, cascaded around her shoulders. If this was what she wore to her interview in Albany, then Toni was not surprised Emma was offered the position. Toni would have hired her on the spot.

Emma nodded. "I'm here to see Cathy."

Toni read the nervousness that entered Emma's expression. "You're not here to get your taxes done, are you?" she said.

Emma shook her head.

Cathy piped up again. "I'd advise you to sleep on your resignation, Toni." There was a slight pause during which Sue made a gurgling sound as if she was about to cough up a fur ball. "Emma . . . shall we?"

Hazel eyes met Toni's. "Wish me luck."

"Good luck."

The green flecks twinkled, and Emma said with a smile, "And just in case you didn't already know . . . I love you too."

And with that Emma stepped past Toni to accompany Cathy to her office.

Toni watched the empty air they had walked through for a good ten seconds. Then she turned to Sue and grinned like a Cheshire cat. "She loves me."

Sue just nodded, her eyes still wide but her hand already reaching for the phone. Toni knew Sue had reached gossip overload and couldn't wait to tell someone . . . anyone.

Sure enough, even before Toni had taken two steps toward the passage, she heard the rabid pressing of buttons. Briefly, Toni wondered who would be first to hear the news, but that thought was soon overridden by anguished curiosity at the proceedings in the office next to hers.

She sank into her office chair and began it on its slow spin. Where would Emma be in five weeks' time? In Albany, or still in Perth? Toni realized it didn't really matter, because wherever Emma was, Toni would be right there beside her.

EPILOGUE

Three months later

"So." Emma watched Pete swirl a spoon through his hot chocolate, raise the utensil to lick it clean, then drop it back into his drink. "How's our favorite vet?"

"Same as ever." Pete screwed up his nose. "Still click-clacking around in her high heels." He grinned. "But at least we all know when she's coming."

"And Tom?" Emma asked, referring to her replacement at Colleen's practice.

Pete shrugged. "He's okay. Quite good actually."

"Oh. How good?"

"Stop fishing, Em." A quick swirl of the spoon, three large gulps and Pete's hot chocolate was gone. "You know, it's hard to believe you've only been gone three months. It seems like forever."

"Not to me." Emma wrapped her hands around her mug, feeling the warmth seep through her palms. "I've been so busy, half the time I don't know whether I'm coming or going. And Maggie's almost ready to mutiny."

Emma paused deliberately, waiting for Pete's reaction to the news that the assistant she shared with Tricia was finding the increased workload a strain. It was as expected—fresh hope glimmering in his eyes. Pete was still actively looking for work, but it seemed vet assistant vacancies in Perth were as rare as vet vacancies. He had been offered part-time employment at a practice in a newly created suburb along the northern coastal strip, but he couldn't afford to live on the part-time wage that came with the position.

Pete sat up straighter. "So all my name-dropping has done some good then?"

Despite warning Pete away from letting her old clients know where she was now practicing, he persisted in "just dropping it into conversation." Surprisingly, even though her new practice was a good few suburbs from Colleen's, almost a third of her current customer base consisted of past patients. Emma nodded. "If Maggie found out you've been contributing to her extra load, your name would be mud. So you'd better not mention it. Not for your first few weeks anyway."

Again Emma paused, this time to see hope turn to astonishment. Pete's eyes widened, "Are you saying . . . ?"

Emma nodded, thoroughly enjoying this, her first official recruitment, since becoming a partner. "When can you start?"

"I . . ." Emma could see Pete's mind madly ticking over. "I really do have to give at least two weeks' notice." Worried eyes settled on hers. "Is that okay?"

Emma had already figured Pete's genuine concern for the welfare of his charges would not allow him to just up-sticks and leave. That's why she'd arranged for the veterinary science student currently on work experience to stay a few more weeks, but in a part-time, assistant capacity. With pay.

"Oh, I think Maggie may just be able to hold out for a little while longer." With Pete's relieved expression Emma assumed a serious tone. "There are a few conditions to your employment though. There'll be none of this Saturday stock-take business. And unless it's a screaming emergency there'll be no working through your lunch break. And when the situation calls for it, you'll use the office phone to make personal calls. Local calls only though," she warned.

The smile that had formed and spread while Emma "laid down the law" assumed a cheeky crookedness. "You strike a hard bargain, Em, but I guess I can live with that."

"Excellent." Her motive for arranging a late Saturday afternoon café catch-up achieved, Emma stood, checking her watch as she tossed money for their drinks onto the table. "I'll call you sometime next week and we'll set a time to get all the paperwork out of the way, but for now I've got to fly."

"My turn." Pete shoved the note back into Emma's hand. "Another wedding rehearsal?"

Emma shook her head. That little torture was scheduled for Monday night, Justine's wedding the following Saturday afternoon. "No. I have to go pick up the cake for tomorrow."

"Ahh, yes." Pete nodded, grinning. "The *official opening*."

"That's right." Toni's cat run had been erected at least six weeks ago, but now that both the decking and the landscaping were also complete, she'd decided it was time to present her masterpiece to the masses.

Once outside they hugged their good-byes. The embrace was swift, but Pete's heartfelt "Thanks, Em" gave her a happy glow that lasted well into her journey to the patisserie located in the next suburb.

With the patisserie cake safely deposited in the middle of Toni's large kitchen table, Emma followed the human noises coming from the back room. She got there just in time to see Toni's head disappear through the cat flap that led to the run. The flap was close to ground level, and Toni was splayed out on the floor, propped up by her elbows. Her denim-clad behind wriggled appealingly as her head popped back into the house, then almost immediately out to the run again.

Stifling a laugh, Emma loudly cleared her throat, "Um, Toni. Just exactly what are you doing?"

Toni's behind stopped its wriggle. Then her head slowly reappeared and she looked up to Emma with a sheepish expression, "I was just playing peekaboo with Virgil."

Emma glanced out of one of the windows facing the backyard. Virgil was sitting on the decking, front paws tucked under her chest, facing the cat flap, but with a look of complete disdain. It seemed Virgil had not quite grasped the rules of the game.

Emma helped Toni scramble to her feet. "You're completely mad, you know."

"I know." Toni's mouth stretched into a grin and she planted a kiss on Emma's nose. "But you're still here, so what does that say about you?"

"Speaking of being here . . ." Emma followed Toni into the kitchen and watched her lift the lid on the cake box. "I hope you don't mind me letting myself in."

"This looks great. Thanks for picking it up." The lid was closed and Toni frowned at Emma. "Why should I mind you letting yourself in?"

Emma's glance fled to the set of keys she'd placed on the kitchen bench, next to the kettle. Her hesitation at Toni's front door had not been entirely due to the balancing act she had to perform with the large cake box while she fumbled with her keys. It was because, as well as having to pick out Toni's key from the ever increasing array she carried, Emma was not quite sure if she should be using the key at all. She and Toni had only recently swapped house keys and Emma was still battling with the finer points of house key etiquette. The question was, knowing Toni was home, did she just let herself in, or should she knock? The shifting weight inside the cake box, however, forced a decision and Emma, imagining the disaster of an upturned catering-size mud cake, turned the key in the lock. "I just wasn't sure if, when you're home, if I should use them or not."

"Of course you should, silly. I wouldn't have given them to you if I didn't want you to use them."

"But what if you weren't expecting me and you got a fright—"

"You could always try the old 'honey, I'm home,' routine." Toni interrupted, grasping Emma by the hand and leading her down the hallway to the front door. "Go on. Give it a try."

The door was opened, and before Emma knew it, she found herself staring at the wrong side of the wood. She reached into her pockets but found them empty, her keys still on the bench next to the kettle. So she knocked instead.

The door opened and Toni rolled her eyes skyward. "Jeez, for a vet you're not very smart." The front door closed again before Emma had a chance to explain she had no key.

Emma knew Toni wouldn't be able to resist looking through her peephole, and when she did, she'd see Emma holding out the insides of her pockets, displaying their emptiness. Sure enough, in less than a minute Emma heard the scamper of footsteps down the hallway, followed by their quick return. The door opened a fraction and Emma's keys dropped onto the front mat. Then the door closed again.

Emma turned the key in the lock, wondering how on earth she'd gotten herself involved with such an oddball. At least life promised to remain interesting. She eased the door open and found the hallway empty. Toni must have tiptoed away.

"Hi, honey, I'm home," Emma called, heading toward the kitchen.

Toni caught her halfway down the hall, suddenly appearing out of the doorway that led to her bedroom. Emma wasn't expecting it and almost jumped out of her skin.

"See." Laughing, Toni gathered Emma into her arms. "I wasn't frightened at all."

"Don't think you can win me over like that." Pretending hurt at Toni's practical joking, she tilted her head upwards, to avoid Toni's lips making contact with hers.

"Kiss me."

"No." Emma continued with her charade, despite Toni's attentions to her neck quickly dissolving her resolve.

"Then I'll send you home before our visitors get here tonight."

"We have visitors coming?" Emma chuckled at Toni's empty threat, but also felt a little deflated. She had hoped this evening would be just the two of them. They would, after all, be seeing just about everyone they knew at tomorrow's grand opening.

"Mmm." Toni returned her attention to Emma's neck, but her little bites were half-hearted. Emma could tell she was just bursting to tell her something.

While her curiosity was aroused, Emma also knew she did not need to dig for it. Sure enough, Toni could not stand keeping the information to herself any longer and blurted, "Cathy and Lisa!"

"Oh." Emma shrugged, confused. "Why? Aren't we going to see them tomorrow?"

"Yes. But apparently they have some news they want to share with us without everyone else around."

It took Emma about ten seconds to figure it out. "Do you think they've found a donor?"

Toni nodded vigorously. "I think so!"

As they excitedly hugged each other in anticipation of the good news, another thought occurred to Emma. She held Toni at arm's length. "Maybe they'd already found a donor and didn't tell us in case it didn't work out . . ."

Emma left her thought hanging and Toni caught onto it almost immediately. Her eyes opened wide. "You think Cathy may already be pregnant?"

"Maybe. We'll just have to wait and find out I guess."

Toni checked her watch and groaned. "It's *ages* till they get here. God, I want to know *now*!"

"Me too," Emma agreed, pulling Toni through the bedroom door. "Let's see if we can find something to keep us amused until they arrive . . ."

Publications from
BELLA BOOKS, INC.
The best in contemporary lesbian fiction

P.O. Box 10543, Tallahassee, FL 32302
Phone: 800-729-4992
www.bellabooks.com

OUT OF THE FIRE by Beth Moore. Author Ann Covington feels at the top of the world when told her book is being made into a movie. Then in walks Casey Duncan the actress who is playing the lead in her movie. Will Casey turn Ann's world upside down?
1-59493-088-0 $13.95

STAKE THROUGH THE HEART: NEW EXPLOITS OF TWILIGHT LESBIANS by Karin Kallmaker, Julia Watts, Barbara Johnson and Therese Szymanski. The playful quartet that penned the acclaimed *Once Upon A Dyke* are dimming the lights for journeys into worlds of breathless seduction.   1-59493-071-6 $15.95

THE HOUSE ON SANDSTONE by KG MacGregor. Carly Griffin returns home to Leland and finds that her old high school friend Justice is awakening more than just old memories.   1-59493-076-7 $13.95

WILD NIGHTS: MOSTLY TRUE STORIES OF WOMEN LOVING WOMEN edited by Therese Szymanski. 264 pp. 23 new stories from today's hottest erotic writers are sure to give you your wildest night ever!   1-59493-069-4 $15.95

COYOTE SKY by Gerri Hill. 248 pp. Sheriff Lee Foxx is trying to cope with the realization that she has fallen in love for the first time. And fallen for author Kate Winters, who is technically unavailable. Will Lee fight to keep Kate in Coyote?   1-59493-065-1 $13.95

VOICES OF THE HEART by Frankie J. Jones. 264 pp. A series of events force Erin to swear off love as she tries to break away from the woman of her dreams. Will Erin ever find the key to her future happiness?   1-59493-068-6 $13.95

SHELTER FROM THE STORM by Peggy J. Herring. 296 pp. A story about family and getting reacquainted with one's past that shows that sometimes you don't appreciate what you have until you almost lose it.   1-59493-064-3 $13.95

WRITING MY LOVE by Claire McNab. 192 pp. Romance writer Vonny Smith believes she will be able to woo her editor Diana through her writing . . .   1-59493-063-5 $13.95

PAID IN FULL by Ann Roberts. 200 pp. Ari Adams will need to choose between the debts of the past and the promise of a happy future.   1-59493-059-7 $13.95

ROMANCING THE ZONE by Kenna White. 272 pp. Liz's world begins to crumble when a secret from her past returns to Ashton . . .   1-59493-060-0 $13.95

SIGN ON THE LINE by Jaime Clevenger. 204 pp. Alexis Getty, a flirtatious delivery driver is committed to finding the rightful owner of a mysterious package.
1-59493-052-X $13.95

END OF WATCH by Clare Baxter. 256 pp. LAPD Lieutenant L.A Franco Frank follows the lone clue down the unlit steps of memory to a final, unthinkable resolution.
1-59493-064-4 $13.95

BEHIND THE PINE CURTAIN by Gerri Hill. 280pp. Jacqueline returns home after her father's death and comes face-to-face with her first crush.   1-59493-057-0 $13.95

PIPELINE by Brenda Adcock. 240pp. Joanna faces a lost love returning and pulling her into a seamy underground corporation that kills for money.   1-59493-062-7 $13.95

18TH & CASTRO by Karin Kallmaker. 200pp. First-time couplings and couples who know how to mix lust and love make 18th & Castro the hottest address in the city by the bay.
1-59493-066-X $13.95

JUST THIS ONCE by KG MacGregor. 200pp. Mindful of the obligations back home that she must honor, Wynne Connelly struggles to resist the fascination and allure that a particular woman she meets on her business trip represents.   1-59493-087-2 $13.95

ANTICIPATION by Terri Breneman. 240pp. Two women struggle to remain professional as they work together to find a serial killer.   1-59493-055-4 $13.95

OBSESSION by Jackie Calhoun. 240pp. Lindsey's life is turned upside down when Sarah comes into the family nursery in search of perennials.   1-59493-058-9 $13.95

BENEATH THE WILLOW by Kenna White. 240pp. A torch that still burns brightly even after twenty-five years threatens to consume two childhood friends.
1-59493-053-8 $13.95

SISTER LOST, SISTER FOUND by Jeanne G'fellers. 224pp. The highly anticipated sequel to No Sister of Mine.   1-59493-056-2 $13.95

THE WEEKEND VISITOR by Jessica Thomas. 240 pp. In this latest Alex Peres mystery, Alex is asked to investigate an assault on a local woman but finds that her client may have more secrets than she lets on.   1-59493-054-6 $13.95

THE KILLING ROOM by Gerri Hill. 392 pp. How can two women forget and go their separate ways?   1-59493-050-3 $12.95

PASSIONATE KISSES by Megan Carter. 240 pp. Will two old friends run from love?
1-59493-051-1 $12.95

ALWAYS AND FOREVER by Lyn Denison. 224 pp. The girl next door turns Shannon's world upside down.   1-59493-049-X $12.95

BACK TALK by Saxon Bennett. 200 pp. Can a talk show host find love after heartbreak?
1-59493-028-7 $12.95

THE PERFECT VALENTINE: EROTIC LESBIAN VALENTINE STORIES edited by Barbara Johnson and Therese Szymanski—from Bella After Dark. 328 pp. Stories from the hottest writers around.   1-59493-061-9 $14.95

MURDER AT RANDOM by Claire McNab. 200 pp. The Sixth Denise Cleever Thriller. Denise realizes the fate of thousands is in her hands.   1-59493-047-3 $12.95

THE TIDES OF PASSION by Diana Tremain Braund. 240 pp. Will Susan be able to hold it all together and find the one woman who touches her soul?   1-59493-048-1 $12.95

JUST LIKE THAT by Karin Kallmaker. 240 pp. Disliking each other—and everything they stand for—even before they meet, Toni and Syrah find feelings can change, just like that.
1-59493-025-2 $12.95

WHEN FIRST WE PRACTICE by Therese Szymanski. 200 pp. Brett and Allie are once again caught in the middle of murder and intrigue.   1-59493-045-7 $12.95

REUNION by Jane Frances. 240 pp. Cathy Braithwaite seems to have it all: good looks, money and a thriving accounting practice . . .   1-59493-046-5 $12.95

BELL, BOOK & DYKE: NEW EXPLOITS OF MAGICAL LESBIANS by Kallmaker, Watts, Johnson and Szymanski. 360 pp. Reluctant witches, tempting spells and skyclad beauties—delve into the mysteries of love, lust and power in this quartet of novellas.   1-59493-023-6 $14.95

ARTIST'S DREAM by Gerri Hill. 320 pp. When Cassie meets Luke Winston, she can no longer deny her attraction to women . . .   1-59493-042-2 $12.95

NO EVIDENCE by Nancy Sanra. 240 pp. Private Investigator Tally McGinnis once again returns to the horror-filled world of a serial killer.   1-59493-043-04 $12.95

WHEN LOVE FINDS A HOME by Megan Carter. 280 pp. What will it take for Anna and Rona to find their way back to each other again?   1-59493-041-4 $12.95

MEMORIES TO DIE FOR by Adrian Gold. 240 pp. Rachel attempts to avoid her attraction to the charms of Anna Sigurdson . . .   1-59493-038-4 $12.95

SILENT HEART by Claire McNab. 280 pp. Exotic lesbian romance.

1-59493-044-9 $12.95

MIDNIGHT RAIN by Peggy J. Herring. 240 pp. Bridget McBee is determined to find the woman who saved her life.   1-59493-021-X $12.95

THE MISSING PAGE A Brenda Strange Mystery by Patty G. Henderson. 240 pp. Brenda investigates her client's murder . . .   1-59493-004-X $12.95

WHISPERS ON THE WIND by Frankie J. Jones. 240 pp. Dixon thinks she and her best friend, Elizabeth Colter, would make the perfect couple . . .   1-59493-037-6 $12.95

CALL OF THE DARK: EROTIC LESBIAN TALES OF THE SUPERNATURAL edited by Therese Szymanski—from Bella After Dark. 320 pp.   1-59493-040-6 $14.95

A TIME TO CAST AWAY A Helen Black Mystery by Pat Welch. 240 pp. Helen stops by Alice's apartment—only to find the woman dead . . .   1-59493-036-8 $12.95

DESERT OF THE HEART by Jane Rule. 224 pp. The book that launched the most popular lesbian movie of all time is back.   1-1-59493-035-X $12.95

THE NEXT WORLD by Ursula Steck. 240 pp. Anna's friend Mido is threatened and eventually disappears . . .   1-59493-024-4 $12.95

CALL SHOTGUN by Jaime Clevenger. 240 pp. Kelly gets pulled back into the world of private investigation . . .   1-59493-016-3 $12.95

52 PICKUP by Bonnie J. Morris and E.B. Casey. 240 pp. 52 hot, romantic tales—one for every Saturday night of the year.   1-59493-026-0 $12.95

GOLD FEVER by Lyn Denison. 240 pp. Kate's first love, Ashley, returns to their home town, where Kate now lives . . .   1-1-59493-039-2 $12.95

RISKY INVESTMENT by Beth Moore. 240 pp. Lynn's best friend and roommate needs her to pretend Chris is his fiancé. But nothing is ever easy.   1-59493-019-8 $12.95

HUNTER'S WAY by Gerri Hill. 240 pp. Homicide detective Tori Hunter is forced to team up with the hot-tempered Samantha Kennedy.   1-59493-018-X $12.95